AUThOR'S NOTE

The quotations that begin each chapter are taken from the twelfth-century manuscript called the *Codex Calixtinus*, a compilation of texts about the pilgrimage to Santiago de Compostela in Spain, including a guide for pilgrims, a collection of miracle tales, and a series of prayers and hymns. The compilation of this manuscript and authorship of the pilgrim's guide has been attributed to a Frenchman, Aimery Picaud of Partheney-le-Vieux.

CHARACTERS

At Gistel

Gebirga of Gistel
Liisa, her dog
Alice, abbess of Gistel and Gebirga's great-aunt
Godeleva, Gebirga's mother
Bertulf, Gebirga's father
Mathilde, Gebirga's nurse
Winnoc, Bertulf's brother
Aude, Bertulf's second wife
Theodore, their son
Thomas and Jankin, crusaders
Hillegond, founder of Gistel
Floerkin, Johanna, and Lisebet, servants
Trude, Winnoc's concubine

Flanders

Count Baldwin
Clemence of Burgundy, his mother
Katerinen, his sister
William Clito and Charles of Denmark, the count's friends
William of Ypres, Baldwin's bastard cousin
Eudes, Clemence's messenger

France and Burgundy

King Louis of France
Archbishop Guy of Vienne, later Pope Calixtus,
    Clemence's brother
Pope Gelasius
Pons, abbot of Cluny
Oliver d'Asquins, monk of Cluny
Aimery Picaud, a wandering canon from Parthenay-le-Vieux

PILGRIMAGE

Lucy Pick

Cuidono Press
Brooklyn

PILGRIMAGE

© 2014 Lucy Pick

Cover image © The Metropolitan Museum of Art. Image source: Art Resource, NY. The Life and Miracles of Saint Godelieve, Netherlands, late 15th century; used by permission.

ISBN: 978-0-9911215-3-3
eISBN: 978-0-9911215-8-8

Cuidono Press
Brooklyn NY
www.cuidono.com

Spain

Queen Urraca, ruler of Leon and Castile
Alfonso of Galicia, her son, ruler of Galicia and Toledo
Raymond of Burgundy, Urraca's deceased first husband,
    father of Alfonso, and brother of Clemence
Diego Gelmirez, bishop of Compostela
Bernard, archbishop of Toledo
Bernard, prior of San Zoilo de Carrion
Yusef ibn Cid of Toledo
Berenger de Macon, a monk of Toledo
Gerard, a canon of Compostela
King Alfonso of Aragon, Urraca's estranged husband
Nazarena, a Mozarab in Aragon
Andregoto, abbess of Santa Cruz
Gracia, nun of Santa Cruz
Count Bertran de Risnel, cousin of Alfonso of Aragon
Count Pedro Fernandez de Lara, Urraca's lover
Teresa of Portugal, Urraca's rival and half-sister
Mosse Toledano and Blanca, Jews of Sangüesa
Sason ibn Raguel, Jew of Burgos
Natan and Jamila, Jews of Estella
Father Juan and his dog, Alfonso
Count Diego Lopez de Haro, Urraca's ally
Sancha Raimundez, daughter of Urraca
    and Raymond of Burgundy
Anneke, Aliit, Dirk, Hugo, Pelgrem, Piet
    and Sara, Dutch pilgrims
Robert, canon of Compostela
Bishop Hugo, envoy of Diego Gelmirez

CHAPTER ONE

Pilgrimage

*Let no one think that I have written down all the wonders
and tales I have heard, but only those I have judged to be true,
based on the truest assertions of the most truthful people.*

"It doesn't seem natural how that girl can make her way around
so well when she can't see."

Gebirga strained her ears to hear the group of nuns, taking a
break from their tasks to mutter outside in the July sunshine. Sweat
plastered the thin wool of her dress to her back, though the day was
barely warm. She imagined the nuns standing there, casting sidelong
glances as she entered the monastery gate. She held her head high as
she made her way through the courtyard toward them, a strong grip
on the lead of her dog, Liisa, and a bundle under her other arm. Liisa
would make sure she avoided the worst of the mud puddles from last
night's rain, not yet baked dry by the weak northern sun.

"Sisters," she greeted the knot of women, "where might I find
Abbess Alice? I have the candles from the castle for my mother's
feast day."

"The feast day of Saint Godeleva," an older nun corrected, gentle
but firm, refusing to acknowledge that their saint had first been her
mother. "You'll find the lady abbess in her parlor, doing accounts."

Gebirga shifted her bundle from one arm to the other, swapping
the hand holding Liisa's lead as she did so. The bundle was not heavy
but she would be glad to be rid of it. The gesture bought her time
to fix the plan of the monastery grounds in her mind before she
headed away from the women toward the outbuildings that served
as the abbess's quarters. Behind her was dead silence.

She reached the abbess's rooms and gathered her courage. The sound of a quill scratching on parchment could be heard through the oaken door. She stood a little straighter and knocked.

The quill stopped. "Enter," a sharp voice called. Gebirga felt her unruly hair starting to escape its tight white coif, but it was too late to worry about that now. She opened the door and motioned Liisa forward. Alice would not like the dog tracking mud on her spotless floor, but Gebirga was not going to make Liisa wait outside. Her aunt greeted her from where she was seated.

"Gebirga. All is well at the castle, I trust? You must have the candles for the feast day with you. Show them to me." She spoke in an elegant French instead of the local Flemish, and she did not invite Gebirga to sit.

The monastery relied on the castle at Gistel for much of its sustenance, but tried to keep itself aloof. Contact was infrequent except when it could not be avoided, like each year at the celebration of the feast day of the woman who bound castle and monastery together, Saint Godeleva, Alice's niece and, whatever the nuns said, Gebirga's mother.

Gebirga opened her bundle, Liisa sitting patient at her feet. "Here are the candles, four good, tall ones, made from our best beeswax." The fragrant scent of fresh wax rose in the air.

Alice took the candles and Gebirga heard her fingers slide up and down their length. "There's a flaw in this one. Sloppy work. Never mind. We can turn it around to the back. What else do you have in there?"

"This," Gebirga said, and unfolded a large rectangular cloth onto Alice's table, lovingly smoothing its creases. Woven from their finest wool, Gebirga and her women had bleached it in the sun before covering it with embroidery in every color they could draw from their dyes—nettle, marigold, coltsfoot, chamomile, walnut, juniper, and many more. "We made this altar cloth for my mother's feast. See? These are all the miracles my mother has performed since her death."

Alice was eager. "Yes, Godeleva looks just as I remember her here in the center, surrounded by the glow of the Holy Spirit. I suppose you got the gold thread in Bruges. And here are the thieves who tried to steal our harvest until Godeleva swamped their boat. Who is the crowd around her in the image at the top corner?"

"That is when she healed the woman with falling sickness. The woman's family is in the background." Gebirga said from memory. Her hands knew every inch of the cloth. She was a fine needlewoman, creating tapestries of texture through her sense of touch. When her nurse, Mathilde, was still alive, she taught Gebirga how to use different stitches for each shade of wool, and gave her a special frame to keep the colors organized. The cloth was Gebirga's idea, though other women at the castle helped her design it and plan the colors, and they all helped with the stitchery.

"Very nice, and I like the scene at the bottom where she miraculously sews the shirts for the peasants. But what's this down here?" Alice's voice turned acidic. "A woman and a dog? Is this supposed to be you? That's no miracle. You're still blind. Well, we can always pick it out."

"You won't do that." She might have to endure petty insults and pin pricks, but Gebirga knew they would never risk such an open slight to the castle. She had wondered how long it would take Alice to spot that she had put herself and Liisa into the embroidery. They were over to one side, but plainly visible if the cloth were hanging over the altar. Gebirga would never see it, but she would know she was there, visible, not forgotten or brushed aside.

"Is that all?" asked Alice, ignoring her last words as she folded the cloth back up again, "Because I must get back to work."

The abbess started writing again before Gebirga reached the door. Once outside, she paused to orient herself and then directed the dog, "This way Liisa. Straight forward, and don't let me trip over a chicken." One last errand remained before Gebirga could leave the monastery grounds. She reached her destination, the small chapel that served the nuns' needs, and commanded Liisa to wait outside. A low stone box with a barrel-vaulted roof and an arched doorway in one side, the chapel had been the main hall when Gebirga was a child. Before her mother died, and they moved up to the castle, and her father, Bertulf, vanished on crusade, they had all lived here together.

She entered the church and felt for the statue of Mary that stood on a small altar to the right of the door. With her hands she traced the contours of the virgin's smooth wooden face and the Christ child sitting stiffly on her lap, and she remembered how, when she was little, Mathilde used to lift her up so she could touch the statue, which was a parting gift from her father to the nuns. On her mother's feast day, the necklaces, rock crystal bracelet, and gold circlet her mother had worn in life would deck the simple painted wood. Gebirga had not come here for Mary or her mother, however, but to light a small candle for Mathilde who had spent the last few years of her life in the monastery. She had died a half dozen or so years before, but Gebirga never missed bringing her a candle when she was forced to the monastery on an errand.

The statue helped her find her bearings, and she crossed the narrow aisle of the church to the sarcophagus where the bones of her mother were placed after her body was raised by the bishop from the cemetery to its final resting place in the monastery church, in official recognition of her sanctity. Without Liisa, Gebirga misjudged the distance, and stubbed her toe on the unadorned stone. She rubbed her foot gingerly through her leather boot, and then felt in her now almost empty bundle for her tinderbox and a short candle, this one of tallow, not precious beeswax. A burned-out stub left by a previous petitioner was displaced so she could wedge the candle in a crevice in the surface of the stone tomb. She struck the flint with practiced skill and a faint charred odor told her when a spark lit the tinder. The tinder lit the wick of the candle, and when the scent of melted tallow indicated it had caught, she cupped her hands around its gentle glow, willing it to stay alight.

Mathilde would be pleased to have her candle here. The Virgin Mary was all very well, but Mathilde had been Godeleva's nurse as a child, coming with her to Gistel when she married Bertulf, and she had loved Godeleva more than anyone living or dead, on earth or in heaven. Gebirga came a respectable second in Mathilde's affections. She kneeled on the hard stone floor, ice cold even in midsummer, and tried to offer a prayer for Mathilde, but her mind kept wandering to the image of her mother she had been told was painted on the wall above the sarcophagus. Egg tempera on dampened rough plaster, it had been commissioned from a wandering painter heading to Bruges to work on the cathedral several years before, based on the memories of Alice and the few other nuns who had known

Godeleva. They said Gebirga looked nothing like Godeleva, who had been slight and dark where Gebirga was sturdy and fair, with freckles and honey-colored hair—adding fire for those who would deny a blood connection between them. She wished she could see the image for herself. A flat surface, she could never learn it with her hands the way she could the Mary statue.

A sound from behind distracted her.

"Oh it's you, Gebirga. I wondered who was kneeling here alone in the dark." A nun's voice tittered. "I'm here to polish the candlesticks and chalice for the feast day and to do a little dusting. Don't mind me."

"I was just about to leave," Gebirga said politely to the woman who had disturbed her silence, then rose to her feet. Liisa was glad to be collected at the door, knocking Gebirga's knees with her wagging tail in joy to be on their way again, and Gebirga relaxed too when the monastery gate finally closed behind them. She massaged a knot of pain that had settled at the back of her neck.

"Come on, Liisa. You've been so good. Let's go to the river, and you can have a bit of a run." They took, not the path that led back to the castle, but a narrow track that wound its way along the river before it met the main road. Liisa began to whine when they reached a willow tree that stood sentry in the flat, watery landscape.

"Very well, have your run. But don't be too long. I'm trapped here until you come back," she said, unclasping the dog from her lead before Liisa tore off. She sat under the canopy of the willow and hugged her knees to her chest against a sudden chill from the distant North Sea, a breath of wind with an ammoniac, briny tang that taunted her with oceans she would never see and journeys she would never make. The protests of sheep in a nearby field, rebelling against their shepherd, fought with the dull bell of the monastery, now calling the sisters to prayer in the chapel she had just left. She would have to return there in a few days for her mother's feast, but then she could avoid it for many months, thank God. If only she could have sent a servant on her errand with the candles, but it was a duty expected of the daughter of the house.

Gebirga often came to shelter under the willow at this bend in the shore when she needed to escape the demands of the castle. Mathilde brought her here when she was still just a child, to play ɔy its shade on hot summer days. As she grew and became more independent, she started coming alone because it was the last place on earth she could remember seeing with her own eyes, before the blindness came and took her sight.

The last thing she remembered seeing was the death of her mother, twenty years ago and more now. The murder of the blessed virgin, saint, and martyr Godeleva, the nuns would correct, the same nuns who believed that her blindness was a judgement on the family, brought on at the very moment of her mother's death. The monastery was at the place where they pulled the bloated and bedraggled body of her mother out of the river, but it was right where Gebirga was sitting that she had seen her mother enter the water.

Some things she was sure she could remember seeing that day, the green of the fields, thick grey clouds scudding across the sky. It was a strange July afternoon, full of uncharacteristic mists and fogs following a spring of floods, and she had been out with her mother and father. She was little and her legs were too short to keep up with her parents, who were walking quickly, as people do when they argue, so she plopped down on the bank in the shade of the willow while they marched away. She threw sticks into the rushing river and watched them disappear into the mist shrouding the stream until she became bored of this game. Daisies grew in the meadow by the river, and she collected as many as she could. She still recalled their sunny golden faces and white petals, and how she tried to plait them into a wreath for her hair like Mathilde had showed her. But her fat fingers could not copy the deft hand motions of her nurse, so she gave up and threw the damp and wilting flowers onto the bank. She stood to look for her parents, and she was sure she recalled her father grasping her mother by her upper arm. Gebirga could remember her mother's fat black braid snaking over her shoulder, but try as she might, she could draw forth no clear memory of her mother's face, nor of how she looked as she stared up at her husband, entreating or mocking him with words Gebirga could not hear.

But then the images became confused and contradictory in her memory. Had she seen her mother pull away with such force that her father toppled backwards, and her mother fell crashing down the bank into the swollen river? In this version, her father ran down the bank trying to see where her mother had drifted. Had her father shaken her mother by the neck until she hung like a limp rag doll, and then flung her slack body into the river with rage? In the version the nuns told, Bertulf had secreted two men-at-arms along the shore, and it was they who had strangled Godeleva and tossed her in the river, leaving her father's hands as clean as those of Pontius Pilate. But Gebirga had no memories of anyone other than her parents there that day. Sometimes though, the images in her mind revealed her mother backing away down the river, taunting and teasing Bertulf to catch up with her, and always just slipping out of reach, before finally jumping to her death.

She had been questioned over and over as a child about what she saw, and each questioner knew what story they wanted her to tell, whether it was Mathilde, or the priest sent by the nuns, or her father's brother, Winnoc, until she had no idea what was true. Better not to think about it, not to wonder what had happened, why her mother left her, and who was at fault.

Gebirga remembered no more of that day. She knew Mathilde came to fetch her, because her nurse told often of how she found Gebirga screaming by the edge of the river under the willow, forgotten by her father and everyone else, and how she brought her home and held her close to her plump bosom on the straw mattress they shared in the women's quarters.

Whatever force impelled Godeleva into the river, the current must have wedged her body under the waterlogged roots of the low scrub that concealed the water from sight downstream. That was why no one could find her body until it washed up hours later just before dusk at the staithe by their house. By the time her corpse was drawn out of the water, no distinction could be made between bruises it had received by the buffeting of the current and any wound inflicted beforehand. But all that was long ago now. Godeleva became a saint and her father went on crusade in disgrace and never returned, leaving his brother in charge of the castle.

At last Liisa returned from her run, racing back as quickly as she had left. But when Gebirga rose and hooked the lead back onto her collar, the dog lifted her woolly white muzzle and woofed softly, resisting.

"What's the matter?" she said, "There's nothing out there but rabbits." Gebirga's dusky brown cloak made her almost invisible against the landscape around her. She pulled it tight to her chest and gazed sightless in the distance, absently caressing the head of the dog at her feet.

Liisa growled softly and before long Gebirga heard the far away clip clop of horses, quite a number of them, approaching the castle from the main road above the river. Fear prickled between her shoulder blades, and she gripped the dog's lead tightly, drawing courage from the animal as she decided what to do.

She considered who could be riding on the lonely road that led through bog and meadow to the castle, none of the possibilities good. Thieves hoping to nab a few unprotected sheep? Cousins come to make trouble? Even if it were just visiting neighbors or traveling churchmen looking for a bed and entertainment for a night or two, she did not welcome the interruption. Could she make it back to the castle before they reached her? Woman and dog hastened up the path to the road, but once there, Gebirga realized she had badly misjudged the distance of the riders. There was no time to reach the protective gates of the castle before they were overtaken, and there was nowhere to hide in the flat and open landscape, so she stood on the road and faced the sound of the approaching horses.

Before they reached her, the horses halted. "Greetings in Christ's name!" she called out, fighting to keep her voice forceful as she heard one of them dismount. "You are on the domain of Bertulf the Cross Bearer and his brother, Winnoc. I am Gebirga, daughter of Lord Bertulf. We give welcome to all those who come in peace." She was waiting for a similar salute when she found herself clasped in the fierce embrace of a strange, large man who smelled of travel, horses, and sweat. She went rigid.

"Gebirga, little lass," the man stroked her hair, "I never thought to see you again. It is Bertulf, your father. I am back from the Holy Land, back to the castle, for good. And I've brought someone home with me."

Gebirga found herself released and her right hand placed in the small, soft hand of a girl, still seated on her horse.

"This is Aude, my wife and your new mother. Come, let us all go to the castle together."

Whatever Gebirga had feared, it was not this. The buried past, brought too close for comfort by her visit to the monastery, threatened to rise up anew. She made her way back to the castle with her long-lost father, only half-aware of his excited questions and her own distracted answers.

CHAPTER TWO

Reunion

*When stories about the saints are recounted by the
skilled, the hearts of listeners are moved piously toward
the sweetness and love of the heavenly kingdom.*

Did she lose her sight the moment her mother died, like the nuns said? Did it vanish all at once, or did it slowly fade? Gebirga could not say. She remembered those somber days, the confusion and panic as she attempted to negotiate a world now dark, the insults and careless cuffs from the servants when she got in their way. Unattended, she would trip and fall or knock things over, once a lit brazier that caught the rushes on the floor and almost ignited the hall, so when Mathilde had duties elsewhere, Gebirga had to be tied to a chair or a bed. There, she would shriek in loneliness and frustration until someone came for her, impatient at being drawn from important tasks by a little girl who was perfectly safe where she was.

"I don't want you. I want Mathilde!" she would cry, kicking out at her rescuer.

When she was isolated by darkness and grief, Mathilde remained her rock. The nurse was in a strange intermediate position in the family. She was a servant, but also a relative, a by-blow of Godeleva's grandfather, and so a half sister of Alice, the abbess, and a kind of aunt to Godeleva. Bereft of Godeleva, Mathilde poured all her lost love into her daughter and fought for her like a wildcat when the other servants muttered about demonic possession after one of Gebirga's screaming fits.

Memories from the time after her mother's death came from her other senses, the sound of the wailing cries of the women as they laid Godeleva out for burial, the pungent scent of the herbs they wrapped in her shroud. Mourning and burial were women's work, and Gebirga could not be kept away when they washed the corpse, tut-tutting over the ribs that showed under her skin and the bruises that mottled her wasted flesh.

"Look how thin the poor dear is. Mark me, they've been starving the girl. And see these scars where that brute of a husband used to beat her," said Mathilde. The other women nodded sagely at this pronouncement, and Gebirga drank it all in. Mathilde's words gained broader currency when the women whispered them to local peasants, visiting the back door with a chicken or a comb of honey to sell. They remembered Godeleva's generosity to them in times of want and her healing remedies when they were sick.

But most of what Gebirga knew about these events came from the stories these women told long after Godeleva was in her grave, gossipy tales over loom and embroidery frame, or brave adventures to enliven a dull dinner on a rainy evening, like the story of how Bertulf's mother dropped dead at Godeleva's funeral at the very moment the priest was saying the blessing over the grave.

"She fell to the ground in a fit," they said when they repeated the tale in horrified whispers, "And she seemed to be pushing something away with her hands." They told how, twisting her head from side to side as if to avoid gazing on some horrible apparition, she shook with a final convulsion, stiffened, and died. Everyone knew she had hated Godeleva and made her son miserable for choosing a Frenchwoman as his bride over one of their neighbors, forcing the couple to live in the small house by the river, instead of with the rest of the family, in the castle. Caught between wife and mother, Bertulf took out his frustrations on Godeleva with regular beatings, even when she was pregnant with Gebirga. In desperation, Godeleva fled home to her father, but he refused to allow her to leave her husband and rightful lord. Back at Gistel, Godeleva fell into a melancholy that only worsened with Gebirga's birth. She stopped eating and paid no attention to her baby, who was left to the loving care of Mathilde.

The kin who might have protested Godeleva's death were distant, and the murmurs would have dwindled eventually, were it not for her mother-in-law's dreadful death. The common folk gossiped that it was a judgement on her for her cruel treatment of Godeleva. The servants started a campaign of insolence and neglect against Bertulf, who was so shaken he did not end the mutterings with a few well-placed floggings, as he once would have. The local people took earth from Godeleva's grave to make healing plasters, claiming the earth healed their fevers as well as the tinctures Godeleva had dosed them with when she was alive. Gebirga's blindness was woven into the story of divine retribution against a wicked family.

Bertulf's father died a few months later, and the castle became Gebirga's new home. She could remember no other. But if Bertulf had thought a move from the river house to the castle would quiet people's mouths and stop the gossip, he was soon proven wrong. The talk only increased, and more bad luck dogged him, a string of disasters that the women recited like a litany. First the sheep caught murrain and had to be destroyed, and the wool they had to import from England to feed their looms put them in debt. Without a mistress to supervise the spinners and weavers, the cloth was of such poor quality it could not be sold in Bruges for any profit. Then one of their men was killed and another maimed in a scuffle with some cousins who wanted to encroach on their property. The kitchen caught fire during the Christmas celebration, followed by a long, wet winter when everyone fell ill. Gebirga caught a fever in her chest and was so sick, the priest was called to give her last rites. The elements of the tale that made Godeleva a saint came together and the women of the castle prayed for her to intercede for them in the court of the Heavenly Judge.

Bertulf seemed oblivious to these reverses, spending most of his time kneeling at the small altar in his chamber with the candles guttering smoke before the small statues and painted saints that had belonged to his mother. The bluff, hearty man everyone remembered, always looking to pick a fight, or go hunting or carousing with his men-at arms, became a chastened meek figure who moved like a ghost through the hall, growing thinner before their eyes.

"Mathilde, where's Mama?" Gebirga still asked at least once a day.

"She's in heaven with all the saints, just like I told you, looking down on you to make sure you are being a good girl."

"Where's Papa?"

"Shh, don't disturb him."

Discovering that Gebirga could not see, Mathilde tried to help her become mobile and independent again. When one of the sheep-herding dogs whelped, she decided that Gebirga should be given one of the puppies, Liisa, mother of the current Liisa. She told Winnoc that if a dog could prevent a sheep from drowning in the river, it could stop a little girl from falling into the duck pond.

He agreed and one morning, she brought Gebirga down to the stables and had her kneel down in the straw beside the mother and her pups. Gebirga reached out her hand and felt the soft, wet slap of a brave puppy's tongue licking it, followed by the grip of needle-like teeth. A knot of anger, inside her since her mother's death, softened. She drew the dog onto her lap, to the mild protests of its mother, and cradled it in her arms. Dog and girl grew up together, learning to maneuver around the castle and its grounds, until they could be trusted to journey further afield.

The dark rumors about Godeleva's death reached distant France and Godeleva's father pressed the count of Flanders, Bertulf's over-lord, for an investigation and the return of her dowry. Commissioners came from the count to investigate. Winnoc showed them the slippery part of the bank where Godeleva went into the river and spoke darkly of his sister-in-law's instability since the child was born, of her moods and sulks and unpredictable behavior. The two men-at-arms whom rumour blamed for perpetrating the deed were unavailable, said to be off hunting. But others were brave enough to testify to the mistreatment of Godeleva and the misfortunes that followed her death. Gebirga remembered being trotted out before the commissioners, who tried to get her to tell what it was she had seen that day. But the men who questioned her were loud and strange and smelled bad, and she had heard so many stories about what had happened and what she was supposed to have seen that she just stood before the men and sobbed in confusion and fear. Bertulf, dazed, answered questions vaguely or not at all.

Then, on a cold day in January when frost rimed the trees and Gebirga carried her rabbit fur muff indoors and out, Bertulf was summoned to the count's great council in nearby Bruges to answer the case against him put forward by his father-in-law. He returned a few days later rubbing his fingers together against frostbite, with a strange light in his eyes and a piece of red cloth in the shape of a cross roughly stitched to his jerkin. No one, not even Winnoc, dared risk his short temper or disturb this strange mood by asking what had happened. They gathered in the hall for the main meal of the day, boiled salted beef and basins of cabbage soup cooked with a mutton bone to warm their insides, served in the late afternoon to make the best use of the few hours of wintery daylight. When servants collected the empty platters and threw the trenchers to the dogs, Winnoc could wait no longer. "And so, brother, what are we to expect from the count?"

Bertulf dismissed the question with a wave of his hand. "That has all been settled. Far weightier matters were spoken of in Bruges these past days."

He rose to his feet and addressed the whole of the long table that dominated the hall, his gaze moving from his family at the top all the way down to the youngest serf seated at the end of the room furthest from the great hearth and the braziers that took some of the chill off the day. His face glowed in the rush lights already lit against the fast approaching dark. "My lord the count, may God bless and keep him, summoned us to Bruges to hear a letter sent to him by Pope Urban."

"What care have we for the doings of popes?" asked Winnoc.

Bertulf ignored the interruption, his eyes shining. "The pope is planning an expedition to the Holy Land, where Christ himself walked, to liberate it from the filthy pagans who have stolen it from its rightful Christian heirs. His letter told of how the barbarians in their frenzy have invaded and ravaged the churches of God in the east and how they have seized Jerusalem itself." Bertulf paused to take a draught of ale. "The pope has promised he will remit all the sins of those who take part. Our count has pledged to go to Jerusalem to liberate the Church of God and many of his vassals have followed suit. As have I. The cross I wear on my jerkin is a testament of the oath I have sworn to be part of the armed host. Any of our men who wish to join me on this expedition may swear likewise. We set out from Lille on the feast of the Assumption of the Blessed Virgin."

Winnoc leapt to his feet amidst the astonished clamor that broke out the moment Bertulf finished speaking. "This is madness,

Bertulf! Our lands are flooded and frozen, and our sheep are sick. This is no time to quit the castle and take our best men to go on a fool's errand."

The old Bertulf would have answered this interruption with a shout and a roar. The new Bertulf responded patiently. "Winnoc, my dear brother, I will be helping the castle every moment I am away. Winnoc! All of you! Do you understand what the pope's promise means? This is a journey commanded by God, through his vicar on earth. The pope will forgive all my sins, and the sins of all the holy men who make this armed pilgrimage. For the first time in the history of salvation, a fighting man can be redeemed through feats of arms rather than prayers. The castle and all those who shelter within it will benefit from what I do."

Winnoc persisted, "But what of Godeleva's father and his suit against us? How can we possibly fight it with you so far away?"

Bertulf smiled. "Godeleva's father has taken the cross as well, and because all men in our company must be at peace with one another, he has agreed to drop his suit. In exchange, I have pledged to endow a monastery in the river house, with all its lands. Godeleva's Aunt Alice, his sister, will be its abbess and will bring women with her to form a community."

The hubbub in the hall grew even louder. Bertulf was as good as admitting guilt in the death of his wife by granting the house and lands where he and Godeleva had spent their few unhappy married years to her family to found a monastery, and by setting forth on a penitential journey from which, like as not, he would never return.

"Silence!" Bertulf commanded in the old tone of voice they remembered from before Godeleva's death, and the murmurs subsided.

Was Gebirga at the table to hear Bertulf's fateful speech, picking at her food, or burying her face in Mathilde's lap? She heard the story of this meal and her father's surprise announcement many times after her father left, since it was a favorite of the old women to tell by the fire in the evening, when it was too dark for anyone but her to sew.

They had all worked their fingers to the bone getting the property ready for haughty Alice and her fancy French companions, turning the river house into a chapel by placing a stone altar at one end and newly whitewashing its walls. Bertulf returned from Bruges with the wooden statue of the Virgin that still stood in a place of honor. Once they had been thoroughly cleaned, the out-buildings became rooms where the nuns could sleep at night and chatter in the day, the wooden walls hung with Godeleva's embroidered tapestries to protect the women from drafts. The church was consecrated at a celebratory Mass attended by the inhabitants of the castle and the new nuns, who all looked on as Alice signed her name while her brother and Bertulf put their marks on the document prepared by the chaplain who was to serve the sisters. Before long, the local people sought the solace offered by their prayers and the bitter healing possets they made according to Godeleva's family receipts, and it was hard to remember a time when their bell had not tolled out the hours on the flat plain.

Gebirga knew she had been there to hear the women weeping and the horses stamping and jangling, impatient to be off, the day the pilgrims left for Jerusalem. She also remembered her father one evening before he left, surely drunk on ale, climbing the stairs up to the gallery above the lord's chamber, where the women slept under the thick thatch of the roof. He kneeled by the bed where she lay, Mathilde snoring beside her, and clutched her tightly, the bulky weight of his chest pressing down on her small frame and scratchy chin abrading her cheek. He begged her to forgive him, persisting until she gave her puzzled assent.

Tales of the count's host as it moved south through France and Italy drifted back from time to time, but after the army set sail for the Holy Land, the people of Flanders heard no more of the fate of their lords, husbands, sons, and brothers for two years, when the joyful news came that the city of Jerusalem had been captured from the pagan infidels. Gebirga was only six, but she remembered being chivvied into the monastery chapel for a hastily arranged celebratory Mass, bells ringing and clouds of the best incense wafting over the congregants. And indeed Bertulf's departure seemed to restore the fortunes of the castle, and the coins spent liberally to ready him and his men for their journey were replaced one by one.

When the count and what remained of his armies returned to

Flanders a couple of years later, they were greeted as holy heroes and questioned again and again about what they had done and seen, and what had become of their fallen comrades. The returnees told of famine at the siege at Antioch and bloody slaughter at Jerusalem, of miraculous victories in the dust and heat. Gebirga listened to all of these stories with the rest, nestled in the warm folds of Mathilde's plump lap. But scant news of Bertulf drifted back to Gistel. Winnoc spoke to someone at the yearly cloth market in Bruges who thought he had seen Bertulf alive after Jerusalem, but her father did not return with the count.

Gebirga was nine when their neighbor's youngest son, Thomas arrived at the gate. They hardly recognized in him the youth who had left years before, hardened now by battle, disease, and the death of his older brother, but he was ushered into the hall and put at the head of the table with a mug of their best beer. Everyone who could be spared gathered to hear what he had to say. The news was brief; Thomas had never been much of a talker. Bertulf had asked him to bring word to Gistel that he was well, but he was not coming home yet. There was a fortune to be made in the Holy Land by a Christian with a strong sword arm. Then Thomas reached into a bag he had brought with him and pulled out a small silver casket, which he placed on the great table. Mathilde held one of Gebirga's fingers to the little chest so she could feel its decorations. The casket was rectangular with a peaked lid, like a little house, and beaten into every surface in relief were intricate, decorative images and shapes. Every time she touched something different, Mathilde told her whether she was touching birds, hunters on horseback, vine scrolls, or other wonders. Finally she touched something Mathilde could not identify.

"What is this?" Mathilde asked Thomas about the row of upright joined lines, loops, bars, and dashes that ringed the top of the casket.

"That's their writing," said Thomas.

"Whose?" piped up Gebirga, "Whose writing?"

"That's Arabic writing. That is the way the infidels write. They decorate everything with it, even buildings."

"What does it say?"

"I don't know. Something about their miserable Mohammed, probably. That's usually what it is about."

"You mean this is a heathen object?" one of the sillier women of the household said in horror.

Thomas smiled. "Not anymore. Look inside. But just for a moment." He opened the casket and they all caught a flash of silk woven in patterns as elaborate as the silver on the outside of the casket and in colors their dyed wool could never match. The lush silk made a striking contrast to the object cradled in the casket, the dried and darkened finger bones of someone who had been dead for a very long time. Everyone gasped, immediately understanding the significance of the grisly object. Thomas closed the casket as Gebirga demanded, "Tell me, tell me! What are you all looking at? What do you see?"

They ignored the little girl who was always asking others to be her eyes. "Who is it?" Winnoc asked, "Which saint?"

"This is the forefinger of Saint Nicholas," answered Thomas. "It is a gift for the ladies of the convent from Bertulf. They are to remember him in their prayers."

"How wonderful," one woman breathed as everyone drew closer, attracted by the holy chest.

"And more than that," Thomas continued, "Bertulf asks the ladies of the monastery to take his daughter with the chest as a gift, as an offering for his sins. The chest is her dowry to the sisters."

The crowd broke into excited chatter. Everyone had expected Gebirga would enter the monastery one day. What other future could there be for the blind daughter of a lord, cursed by a saint? It was not likely anyone could be found to marry her. Bertulf was sure to return home eventually and sire more children, sons who could inherit, and then what place would there be for Gebirga? But no one had expected her to leave so soon, or bear such a spectacular treasure with her.

Gebirga shrank into Mathilde's arms at the mention of the convent where her mother's bones lay, not understanding what was going on, or why she was suddenly the center of attention but drawing strength from the older woman. Gebirga hated the monastery, the cold damp of the stone chapel, filled with the stale smells of incense and old women, and she imagined the eyes of all the nuns upon her as she kneeled with Mathilde at Mass each Sunday, her nurse praying fervently to her mother for Gebirga's sight to be restored after paying a meager coin for a candle offering for the saint. Mathilde was always welcome at the convent, as a former servant of the sainted Godeleva, and a French speaker in the land of the despised Flemish, not to mention a sister of Alice, albeit from the wrong side of the blanket, but Gebirga did not fall under their welcome. She could tell they had no hope that her eyes would one day be healed by prayer. To them, she was the daughter of a man who killed a saint. They pinched her when she got in their way.

So when Thomas said that the silver chest with its grisly cargo was to serve as her dowry with the monastery, even though she did not really understand what a dowry was or why everyone was so excited, she became so distraught that Mathilde had to take her from the hall. As they left, one woman murmured, "Ungrateful wretch! Such a reaction to hearing she will spend the rest of her days living with the ladies in the convent, waited on by servants with no husband or screaming children to worry about."

"She truly must be a child of the devil," another replied, surreptitiously making the sign against the evil eye.

Mathilde tried to explain to the weeping nine year old, "Gebirga, this is wonderful news. You'll live with the nuns and have a home and I'll go with you and we can always be together, even when you are grown up."

"They don't like me. They don't want me. And I don't want them."

"Nonsense. You're Godeleva's daughter, her only daughter. They will love you as I do. Your place is there with them."

"No! I belong here with Winnoc and the rest. I want to learn how to weave and sew, and I want to take care of the castle and carry a big ring of keys at my waist. I don't want to be a nun and pray and be sad all the time."

But Gebirga had no say in the matter. She was told she was lucky to have such a comfortable place open to her so close to her home. Winnoc, when appealed to by little Gebirga, refused even to think of going against his brother's wishes, accompanied as they were by the sacred relic, though he admitted he would miss the girl. So the next day, Winnoc bearing the small chest and Mathilde, holding the hand of the little girl in her best dress, made the short journey to the convent. There had been more weeping when Mathilde told Gebirga that Liisa would have to stay behind, that small girls in monasteries did not have dogs, but finally Gebirga's tears were wiped away and they left with the sound of the dog howling in the background, knowing something was wrong with her mistress.

Alice was used to seeing Mathilde and Gebirga at odd hours, but Winnoc's presence was much more unusual, so she ushered the three into her private parlor. There were only two chairs, so Mathilde and Gebirga stood while Winnoc unwrapped the silver casket from its coverings and put it on the table before Alice. "Bertulf sent this from the Holy Land."

Alice knew the moment she saw the casket that it was a saint's reliquary. She fell on it with covetous hands. "Whose bones are in it?"

"It contains the finger bones of St. Nicholas. You can look inside."

Alice fumbled with the clasp and took a peek before quickly closing the lid. "Where did Bertulf get this from? Did he send a letter, some written attestation proving whose bones these are and where he got them? The city of Bari claims to possess the whole body of Nicholas, you know."

Winnoc did not know. These nuns and their desire for written documents all the time—what was wrong with a man's word? It was getting so every time you sold someone a cow, it had to be all written down and signed by a priest.

"Never mind. We can have someone here write something," said Alice, "This is a gift for the monastery, I presume? Bertulf is most generous."

"Yes, it is a gift," Winnoc said, "It is a dowry for little Gebirga here. She is going to join you here with the other sisters."

This dampened Alice's enthusiasm. While she greatly desired the silver box, she did not at all want Gebirga, daughter of the hated Bertulf, and blind and useless to boot. "I hardly think that is suitable. I loved Godeleva like my own daughter and to admit the child of the man responsible for her death would be an insult to her memory."

Winnoc said, "Bertulf was the benefactor of this monastery and his wishes deserve respect.

Alice raised her voice, "He was a very devil, and he killed my precious girl!"

Gebirga had heard no story more often in her short life than the tale of her mother's death, as it had slowly taken shape in the minds of the local people and been preserved by the priest who had come to write it down so it could be read and remembered on her feast day. Told and retold, Gebirga could recite it by heart, including the part when a pregnant Godeleva was cast out by her own family to return to the husband she feared. She said to the abbess with a shrewdness beyond her nine years, "Tante Alice, you didn't love my mother. She came home to her family for help, and you all sent her back to her death."

The abbess spluttered. No one spoke to her like that, ever, and Gebirga's story cut deeper for being true. When Godeleva had returned to her family, desperate and pregnant, none of them raised a finger to keep her there in safety. But in Alice's mind, this rudeness was proof of something the older woman had been shaping in her mind for years, that this Gebirga was no daughter of her niece.

"Limb of Satan, you don't belong here with Christian women. I won't accept Bertulf's bastard child in the house dedicated to his sainted wife. Take her home, Winnoc, and find a place for her by your fire. She'll have none of ours."

Winnoc was placid by nature and remained calm. Besides, he had been none too glad to have Gebirga leave. She had become a winsome little thing under Mathilde's care, and he liked seeing her playing in the castle yard with her big dog, and learning to spin by the fire with the women. So he said diplomatically, "No need to get into such a taking, Abbess. Gebirga is welcome to abide with us. But we'll take the relic back too, and its casket. That was intended for Gebirga's dowry, and it will go wherever Gebirga goes."

This gave Alice pause. She coveted both the unusual reliquary and its sacred cargo. Relics drew pilgrims who made donations, and while she already had the complete body of one saint, the finger bones of St. Nicholas would confer glory on her house and draw even more people to visit.

Mathilde could no longer keep silent. "Gebirga is Godeleva's child! I was present at the wedding night and saw the blood on the sheet the next morning along with everyone else. I tended her all through her pregnancy, and I was there at the very moment that Gebirga was drawn from her body. And how can you forget the two of us returning to your brother's hall, my blessed darling heavy with child and barely able to stand?"

Alice had erased her memories of pregnant Godeleva begging for help in her father's hall, and remembered only what she knew about virginity, and how much more pleasing virgins were to God than married women. Godeleva's holiness made sense if she had been protecting her virginity from a rapacious husband; it was far less impressive if she were just another married woman with a child and a violent husband. Why, if that were enough to confer sainthood, half the women in Christendom would be saints. Alice wanted to protect the special status of Godeleva, and of the house she ruled as abbess. But she also wanted the reliquary casket. She resolved to let God decide.

"These matters are beyond the discernment of ordinary mortals. God, who has built this house and provided for all our needs will guide us now. We will go to the chapel and pray for a sign." Alice scarcely knew what kind of sign she expected, but she was a woman of faith. If Winnoc thought that his brother Bertulf did more to build the house and provide for the nuns than God did, he gave no indication, and agreed to follow the abbess to the chapel.

Alice called the nuns to the church with the bell, and they entered one by one, surprised and put out to be taken away from their tasks and gossip without warning. Standing at the front of the church, Alice summoned Gebirga to her side while one of the nuns lit the candles; not the good beeswax ones they kept for feasts, but simple rushlights dipped in tallow. She turned Gebirga to face the assembled nuns and placed her hands on the girl's shoulders. Gebirga fancied they were the claws of some huge bird of prey, snatching her away from her home and friends. Alice began to pray in Latin, asking God for guidance. Gebirga looked out unseeing towards the crowd of women she knew were before her. She imagined the disdain of the nuns called away to attend a girl whom none of them liked. Gebirga never joined in Mathilde's prayers before the image of her mother, not even silently to herself, but suddenly she prayed as she had never done before.

"Mother! Mother, protect me from these women. I don't want to be a nun. I want to go home and live in the castle."

Gebirga knew her native Flemish and spoke French with Mathilde, but the unfamiliar Latin made her head hurt and her eyes, though sightless, smarted from the smoke of the cheap rush candles in the chapel. The room, crammed with too many people, was airless, and her stomach churned from fright and emotion and the strain of the day. Unable to bear it, she made a sudden turn away from the watching company towards the abbess and was violently sick all over the front of Alice's habit.

The nuns gasped while Mathilde rushed to care for her precious girl. This was all the sign Alice needed. She did not shout, because she was in church, though she would sorely have liked to. She simply told Winnoc to take Gebirga and go. Winnoc had the presence of mind to scoop up the casket of relics on his way out.

Gebirga, Winnoc, and Mathilde walked back to the castle in silence. Finally Gebirga asked timidly, "Winnoc, is it true? Am I really the daughter of a devil?"

Winnoc smiled. "A devil? No, but you're the daughter of my brother and maybe that is bad enough. Never you mind what those cats say. Mathilde and I well remember the night of your birth. First your mother screamed and then you screamed and it was all over." He started to laugh and once he began, he could not stop. "Oh, I'll never forget the look on the face of that Alice when you were sick all over her habit. It was worth the walk just to see that. She'll be sad when she realizes she's lost the casket forever though." He was so hearty that even Mathilde began to see the funny side of the day's events and it was in much better cheer that they arrived back at the castle.

Mathilde stopped bringing Gebirga along on her frequent visits to the monastery, though she never ceased praying for Gebirga's sight to be restored. Mathilde fervently believed that one day Godeleva was sure to intercede with Christ on her daughter's behalf, and Gebirga would be healed. She told Gebirga about every miracle attributed to Godeleva, how she cured that lame boy whose family lived over by the dyke, and found the chaplain's cow that had gone missing.

But every visit she was disappointed. Fortunately, her other plans for Gebirga's future were more practical. If Gebirga was not going to marry and she was not going to become a nun, then she might as well learn to be useful.

Mathilde had already taught Gebirga how to use her sense of touch and hearing to take care of herself, to comb the tangles out of her thick hair, and wash the dust off her freckles, and eat like a young lady. Now she persuaded Winnoc to teach the young girl how to ride, at first on a long leading rein, and later on her own. And every day she instructed her in the business of the women of the castle, how to clean and card the wool of the sheep, and then how to use a drop spindle so the thread was long and fine and smooth, with no lumps, breaks, or tangles.

Gebirga learned to weave standing before a big warp-weighted loom, first the plain undyed cloth that was the staple of the castle, then the patterns and colors distinctive to the Gistel looms. Gebirga found weaving dull, so she rejoiced when Mathilde started her on embroidery work. With the other women of the castle, she began an ambitious scheme to replace the worn and tattered tapestries that hung on the walls of the hall with scenes of family and local legend. Their first masterpiece was Bertulf at the siege of Jerusalem, with the casket holding St. Nicholas's bones done in silver thread. The real casket sat tarnishing on the small altar in the lord's chamber.

Then, Mathilde began teaching her how to manage the household. Gebirga learned how long to malt the barley before it was crushed for beer, what meat to smoke and what to salt, how to heal a pig with swine pox or a boy with toothache, and all the thousand and one things that needed to be done lest the castle descend into chaos and decay. One day, when her contemporaries were marrying and setting up homes of their own, Winnoc rewarded her with the great ring of keys that showed her to be mistress of the castle, and Mathilde tucked her hair into the tight white coif that signaled a woman's passage to adulthood. Where once the castle dwellers had muttered about devil's spawn and judgements on the family, they now spoke of miracles and the blessing of Saint Godeleva on her daughter. Her job at raising Godeleva's child done, Mathilde slipped away to spend her last few years of life in the monastery dedicated to her beloved.

It was the life Gebirga had always hoped for—making sure everyone was fed and dressed and warm, supervising the making of the bread and the beer, managing the weaving and dying of their cloth, responsible, indispensable, and even loved by her community. If the sudden scent of salt on a northern breeze made her think of journeys like her father's, if the desire for adventure that sent him across the seas ever burned in her own breast, she never told anyone. What sort of adventure could be possible for a blind woman? Why, even the prospect of a short trip to neighboring Bruges panicked her. Surely she was lucky to be where she was, and when work made her weary, she could always escape for a few moments to walk by the river and give thanks for how her life had turned tragedy to contentment.

In all those years, Bertulf never sent any word from the Holy Land after the time Thomas came with the saint's relic in the Muslim casket. In the long winter evenings, when the hall was dark and the women were telling tales, "And he was never heard of again," was the way they ended their stories of Bertulf and the crusade, and this was how Gebirga thought of her father, as a character in a tale, real but absent. But now, twenty years and more after he had last been seen, her father was walking beside her as if he had been gone no longer than a few months, asking questions about everyone he saw. And he had a new wife.

Gebirga did her best to respond. Yes, Winnoc would be there. Yes, the castle was prospering. The closer they drew to it, the more distracted her father became and the less he attended to her answers about how many bolts of cloth and bales of wool they were producing. She sensed him looking eagerly about, scanning for the first time the home he had not seen in twenty years. Apart from re-digging the moat and repairs to strengthen the palisade, the castle and the country surrounding it had changed little since he left, the countryside still a crazy patchwork of fields farmed through the ages by the same peasant families.

Bertulf remarked on the changes he saw to his bride, who remained mounted on her horse while Gebirga and Bertulf walked.

She replied in monosyllables. It emerged that Aude was as young as she seemed, that she was the only daughter of one of Bertulf's allies in the Holy Land, recently dead, and that they had returned to claim her inheritance.

Most disturbing was Bertulf's sudden recollection that Gebirga should not have been roaming the countryside at liberty. "But didn't Thomas arrive with the casket? I expected to find you a pious little sister, praying at the monastery for the good of your father's soul!"

He did not wait for an answer, and turned to other subjects. But his words made Gebirga realize that her father's return would bring many changes to her life, not all to her liking.

CHAPTER THREE

Gistel

Pilgrims returning from Jerusalem carry palms to show they have
mortified all vices. Therefore drunkards, fornicators, misers, the greedy,
the litigious, the extravagant, usurers, adulterers, and other wicked people
who are still at war against sin should not carry the palm, but only those
who have wholly overcome their vices and have adhered to virtue.

The castle dominated the surrounding countryside from its perch
on a motte of hard packed earth, daring all who approached to
attack at their peril. The motte was scarcely the height of two men,
but from the top of the castle a watch could be kept for miles around
because the surrounding countryside was as flat as the pancakes
Mathilde made Gebirga when she clamored for food between meals
as a child. Even Bruges was visible, distant in the east, on a clear
day. While Gebirga munched on her pancakes, Mathilde would tell
her the story of the giantess Hillegond who went to the beach one
day to fill her skirt with sand to build up the soil at the place by the
river downstream from Bruges where she wanted to build her castle.
Before she got there, however, her skirt ripped open and all the sand
fell to the ground, so she had to build her castle there at Gistel.

The truth was the motte had been built by hard labor. Hillegond
was an ordinary woman, not a giant, and she had been married to a
fisherman. When he died on the cold North Sea, like his father before
him, she did not want her three strong boys to follow their craft.
So they went inland and claimed as much of the marshy, swampy
land for themselves as they wanted. They built ditches and dykes to
drain the land, and collected a group of bullies who intimidated the

local peasants in exchange for food. The peasants built the motte in exchange for not having their heads bashed in. Once the motte was piled high, they surrounded it with a wooden palisade and dug a water-filled ditch around that. On top of the motte they built a big one-roomed house out of wood where Hillegond and her sons lived with their strongmen. The peasants were set to work building more ditches and dykes, which gave them good earth to cultivate, so they were content enough to farm the land and give over some of its fruits each year to Hillegond and her sons, and to work on the harvest each autumn. The land prospered, and all had some share in it. Hillegond settled disputes and meted out justice from the big house, and her sons and their men made sure it was carried out. But the middle son cleaved through the skull of the eldest with an axe in a fit of rage over a woman. The middle son fled, and the youngest inherited the whole property. He passed it to his eldest son who in turn passed it to his eldest, Bertulf's father.

By his day, the family pastured sheep for their wool, which was spun and woven into cloth by the female domestic serfs, little more than slaves. They sold the cloth in nearby Bruges and used the profits to draw more men into their employ, strengthening their dominion over the lands around them. Bertulf's father received permission from the count of Flanders to expand his castle. He built a much larger home for his family on the motte, with a new ground floor of stone and slit-like windows for shooting arrows at attackers, and a big thatched barn for their horses and other livestock and the bales of wool they now imported from England so they would have enough raw material to weave. He dug a bigger moat, and put up a wooden tower house to guard the gate.

Gebirga and her father's company finally reached this gatehouse. When the young man guarding the tower realized that Gebirga was among the strangers, he climbed down and lowered the gate, calling to her, "Lady Gebirga, you left alone, but I see you return from your errand with companions."

It was Floerkin, she knew from his voice and from his farewell to her when she left earlier in the afternoon. He was a couple of years younger than she, and so still a babe in arms when Bertulf left on his pilgrimage. He would have no way to recognize this was his lord, returned home after so many years. What she said next would set the tone for how the castle received their long-lost castellan.

"Floerkin, you are the first of our people to hear the news of this wondrous day. This is my lord and father Bertulf, returning from the Holy Land at long last to be restored to his people, together with his lady, Aude." As Floerkin stood gawping at the news that this legendary figure stood before him, she added, "You may remove your cap and bow before your lord." Grateful to have something he could do, poor Floerkin made haste to obey.

"Floerkin. You must be Hugo and Griet's long-awaited chick. Did any more follow your birth?" asked Bertulf.

"Sir, I have seven brothers and sisters," answered Floerkin.

"Seven!" said Bertulf, "Let's hope all my domain has multiplied in this way."

They passed through the gate and into the courtyard, and immediately caused a stir. Most of Bertulf's small entourage were strangers to Gebirga, presumably new men taken up in his travels to replace men from Gistel whose bones now rested in a distant land. Still, two of his company shyly identified themselves to her as men who recalled her from their own distant youth in Gistel. They were soon looking for, and finding people at the castle who remembered them. Screams and hugs from the weaving women and the men in charge of the byres and stables erupted all over the courtyard as long-lost cousins and friends were reunited, introductions were made, and people were called from their work to greet the surprise return of the exiles.

Bertulf helped Aude down from her horse and brought her to where Gebirga was standing in the middle of the hubbub. He was quickly surrounded by castle residents who longed to see and touch their returning hero. The excitement made Liisa start barking. Aude moved away. "The yard is so mucky. And that dog! Make it stop that noise!" she said in a high, juvenile French, instead of the local Flemish.

"She's just excited; she doesn't usually bark at all," said Gebirga, nettled. Most people in the region could speak a few words of French, in addition to their mother tongue of Flemish, but Gebirga was fluent in both, having learned her mother's French from

Mathilde. Gebirga tried to soothe Liisa by stroking her, without much success.

"I hate dogs. Horrible animals," responded the young girl.

Gebirga had more serious worries than the happiness of her new step-mother, however. With all the noise in the courtyard, everyone in the castle would soon know about their lord's return. She grabbed a passing boy, "Where's Winnoc?" she hissed, "Take me to him!"

"I think he's in the chamber with the steward," said the boy, "Come with me, and I'll find him for you."

They climbed the external staircase up to the second floor of the castle where the living quarters of the castle were; the great hall, the women's gallery, and the lord's chamber. The chamber was divided from the main hall by movable partitions of woolen cloth, brightly painted on both sides, stretched over wooden frames. Here was the only real bed in the castle as well as the small altar where Gebirga's casket sat. Winnoc slept in the bed along with his most recent concubine, while the rest of the castle slept on straw mattresses. But Winnoc would not be sleeping there any more, not with the return of his older brother. Gebirga needed to tell him as soon as possible before he learned it from someone else.

She followed the boy into the chamber where Winnoc was working. The summer fair in Bruges was coming up, and it was time to decide what they had to buy and sell, and whether they needed to borrow more money, or if they could pay off something of their debts. The steward, seated at a table, scrawled out each item on a scrap of parchment at his dictation. Winnoc broke off when he saw her.

"Gebirga, back from the monastery? Good thing because I've been pestered all afternoon by women with questions only you can answer, and I want to ask you what we need to do for this fair. Are we going to sell those bales of wool from our best sheep as we planned, or will we keep them and weave them ourselves? With Johanna's sudden death and Lisebet's illness, we don't have the weavers to make use of it. At least Lisebet has recovered."

"Winnoc, we can't talk about that now; something has happened." She drew him out of the room away from the curious ears of the steward. "Can you hear the noise from the courtyard? Bertulf has come home; he's returned from the Holy Land."

"Bertulf? You're not serious. After all these years? I swore he was dead by now." Gebirga kept silent and he continued, "He's outside you say? Why didn't he send word he was coming? We'll have to have a feast, maybe invite all the neighbors. Holy Mother of God, my brother back with us again! How does he look? Is he well?"

Winnoc hurried to the door of the hall. Gebirga put her hand on his arm as he passed. "Winnoc, he has brought a wife home with him, a young wife."

This news brought him up short as Gebirga expected. The return of the blustery, loud, and sometimes violent Bertulf was going to bring changes to their peaceful, orderly way of life at the castle. Not all these would be bad—sometimes Gebirga felt that life was too orderly, too stable, and her father at least promised excitement, even if it was only by vicariously living through the stories he was sure to tell. But the advent of a wife who might provide Bertulf with an heir changed everything for both of them. What if he begat a boy, a son who would inherit one day? Winnoc's position in Bertulf's absence was ambiguous, since he could never fully claim the castle that was his brother's. Gebirga was his brother's heir, and under normal circumstances the land would pass to her and her husband. But while Bertulf was gone, Winnoc had had no incentive to marry her off and render himself homeless and landless. Moreover, the stigma of her blindness scared away the young men.

In Bertulf's absence, this had not mattered, especially since none of the young men had much appealed to Gebirga and she had no desire to leave home. Winnoc and she could stay at Gistel in peace and prosperity to the end of their days. She had never much thought about who would inherit the castle after her death. Perhaps Winnoc would have eventually recognized one of his many bastards who drifted around the castle as his own, and raised him to be lord. But with a son of Bertulf's body, all this security vanished.

The two descended the stairs from the castle to greet their returning lord. Bertulf was joyful when he saw his brother. "Winnoc," he embraced his brother and held him tightly, "You've lost all your hair!"

"And you've grown fat," said Winnoc, breaking free from his embrace and smiling at the man before him.

"Ha! I was always fat," said Bertulf, "Winnoc, may I present to you my wife, Lady Aude de Bergeval."

"My lady, I am delighted to meet you. Welcome to the castle of Gistel." Winnoc bent low over her hand.

"Je vous remercie, mon sieur," she replied. "I thank you," she tried in halting Flemish.

"A French bride, how wonderful," said Winnoc, his voice sounding strained. The last French bride brought to this castle was Godeleva, and look how that turned out.

Gebirga decided that they had spent long enough standing in the courtyard letting people stare at them so she said, "You both must be tired after your long journey. Why don't you come to the bedchamber and I will ask someone to bring you some hot water. I could send for some food also, but we will eat shortly in any case."

"Excellent idea, daughter," said Bertulf, "Oh, I have missed that bed, sleeping in tents in Outremer and on what passes for beds in that place. I will sleep well tonight."

Gebirga felt Winnoc jerk beside her. Yes, you will be losing your bed and your chamber, she thought. But Bertulf was the lord; there was no way around it.

Room for Bertulf and Aude also had to be found at the head of the long table that filled the great hall. Winnoc and Gebirga were accustomed to sit side by side at the end of the table, as befitted the titular master and mistress, with the rest of the household ranged down its sides according to rank. Gebirga had benches brought so she and Winnoc could flank the real master and his lady. But when she moved to sit next to the young girl, Aude squealed and refused to sit anywhere near Liisa. Conflict was averted by having Gebirga sit next to her father, but every time Liisa shifted on the rush-covered floor, Aude jumped, and she did not dare feed Liisa the little tidbits she was used to, lest Aude take fright at the dog's slavering jaws.

Conversation at the table was stilted at first. Gebirga heard Winnoc trying with his poor French to make conversation with Aude, but she rebuffed all his kind overtures. He finally gave up and spoke over her head to Bertulf.

"Brother, tell us of your adventures. We have heard many stories about the expedition from those who have returned from Jerusalem, but we all want to know what happened to our very own lord." His invitation caught the attention of the whole table, longing for stories of peril and bravery.

Bertulf rose to the occasion. "The journey to Italy was pleasant enough, with much wine and feasting on what we found along the way. Not so pleasant for the people we took it from perhaps, but we were doing God's work. Things turned when we took ship. The devil raised storms against us, and we feared shipwreck, but our prayers to St. Donatien were answered, and he calmed the waves enough that we could cross the Adriatic."

"The trek to the city of Constantinople was long but, Mother of God, the end was worth any hardship. Constantinople shines like the heavenly city of Jerusalem itself. You've never seen such riches in one place, statues covered in gold and studded with gems sitting out in public view, churches decorated with glittering chips of stone instead of paint, people covered head to toe in silk the way we wear wool. And the size! It makes even Bruges look like a sheep run. I think their emperor got more than he bargained for with us though. When we took Nicaea, he wouldn't let us sack it, so that was the end of our friendship with him. The Turks chased us down, but we taught them the strength of a Christian sword. We routed them, but that was the battle we lost poor Jankin at," he said, nodding at an old woman he recognized as Jankin's mother, sitting way down the side of the table. She hung on each word he spoke like everyone else, hoping to hear news of fallen friends and relatives.

"Then we besieged Antioch and God tested us mightily. I still have nightmares about it sometimes, the dust and the flies. A loaf of bread was a penny, if you could get it, and an egg cost ten. We lost more men to famine than to Saracen arrows. Worse than the heat was how the great lords fought with each other. The count of Flanders had enough of the squabbles, and we set off with him to raid and harry the Saracens on our own. We'd come to kill Muslims, not fight with our Christian brothers. It was on one of those raids that I got the relic chest with St. Nicholas's bones that I sent back with young Thomas."

This recollection brought him back to the present. "Did Thomas ever bring it to you? There'll be blood spilled if he kept it for himself.

I told him it was for Gebirga's dowry with the nuns. I thought that grasping Alice would not be able to resist the bones of a real saint from the land where God walked. But why is Gebirga still here? You didn't let those nuns cheat me, did you, Winnoc?"

"No need to threaten Thomas, Bertulf. He brought the casket just as you asked, and we did our best to follow your wishes. But Alice..." Winnoc weighed his words. "Alice declined your gift, and thought it best not to admit Gebirga into the monastery. She felt Gebirga was not suited for the monastic life. So the casket is still here, sitting on the altar in your chamber."

"Not suited for life as a nun? God's teeth, brother, she's blind—what other life is she suited for? She'll never marry, no husband would take her, and there is no need for her to bear children now I have my Aude." He gave his bride a squeeze. "I'll talk to Alice right after Mass on Godeleva's feast day—no, I hadn't forgotten about it. That's why we arrived when we did. Not take my daughter, indeed! I'll soon remind Dame Alice what she owes to me!"

Gebirga struggled to keep the distress from her voice. "Sir, father, I have been living these past years very happily and usefully in your household, assisting Winnoc. I would be most content to remain here under your roof."

Winnoc took Gebirga's part. "I don't know what I would have done without Gebirga all these years. Everyone from the least scullion to our bravest fighter looks on her as the mistress of the household."

"That is the problem," Bertulf replied, "I learned from my first marriage that you can't have two mistresses in one house. And Aude, as my wife, must be mistress. Gebirga can stay for a while to show Aude how things are done here but then she must take her place at the monastery. And that reminds me, Gebirga, do you keep the household keys? You must give them to Aude."

Bertulf's tone made it clear he meant her to hand them over right away. Gebirga's hands shook as she slipped the iron ring of keys off the leather girtle she wore about her waist and handed them to young Aude who almost snatched the ring from her hands. The keys opened every locked door and box in the castle. Gebirga would unlock the storehouse in the ground floor of the castle and be overcome by the different food smells—the beery scent of the grain used for bread and ale, the smoke of the hams and bacon hung from the ceiling, even the half-rancid smell of the sheep tallow they kept for candles. Her domain included all the chests and coffers that ringed the hall. One stored items too costly and sensitive to be kept in the ground floor, like their precious salt and sugar and their meagre cache of spices, all purchased at great expense in Bruges; others kept linens, blankets, and furs free from moths, while still more held cups, kettles, wooden trenchers and knives. When Winnoc gave her the keys to the castle, she had been proud to fetch what was needed, memorizing each location by feel and smell. Losing the keys to Aude meant forfeiting her very identity at the castle.

"My lord, please tell us about Jerusalem! What is it really like? Was the battle to take it as bloody as everyone says?" someone spoke up from further down the table, bored with these domestic questions and impatient to get back to Bertulf's story. Bertulf took up his tale where he had left off and Gebirga was grateful for the interruption. She heard with only one ear Bertulf's tale of sieges and prayerful processions around the city, followed by slaughter in the streets and massacre on the very Temple Mount itself as the Christian warriors cleansed the defiled holy places with Muslim blood. The rest of her was reeling in fear for her future. Was she going to be sent to the monastery after all these years? And how could she cope without Liisa with her, guiding her steps? She would be by far the oldest novice, not to mention the only one unable to learn how to read. Unable to follow the chant and the liturgy, she would be more like one of the lay sisters who did the hard work around the community than one of the choir sisters, the elite of the convent. Hardly suitable for the daughter of the castle. Of course, in Alice's mind she was nothing more than Bertulf's bastard. She was trapped though, with nowhere else to turn if Bertulf would not let her stay. Her mother's relatives would have no use for her and it would be even harder for her to marry now, her only dowry a casket of bones. Even her mother could not protect her a second time from life in her monastery, no matter how fervently she prayed.

She heard Winnoc ask Bertulf why he had decided to stay in the Holy Land and not return with the rest, and how he came to marry

Aude. This was a story she wanted to hear so she pulled herself from her thoughts and listened.

"You know Flanders; wealthy and fruitful but cramped and small, a place where too many men fight for too little land. In the Holy Land there was room for anyone with a strong sword and a good horse. I took my men who had survived the struggles for Antioch and Jerusalem and found a few more who had lost their lords but wanted to stay on, some of whom you see tonight." Here Bertulf toasted a couple of the men he had brought with him who were scattered along the big table, and downed a big draught before continuing. "I joined with a few more lords like myself, including Aude's father and we formed, well, a kind of protection service. We protected each other's goods and also any merchant trains who wished for our services. But when Aude's father died, it was she who needed protection, not to mention help securing her inheritance. She's the only child and sole heir of her father," he winked at his listeners, "So we returned to claim the castle Bergeval in her name and now we are here."

"Would you ever go back?" asked Winnoc.

"You'd like that, wouldn't you," Bertulf said shrewdly, "No, I'll spend the rest of my days here, watching my children grow. But maybe one of them will return, and you younger people should think about it," he gestured around the table. "There are fortunes and a name to be made fighting the Saracens there, or even in Spain."

"Spain?" questioned one of the castle men.

"Yes, I hear the rulers of Spain will pay good money for people who go down to fight for them, and give them land too. Why, the Countess of Flanders' own brother went down and was given the hand of the princess, Urraca. Too bad he died before Urraca became queen. The women in Spain use their men harder than the Saracens do!" Bertulf laughed at his own wit.

His laughter was punctuated by the noise of Aude vomiting copiously onto the floor. Before Gebirga could move to help her, Lisebet, a servant who could speak a little French was by the girl's side, comforting her and ordering milder food, currying favor with the new mistress.

"Poor dear. With a lusty man like Lord Bertulf, odds are you are pregnant. Don't worry, it just means the baby is strong in you. You'll start feeling better soon. I am Lisebet and I will take care of you."

Gebirga froze at Lisebet's words. Aude, pregnant already? She barely registered Bertulf's overjoyed announcement to the table and the cheers of the others as they toasted their new mistress.

The meal mercifully ended. Gebirga found Bertulf's new men places to sleep, unpacking blankets and finding them straw pallets from the store in one of the lofts. Some pallets were badly mouse-eaten and Gebirga noted she must have new ones made before she remembered that this would be Aude's task from now on, not hers.

Usually the castle settled quickly in the evening, tired after a long day of work that began at dawn, but tonight small groups remained in the hall well after sunset, some playing tunes on whistle and drum while others clapped along, most listening to the stories of Bertulf's men about the East, about camels and other odd beasts, assassins who would slit your throat, and buildings that shone with gold and precious stones. Finally the boys who slept in the stables returned to their piles of straw and the rest settled for the night.

Gebirga did not sleep, disturbed by the snores of the other women in the sleeping gallery, as well as by her own thoughts. The gallery was above the lord's bedchamber and she heard her father going to bed. Sound traveled easily through the castle, and she was used to hearing Winnoc grunting with his women and the laughter of whoever else had found a partner for the night. She heard her father wake Aude and force his attentions on her, and listened to Aude's protests that it was bad for the baby and a sin besides, to have sex with someone already pregnant. Her French words would be understood by few others. Aude's protests did not dissuade Bertulf; in fact he seemed more inflamed by her scuffling and weak resistance. Gebirga heard Aude sobbing quietly after her father was finished. Possibly there were worse fates than being sent to live among the nuns.

CHAPTER FOUR

Bruges

There are certain fish in the sea of Saint James, which the people call scallops. They have two shields, one on either side, between which the fish lies, as if between two shells in the manner of an oyster. These shells are shaped like the fingers of a hand.

"You will destroy everything I have built here over the past twenty-five years!"

Winnoc's voice rang through the great hall, and the women looked up from their woolwork in surprise. "That didn't take long," muttered Gebirga to herself. She had spent the morning showing Aude around the castle and its grounds, trying to teach the girl her new duties, and had just settled down to her embroidery with the women spinning and weaving in the hall when their peace was disturbed by Winnoc's shouts.

"It is the only right thing for us to do. We're knights, not merchants," came Bertulf's angry response. The two men were arguing in the lord's chamber. They were making a spectacle of themselves, so Gebirga hastened to see if she could calm them down before the whole castle heard.

"What's wrong?" Gebirga asked, entering the chamber, "They can hear you down at the convent, the way you're both shouting."

"Remember yesterday when I spoke about taking our cloth and wool to Bruges to sell at the fair?" Winnoc asked, lowering his voice a few notches. "I asked you if you thought we should keep our best wool and weave it, sell it to pay down debt, or exchange it for lower quality wool for us to weave. Bertulf wants us to sell the wool and acquire more debt."

"Why, father?"

"It's to build up our family name and reputation, daughter. We need more arms. My men are adequately armed but the arms and armor at the castle are out of date, when they're not rusty and more of a danger to the man who uses them than the man he is attacking."

"But father, surely we don't need arms that badly. The land is at peace, and we are able to protect ourselves with what we already have."

"That's what I have been trying to tell him. In fact, Bertulf should turn off some of the men he has brought with him. They look like they'll want more adventure than our little corner of the world can provide."

"Are you mad? Turn off men who have fought with me bravely for years, and who have followed me across the world because I promised them a good life here?"

"But you'll bleed the rest of the castle dry to pay to keep them," said Winnoc, "We make our living from weaving and from our sheep and what we can get for both. We don't make our living from fighting."

"That's the problem. We are knights. We do live from fighting. You want to turn us into merchants and tradesmen. Oh, it is good to have a few sheep, and weave a little wool. It keeps the women busy when their husbands are off doing more important things. But you'll make us all womanish. By the strength of our armed following we are known to our superiors, to our liege lord Baldwin, the count of Flanders, and to his enemies. Besides they won't be idle. When we are not serving the count, they will help me expand our influence here. Booty and plunder are the honorable income for a knight, not wool profits."

"Count Baldwin is mixed up in the quarrels between France and England about who is to rule Normandy now the son of the Conqueror is dead. Will you die, Bertulf, to make William Clito, the duke of Normandy?"

"If my count asks it of me, I will consider it an honor. And I won't die. I've survived until now, haven't I? I'll return with the gold of the Norman burghers in a big chest under my arm and a charter from a grateful Count Baldwin for a village or two in my hand. That is the way our kind was meant to live. And that is all I have to say about this matter. Sell the wool and buy the arms."

It was not all they said, of course. The two bickered constantly about their different visions for the castle while the wool and finished cloth were baled up for shipping, and plans were made for the journey. Their quarrels cast a pall over the whole castle. Mealtimes were silent lest a careless word set them off again. Eventually Winnoc realized it was no use arguing and became morose and remote, saving his criticisms for Bertulf's bride.

"Don't know why, with all the women in Palestine to choose from, he had to pick Aude, skinny and brown-haired as she is. She's all nose, elbows, and opinions, that one." Winnoc was known to prefer his own women blonde, plump, and brainless.

Gebirga had her own concerns and was as withdrawn as her uncle. Aude showed little signs of mastering the household, and demonstrated a disturbing tendency to rely on the steward, a man who worked well when closely monitored but who was inclined to be dishonest. He ingratiated himself with his superiors in a way Gebirga found distasteful, and was overly harsh on those under his power. But he spoke French so perhaps it was no wonder Aude relied on him.

Aude was having a hard time settling in. Peevish and ill from her pregnancy, she complained about everything from the stink of the pigsty to the barley bread they ate and the blandness of their spices. She was disgusted by the tallow and lard they collected for cooking, and told them everything in Palestine was cooked in an oil that came from a fruit.

"Oil from a fruit?" the head cook scoffed when Gebirga translated during a tour of the kitchen. "You can't get oil from a fruit!"

Gebirga feared that Aude was about to demand the man's ears be cut off, or whatever they did to disobedient slaves where she came from, so Gebirga intervened and asked her to tell them about it.

"They are called olives and they grow on trees all over the Holy Land. It is even in the Bible; you can ask your priest about it. They pick them from the trees and then they put them in a basket in a press. When the press is turned, the oil flows out of the holes in the basket and is collected in jars. It tastes lovely, and it can be used to make soap and also for oil lamps."

"Maybe we could grow a few olive trees at Gistel," Gebirga said politely.

"At Gistel? It is much too cold and miserable here for that. They like it hot and dry. Here they would wither and die, just like I am going to do."

More troubling was the news from the convent. Godeleva's feast day Mass was even more awkward than usual. The chapel was packed and, as promised, Bertulf stayed after Mass to confront Alice about Gebirga's future. He returned to the castle later that afternoon and told her grimly that she would leave for the monastery as soon as Winnoc returned from the trip to Bruges. "Alice tried to resist me," he said, "But I told her a thing or two." Part of her wished she had been there to hear her father telling off Alice, but her heart sank thinking of the reception she would receive. He could force them to accept her, but he could not make them welcome her.

She was surprised to be summoned to talk to Winnoc and her father the day before her uncle was to leave for Bruges.

"Gebirga," Bertulf began, "Winnoc has asked me if I would consent to let you go to Bruges with him to sell our wool and cloth. I have some misgivings about the trip, but I am going to let you go."

"But why, what help can I be there?" she said, her heart beating as she tried to keep the panic out of her voice. Winnoc made the journey to Bruges every year at this time, to sell their wool, borrow money, pay down debt, and buy what the castle needed and could not make. Gebirga had been there just once. At home, with Liisa's help, she was able to find her way all over the castle and the surrounding countryside without any difficulty. But in the strange streets of Bruges, with their stench of unfamiliar unwashed bodies and cacophony of carts, hawkers, horses, and beggars bickering with each other for dominance, she was disoriented, and Liisa was confused. After that one occasion, Winnoc went alone.

"It will be a tremendous help for me to have you there," said Winnoc. "As daughter of the house, you have an authority none of the men I take with me has, and you know better than I do what provisions the castle needs from Bruges."

Gebirga appreciated his kind words, but she did not believe a word of this speech and wondered what he was up to.

"I don't understand this buying and selling business. But I suppose Gebirga should have a chance to experience more of the world before she enters her convent. And it will help Aude to have a chance to command the household on her own," Bertulf said, "Now, go organize whatever you need for your journey."

Gebirga's fear must have shown on her face because Winnoc, normally undemonstrative, put a hand on her shoulder. "It won't be so bad, you'll see. I'll make sure someone is with you all the time. And we'll be gone for just a few days, if all goes well."

When the people of the castle heard she was leaving for Bruges with the wool boat, there was scarcely a one who did not come to her with some special request for a purchase, the coins for it screwed up in a bit of cloth. They were too shy to ask Winnoc to perform their commissions, but Gebirga was different. She promised she would do her best to remember their buttons and needles and small tools. There was barely time to get her own pieces in order, tied up in a neat bundle, before she boarded the boat the next day, and her journey began.

The boat was the pride of the castle. The kind used for inland water travel and transport in their area, they were the only ones among their neighbors to own one themselves—most transported goods in borrowed or shared boats or sold their wares to traveling merchants. Gebirga's grandfather had the boat built, sacrificing one of the few large oaks that grew on higher ground for its sake. The oak had been hollowed out and then lengthened fore and aft by adding boards. The sides were built up with strakes overlapping clinker-fashion and fastened together with wooden nails. Then the interior of the boat was reinforced with forty ribs that ran in parallel up and down its length. Some boats used a short mast and a sail, but theirs did not have a mast, so it was punted by two men using poles in rhythm the short distance from Gistel to Bruges. The boat had a shallow draft, essential for navigating the marshy waters. Since the Great Flood just two years before Bertulf left on crusade, the waterway threading through the flat fields to Bruges had been growing shallower each year. Already the bigger ships were unable to make it down as far as Bruges, and the river at Gistel was beginning to silt up. But while they could still navigate, the boat made them the envy of their neighbors.

It was packed to the top with bales of wool and bolts of woven cloth, most wanting the last stages of fulling and dying, which would be done by their purchasers in Bruges. Gebirga was the last to board, bracing herself as the boat gently rocked after Liisa jumped on. She greeted the boatsmen and the others traveling to Bruges, unsurprised to find one of Bertulf's new men on the ship. He must be there to guide the purchase of the new arms her father thought they needed.

But then an unexpected female voice hailed her. "Lady Gebirga, come sit by me. Winnoc has arranged a very comfortable bale of wool for us to recline on as we pass down the river."

It was Trude, Winnoc's latest mistress. Gebirga knew her by her voice, and also by her scent, like lavender and honey. Now why had he brought her along? Winnoc had been with Trude for the past two years, ever since his last mistress had died in childbirth. Gebirga liked her. Most of Winnoc's women were more or less interchangeable, buxom, loud, and cheerful, but Trude was different. She had intelligence and wit, along with what passed as a reputation for beauty in their narrow circle. That put her into quite a different category and Gebirga wondered that her family allowed her to get involved with Winnoc when they surely could have arranged a respectable marriage for her. In any case Gebirga was glad the other woman was there. If Trude would help her do her errands, Bruges might be a less fearsome place.

They cast off, and everyone at the landing to see them off cheered as they began moving down the river. It was a fine July day, hot and hazy, and both women wore the wide-brimmed straw hats that peasants used in the fields, to keep the sun from burning their noses. The rhythm of the punt was gentle and relaxing and the day stretched lazily for everyone but the two doing all the work, who were spelled by others in time so they could have a bite of bread and cheese and a rest. Gebirga remained beside Trude. Every time a new settlement or a castle belonging to one of their neighbors came into view, Trude seemed to know some gossip. "We're passing Thancmar's place," she would say, "I can tell it hasn't prospered much since he disowned his eldest. The twins were killed in a drunken brawl the very next month and now I don't know what he's going to do for an heir. They say he's trying to get one on his cook. But I see Odger has been building dykes and draining new land, a sure sign of success. He must be borrowing money from the monks; he doesn't have the men to do it on his own."

As the shadows began to lengthen, they reached their destination for the night, a hamlet about half way between Gistel and Bruges. The men would stay on the boat at the jetty to guard the goods, taking turns sleeping and keeping watch. It was lucky for them it promised to be a clear night. Gebirga, Trude, and Winnoc were to stay in the guesthouse of the Abbey of St. Peter. The three shared the guesthouse, a single room with a hearth at one end. From the smell of mouse that hung about the room, Gebirga feared their straw mattresses were filled with vermin, but it was better than sleeping on the boat. The abbey cellarer settled them in and brought them food but soon disappeared to take part in the evening liturgy. At last Gebirga was alone with Winnoc and Trude. She wasted no time.

"Winnoc, what is the real reason you wanted me on this trip? Not for the simple delight of my company surely, since you have Trude for that."

Trude murmured to Winnoc, "We might as well tell her. You have to confide in her some time and we're far enough from Gistel now."

Winnoc spoke. "Gebirga, after we finish our business in Bruges, I am not returning to Gistel. Neither is Trude. I was afraid to tell you there lest you try to stop me or even tell Bertulf. But I couldn't leave you without a word, so I brought you with us."

"Not returning to Gistel? But wherever are you going? And Trude?"

"Trude and I got married. We did it last week; it was a secret marriage. The Church doesn't much like them because the priests want to get their hands in everything these days, but it was valid. And she's pregnant, we think, not much more than a couple of months. As for where we're going, well, it is far away."

"Not as far as Constantinople I hope," said Gebirga, dismayed by his news, and afraid he had taken her father's words on adventure too much to heart.

"No, and not to Spain either. I'm not a fighting man by choice, though I can give a good account of myself if I must. I'm a householder and a farmer as well as a knight, and I'm going to settle land for the archbishop of Magdeburg, east of the Elbe river. They need peasants to farm the land they are taking from the pagan Slavs, and they need knights like me to keep them in order. The archbishop's men were recruiting in Bruges last year, and I met them when I was selling our wool. They promised me more land than you could imagine, but I didn't give it a moment's consideration until the last few weeks, when your father came home and everything started changing, and then finding out Trude was pregnant. It was time for me to make something for myself for a change instead of tending another man's land."

Gebirga could not disagree despite her dismay. His words began to sink in. Gistel without Winnoc? After her mother died and her father left, even after Mathilde died, Winnoc had always been there, solid and steady. She grasped at hope. "But what if the archbishop's men aren't there this year? Or don't need you?"

"We'll go anyway. Someone will want us. It's a wild country with room and opportunity for someone who knows how to build a dyke and drain a field. I sold that piece of land I inherited from my mother to the abbot here, and I've brought the bits I've saved over the years so we can pay for the trip. It's by cart the whole way so the journey will be slow, but that can't be helped; we'll get there sooner or later and Trude's baby will be born on his father's land."

"Just like a man, he can't imagine a baby who isn't a boy," Trude said, trying to lighten the serious mood. But Gebirga had more questions.

"Father—he doesn't know? How do you think he will react when he learns? Oh!" she had a sudden thought, "I suppose it is going to be my job to tell him."

"I think Bertulf half suspects already. That doesn't mean he won't explode when he learns the news for certain. I am sorry to put you through that, Gebirga. To be honest, I am going to miss him. I'll miss everyone at the castle. It is strange leaving the land our family has held for years for a place where no one has ever heard our name or knows our history, now he has returned after so long. But I know it is best. Maybe it isn't God's will for us both to be in the same place at the same time. I am going to send a letter back to him explaining what has happened—the scribe who prepared the deed for the land I am selling will write it for me and the steward can read it to Bertulf. I told the scribe to make his writing clear and not to use big words."

Trude reached forward and took Gebirga's hand in her own, "Gebirga! Don't go back to the castle. There's nothing for you there. You don't want to go to the convent with all those French women twitting you about your accent and keeping you on your knees all day. Come with us instead! It will be an adventure. You can help me with the baby. And perhaps we can even find a husband for you, a nice one who will treat you well, not like the fools around Gistel."

Gebirga felt a flutter of panic mixed with something like hope, "I don't know what to say." She withdrew her hand from Trude's and nervously scratched a flea bite on her wristbone.

Winnoc spoke, "Trude is right. You should come with us. It would be good for Trude to have a familiar woman's face around while she is expecting. And I know you won't be happy at the convent or at the castle now."

All Gebirga's fears fought with a little voice inside asking her, why not go with them? "But I have hardly any of my things with me. I thought I'd be away for a week, not the rest of my life. And father would be furious."

"I know he's your father, Gebirga, but he did leave you for over twenty years. He has a whole convent to pray for his sins already; will your added prayers really make a difference? And as for your things, we can buy whatever you need in Bruges. Please promise you will think about it."

Gebirga promised and the three made their way to bed, tired from their travels. Liisa stretched out full length before the hearth out of habit, though it was not lit on this pleasant spring evening.

A young lay brother woke them early in the morning, coming to empty the slops. He was followed by the cellarer bearing beer, bread, and three big wedges of strong, ripe cheese from their own sheep. Trude took one look at the cheese and ran outside. Gebirga would have followed her but Winnoc held her back, "It is just the baby sickness. It comes every morning but it passes quickly. Trude prefers to be alone when it comes. It's a good sign. The midwife says sickness in the morning means it is sure to be a boy."

"A boy!" said the cellarer, "In that case you must name him after our patron, Saint Peter."

Winnoc, a little flustered, promised he would.

"Oh dear, what have I done?" he said when the monk left, "Trude will be furious, she wanted to name him after her father."

"You'll just have to give him two names. Or maybe you'll be lucky and it will be a girl" she teased, nibbling on her cheese.

"Never!" he cuffed her playfully. At that moment Trude came in, still fragile, but saying she felt much better. She proved this by drinking a little of the beer and taking a hunk of bread with her to chew on the way. They bade farewell to their monastic hosts and returned to the jetty where their men were making the boat ready to leave.

The air was chill and a soft fog hung about the willow trees that lined the river. They made good speed and were already far from the monastery by the time the sun shone through the thin blanket of clouds, burning through the mist and drying the dew on the grass that grew down to the riverbank, cropped close by sheep on both sides. They floated through the vast expanse of flat land and low sky, stopping around midday to stretch their legs, and reached Bruges well before nightfall. The men punting descried its tall steeples and castle from many miles away, and Gebirga smelled the rank river odor of weed and decaying vegetation give way to the city stench of raw sewage. They approached the town from the west and circled it on rivers and stagnant man-made canals, punters poling carefully to avoid dead rats and other dubious river refuse, to reach the harbor on the east side.

"Not far now; I see the steeple of St. Walburg's." Winnoc explained, "St Walburg is the patron saint of the merchants of Bruges and her church is at the port. We can tie up there, but we'll leave the business of selling for tomorrow. It is hard to get a good price at the end of the day, even during a fair." The men were to stay with the ship while Winnoc and the two women found an inn.

The port smelled of the ghosts of long-dead fish and Gebirga was disoriented by the fishwives calling their remaining wares, and burghers jostling to get home. Once Winnoc and the two women left its open space to enter the warren of tiny streets, the din only got worse. With Winnoc holding tight to one arm and Liisa's lead firmly clasped in her fist, she felt almost safe. The cobblestones amplified the clatter of horses' hooves on all sides. More than once she had to press herself up against a wall to allow a cart to pass in the narrow street, the iron rim of its wheels screeching on the cobbles. Trude, who had never been this far from Gistel, chattered about the sights of the town. The shops, little more than open-fronted stalls, were closing for the day, so most of her attention was on the large castle that dominated the town, protected by a ditch and the river on two sides, and surrounded by a thick stone wall. She asked Winnoc about it.

"It is called the Burg and the two buildings you see above the wall are the church of St. Donatien and the residence of the count."

"Is the count in Bruges? Might we see him?" asked Trude.

"Count Baldwin is probably off looking for battles to fight with his friends Charles of Denmark and William Clito. But his mother, Clemence, may be here. Some say she is the real power behind the count. She doesn't so much as let him sign a document without putting her mark on it, and she mistrusts Baldwin's friendship with Charles. Charles is a cousin and Baldwin's successor until he has a child of his own, and she thinks Charles is distracting Baldwin with warfare to stop him thinking about getting married and begetting an heir. Neither Charles nor William Clito are married."

They took a sharp right into a narrow alley, rutted and dusty after days of summer heat, and entered a hostel opposite the wooden church of St. Walburg. "The Sheep and Lamb," Winnoc said, "This is where I always stay. It's not fancy but it is cleaner than most."

Roosters and church bells woke them at dawn the next morning, and they returned to the boat, passing milkmaids taking their herds out of town to pasture in the surrounding meadows. Selling their merchandise was a slow process, trooping around to each of the wool merchants whose warehouses and shops ringed the market square. Gebirga had a long, hot day of listening to talk of prices and grade and quality, while they stood in shops consuming the mug of beer and biscuit or pasty or tart served by the merchant's wife, and breathing in the faint but persistent scent of the sulphur, lye, and stale urine used in the cloth trade, drifting in from the workrooms. It took until the end of the day for Winnoc to finish selling the very last bolt and bale.

The next morning the company split off to spend the money amassed the previous day. Winnoc went with Bertulf's man and a purse full of coins next to his skin to buy weapons. He also planned to contact the archbishop of Magdeburg's men. Those tasks would keep him busy the whole day.

Gebirga and Trude went shopping for the castle with Liisa trotting happily beside her mistress, sniffing the unfamiliar and fascinating town smells. Gebirga clung tightly to Trude's arm, assaulted by noise and stench and jostled by crowds of shoppers and pickpockets. With her other hand she tried to keep hold both of Liisa's lead and her purse. Trude warded off the beggars who, drawn to town by the fair, waved limbs diseased by nature or artifice in their faces and demanded alms. They lunched on a mess of steamed mussels, then were tempted by the warm scent of yeasty bread to a bakery stall to buy a sack of buns. "Local speciality!" they were told.

"Keep them with you, Gebirga," said Trude, "We may be hungry later."

Full of food, they started their shopping. They bought the big items first—a loaf of sugar, pots the cook had requested, pieces of leather that could be made into shoes—and sent them back to the inn with a boy hired for that purpose. Most items could be acquired at the market beside the castle, but when Gebirga told a woman selling them a bracelet of glass beads her father wanted for Aude that she needed to buy needles and buttons, the woman sent them to a bone shop out of the center of town.

"You go further down the Hoogestraat and then turn left onto Mariastraat. The shop is just beyond the church of the Holy Virgin. You can't miss it. They'll set you straight if you go there. Jankin makes the best articles out of bone in the whole town. His buttons never split and his needles stay sharp, not like some I could mention."

Once the women left the main street to turn down to the bone shop, Trude began to feel ill. They were in an area of butchers, sausage makers, and slaughter houses, which all disposed of the blood, entrails, and carcasses of their profession by tossing them in the stagnant canals, and the stench in the hot summer sun was too much for her delicate stomach to bear. They reached the shop without trouble following the woman's directions but Trude balked at entering its close quarters.

"Oh Gebirga, I do feel so ill."

"Is it the baby?"

"Yes, or maybe one of those mussels was bad. I'll stay outside here in the fresh air while you do the shopping if you don't mind. I'm sure I'll be well in a minute."

Gebirga doubted whether the air outside qualified as fresh, but she supposed she could manage this little bit of shopping on her own, so she went in with Liisa. It took her longer than she expected to buy the few things she needed. The man, taking advantage of a blind woman, tried to offer her blunt needles and cracked buttons.

When she finally left the shop, she found herself alone in the small street. "Trude?" she called tentatively. No answer. Perhaps she had felt better and had gone into one of the other shops. Surely Trude would not abandon her here. She called again, and again, louder each time. Apart from the distant sounds of men and women working, only silence met her shouts. She began to worry. What if Trude had been taken seriously ill? Then a new thought came to her. How was she going to get back herself? The first fingers of panic touched her. It had been so easy walking around with Trude, she had almost forgotten her old fears of the town. She fondled Liisa's head to help calm her nerves. Liisa would make sure she did not walk into a wall or worse, fall into a canal. It could not be that hard. All she needed to do was go back up Mariastraat and then turn right onto Hoogestraat, which she would know by its cobbles, to get to the market. There she could surely find a boy to escort her back to the inn.

Gebirga set out cautiously up the street, keeping Liisa on a short leash so the animal could protect her from obstacles. They walked for what seemed like ages, though it was probably not much more than fifty yards or so, before she was hailed by a voice to her left begging for aid.

"Some food for an old man? It has been long since I ate last."

Gebirga was startled to be addressed, but she reached into her bag and pulled out one of the buns she and Trude had purchased, motivated by hope that the man would help her if she fed him. "Here, grandfather. I'm told these are the specialty of the town."

By the way the man wolfed it down, he had been speaking the truth when he said he was hungry. Gebirga had pity on him, and offered him her bottle gourd. "Grandfather, I have some weak ale as well. Please take some."

The man took a long draught and handed it back to her. "This is a bottle gourd like pilgrims carry. Are you a pilgrim then?"

"No," she laughed, "I'm no pilgrim, although I do come from out of town."

"I think you are a pilgrim. And you have a long way to travel, following the Milky Way the whole journey to Compostela in Spain."

The Milky Way? The stars in the sky she could not even see? That made no sense. But she had heard of Compostela. The bones of St. James were buried there, at the ends of the earth, and people traveled to Compostela from all over, by horse or on foot, the sick seeking healing, the sinful seeking absolution for crimes committed and confessed, and the curious seeking adventure, bringing scallop shells home with them as a sign of their journey. It was third in importance only to Rome and Jerusalem as a place of pilgrimage. She had learned them in a jingle from the local priest—the three great pilgrimage sites, the four cardinal virtues, the five wounds of Christ—before he grew bored with teaching her. One was God, and two were the Old and New Testaments, but she had forgotten six and seven.

Gebirga decided the man must be mazed in the head with his talk of stars and Spain and doubted he could help her, but still she asked, "Sir, I am no pilgrim. How could I be a pilgrim; I can't even find my way through Bruges. I am trying to reach the market, and I am lost. Can you help me?"

"You are a pilgrim. Off to see St. James, or Santiago as they call him in Spain. Saint Jacques, Sint Jakob, it is all the same. And you are not lost; you are on the right road for where you are heading. In fact, I think you will be just in time."

"In time for what?"

"In time to make the next step."

This puzzled Gebirga even more and she was about to bid him farewell and go on her way when he took her hand, startling her. His hand was gnarled and old, but strong.

"Wait! We are going to meet again but I see you are blind and I want to make sure you know me when we next meet. I am a pilgrim too, you know."

Before she could demur, he used her hand to trace the contours of his face. A face like tree roots, old but nothing soft about it, big nose, short, straggly beard, it was a face like many and she doubted that she would be able to tell him again from a thousand other old men who smelled like hunger and unwashed clothes. Then he put something in her palm. "You'll need this," he said.

She took it, glad to be released. As the man shuffled off in the direction from which she had come, she inspected the surface of the object in her palm. Rough on its convex side but smooth as pearl in the interior, it was a flat shell, a scallop. Worthless, but Gebirga put it in the purse she wore on the leather girdle about her waist before she continued in the direction she was going before he stopped her, feeling her way down the road.

After some time she grew concerned. Surely she and Liisa should have reached the high street by now. She was certain she would recognize it from the noise. She noticed a new smell in her nose, replacing the former stench of animal parts and hides. It was burnt wood, but not from a householder's hearth fire, more like a whole building that had burnt down and had been left to sit in the weather for a long time, a big building from the magnitude of the odor. If she had passed it on her way to the shop, she knew she would have noticed it before. There was no question about it; she was lost.

CHAPTER FIVE

Katerinen

O, how blessed are those who have such an intercessor before God, and such a pardoner! Why then, O lover of Saint James, do you delay in going to his abode, where not only all nations and languages, but also the angelic hosts gather, and where the sins of men are forgiven?

er heart thumped and beads of sweat pooled between her shoulder blades under the thin wool of her dress. Now her panic was full fledged. "Come on," she spoke to herself sharply out loud, as if the sound of her own voice might brace her, "You are not in the middle of nowhere. It's a city; there are people here, and you have friends close by. Find someone to help you." Should she try to go back to the old man? No, he was worse than useless with his strange messages, and shells, and tales of pilgrims. He was clearly mad, and maybe talking to him was what had set her on the wrong path in the first place. Surely someone else was near. Beggars never strayed too far from their patrons. With that she stopped and listened. She heard a rumble of voices not far away and she headed slowly in that direction, straining every available sense in an effort to orient herself. The rank odor of stale beer almost overpowered her as she drew closer to the sound. The noise was coming from a tavern and, by its stench, one that did not place a premium on cleanliness. The closer she got the more it sounded like there was a small-scale brawl going on inside, but she did not have much choice. She aimed for the place where she heard the loudest blast of noise in the hopes it was an open door. Liisa would stop her if it were not. Just before she walked in, she heard an unexpected feminine voice among all the men and she distinguished fragments of conversation.

"No! Don't touch me! I tell you, I'm the sister of the count and he'll have you all boiled in oil!" the girl was shrieking.

"The count's sister is it? And I'm the king of France so let's get married. But first give us a kiss. In fact, these are all my courtiers so why don't you give them all a kiss. And then we'll decide what to do with you next depending on how nicely you kiss us."

Gebirga took a deep breath. There was already one damsel in distress inside, and they were unlikely to help a second one. She should stay out of it, really she should. Surely whoever was in there could take care of herself. Gebirga walked into the room.

The stuffy scent of unwashed men, spilled beer, and old food hit her like a wall. Then she was almost knocked over as a small, scared thing hurtled into her and held on for dear life. It was the girl, seeing a female face and hoping for an ally. The girl clung and sobbed, "I am so glad you are here!" Gebirga reflexively held her close, all sharp angles and heaving shoulder bones.

"Hey, who are you? What are you doing here?" another of the men asked.

It helped she did not know how many men there were in the room. If she knew there were twenty she might lose her nerve, but she could pretend there were five and try her best to bluff them.

"I've come looking for my sister. Sister! Wherever have you been and what are you doing in this nasty place? Our brothers have been looking for you all afternoon," she addressed the shrinking girl, who quivered like a frightened animal in her arms. Gebirga hoped she was conveying the impression of a crowd of angry young men furiously combing Bruges for their beloved sister. "You mustn't wander off like that. Let's go home."

"Oh yes, let's!" the girl played along.

"Wait a minute, we were just getting started. Your sister can join in the fun. Who's she? The queen of Spain?"

Liisa very helpfully started a slow growl deep in her throat at the man's words. Liisa was a great big sheep-herding dog, and her thick, shaggy, white coat made her seem even bigger than she was. She looked like she could rip the throat out of you without a struggle if she chose. But she could not protect them alone. Gebirga drew herself up to her full height and stared down the man, or at least stared down the place where she thought he might be standing.

"Good sir, I have no idea what games you are planning but you will have to enjoy them without us. My dog is easily enraged, as you can see, and we must leave."

Liisa barked and strained on her lead. Gebirga let it out a fraction and heard the men draw back.

"Now never mind all that," a third voice said anxiously, "You just take your dog and be on your way."

Gebirga did not wait to be invited twice. She turned quickly, girl in one hand and the dog in the other.

"Now," she said to the girl the minute they got out the door, "Do you know Bruges at all? If so, take us some place fast where we will be surrounded by lots of people. We've surprised those men for now. I suppose they weren't expecting a mystery sister to come rescue you. But I wouldn't put it past them to follow us and I'd like to be somewhere public if they do."

The fresh air seemed to restore the girl's spirits, "That's easy, just round here, come." Still holding Gebirga's hand, she led her a short way around a corner. Gebirga heard the sounds of town bustle and people, and began to relax, though she was uncomfortable holding the young stranger's hand and not just because it was still sweaty and cold with residual fear. She did not like being touched, especially by people she did not know well.

"By the way," she asked the girl, detaching herself, "Where does that strong smell of burning come from? What is it, it seems quite close?"

Puzzled, the girl answered, "Why it is right beside us. It is the church of the Holy Savior that burned down a year ago. Can't you see?"

"No, actually, I can't see. I'm blind. Is there somewhere we could sit down nearby and catch our breath? You've needed my help and I'm going to need yours. Once we get you back to where you belong, I hope you will help me get back where I belong."

The girl led her to a low stone wall that ringed the burned wooden church and they sat down. "You really can't see? You seemed so brave, marching into that tavern back there and rescuing me."

"No, I can't, though I can figure out a lot of things without sight.

For instance, from your size when I held you and the sound of your voice I would guess you to be about fifteen. I also remember your long hair is loose over your shoulders. But I can't tell what color your hair is, or your eyes, or whether you have dimples or freckles."

"That's very good," said the girl. "I am fifteen. And my hair is blond and my eyes are blue. I am told I am very pretty," she finished proudly.

"How lovely for you."

At this point, Liisa evidently decided that all immediate danger was passed and settled down at Gebirga's feet, yawning noisily. The girl squeaked at the sound, "Your dog—is she dangerous? Will she bite me?"

"Liisa has never bit anyone in her life, but those men back there weren't to know that. It is lucky for us that she can look fierce when she chooses to. Here, let me show you what she likes." She took the girl's hand and bent down to rub Liisa's tummy. Liisa whimpered and rolled on her back to give the girl better access.

"She likes me," said the girl.

"Yes, she does," said Gebirga, and sighed.

"Why are you sighing? Are you sad?"

"Oh, I'm sad and also worried. When I get home I am supposed to go to a convent and I don't think they will let me take Liisa with me. I don't know what is going to become of her, or of me, for that matter. I use Liisa to help me get around. She makes sure I don't fall in ditches or trip over boulders."

"What would you rather do? Stay at home?"

What would she like to do? Gebirga was nonplused. No one had ever asked her that question. "I don't know. I don't really want to stay at home, and I am too old to get married, even if I wanted to. I grew up hearing stories of my father and the others on crusade, and I always wanted to follow them and have adventures. I used to embroider the stories I heard, and imagine I was there on the walls of Jerusalem. But of course that is out of the question for a blind woman."

"Why? I think you should be able to go off and have adventures if you want to. You were able to rescue me from those nasty men. You can't be that helpless."

"No, I can only live somewhere I know very well. Even Bruges intimidates me, and I was lost before I found you. At least the monastery will be familiar and well-regulated."

"Maybe, but I think it sounds dull and horrible too, not letting you keep your dog. Why don't you both come and live with me? That would be a little adventure at least."

This girl was sweet but she seemed much younger than her years, especially compared with Bertulf's hard-edged Aude. "I imagine your mother would have something to say about inviting a strange woman and a great big dog to come live with you."

"You're probably right. Mother is quite fierce. But if I screamed loud enough, I could probably get my way. Mother hates it when I scream because sometimes then I have fits and they scare her because they make everyone think a demon is inside me and people make the sign of the evil eye around me. So she often lets me have my way. I think maybe if you lived with me, I wouldn't have so many fits."

Gebirga had been accused often enough in her own childhood of being possessed by the devil, especially before Mathilde taught her how to function with her blindness, that the girl's description struck a chord. "Why do you think you have fits?" she asked.

"I don't know. Sometimes I am very sad and then I get very happy and it all goes out of control. Maybe it is the devil," the girl said, sadly.

To distract her, Gebirga brought the conversation around to something more pressing. "Right now your mother must be worried sick about you. How ever did you come to be in that tavern in the first place?"

The girl's mood stayed melancholy. "That is my brother's fault. He is older and he is always teasing me about how scared and useless I am. He pinches and I scream. I thought I'd show him I could be brave too. He boasts about how he dresses up and visits taverns with his friends in secret, so I thought I would do the same and it all worked fine, except I suppose I picked the wrong tavern. The way he describes them, they are all fun and singing, but no one was singing in there. I suppose you can't see it, but I borrowed my maid's dress for the day. She was delighted to be able to wear my soft wool instead of her homespun and I can't blame her; this scratches terribly. Still, if anyone sees her in my dress, she will be in big trouble."

Gebirga was hard put to follow this story of maids and dresses and brothers but she grasped at the reference to trouble. "I am afraid you may be in trouble yourself if we don't get you back where you belong quickly. Can you let me take you home?"

"I'll gladly let you walk back with me but I'll have to leave you outside because I will want to sneak in without getting caught. I'm not supposed to leave the castle grounds without an escort but that is just mother being silly."

"The castle? Who are you?"

"My name is Katerinen. I am the sister of the count."

Sister of the count? It was what she had heard the girl telling the men in the tavern. But that was ridiculous. "Katerinen, I know you told the men that because you were scared. But honestly, I am not going to hurt you. I just want to help you find your way home." And then have you help me, she thought. "Are you afraid to go home for some reason? Don't you have a home? Please, let me help."

"I do have a home, a very rich and beautiful home, much nicer than anything you have ever seen," the girl answered crossly, "Why won't anyone believe me? First those men and now you. Who are you anyway?"

"My name is Gebirga of Gistel. My father is castellan of Gistel and he accompanied Count Robert on crusade. So I have a very nice home myself."

"Ha! Your family doesn't even want you there; you said they're sending you to a convent."

Gebirga was silent. What the girl said may be true but she took back her notion about Katerinen being sweet. Really, she was a brat. Maybe she actually was the count's sister.

"Gebirga? Gebirga?" The girl put her hand on Gebirga's forearm, trying to reestablish the connection between them. "I'm sorry, I didn't mean to hurt your feelings. Mother always threatens to send me to a convent too when she is angry with me, which is often, though I know she won't do it because she wants to marry me off to someone powerful. Only, it is horrible having no one believe me about who I am. Mother and the priests say that true nobility shines out from a noble woman and she can be recognized by everyone, but as far as I can see from today that isn't true. Maybe if you weren't blind you'd see my nobility. Come to the castle with me and help me sneak in and then I'll find a boy to take you wherever you need."

Gebirga softened under her charm, "Very well. But if you really are Count Baldwin's sister you shouldn't be hurtful like that. You need to be kind and gracious to everyone."

"I know. Everyone tells me that too. Come on, let's go."

Gebirga was not sure she believed Katerinen's tale of her identity, and she feared a trick played on her by this capricious young lady, still she had no choice but to follow, so they walked together over the bridge and through the walls of the Burg. No sooner had they entered the castle yard when they were accosted by an anxious older woman.

"My lady Katerinen," she hissed pulling the girl into a dark corner in the lee of a building as Gebirga followed, "Where on earth have you been? We have barely been able to hide from your mother that you haven't been in the castle. And then your maid turned up wearing your gown with a big stain on it. If your mother sees her, we'll all be sunk."

"Drat that girl. I told her to keep it clean. You see Gebirga, everyone is afraid of mother," Katerinen said cheerfully. "As you see I have been perfectly safe, strolling about the town of Bruges in the company of the gentlelady Gebirga of Gistel, daughter of one of my poor deceased father's holy companions in Jerusalem. And now we're back, safe and sound."

The woman ignored Gebirga and focused on her charge, "Strolling through Bruges! Among the cut purses, drunkards, and murderers? You're lucky you weren't robbed and raped and returned without a stitch of clothing! Let's get you inside before your lady mother sees us. We can pretend you were praying in the chapel out of sight all afternoon." She made as if to drag Katerinen inside.

"Wait!" said the girl, "I must find an escort for my friend." She quickly commissioned a passing stable lad to take Gebirga wherever she wanted to go, then squeezed her new friend in a bone crunching hug sealed with a big kiss. As her captor started to pull the naughty Katerinen behind her, the last thing Gebirga heard was the young girl shouting, "Good bye! But not for long—I know we are going to meet again some day!"

The boy took Gebirga's arm in his and soon they were marching towards the inn where Gebirga was staying. Gebirga pondered her recent encounter. So Katerinen was the count's sister after all. She had heard Count Baldwin had a sister, but knew nothing about her. Poor thing. Though Baldwin was as yet wifeless and childless, he had so many powerful male cousins that Katerinen would never inherit. Her fate would be a distant marriage or maybe even a convent like Gebirga.

When they arrived at the inn she reached in her purse to give her guide a small fraction of a coin as reward. Her hand brushed against the scallop shell, forgotten since the old man gave it to her. It reminded her that both the new people she had met that day had promised her, against all likelihood, that they would meet again.

She entered the inn, to be greeted by Winnoc and Trude who were sitting around the fire.

"Trude, what happened to you? Are you all right? I was so worried; I was afraid you'd been taken seriously ill."

"I'm fine now. I felt so queasy waiting for you outside the shop, that I went down to the river, but when I tried to come back to meet you, I got totally lost. By the time I found the bone shop, you had gone. Did you get lost too? What a pair we are! Bruges is so confusing, isn't it?"

Gebirga was hurt that Trude would equate their difficulties finding their way around. Did she not know that being blind in a strange place was not the same thing as simply taking a wrong turn? "I did get lost," she answered, "And you can imagine that it was even harder for me to find my way back than you."

"Oh, I'm sorry, Gebirga. But everything turned out well, didn't it? I mean, you're back safely with no harm done."

"Never mind all that," Winnoc broke in, "We have to talk about tomorrow and tell you our news. The archbishop of Magdeburg's men are in town, luckily enough. Their offer to me still stands but they're leaving tomorrow, and so too must we, if we are to travel with them. Gebirga, are you with us?"

He seemed sure Gebirga would throw her lot in with them. And perhaps she would have, if it were not for her adventure of the afternoon. At least the convent at Gistel was familiar and there was no chance of her losing her way there. She shuddered at all the new places she would have to get used to in the dark if she traveled with Trude and Winnoc. Could she trust them to take care of her as they started a new life? She feared she would always be out of place, an extra third to be accounted for and to get in the way. And could she disappoint her father by leaving without a word? She also admitted to herself a vague sensation that there might be some third option, some new possibility as yet unguessed at. "I wish both of you the very best and I am sure this trip to the East will be successful," she replied to Winnoc. "I'll pray for you on the journey and that your babe may come into the world easily and safely, boy or girl. But I won't be going with you. It's not my place; I can see that now. I'll be going home to Gistel with the boat and the men. I'll take the letter to Bertulf. I'm not afraid of him and it is right that the news should come from me."

Winnoc could see that her mind was made up and did not try to persuade her to change it, though Trude was aghast and said so. But Winnoc stopped the conversation by saying that they had much to do before they went on their separate journeys the next day, and all needed to get to work.

It was lonely for Gebirga on the trip home, especially the night she spent with only Liisa for company in the abbey guesthouse where the three of them had such fun on the way up. She missed Trude's lively speculation about every person she knew and each thing she saw. How would Trude fare in a place where everything was foreign to her and all the people and customs were strange? Many times Gebirga asked herself whether she had made a mistake not going with them. All the comfortable bales of wool and cloth had been sold, so she sat on the hard oak of the boat, back uncomfortable against Bertulf's new weapons. To make matters worse, she had come down with a summer cold. Head throbbing and nose streaming, she drifted down the river, heading back to Bertulf, Aude, and the convent.

Her spirits lifted when they arrived at the jetty at Gistel and the familiar people of the castle rushed out to meet the boat. There was loud chatter as everyone asked for the news from town, and pestered to see what the wool and cloth, produced so arduously by all of them over the preceding year, had purchased. Amidst the crowds of people hugging, opening parcels and heaving bales out of the boat, Bertulf saw immediately who was missing.

"Where is Winnoc?' he asked his daughter.

"Winnoc didn't return with the boat. He is traveling with the archbishop of Magdeburg's men to build a new settlement in the lands of the Germans and the Slavs. He asked me to bid you farewell and he gave me this letter explaining his decision." She held the parchment out but her father did not take it.

"Hmmph, I suppose it can't be helped. What of that bit of land near the south pasture?" he said, referring to the land that Winnoc had sold on the way down.

"He sold it to the monks of St. Peter's in Oudenburg. The letter will tell you everything."

Bertulf took the letter now but did not look at it. He wadded up the heavy parchment into a ball and Gebirga heard it splash as he tossed it into the river, unread, before turning to walk slowly back to the castle.

At dinner that night, Bertulf remained taciturn and Aude pretended Gebirga did not exist, as would soon be the case in fact because Bertulf informed her that the nuns would be pleased to receive her the following day. Lost in the fog of her cold, Gebirga could only pick at her food, surreptitiously tossing scraps of tough boiled mutton to Liisa. The food, cooked under Aude's housekeeping, was close to inedible. Again she wondered if she should have followed Winnoc despite the novelties and dangers of travel. But she imagined strange beds every night and strange people the next morning, and never knowing where to find the privy. Better to stay close to home.

Their meal was interrupted by the flustered arrival of one of their sentries.

"Sir! Armed men from the count are at the gate, traveling from Bruges! They say they have a message for you and wish to enter." This was unexpected. They rarely had visitors of any kind at the castle, and never from the count.

"How many?" asked Bertulf, rising.

"Only five, sir, with a couple of extra horses."

"That doesn't sound too threatening. Better let them in. I expect they are planning to stay the night, so offer to stable their horses and bring them in here. Women, we'll need some more places at the table and more food. Get to it, before our guests arrive."

Five powerful men entered the hall. They were greeted by Bertulf and Aude and seated at the table. But it was not until after dinner, when Bertulf, Aude, and Gebirga were sitting with the five men cracking nuts and eating sweetmeats hastily prepared by the cook, that Bertulf said, "I understand from my man that you have a message for me from Count Baldwin."

"Not from the count, my lord, but from his lady mother, Clemence. We come from Bruges, where the lady is in residence with her daughter, Katerinen."

Gebirga, who had been paying little attention to the men, meditating on her convent-bound future and the awful pounding in her head, was startled to hear that name.

"The lady Katerinen is moving from girlhood to young woman-hood and she is in need of a new waiting-woman to replace the nurses and governesses who have attended her before. It is expected that this waiting woman will follow Katerinen to her new marital home wherever that should be. Lady Clemence requests that your daughter, Gebirga of Gistel come with us to Bruges on the morrow to serve as waiting-woman to lady Katerinen. The person known as Liisa must also come too. Lady Clemence, well really Katerinen, was most emphatic about that last part," he finished.

Neither Bertulf nor Aude had made any effort to learn the name of Gebirga's dog so they ignored that part of the message. Aude spoke first. "She is going to go live in a palace in Bruges with a countess while I freeze here in this damp castle?"

"They won't always be in Bruges. Sometimes the court goes to Oudenaarde, or Ghent, or Saint-Omer. And of course Katerinen will join a new court when she marries."

Bertulf was next. "But Gebirga is promised to the nuns at St. Godeleva's. They expect her to join them tomorrow."

The man said nothing this time. Gebirga could imagine Bertulf weighing his options. His hopes for her were moot when the countess had her own plans. Besides, whatever the advantage of a daughter engaged in full time prayer for his soul after his death, the benefit on this earth of a daughter well-placed at the court of Flanders was considerably greater. Heaven could wait, she envisioned him calculating.

"Right then," he answered the man, "Gebirga will be ready to leave tomorrow." Aude made a moan of disapproval, as if she had expected him to refuse the order, but it was Gebirga who spoke.

"Father, you don't mean it. I can't possibly manage at court."

She was ignored by both her father and the countess's man who said, "We must leave first thing in the morning."

"Then that's when she'll be ready, you hear that Gebirga?"

She thought of the crowds, the castles many times the size of Gistel, the strange customs, and new rules. It would be much worse than going east with Winnoc, and even the convent started to look like a better proposition. Then under the table, Liisa put her muzzle in her lap and gave her hand a quick lick as if to comfort her (though possibly just scenting a stray bit of gravy). At least Liisa would be there. Bless Katerinen for remembering the dog. And she would not have to live with Alice. "Yes father," she answered.

"Then why are you dallying here? Surely you must have packing to do and farewells to say."

She got up from the table without another word and went to bundle up her things, a couple of dresses and shifts, probably nothing good enough to wear in her new life, clean coifs, her thick wool cloak and hood as well as her second best cloak, a comb, a few bits of bronze jewelry from her mother, some brooches and clasps and rings, not very valuable. Bertulf had given all the good pieces to the monastery years before. She also packed her embroidery wools in the small frame Mathilde had made for her years ago. She could get linen in Bruges, and it would be good to have something to occupy her hands. Court life was not going to require as much effort from her as running the Gistel household. She sorted through her purse, and decided to keep the scallop shell. The old man had been right in one way—she was about to begin a journey.

When her bundle was ready she got into bed, pulling her shift off last when she was already under the covers as she had been taught to do by Mathilde. She lay there not sleeping, listening to the castle settling down for the night, the distant noises of animals in their stalls, pens, and byres, and even further away, the river at night, birds and small animals rustling in the reeds. She might be hearing these sounds, her steady companions since birth, for the last time. The chance encounter of the previous week bade fair to transform her entire life.

The next morning she felt even more ill. She had become feverish in the night and her head felt like it was packed with wool. Nevertheless, she was up early and breakfasting on bread and beer when she heard the men from Bruges outside readying for the journey. She joined them, carrying her bundle, and with Liisa in tow, followed down the stairs by her father.

"Gebirga," he said, and she turned around, "I have something for you." He put a small casket in her hands. She recognized it from its raised decorations as the relic chest he had sent home from the Holy Land, the one intended to go with her today to the convent, if things had turned out otherwise.

"This is your dowry. You should take it with you, you know, because it is yours. You may still find a use for it."

She packed it deep within her bundle and when she was done, he grasped both her arms, "Little one, I remember the day you were born. How you howled! And now you are going so far away, I may never see you again. I thought at least at the convent you'd be close by. I always hated the thought of marrying you off to some other person's family, a family that might not treat you well, and this seemed a good way to keep you close. But first Winnoc and now you . . . I came home to die among my kin, and my kin are leaving me."

Strange words, given the sad end of her mother and his first wife, but perhaps who better to know the perils of marrying far away from kin? She released herself from his grip. "Father, you are going to have new kin, a whole line to follow you and care for you in your old age. Besides I am not going as far as all that, only to Bruges. And even if I follow the court to Saint-Omer, that isn't very distant either." How odd it was that she had to comfort him about her departure. But neither had control over her destiny now the countess had taken an interest in her.

He sighed and kissed her on the forehead, "Go with God, daughter."

Her bundle was tied to the back of her saddle and one of the men helped her up. Some ladies rode side saddle but riding blind was enough of a challenge; Gebirga rode astride. She warned them against setting an excessive pace both because of her disability and because Liisa would not be able to keep up.

"That's right, Liisa. Where is she? We have a horse ready and saddled for her also. Is she still inside the castle. She must hurry. We plan to reach Bruges before nightfall."

"Liisa is my dog. I don't think your horse would appreciate having her on her back. She'll follow behind as long as you go slow enough and give her time to rest."

Nonplused, the man in charge nevertheless gave the order to move. The castle dwellers shouted and cheered her departure, and that was the last contact she had with the castle, deprived by her blindness from taking a fond backward glance.

They covered quickly by land all the country Gebirga had so recently traveled more slowly by boat. Gebirga was not used to riding so far, however, and with her senses of hearing and scent diminished by her illness, she felt trapped in a dark fog, shivering despite the summer day. Long before they came to the bridge over the Sands, the wasteland on the west side of Bruges, she was exhausted and Liisa was too, from the way she was panting. But soon they trotted over the main castle bridge and passed under the portcullis into the walls. Gebirga had barely dismounted beneath the imposing stone mass that served as the count's palace when Katerinen, who must have been waiting for their arrival from a window, hurtled into her, almost knocking her off her feet for the second time.

"Hooray, hooray, you're here! And you have Liisa with you and you don't have to live in a horrid convent. Wasn't I clever to arrange all of this? Come, let me show you our room. You'll be sleeping with me. The woman who used to sleep there will be glad to go somewhere else. She says I snore, but it's a lie." Katerinen dragged her forward. Gebirga scarcely felt equal to Katerinen's enthusiasm, but it was good to feel wanted by someone, even this rather over-excited almost stranger.

"My orders were to bring the Lady Gebirga straight to your mother, Lady Katerinen. And also the woman Liisa, but since Liisa is a dog . . ." his voice trailed away, uncertain.

"Oh yes, she wanted to inspect you before I found you so she could send you back if she didn't like you. But that won't happen; she will love you just as I do. And we'll bring Liisa with us too. Come."

Gebirga was too ill to care that she would have to pass some kind of test with Katerinen's mother. She followed the young girl and the men who had brought her from Gistel into the palace and up to the great hall where Clemence was holding court. At the door they were met by a servant with a towel and a basin of water to wash off the grime of the journey. Another handed her and Katerinen each a glass filled with spiced wine. Gebirga was more awed by the glass than its contents. At Gistel, they had one chalice of glass, given to her grandfather by a long ago count, which Gebirga did not trust herself to touch, leaving it to be dusted by someone who could see. But here it was used as an ordinary drinking vessel. It felt cool and smooth against her lips, so different from wood or rough earthenware. In her exhausted state, one sip of wine went straight to her head.

The leader of the men announced her arrival to Clemence, who was sitting in a circle of women at one end of the hall.

"My lady Clemence, I present you Gebirga of Gistel. And her dog, Liisa, as I was directed," he finished, washing his hands of the affair.

"Her dog?" Clemence spoke, "Katerinen, you didn't tell me it was a dog. We can't have people bringing their animals here. This is a court, not a menagerie. Gebirga, girl, come here and let me take a look at you."

The hall was noisy and Gebirga's hearing was dulled by her cold. She went in what she thought was the right direction, trusting Liisa to help her avoid obstacles. Obviously she misjudged it for Clemence's next words were, "Over here, you fool! What is wrong with you, can't you see?"

Gebirga turned a little to her right, aiming more closely for the direction of the irritated woman's voice. This was not a good beginning, and she tried to keep the shaking out of her voice as she responded, "I beg you pardon, your grace, it is true that I am blind and can't see you. That is why I travel with my dog. Her eyes perform some of the functions that mine cannot."

"Blind! Katerinen, whatever were you thinking? A blind girl can be of no use to you. You need someone who can care for you and dress you. And there will be traveling, and meeting important people, and then when you are married, a household of your own to run. No, this won't do at all. Gebirga, we will keep you here for the night, but tomorrow you must return to your people in Gistel. There's no place for you here. Your dog can sleep in the stables."

Gebirga was so ill and exhausted from two consecutive days of travel, and overawed by the strangeness and grandeur of her surroundings that she would have agreed to whatever the countess ordered without protest, though inside she sank at the thought of returning home, and Aude's glee at her speedy fall from glory. Katerinen had other ideas, however.

"Mother! I don't want Gebirga to leave; I want her to stay here with me. She's the only waiting woman I want. Mother, you promised."

Clemence raised her own voice. "I did nothing of the kind. I said we'd bring her here and see if she was suitable. And she's not, which you yourself should have known. No more of this. I have spoken."

But Katerinen was not finished. "You promised, you promised, you promised!" she cried, her voice getting ever louder until she started shrieking at her mother. "I want her to stay here with me, I do!" She must have thrown her cup to the floor because Gebirga heard the tinkle of breaking glass. Katerinen stamped her foot and an answering yelp from Liisa suggested the girl had landed on the dog's tail. No one moved to halt her or control her fit in any way.

Gebirga was tired and hot, thirsty and hungry. All she wanted was to lie down on a cool bed, rest her aching head, and die. She was dreading a long night in a strange place followed by yet another journey on the morrow. She had dealt with many fifteen-year-old girls in her time as chatelaine of Gistel, girls who would not eat, or got pregnant, or went into hysterics, or fell in love, or who made a mess of their weaving. To Gebirga at that moment, Katerinen was not a count's daughter but only another young girl needing a sharp talking to before she got herself in real trouble, and who, moreover, had just hurt her dog.

"Katerinen!" she called, illness and anxiety forgotten, her strong, clear voice cutting through the younger girl's screams, "You are making a spectacle of yourself. Pull yourself together." At the sound of Gebirga's command, Katerinen stopped screaming.

"That's much better. Now beg your mother's forgiveness for breaking her glass and making such a display in her hall."

Katerinen slowly did as she was bid, "I'm sorry mother," she gasped between sobs.

"And you can apologize to Liisa too, for crushing her tail."

"Did I hurt Liisa? I didn't know. I'm so sorry," Katerinen was instantly repentant. She sat down on the floor next to the dog, hugging the animal and whispering apologies. Liisa was forgiving and Katerinen's last sobs ceased as she embraced the animal, her breathing slowing down to match the steady respiration of the dog.

Clemence had not said a word and the whole hall was silent. It was hard to tell if they were more startled by Katerinen's fit, or by Gebirga's ability to get her out of it. Finally, Clemence spoke. "Gebirga of Gistel, it seems you have skills after all that Katerinen could make use of. What is your parentage, girl?"

"My father is Bertulf of Gistel. He traveled to the Holy Land in the service of Count Robert, your husband, rest his soul, to liberate Jerusalem from the pagans."

"Ha. A waste of men and money. Never mind. And your mother?"

"My lady, she was Godeleva, daughter of Heinfrid." After a pause, Gebirga added, "She is now known as Saint Godeleva."

"Yes, I remember the story. The crusade did remove some of our more violent knights to a place where their violence could do some good for Christians, rather than harm. Flanders under my rule while Robert was gone was a more peaceful place than it was under him. Or than it is now under my son Baldwin, for that matter." Her ladies tittered gently. Obviously complaints about her son were familiar to them.

Clemence ignored them and said to Gebirga, "If you can continue to deal with Katerinen's moods as you did this evening, you may remain. We shall keep you here for a trial period and see how that works out. You'll need new clothes, of course. You can't wear that dress at court."

Gebirga blushed. It was one of her best. Still, before the countess turned back to her own concerns, Gebirga pressed her narrow advantage. "And my dog? Truly I would not be much use to Katerinen without her. She has lived in a castle all her life and knows how to behave around gentle people. I'm sure she will cause you no inconvenience."

With more reluctance Clemence assented, "Very well. The dog can stay on trial too. But I fear it will be in vain. Katerinen is deathly afraid of dogs."

"No I'm not mother," piped up Katerinen, now fully recovered from her fit with the happy news that her friend would stay, "Look!" And the big dog licked her face.

"Truly, Gebirga, you are a miracle worker," said Clemence dryly, "We shall see if you fare as well preparing my daughter for the marriage bed."

Katerinen took Gebirga up to the room that was to be theirs through a maze of corridors and wooden stairways set into the thick stone of the palace. Gebirga knew she would be lost if she tried to make her way back to the hall on her own, and hoped that Liisa was paying attention. Feeling alone and strange, but relieved to be away from the crowded hall, she unpacked her few belongings, hoping the familiar objects and clothing would make it more like home. But they felt odd and out-of-place: too few to make a difference and too humble for their new environment. She asked Katerinen for food, and the girl tried to summon a servant. The boy who came at last was on the edge of insolent and served them sloppily when he finally returned with something to eat and drink. The hot broth Gebirga had requested was barely warm. Gebirga was puzzled by his attitude and noticed things about their room that also spoke of neglect. The rushes on the floor were musty and almost crumbled to dust with age, and a faint scent of decay penetrated even her blocked nose and muzzy head, as if a dead bird had got caught in the chimney and no one had thought to clean it out. She stroked the bed linens. Though they were of the finest linen, better than even what went on the lord's bed at Gistel, they were filthy. All this was at odds with the order and luxury she had sensed in the hall, so she questioned Katerinen about it.

"The servants don't like to clean here," she answered, fidgeting with one of Gebirga's brooches, hooking and unhooking it, "They're afraid of me because I get so angry sometimes, like in the hall this evening. They whisper that I am possessed by a demon. I don't know; maybe I am. They won't come in here except when we are gone, living at one of the other castles. I don't like to complain to mother, because she has so many other worries, and I cause her enough trouble already."

Gebirga remembered how some of the servants at Gistel avoided her when she was little, fearing her blindness was a manifestation of her father's sin against a saint, and how their neighbors still whispered about her, not to speak of the nuns. Well, lazy servants were something she knew how to deal with, strange castle or not. Maybe she would feel better after a good sleep and then tomorrow they would have the whole room scrubbed, all the hangings changed, and someone would track down that dead smell, or she would know the reason why.

The tepid broth must have done its work, because Gebirga did feel much better the next morning. Her fever was gone and her head had cleared, so they spent the day in a binge of cleaning. Fresh rushes brought the scent of a meadow into the bedchamber, and a whole family of mice were excavated from the chimney. Clemence had sent down a new dress for Gebirga to wear. Katerinen exclaimed over the color, rose madder, but Gebirga appreciated the fine texture of the smooth wool and the care of its stitches. It only wanted some embroidery around the neckline, and perhaps smocking beneath the bust.

Gebirga started to feel at home, at least until it was time to join the rest of the castle in the hall for their big meal of the day. She found the hall without difficulty, thanks to Katerinen, but then the two were separated because Katerinen sat at the top, near her mother, while Gebirga was sent further down. Instead of the pease pottage and roast or boiled mutton that was the everyday fare she knew, here she was served two courses of several dishes each, sweet as well as savoury, poultry, meat, and fish. The aromas of saffron, ginger, and cardamom rising from the dishes before her displayed the wealth of the court and the trading power of Flanders. Even

Aude could have no complaints about their quality. At home in Gistel, the food had been warm and filling. Here, it had been raised to a subtle art, like one of her tapestries. The problem was getting any of it to her mouth. She was used to being served by people who knew of her disability but now she had to fend for herself.

"I pray you sir, would you . . .," she began when she heard a platter placed before her, but the busy servant paid no attention. Timid appeals to her neighbors for assistance were also ignored as they chattered with their friends. She reached out to find the platter, and miracle of miracles, the serving spoon was right there. She took a ladle of whatever it was and moved it to her trencher, only to slop gravy all over the table.

"Charming country manners," someone drawled while another tittered. Gebirga felt the color rise to her cheeks.

After the meal was finished, instead of the man with a wooden flute they had at Gistel to amuse the table, there was a parade of entertainers and Katerinen moved down to join her. A lord named William of Ypres, a descendant on the wrong side of the blanket of Clemence's deceased husband, presented a farce about the current count, Baldwin and his two friends, Charles of Denmark and William Clito, all three of whom were absent from Bruges at the time. The three actors chased each other around, making pratfalls and somersaults and poking each other in the arse with inflated pig's bladders in a way that, Katerinen whispered, was intended to mock the trio's supposedly unorthodox sexual tastes. The shrieks of laughter from the audience showed that these three were popular targets in Clemence's faction of the elite of Flanders. But unable to see their japes, Gebirga got little out of this mummery, and she could not appreciate the jugglers and acrobats who entertained on the following nights. She did like the musicians and singers who told stories about the old legends and fables of Flanders, and the lives of the saints.

Gebirga discovered why many were grateful to have her steady hand governing Katerinen after the tantrum she had witnessed on the first day was repeated again and again, sometimes over the most trivial of reasons. One day she did not want her hair brushed, saying it hurt her head, and screamed at any of the maids who approached her, before Gebirga arrived to take the situation in hand.

"What do you think you're doing, Katerinen?"

The girl stood there weeping. "I don't know. I don't want everyone fussing over me."

Gebirga had heard this before. The previous day Katerinen had refused to wear shoes even though they were to go to the church of St. Donatien for a special mass. When the servants tried to compel her to put them on, she began removing the rest of her clothing as well, and they had to leave her in her room. Clemence had been furious. Now the girl's breath was coming in big gasps and Gebirga placed her hand on her chest. Katerinen was shaking and her heart was beating rapidly, as if in panic.

"Come, sit down next to me on the bed, Katerinen. There's no point getting yourself into a state. Look, you're worrying Liisa." She put the girl's hand on the dog's head and moved it to stroke the animal.

Slowly, Katerinen stroked the dog herself and then scratched Liisa's square muzzle. The dog was in ecstasy, and Gebirga could feel Katerinen begin to calm down. Gebirga gently began to comb the girl's hair, crisis averted again, until the next time. Some days handling Katerinen was more work than running the entire castle at Gistel.

Nothing more was ever said about her or Liisa leaving Katerinen.

CHAPTER SIX

Ghent and Lille

The pilgrim must mortfy his flesh, with its vices and evil desires,
through hunger and thirst, through many fasts, through cold
and nakedness, and through many insults and hardships.

The cart creaked and pitched, one wheel sinking deeply into a hole in the rutted road, before it lurched out again.

"I think I am going to be sick," said Katerinen. Gebirga felt much the same but hoped keeping silent would help the nausea pass.

Gebirga had just begun to think she might survive life in Bruges, when she learned they would leave for Ghent at the end of August. Clemence was joining her son, Count Baldwin, for a court of law, and a council of war was also rumoured. The chore of packing up and transferring the court even the short distance between Bruges and Ghent was a triumph of logistics. All their necessities and quite a few of their luxuries were bundled up and loaded on mules. The men rode, but the women were crammed into covered wagons, sitting in rows on hastily constructed wooden benches facing each other, wool dresses sticking to their backs in the late August heat and splinters from the new wood piercing their thighs. For sightless Gebirga, trapped among the hot, pungent, mass of women, this means of travel was a kind of hell, and she envied Liisa who trotted along behind. Katerinen was no more happy in the cart than she was, and kept asking why they could not ride like the men.

It took them two days to reach their destination, and another to settle in completely. Unlike Gebirga, the others were used to this life of travel from castle to castle. They quickly settled into old haunts and revisited favorite market stalls while Gebirga was still trying to memorize the route from the bedchamber to the latrines that emptied their contents over the river. She also had to deal with Katerinen in the presence of her brother for the first time.

Count Baldwin had arrived with his retinue in Ghent a day or so before the women. Born before his father left for the Holy Land, he was in his mid-twenties, just a little younger than Gebirga. He had been count since his father's death half a dozen years before, sharing power uneasily with his mother whose bridegift possession of twelve strategic Flemish castles made her the most powerful noble in the county after him. The count paid no attention to Gebirga and indeed avoided his mother and all her circle as much as he could, which was difficult when they were all living in such narrow confines.

Baldwin did seek out his younger sister, however, delighting in pestering Katerinen and teasing her, telling her she was ugly and playing silly tricks, like leaving nasty things in the bed she and Gebirga shared. One day Gebirga had to shoo him and his laughing friends out of their apartment, and remove a bloody pig's head from their mattress. This was behavior she might have expected in a boy half his age, but it was not at all becoming in a man of his station and with his responsibilities. She tried to comfort Katerinen who was gibbering with fright in one corner after finding the monstrous object. He knew exactly how to play his sister's volatile mood swings and enjoyed reducing her to hysterical cries or shouts of rage. Katerinen, no fool, tried to avoid him, but they were thrown together at the many public occasions required by their presence at Ghent. Gebirga was moved one day to ask Clemence if she could restrain her son. Clemence answered her plea with some gentleness under her usual asperity.

"Girl, if I could protect my daughter from Baldwin, would I not have done so long ago? But I am grateful that you are aware of what is going on, and I ask you to continue to do your best for my daughter."

When not persecuting Katerinen, Baldwin spent most of his time with his two friends, Charles of Denmark and William Clito, ignoring the giggles and rumours about their close relationship. William Clito hoped to succeed to his father's dukedom of Normandy against the claim of his uncle, the king of England. Charles had lived at the court of Flanders since the day as a young boy he saw his father, the king of Denmark, hacked to pieces by his enemies before the altar of a church. Some ten years Baldwin's senior, he had served as mentor and guide to the younger man after the count's death. Clemence feared his influence over her son and blamed him for the strain in relations between mother and son, who shared an uneasy balance of power in Flanders. It was count's justice that held sway though, and it was his court at Ghent that drew the powerful of Flanders. They hoped to get the count to make decisions about inheritances, put bullying neighbors in their place, and punish violent criminals.

Baldwin held his courts of justice in the grounds outside the castle building, seated on a dais shaded by a canopy, surrounded by his family and councilors. The remaining knights, nobles, and spectators stood unprotected from the noonday sun while their pennons and banners flapped behind them in the breeze. Clemence was on one side of him, and Charles was on the other. Gebirga was there too, sitting right behind Katerinen and her mother, because Clemence had asked her to keep an eye on the girl. "It might get upsetting for her. She'll be easier if you are close."

Plaintiffs, defendants, witnesses, and advocates streamed before Baldwin, hoping for justice or mercy, depending on their perspective. The latter was in short supply. From time to time, Baldwin consulted Charles before levying a sentence. Three men were branded for petty theft while two more lost a hand for more serious larceny. Punishment was carried out right there before the assembled crowd by an executioner in a black mask. Although Katerinen jumped at every scream and groan of the chastised, Gebirga was used to this kind of justice, which was replicated on a smaller scale in every castellan's court in Flanders, including Gistel. The sound of steel hacking bone when a man lost his hand to justice was meant to deter others, and she supposed it worked. Still, even she had never heard such screams in her life as those that issued from the man castrated for raping a nun. But worse was yet to come.

The last accused prisoner brought out of the dungeon for trial was a knight, oddly clad head to toe in full armor. He was dragged before Baldwin by two armed guards. Gebirga sensed Clemence in front of her go rigid as the man approached the dais. Suddenly two women shot forth from the crowd. They flung themselves before the count and begged him, "Mercy, mercy! Your grace, have mercy on him, for the love of Mary." It was common for a woman—wife or mother, or even Countess Clemence on behalf of some favorite—to intercede on a prisoner's behalf. Heading their pleas allowed Baldwin from time to time to let a powerful captive free, without losing face. But this time there would be no mercy forthcoming. The two women were restrained by guards, and taken away from the dais.

A peasant came forward to make his complaint. "Your Grace, late last spring when I went into the byre to milk the cows I saw that my two best cows were missing, stolen in the night. My sons and I searched the countryside around our farm, and found them in the herd of the knight, Siger. When I made my complaint to the knight and demanded they be returned, he refused."

"Do you see Siger here?" the count asked.

"Yes sire, he is here before you, restrained by these guards."

"Siger, do you have anything to say?"

"My lord, the cows were my lawful property. This peasant and his family have been serfs of my family for ages past and they owe us rents and the first fruits of their best animals. They have refused to pay us what they owe despite being ordered to many times. I took what was owed to me and mine."

"Peasant?"

"Your Grace, that is not true. My family has always been free. We owe nothing to this knight."

"Do you have any evidence to support your claim?"

"Yes sir, twelve good men to swear to my free status."

"Bring them forward."

Twelve peasants were brought before the dais, overawed by the company they found themselves in. With the help of a priest carrying a bible, they each swore that the peasant was a free man, as he claimed, as were his father and grandfather before him. After they shuffled out again, Count Baldwin again consulted with Charles. While he was thus occupied, Clemence jumped to her feet.

"It's a lie! They are lying through their teeth to discredit the knight, Siger. And it is you who have put them up to it because you know Siger is my man."

"Silence, woman! This is the count's justice," answered Baldwin and got to his feet to pronounce the sentence as Clemence sat down, shaking with rage.

"We find the knight, Siger, guilty of robbing two cows from this free peasant. As punishment for his theft, and for breaking the count's peace, we sentence him to be boiled," pronounced the count.

"Boiled?!" said Clemence, but she was ignored.

Preparations for this unusual sentence got underway immediately. A cart was wheeled in bearing firewood, a man-sized cauldron, and an iron frame to support it over the fire. It took many men to place the cauldron and to fill it from skin bags once the fire had been laid. A fire was started under the cauldron, and the unfortunate knight was raised up and flung into the pot. Gebirga heard the splash and the spluttering of the man coming again to the surface. The fire began to rage but it takes a long time for a cauldron of water to grow warm, far less hot enough to cause pain. The knight struggled to free himself but the weight of his armor prevented him from hoisting himself out of the pot. The man cursed and swore after several failures to pull himself up out of the neck-deep cauldron.

"Does the water grow hot, sir knight?" said Baldwin, laughing at his struggles, "Why don't you call upon my mother to intercede for you to protect you from this punishment? You have certainly assisted her many a time against me."

But the knight refused to humiliate his mistress by asking for a mercy she had just shown she could not procure for him. The men continued to stoke the fire lapping at the sides of the cauldron. The knight held out for a while, and Gebirga could hear him redoubling his efforts to clamber somehow outside of the cauldron, though it was hard to know what better fate he thought he would endure on the outside. Soon the heat grew too much for him and he began to scream the screams of the damned. Gebirga for once in her life thanked God she was blind and there were some things she could not see. In front of her, Katerinen began to whimper and then started moaning more loudly, but her distress was concealed from most by the cries of the knight. Gebirga reached forward and took her hand. The younger girl held on so tightly her nails pierced Gebirga's palm. Her brother broke off his merriment to hiss at her,

"This upsets you, does it, you little coward?"

The shrieking ceased as the knight was carried into the merciful arms of death. But then, almost as bad, a horrific stench began to rise from the cauldron, mingling with the smoke from the fire. Its horror lay not in its awfulness but in its very sweetness because it smelled for all the world like good boiled pork, cooked to a turn. Gebirga felt the bile rise in her throat.

The cauldron boiled over and put out the fire, ending the gruesome execution. What was left of the man's body was fished out. His head was saved to adorn the castle gate but the rest of his body, a dubious prize, was restored to the two women who had begged mercy for him, to bury as they could. As the women were leaving the older one spat, "May you feel in your death everything he felt in his and more!"

Baldwin ignored the women, used to the rage of his victims, and he and his friends rose and left the dais. As he was leaving, he said to Clemence, still seated, "So die all traitors to me. I suggest you remember it."

Gebirga took Katerinen to their bedchamber and ordered up from the kitchen a pitcher of beer and a basin of bread and hot milk. The girl, who wept if she saw two dogs fighting in the courtyard, was in a state of shock after the spectacle they had witnessed. She sat mute on the bed and Gebirga tried to feed her bits of bread and milk, and small sips of beer, with no success. Gebirga was at a loss; even Liisa would not be enough to cheer the girl up this time. She tentatively stroked her hair and the younger girl reached out for her, and took her in her arms. Gebirga was at first stiff in the unaccustomed embrace but forced herself to relax so she could comfort the girl, stroking her thin, frail back. Katerinen wept, first softly then louder, until finally she was done. Gebirga herself found comfort from holding the girl, her longest physical contact with another person since Mathilde died, but she had her own questions.

"Why?" she asked Katerinen when the girl had calmed down enough to listen, "Who was that man? And why so very cruel? I know justice is justice and it must be done if we are not to live in a lawless society where the big folk crush the little at every turn. And I know men are sometimes vicious, and women too. They'll laugh to see a madman play the fool or pay a coin to watch someone possessed by demons writhe in agony. They'll set two animals against each other and grin as they watch the beasts tear each other to pieces, betting on the outcome. But this? Why did he do it?"

"The man was one of those loyal to my mother when my brother inherited the county. I was a child at the time, and I stayed at the convent of Bourbourg, but my mother led a rebellion so she could keep control of the lands and rents my father gave her when they married. It was Charles's fault; when Baldwin became count, Charles convinced him to refuse to return mother's marriage portion to her independent control. She lost and made peace, and this was all years ago now, but my brother still delights in hunting down and punishing the men who joined her. As for why it was so cruel, well, my brother is cruel. He likes punishing people and enjoys thinking up new ways to do it. Why, once when ten knights disturbed the peace at the annual fair at Turnhout, he punished them by getting each of the men to hang the previous one. When it came to the last one, Baldwin himself kicked over the barrel supporting him, and laughed. It was said some of those knights had also been supporters of my mother."

"How can Lady Clemence endure this?"

"Mother isn't without power and influence. She has her twelve castles still, and he needs her to run the county when he is off fighting battles with his horrible friends. She signs almost every document he issues so he can't make a move without her. He hates that, and it means that when he does have the power, he uses it. I wish I didn't have to go to the council meeting tomorrow; they'll be talking about war and battles, and my head will hurt. But mother will insist. She says I need to learn about high politics. Gebirga, please do say you'll come with me?"

Gebirga assured her she would, if she were permitted.

It was a small group that met the next day around a long table to discuss the involvement of Flanders in the succession crisis in Normandy. The only women among the councilors and churchmen were Clemence, Katerinen, and Gebirga, who sat behind the other two. Katerinen grew bored quickly, and spent most of her time playing with Liisa, who was sitting quietly beside her chair, but Gebirga was fascinated by the talk.

The issue was Normandy, and who was to rule it. It was obviously a problem the council had discussed before, but to Gebirga it was all new. William Clito declared that he had been wrongfully done out of inheriting Normandy by his uncle, King Henry of England and he wanted his cousin Baldwin to help him recover it, speaking passionately to the council about the oppression of peasants in Normandy and the tyranny of the nobles under his uncle's rule. Clemence muttered under her breath that his father had certainly done no better in that regard than his uncle. He evoked the bonds of kinship and of love that bound him and Baldwin of Flanders, and told of a battle that would be pleasing in God's sight, in which men could win honor and booty fighting to restore its natural lord to the seat of Normandy. Charles of Denmark spoke, as one whose entire fortune resided in Flanders, of the duty of the county to help its neighbor, Normandy, resist the occupation of mighty England. Count Baldwin listened, and pretended to weigh the adventure proposed to him, though Gebirga knew he would quickly accede to whatever his two friends proposed.

Some dared speak against the proposal. The abbot of the monastery of St. Bertin suggested sending only a small force, to show good will without draining their own resources. William of Ypres, the bastard cousin of Baldwin and Katerinen whose farce directed against the count had so amused Clemence's court in Bruges, protested more vigorously.

"What has Normandy, or William Clito for that matter ever done for us that we should go die in the Norman mud for it? It is coming on September, with the harvest upon us and I have no mind to strip the countryside for William Clito," he spat the young man's name. "For that matter, to put it bluntly, what are the chances of success for this campaign? The Norman barons all support Henry. Why, they invited him to take Normandy in the first place because this boy's father was making such a hash of being duke. They are there, entrenched in castles, on terrain they know well. What do you propose to do, knock on their doors and invite them out to fight on land of our choosing? No, they'll stay locked in their strongholds until they have us where they want us, and only then will they engage in battle. In the meantime, we'll have nothing to do but harry and plunder the countryside, and that will hardly endear the common folk to our cause. You can't defeat an enemy on his own ground when the populace has grown to hate you, everyone knows that." He pounded the table for emphasis.

The end of his speech was Clemence's cue to speak. "All know I have grave misgivings about this adventure. The points my nephew, William of Ypres, makes are good ones. I will add a few more. When we fight for William Clito and against Henry, we do not just fight against Henry but against all England. And I would submit that England is not our enemy, but our very good friend. When we need wool we cannot produce ourselves to supply our looms in Ghent and Bruges, where does it come from? England. And when we sell our finished cloth, to whom do we sell it? Yes. And we don't just sell England cloth. We also sell her the wine, spices, salt, and oil that come to us from merchants in France, Spain, and Italy. War with England means artisans who can't practice their skills, and merchants without anything to trade. It means poverty, and poverty for our people means poverty for our coffers and without money we cannot buy the arms or the horses we need to maintain ourselves."

Count Baldwin spoke last, lazily rising to his feet. "My lady mother, these are the arguments of merchants, men without honor, dirtied by the filth of their coins, men who grow money from money, rather than from honest labor or battle. It is dishonorable to utter these arguments to men devoted to honest fighting. You would have me be a coiner or a usurer, rather than a warrior like my father, vanquisher of Jerusalem."

This, on a large scale, was the argument Gebirga first heard at home in Gistel between Bertulf and Winnoc. War or wool, on which was the future prosperity of Flanders to be built? But as Clemence had pointed out, it was not a case of one or the other, and Baldwin was ignoring that part. The ability of Flanders to make war was tied to its ability to work wool and it could not have the former without the latter.

He raised his voice. "But the matter of our allies and enemies is not simply being with William Clito and against Henry of England. When we fight with William Clito we also fight with King Louis of France who supports and fosters this campaign. And it is Louis of France, not Henry of England, who is my liege lord and to whom I owe service, and he has demanded I support William Clito. When he commands me to battle, I must answer his call."

This was true, and Clemence knew it. But as a final twist she reminded him, "And what good did it do your father to answer King Louis's call? He died in battle fighting for Louis against Henry seven years ago, and I have no desire to see you following that part of his heroism. Besides, Baldwin, there is answering the letter of Louis's call and answering the spirit of it. The abbot of St. Bertin has wisely suggested the former, sending only enough men to fulfill our minimal feudal obligations."

"My father was an old man when he fell in battle and I would thank God for such an end," Baldwin answered, and she knew she was beaten. William of Ypres continued to resist, however. He asserted they would receive the bare minimum from him, and he would not accompany them himself.

Once the decision had been made, speed was crucial. Ghent emptied as those who had come to attend the court returned home to prepare for the campaign. Baldwin, Charles, and William Clito left to muster men throughout the county. And once the castle was quiet, Clemence decided that she wanted to move her court to Lille, where they would be closer to the action in Normandy and any news from the front.

Katerinen was worse than ever. The disorder and unrest of the beginning of the campaign, coming hard after her collapse following the terrible execution they had witnessed, made her behavior and moods even more erratic than usual. She spent her days sleeping, which meant she was wide awake at night. When she was awake, she was easily distracted and indecisive about little things; she would spend an age deciding which dress to wear and then would not care when it was on. It was difficult to get her interested in any kind of activity, even things she usually liked, such as walking in the castle grounds with Liisa, or visiting the stables. She had little appetite, and no longer even wanted to sneak down to the kitchens to look for treats. She seemed unreachable; even Liisa could no longer cheer her.

It was better once the men were gone, but when Gebirga heard they were to pack up and head to Lille, she worried about the effect of the bustle, discomfort, and disorder of a move on Katerinen. She herself dreaded the thought of another move and a new place to adapt to. She plucked up her courage and went to speak with Clemence about her fears. Clemence was busy looking over accounts, with her steward standing anxiously by, when Gebirga found her in the solar.

"Yes, Gebirga, what do you want?—That will be all, Walter, thank you. See to it that we don't use quite so many candles next month. We must watch pennies now we are at war."

"My lady," Gebirga curtsied deeply, "I am concerned about Katerinen."

"We are all concerned about Katerinen. What is the problem now?"

"My lady, she seems especially dull and slow at the moment. She is very sad, and I fear that the upset of another move will make her even worse. I was wondering if perhaps we could postpone the journey to Lille, at least until she picks up her spirits."

"Postpone our trip, girl, are you mad?"

"Well, it's just that . . ."

"I have to be in Lille. Do you think I want to go there? Surely they must have taught you about duty even in the little place where you come from, where is it, Gistel? We must do the things we must do, even if the tools we have in our hands are not what we would wish. I have a son who needs to be brave and just, and instead is reckless and cruel. He is influenced by wicked men who seek only his downfall. But he is count, and it is through him the county must be ruled. And my daughter," she paused, "My daughter is . . . not well. There are those who tell me she is full of demons and should be shut up in a monastery. Would you wish her that fate?"

Gebirga shook her head.

"So she must do as all women of our station do. She must come and go and appear in public and learn how to control her temper. And she must be married."

Gebirga tried again, "Perhaps if she and I could stay on in Ghent, for a little while maybe, after the rest of you go?"

Clemence turned in her chair to face her directly, "This isn't about Katerinen, is it? This is about you. You don't want to leave Ghent, where you are just now finding your way. I told you this would be a difficult position for a blind woman. Well, don't think I am going to let you go now. You have a duty too, to my daughter, and I'm going to hold you to it."

Gebirga flushed deeply and felt not much older than fifteen herself, hearing the shrewd words of the older woman. Ashamed, she listened to Clemence say, "I need you and Katerinen needs you. I want you to swear to me now that you will love her and protect her and serve her and most of all follow her no matter where she goes, no matter how frightened you are, for the rest of her life. Here, kneel before me and take hold of this crucifix."

Gebirga did as she was bid, eager to prove herself faithful in her shame at the cowardice she had just revealed. Clemence took a heavy necklace off and put its crucifix pendant in Gebirga's hand. She held it tightly, feeling its jewelled surface and carved Christ-figure imprint her palm. "I swear," repeated Gebirga.

"Very well, that's done. Now get up and go pack. We leave tomorrow." Clemence turned back to the table and her work.

The journey from Ghent to Lille was by boat, rather than by covered wagon, floating down the river in a flat-bottomed barge with men at oars rowing against the light current. When the wind was favorable, they used the square sail on its short mast to move them along, and the oarsmen had a rest. Gebirga was relieved she could be outside in the fresh air, and she enjoyed the early autumn sun on her cheeks. She was also glad to see that Katerinen's spirits improved with every mile they went further from Ghent.

The moment they arrived at the castle residence of the count in Lille, Clemence sent messengers in all directions; southwest towards Normandy to glean news of the impending battle; north and east to hear word from the rest of Flanders; and more surprisingly due south for purposes Gebirga could not guess. And then Clemence waited, like a bird in a nest, for her envoys to return home and feed her with information. Scarcely a day went by without someone riding through the gate on a tired, lathered horse, sweating and demanding to be taken to the countess immediately. Clemence paced, while Gebirga tried to distract Katerinen by walking with her in the town where they enjoyed thick waffles dripping with butter, bought from little carts on the street, as well as mugs of beer flavoured with new-fangled hops. But in the back of all their minds were thoughts of the distant war. The days grew shorter and the nights cooler as they moved deeper into the month of September.

One day, late in the month, a travel-stained messenger burst into the solar, where Clemence and the women were gathered listening to a priest read them the Life of St. Eulalia, a tale written in French about a poor girl martyred in distant Barcelona under the Romans. The priest broke off his narration, startled as this apparition from the world of men and action burst into the peace and domesticity of the countess and her ladies. The messenger entered just as Eulalia was making her speech to the evil executioner, and some of the women chafed at the interruption. Clemence, however, recognizing the man and knowing from which direction he was coming, rose from her chair and demanded, "What news from the front, Eudes?"

"My lady," the man collapsed in a deep bow before her, out of breath and gasping, "Not good. A complete rout." He paused and breathed deeply a few times before he could continue. "We were trapped on marshy ground when England attacked and our heavy horses couldn't maneuver in the muck. The Norman lords, de Beauvoir and de Courcy, who had promised to help William Clito regain his dukedom changed sides at the last moment so where we had hoped for a friend on our left flank, we found an enemy. And the king of France came too late with his men. They arrived just as the battle was ending and helped cover our retreat, but that was all they could do. Clito is safe, but Charles of Denmark suffered a sword slash on his left arm. We lost countless men, a host of our bravest knights, from all over Flanders. The songs will sing long of their bravery and tragic deaths."

"Damn King Louis. I knew he was not to be trusted. He's glad to have England and Flanders weaken each other so as to leave him the stronger." Her tone changed, "And my son?"

"My lady, Count Baldwin fought bravely in the vanguard. Many more would have been lost if not for his courage and strength rallying our side, until his horse was killed out from under him . . ."

"He's dead?" Clemence was alert.

"No, my lady, he is alive, or at least he was when I began my wild ride."

"Wounded then."

"Yes, my lady. Grave wounds to his abdomen from a sword stroke and another, less serious, to his right foot from an arrow. The abdominal wounds are shallow but their location is worrisome and he was in great pain when I saw him. I left four days ago, right after the battle. It was not clear then whether he would live or die. Another messenger will follow me in a few days with more news."

"A few days. We don't have that long," Clemence said as if to herself, and then loudly, to her women, "Marie! Catherine! Don't just stand there gawping. Get something for the man to eat and drink, and a basin for him to wash with. And tell one of those men who eat their heads off in my kitchen to come speak with me. I need another messenger. No, bring two. Father, I need you to write a letter for me." The women did her bidding and the priest went to collect ink and parchment. Eudes settled into the place vacated by the two women, and the other ladies asked what he knew about the fate of their own brothers, fathers, nephews, husbands, and sons at the front. Many wept when the news he delivered was bad, and were embraced by their friends.

Gebirga gathered the courage to press through the women and approach him. "Sir, my father is Bertulf of Gistel. What news have you of his fate?"

He took her hand. "My lady it is a sad day when I have to bring so many fair ladies such foul news. I heard that Bertulf of Gistel was felled by an arrow shot through his heart. I did not see him myself. I am sorry, lady."

He released her and Gebirga allowed herself to be jostled aside by the next anxious woman seeking news. So she had lost the father she had barely known. Lost him after finding him again so briefly. And her ties with Gistel were now cut. She spared a thought for Aude, so young and alone and pregnant, only a few months until her child was due. But there was nothing she could do for Aude; her help and sympathy would not be welcomed, and it was her unborn child who was heir to Gistel. She wondered if Winnoc would learn the news. For herself she felt numb, frozen, and envied the weeping women their tears and ability to take comfort from each other. Maybe she would be able to cry later, when she was at last on her own.

But when would she ever be all by herself? Through her grief, Gebirga heard Clemence pacing up and down the solar and Katerinen, sobbing for her hated brother. It was they who needed her most now, and she had vowed to put loyalty to them above her own desires. She found Katerinen and put her arm around the girl and stroked her shoulder, feeling her frail bones through the thin material of her dress. Already the vow she had made to Clemence was shaping how she saw her duty. She listened to what Clemence was doing and saying.

Clemence stopped pacing the moment the priest returned with his portable writing desk. He opened the slanted lid to remove the writing supplies he needed, and then she began dictating. "To my beloved nephew William of Ypres, your aunt and liege lady Clemence sends greetings. As you may know, our brave armies have gone down to defeat in Normandy and my lord Count Baldwin lies gravely ill. For my sake and for his, I ask that you go with a sufficient force to protect his grace in order to convey him to the abbey of St. Bertin in our town of Saint Omer so that the monks there may care for him with their medicine. If, may God protect against it, our beloved son shall have been taken from the chains of this mortal life before you reach him, dear William, we desire that you hasten to protect the comital regalia in Bruges."

The priest wrote this out and Clemence signed her name with a flourish saying to no one in particular as she was doing so, "William's men will be fresh and able to counter any resistance Charles of Denmark might make to the project of taking Baldwin to St. Bertin. The monks there are skilled and if there is any hope at all, they will do what they can. Besides, they are allied with me. And William is clever enough to know that by ordering him to seize the regalia, I am telling him to declare himself Count of Flanders if Baldwin dies. Let us hope that will not be the case, but we must plan as if it might be." The priest folded and sealed the parchment, and Clemence handed it to one of the two messengers who had just arrived, panting from running up the stairs. "Put this in the hands of William of Ypres and no other. He is in Ypres at the moment. If you leave immediately, you will be there by nightfall."

She turned to the second messenger, "You have further to go and a harder task because you will have to remember the message I will give you. I will not take the chance of a parchment being seen by curious or even unfriendly eyes. I want you to seek out my brother, Archbishop Guy of Vienne. He may be in Vienne or he may be further afield in the entourage of Pope Gelasius. Gelasius has spent the last months on the run, traveling through France, unable to enter Rome because of the presence there of the rival pope, the emperor's candidate for the papal throne. But go first to the monastery of Cluny and tell the abbot to expect Katerinen and myself. If my brother is not there, the abbot will be able to tell you where to find him. In any case, once you locate him, tell Guy that Katerinen and I will be coming as soon as we can to Cluny and that we must move ahead with our plans more quickly than we expected. He will know what you mean." With that, she shooed everyone out of the solar, with the exception of Gebirga and Katerinen. Once everyone had left she checked the doors to make sure no one was eavesdropping, and then she spoke.

"Gebirga. I heard what Eudes said about Gistel. I am sorry about your father. You may ask the steward for candles to burn in his memory in the chapel." Sentiment dispensed with, she turned to business, "Now, Katerinen, stop weeping for a moment and tell me what you understand from what we have learned today."

The girl wiped her cheeks, "We lost? And many people died, and everyone is so sad, and Baldwin may die too."

"And what do you think that would mean for you."

Katerinen thought, "Maybe we wouldn't have to travel all over the place any more? Maybe we could stay in one place, like the convent of St. Marien in Bourbourg? I like it there."

"Gebirga? I am sure you see more. Tell Katerinen."

"My lady if Count Baldwin were to die," she crossed herself, averting the bad luck that mentioning this possibility brought, "There would be a new count." A sudden question came to her. "Who would he be, since Baldwin doesn't have any heirs himself? In any case, there would be a new count, not a child of yours, and your position, and that of Katerinen, would be vulnerable." She thought about the possibilities a little more. "Almost certainly you would marry again, my lady, since you would lose your son's protection.

And that, if you will forgive me, could make Katerinen's position even more vulnerable since your new husband might have interests and heirs that would counter hers."

"Very good Gebirga. I knew my faith in your understanding was not misplaced. So how do we protect Katerinen?"

"Customarily there are two ways, my lady. The first way would be to take her out of play, as it were, by dedicating her life to God in a convent. With Christ as her spouse and her community looking after the property she brought to it as dowry, there are few who could threaten her."

"And the second?"

"The second would be to marry her to someone capable of protecting her and of seeing her interests as his own."

"And so much the better if his interests were allied with mine," finished Clemence, "Then we could remain as one family, strong and united. I come from a large family, Gebirga. My father was the count of Burgundy and he had many children. Some of us have married, some of us have had lives in the Church. My brother Raymond even traveled to Spain and married a king's daughter. But we have always helped each other and worked for the interests of the whole family, and that is why we have remained strong. I could send Katerinen into a convent. Indeed, if she were a boy I would not hesitate to dedicate her to a life of religion. But only men can make brilliant careers in the Church, not women. Putting her in a convent would make me like the man in the Bible who buried his talent of gold in the ground. She will better do her duty to my family, and hers, by making an advantageous marriage. And that is my plan. The three of us are going to go to Cluny where, God willing, we will meet my brother Guy, who has been negotiating a marriage for Katerinen with a young man who is his ward. I won't say who, since walls have ears."

"But Lady Clemence," Gebirga hesitated, unwilling to be accused of neglecting her duty again, "I see this is a wonderful chance for Katerinen. But do you think she is . . . up to it?"

Clemence looked at the girl who was paying no attention to either of them and was rocking herself back and forwards while humming tunelessly. "She will have to be," said Clemence.

CHAPTER SEVEN

Cluny

This codex was written in several places, namely in Rome, in Jerusalem, in France, in Italy, in Germany, and in Frisia, and especially at Cluny.

With scarcely time to light a candle for her father and arrange for a hasty Mass from the castle priest, the three women were off and Gebirga left Flanders for the first time in her life, riding south through sullen forests in an autumn turned suddenly frigid with no time to dwell on her grief and confusion at the death of the father she barely knew.

They traveled by horse overland to Cluny in a cold, sleety rain that never seemed to end, riding all day and staying in monastic guest houses at night in beds crawling with bugs, or hard as slate, or once, blessedly, full of fresh new feathers. Their cloaks and other clothing were aired by the fire each night, so the women slept in an aroma of wet wool, but the garments never dried completely, and their hands and feet were sore with chilblains from the damp cold. Gebirga had to get used to speaking French all the time as they passed out of the lands of the Flemish. They took a small retinue of armed men with them to protect them from stray bands of thieves, and a couple of Clemence's hardier women servants, but it was a small party that made the trek through the wooded countryside.

Down to Troyes they followed the well-used roads of the Flanders cloth merchants who journeyed there to the great fairs of Champagne. It took them over a week to reach the city but here they halted for a few days, guests of the count of Champagne at his palace within the city walls, a pleasant change from draughty guest houses and packing up their belongings every morning. Clemence had business to do with the town's many money changers and lenders. She was important enough that these waited on her at the castle rather than forcing her to come to them, and they left pleased with the profit they would earn from enabling Clemence's machinations. Some of them were Christians but others were Jews, the first Jews Gebirga had ever encountered. She crossed herself when Katerinen told her that the man who had just said farewell to both of them so politely was a Jew.

"Really, Trintje? But he sounds just like everyone else in Troyes. What did he look like?"

Katerinen laughed. "He looks like everyone else in Troyes too. What did you expect, a red nose and a tail?"

With its many canals, Troyes resembled the Flemish cities they knew, and the two wandered its streets, Katerinen boldly leading the way and Gebirga shy in yet another new town. Katerinen took her to the lanes where the Jews lived, close to the protection of the count's castle and palace, and dared her to walk down them. Gebirga was not to be drawn in. Strange and aromatic cooking smells coming from the alley were the only thing that suggested its inhabitants might not be completely like all the others in Troyes, but still she was fearful.

Leaving Troyes behind, their journey continued south. The days grew shorter, limiting their travel time, and Gebirga exchanged her summer cloak for her thick winter one of boiled wool. Their pace was too fast for much conversation while they rode, but Gebirga took her chance to ask Clemence about their destination while they supped at yet another monastery guesthouse.

"Cluny?" Clemence replied, "It is the wealthiest and most powerful monastery of all. Its abbots raise popes and topple thrones. But it is more than just a single monastery. Its influence stretches to every county and realm in Europe through the daughter houses under its rule that grateful kings and nobles have handed over to its care. I gave Cluny the monastery of St. Bertin while my husband was on crusade."

"Why did you do that?"

"Prayer," Clemence answered simply. "The monks pray for us while we are alive, and for our souls after we die. How else can we who rule, mired in the tangle of worldly affairs, hope to gain salvation? Not on our own merits."

"So prayer is a commodity, like a wool sack or a bolt of cloth, which you can exchange for a monastery as if it were a sack of gold coins?"

"No, though it might look that way to a mercantile mind. By giving St. Bertin to Cluny and its patron, Saint Peter, I create a bond between us, like that between a king and his nobles. Saint Peter protects me and my house, and in turn I offer him my service. You'll see. We'll be there soon enough." But it was another week and half before Katerinen sighted the towers of Cluny looming in the distance, promising an end to their journey.

Gebirga thought she was beginning to understand towns. They were always located on water—the more important the river, the more important the town—and they were walled for protection. Inside, sometimes within its own wall, was the castle and residence of its lord, and this was the largest and most prominent feature of the town. Churches and even abbeys might be found within the town too, but they were always lesser structures.

Cluny was different. There was a wall, and there was also a river, though it was an insignificant one. There the similarities ended, for Cluny had no castle and had no count. Instead, the huddle of houses that made up the town was overshadowed by the largest monastery with the biggest church in all of Christendom. Katerinen, who had lived her whole life in palaces, gasped in wonder as the full might and size of the complex before them came into view. "Mother, it's so big. It looks like heaven!"

Even Clemence was impressed. "It has been more than thirty years since I was last here," she said, "I knew they were building a new church with the money from Spain but I didn't imagine they would complete as much of it as they have done in that time. Or that it would be so huge. Why, it must be four times the size of the old church, which was not small. And it's twice as high."

They were met in the outer courtyard by the monastery's cellarer, who was clearly expecting their arrival.

"Good, my messenger must have got through." Clemence murmured when she saw him.

The cellarer directed their men-at-arms to the stables so they could tend to the horses, while lay brothers took their baggage. The cellarer then bowed down deeply before the women and gave each one the kiss of peace. "Thanks be to God for your safe arrival," he said, "Let us go across to the guest house. It is new since you were last here, countess."

They climbed the stairs to the central hall that separated the men's side from the large room where the women slept, and the cellarer pointed out the amenities, including cloth-covered frames that screened off a section of the room for their use, to give them some privacy from other visitors.

Their maidservants set to making up beds and arranging their belongings in the screened-in area. The cellarer directed them discretely to the latrines located at the far end of the hall, where there was also a place where they could have a quick wash.

"I am impressed with all the building," said Clemence to their guide.

"Thank you. We had to shorten the men's guest hall because of the new church. But we made up for that by building a palace on either side of the portal of the old church, to house important ecclesiastic guests. We expect our first guests early in the new year, Pope Gelasius with half a dozen or so of his cardinals. They fled Rome, of course, to escape the emperor and the anti-pope he installed in Gelasius's place. Your brother, Guy, will join us also. It will be lovely to have the pope staying here with us. His presence will be a blessing on all our new building work." Then the cellarer's face fell, "But I hear that he is not well. Poor man, what else is to be expected after charging all over France the way he has done since his election last January."

All this was opaque to Gebirga. The pope in flight from Rome, an anti-pope in his place? But it was obviously old news to Clemence because she changed the subject and inquired, "The abbot, how does he fare?"

"Abbot Pons is well. You will meet him in the guest refectory at dinner time. The refectory is below your sleeping chamber and we eat late in the afternoon, of course, in this season. The food, since the abbot will be joining you, will be excellent. In the meantime, please make yourselves comfortable and ask one of the lay brothers if you need anything."

The three rested briefly, then went down to eat. They joined the abbot and those of the abbey's visitors whose station merited a stay in the guest house. "Abbot Pons, I am grateful for your welcome," said Clemence after the abbot gave her the kiss of peace.

"My lady, your presence sheds light on our house. I wish the forthcoming visit of your brother would be as benign a presence." Clemence ignored this dig. She knew her brother had little respect for the current abbot of Cluny, whom he found pompous and not very intelligent.

Clemence was favored by sitting at the right hand of the abbot, and Katerinen was at his left. Gebirga was near enough to follow their conversation, especially since her two neighbors were wholly focused on the food, which was excellent. Each dish was served to her so she did not have to fumble around on the table. Course after course of hare, rabbit, and pheasant, smoked ham, boiled eels with green sauce, black puddings, and liver sausage, were followed by cheeses of all kinds, soft and hard, made of goat and sheep and cow's milk, and then gingerbread and other sweetmeats, all washed down with the best wine of Burgundy. Liisa appreciated the scraps she received. Gebirga tried to cut each morsel into a small bite and use only her thumb and first finger to bring the food to her mouth, as Mathilde had tried to teach her so long ago. One dish puzzled her. It was a simple plate of fried eggs and onions but the sauce tasted like nothing she had ever experienced. There was wine and maybe vinegar in it but it also had an odd oily fruity savour to it. "Olive oil," said her neighbor when she appealed to him, "The stewed veal has been cooked in it too."

Olive oil. So this was Aude's mysterious oil from a fruit. Gebirga tasted it again cautiously. She rather liked it.

"My lady, for how long are we to enjoy your presence among us?" Gebirga heard the abbot say. Did he ever stop sounding so formal?

"For quite some time I expect, my lord abbot. I wish to be here when my brother and Pope Gelasius arrive, though I may have to return to Flanders to deal with pressing matters between now and then. Katerinen and her lady, however, will stay in my absence and await my return." This was the first Gebirga had heard of that possibility.

"I do hope Katerinen will not be bored here. There is little to do for young ladies," he said politely.

"Your concern is well-placed, and I must find her suitable occupations. There is the liturgy of course; I am sure she will wish to attend that. But above all, I would like her to continue her studies while she is here."

Studies? What studies, wondered Gebirga.

"Katerinen could learn a new language," Clemence continued, "You have so many monks from distant parts in your community It would be marvelous if she could learn . . . Spanish for instance. Yes, Spanish. Have you anyone here who could be spared to speak Spanish with her each day? Lady Gebirga who travels with us will learn with her."

Clemence must be expecting Katerinen to live as a bride in a foreign court, Gebirga realized. That was the only reason she would need to learn a new language. But Spanish? Were they going to Spain? And whom was Katerinen to marry? Gebirga raked her memory to recall the little she knew about that distant land, a place more of legend and story to her than anything else. There were Muslims there, just like the Holy Land, that she knew. But was there a Christian ruler too? Or more than one? And had not her father said something about a queen?

"Spanish," the abbot repeated, sounding as surprised as Gebirga, "I couldn't say. We have so many living here now, almost three hundred choir monks from every corner of Christendom, not to mention the lay brothers. I am sure some must be from Spain. But it would be easier if it were someone not yet in full vows. Speak to the novice master and ask him if he has any suitable candidates. You may address him before Mass tomorrow. I will let him know I have given my permission."

Clemence did as he suggested. The novice master pondered for a moment, then spoke with relief in his voice. "I have just the candidate for you. He is a rather troublesome young novice. Oh, no, not misbehavior or anything like that. Quite the reverse. He is almost too pious, if you know what I mean, tending towards spiritual pride—takes on excessive fasts and vigils and makes himself ill. Teaching Spanish could help him learn some badly needed humility. He was born in Spain and lived there all his life until he came to us a couple of years ago, though he will tell you he is French. His father was a Frenchman, one of the many who have crossed the Pyrenees in recent years to make their fortune. The family was originally from Asquins, you know, near Vezelay. Sometimes we think he might fit in better with our brothers at Vezelay, but he insists he wants to remain at Cluny." The master sighed. Gebirga was not at all sure that this misfit sounded like the right person to teach Katerinen but since the novice master had no other candidate, Clemence made arrangements for the young man to begin lessons the following day.

Gebirga would have preferred to avoid the church. She had enough of monasteries back in Gistel. But Katerinen had begged her to join them, and she was curious to hear the famous liturgy of Cluny, so she went along.

The grandeur of the stone building dedicated to Saints Peter and Paul overawed Katerinen. "I feel like a dwarf in here," the younger girl whispered as they walked down the long nave towards the choir, "Like a gnome in my old nurse's stories. It is like walking through an ancient forest that has no end." Gebirga could sense the size of the place from the way it hushed their voices and muffled the sound of their feet. The monks were already in the church, having just finished the office of Terce that preceded the Mass.

The monks began the first antiphon, the older ones chanting the verse and the young oblates with their high, pure voices chiming the response. Voices sounded in unison, building to peaks and crescendos, and then fell away, sounding at the same time both wildly joyful and exquisitely tragic. Reverberating against the stone, the sound seemed to come from all directions at once. All of Gebirga's functioning senses were under siege. The scent of beeswax candles mingled with the rising plumes of incense to create an odor that intoxicated and stunned. When the monks reached the Gloria with its soaring high notes, the music itself seemed to reach inside Gebirga and crack something that had been frozen since she had heard about her father's death, long ago now it seemed, in Lille. She began to weep, silently at first and then louder, though the power of the full choir was such that she could not be heard over it, even by Clemence and Katerinen who were standing near. By the time the Mass ended and the monks filed out, she was calmer, but she waved the two women off and told them she wanted to spend some time in the church alone. A monk or a lay brother, or even one of the other guests of the monastery could help her get to the portal where Liisa waited.

She leaned against the cold stone of one of the heavy piers, drawing in the peace of the huge church, trying not to think, the empty stillness of the building echoing in her heart. Not completely empty. A male voice addressed her. "You were grieving greatly during the Mass. I do hope you were able to draw some comfort from it."

She was shaken out of her reverie.

"I am sorry, I did not mean to startle you," he continued, "But I could see how sad you were and I found I could not leave before I spoke with you."

"I . . . I . . ., yes you are right. I have been grieving. I learned a fortnight ago that my father had died in battle. I barely knew him. It has been hard to know how to mourn. Being here has helped me. I feel better now, though maybe I don't look it."

"I'm glad. You have come to Cluny at the right time to mourn your father. In a few days, on the second of November, the abbey celebrates All Souls Day, when it prays for all of the dead. I am certain they would include prayers for your father if you wished."

"Oh would they?" Gebirga wiped her eyes. "Yes, I would like to do that. It would help. And he had great need of prayers."

"As do we all."

"As do we all," she agreed. They were speaking in French but the man spoke oddly, with a strange accent she could not place. He also had a distinctive and unfamiliar smell, like expensive spices and that olive oil she had tasted for the first time the previous night. "Would you be kind enough to take me to the door? I am blind and I can't make it easily on my own."

"Blind? I could not have told. You hide it well." He offered her an arm that was steady and sure. Gebirga was grateful for that. So many did not know how to guide a blind woman. They tugged and pulled, but this stranger matched his steps to her and they walked gracefully in silence back through the dimmed church. Like dancing, Gebirga thought, irrelevantly. They reached the portal where Liisa was patiently waiting, head on her paws.

"Here is my dog," she said, stroking the animal's head and finding the lead as Liisa pushed at her hip, "You may find it odd, but she helps me find my way about. Thank you so much, Father, for your words and for your assistance."

"Father? Oh! You think I'm a monk," he laughed, "I'm no monk!" But he was gone before she could ask him more.

He must be one of the other guests, she thought. Perhaps he was staying in the hospice for lesser folk, though he spoke in a cultured manner under the odd accent, and his words were more gracious than she would expect from a poor pilgrim or a man-at-arms. But she did not recognize his voice from among those she had heard in the guest refectory the previous evening, though she was sure she would know it if she heard it again.

The next day, Gebirga met the novice who was to give the Spanish lessons in an antechamber off the guest refectory. It was Clemence's idea to have Katerinen join them later, to give Gebirga a chance to decide whether the monk was up for the task, and to back out of it politely if it turned out he was not. Gebirga was not optimistic. The young man, for he seemed about twenty, was rather sulky on first impression. She invited him to sit and tried to draw him out.

"I am pleased to meet you, Brother Oliver, and I am delighted that you are to teach us Spanish. I understand that you yourself are Spanish. We are lucky to have such a teacher."

He drummed his foot on the ground. "I am not Spanish. I'm French. I left Spain and all in it behind long ago."

Oh dear, yes, they had been told he did not care for his origins. She had put her foot in it.

She changed the subject. "Oliver is an unusual name. Where does it come from? I do not believe I have heard it before."

He bristled again, "You have never heard of Oliver? The brave hero who fought and died alongside his beloved friend, the noble Roland, fighting the wicked Moors in the pass at Roncesvalles, saving Charlemagne and the entire French army when they returned from pilgrimage to Compostela? My parents named me for him." Gebirga heard him slump back in his chair, and he settled into contemptuous silence.

"Ah, your parents. And where are they from?"

"They are from Asquins, in Burgundy," he said wearily, as if it exhausted him to even answer such a foolish question, "But if you are asking where they live, if they still do live, they are in Logroño, in Spain. The kingdom of Aragon, actually. Where I grew up. It's a town on the pilgrimage road to Santiago de Compostela. One of their kings invited the French to settle there a couple of decades ago, and my parents took up the call."

The pilgrimage road to Compostela. Gebirga's mind briefly flitted back to her strange encounter with the old man in Bruges who had spoken of the way to Compostela. Oliver was the first person she ever met who was from that strange place. That, and his obvious unhappiness, made her curious about him. She wanted to know what more was there under the surly demeanor. But just then Katerinen came to the door.

"Ha! I found you! This monastery is so confusing."

"Lady Katerinen, may I present to you Brother Oliver d'Asquins, who is going to teach both of us Spanish."

Katerinen greeted the monk politely enough, but the youth seemed to be struck dumb. He stammered out a shy greeting at odds with the bored disdain he had shown to Gebirga. Gebirga knew those signs; he was smitten with her.

The boy was still goggling at Katerinen when Gebirga gently suggested that they start their lesson. He seemed to have no idea how to go about this, so she said, "Maybe you could begin by telling us the different Spanish words for all the things in the room."

"I will teach you the way they speak in Castile," he said, "There is no one Spanish language. There are as many languages in Spain as there are kingdoms." Oh dear, thought Gebirga, will we have to learn all of them and have a fleet of sullen boys for the purpose? Oliver added more optimistically, "But if you learn Castilian, you can make yourself understood in most of the Christian kingdoms." Then they began their lesson. He proved to be a surprisingly good teacher, patient with Katerinen, and skilled at helping them emend their accents.

The chilblains on Gebirga's hands did not heal but cracked and grew more painful as the cold weather deepened. Clemence saw her rubbing goose grease on them one day and took pity on her.

"Here, try this salve the infirmarian gave me," she fished in the purse at her waist, "They make it of beeswax, olive oil, powdered myrrh, and sage. Even if it doesn't work better than the goose grease, it will certainly smell better and Liisa will stop trying to lick your hands all the time."

As Gebirga smoothed the sweet-smelling ointment onto her hands, she took the opportunity of a moment alone with Clemence to ask why she had arranged for the two of them to learn Spanish.

They were alone in one of the small rooms on the ground floor of the guest house. Katerinen was trying to count all the angels in the abbey church, and this was not a mission Gebirga could assist with. Clemence shut the door before she replied. "Why do you think?"

"Since you have expressed a desire to see Katerinen betrothed, it must be because you have a Spanish bridegroom in mind."

"Very good, Gebirga."

"May I know who it is?"

Clemence considered for a moment and then replied reluctantly, "I suppose I must trust you. But you need to keep it completely secret. I don't even want Katerinen to know until it is settled. She'll tell someone and ruin everything." She leaned forward and spoke conspiratorily. "We are trying to marry Katerinen to my nephew, Alfonso of Galicia. My brother, Raymond, married Urraca the daughter of the emperor of Spain, and Alfonso is their son. My brother died, and then Urraca's father died too. My nephew rules in Galicia, but his mother calls herself the empress of all Spain though really she is only the queen of two of its realms, Leon and Castile. Still, he will inherit that when she dies. It is an excellent match for Katerinen."

"So Urraca is like you then—her son rules but she retains power because of the castles or land she possesses?"

"No, it is quite different. She rules in her own right, inheriting from her father. I only married into the house of Flanders. Queen Urraca's position is as if Katerinen became countess of Flanders, were something to happen to her brother."

Gebirga imagined that heady possibility: Katerinen ruling and Clemence the power behind the throne. How different Flanders would be if that were the case. Clemence sounded bitter and Gebirga could tell she was jealous of Urraca's independence, a queen who did not have to answer to any king. But Gebirga had more questions. "How old is this Alfonso?" she asked Clemence, "And how can it be possible for Katerinen to marry her own first cousin? I thought the church forbade such close marriages."

"The boy must be about fourteen now. Close to Katerinen's own age, a little younger but not too much. And as for your second question, that is one of the reasons we are in Cluny. Only the pope can give a dispensation to permit such a close marriage and he is expected to arrive in the next couple of months."

"One of the reasons we are at Cluny? What are the others?"

"My brother, Guy of Vienne, will be coming with the pope. He is one of Alfonso's guardians. The other is Diego Gelmirez, the bishop of Compostela. He is a bishop, but he wants to be an archbishop. Only the pope can make Compostela an archbishopric, so he is sending envoys to Cluny to negotiate on his behalf. While they are here, they can agree to the betrothal."

"Alfonso is in Diego Gelmirez's custody, rather than his mother's?"

Clemence shifted in her chair. "Alfonso was in the hands of Diego Gelmirez for many years, but now he is in the care of Bernard, the archbishop of Toledo, a staunch ally of Urraca and a former monk of Cluny." For the first time, Clemence sounded troubled. "Bernard is a rival of Diego Gelmirez, because if Compostela is made equal to Toledo, Toledo would no longer be the most important see in Spain."

"Could this cause problems for Katerinen's betrothal?"

"Queen Urraca, the boy's mother, may fear a marriage that will allow him to build a power base of his own, apart from her. Archbishop Bernard of Toledo and Bishop Diego Gelmirez of Compostela, are wary of anything that might move Alfonso out of the orbit of the one and into the orbit of the other. That situation is volatile. Bernard is a staunch supporter of Urraca. Diego only supports her when it suits him. But never fear. We shall prevail."

Gebirga considered these words. "So Katerinen is to travel to Spain," she said.

"You too," Clemence answered sharply, "I wish I could send her with an army at her back, but you are all I have." She paused for a moment. "And I have come to trust you. Remember, you swore to stay with her."

"I did swear." And whether it was because of her father's death, or all the traveling she had already done, Gebirga did not feel the terror she once would have about journeying into the dark unknown. She would have Katerinen with her, and Liisa. And Katerinen needed her. "Is it far?" she asked, stabbed by sudden apprehension, mixed with excitement. "Further than Flanders to Cluny?"

"Much further. But it is a well-traveled road because of all the pilgrims. It is better if you keep the purpose of your journey to yourselves until you reach Queen Urraca. You and Katerinen will pretend that you are pilgrims, on your way to Compostela. Many nobles make that journey, so no one will think twice about it. And I will give you this to take now." Clemence put a folded square of parchment the size of a fist into Gebirga's right hand. "Carry this letter with you on your travels. I am sending it to Diego Gelmirez of Compostela and it concerns Katerinen's betrothed. Keep it safe on your person at all times and never let any one else see it or know you have it."

After Clemence left the room, Gebirga's fingertips stroked the smooth surface of the parchment she was unable to read, and wondered what was written there. A blind woman was the perfect courier for a letter whose contents should only be known to its recipient. She folded it into as small a square as possible and tucked it into the purse at her waist, right beside the scallop shell she still carried. She kneeled down on the floor beside Liisa and hugged the dog's strong body, burying her face in Liisa's wiry fur. "It is going to be an adventure, isn't it?" she said. The dog's warm steady breathing was the only reply she received.

Clemence left a few days later, promising she would return by Christmas. She bade a formal farewell to the abbot and told him she was leaving for Flanders to see how Count Baldwin fared. A messenger from the monastery of St. Bertin shortly after they arrived at Cluny told them he was still living, but was grievously ill, and they had heard nothing since.

Her farewell to Katerinen and Gebirga was warmer. "At least Katerinen will be safe here," Clemence said before she left. Gebirga knew what she meant. With her brother weakened and out of action, Katerinen was vulnerable to threats from ambitious nobles who would seize her and marry her and ask for permission later. The king of France might even exert his rights of overlordship to take custody of her as a fatherless heiress. Clemence had been wise to bring them to Cluny, which was in Burgundy rather than France, and where no one would dare to abduct her while she was under the watchful care of the monks.

A cold snap started right after Clemence left. Each night, Gebirga and Katerinen huddled together under the covers for warmth, and in the morning the basin of water they used for washing had a thin layer of ice on the top. Katerinen refused to wash but Gebirga was intractable. "Come on, Katerinen. Under your arms and then your bottom at the very least. Otherwise you'll smell." Grumbling and shivering, the younger girl sponged herself off.

They had little to do with the monks and most of the monastery was inaccessible to them as laywomen. At Katerinen's insistence, they walked in the small town that had grown up around the monastery, bundled up tight against the cold. The stone workers who built the church found new employment raising impressive mansions in the local stone for the town's important burghers, and Katerinen liked to see the buildings going up, though work was slow now that the frost had come. The masons spent their idle time chiselling decorative corbels to be used in spring as roof supports, and Katerinen watched them and asked questions. Gebirga bore it as long as she could, stamping her feet to keep warm, before insisting they move on. They also walked across the river and into the surrounding countryside on days when the weather cooperated, avoiding the area around the abbey midden, though it was less smelly in the freezing cold.

With Clemence gone, they were moved down to lower places at the guest house refectory table where the endless parade of visitors provided some novelty. They continued their language lessons. Gebirga learned, while Katerinen was bright, but easily distracted. Still, she managed to learn some polite phrases in her new language and Gebirga hoped these would impress Diego Gelmirez's envoy, and please Clemence. Oliver's infatuation with the younger girl only got worse. He was brusque and critical with Gebirga's efforts, but endlessly patient with Katerinen, praising her for every word she almost remembered. But it seemed to Gebirga like harmless calf-love, especially after he compared his lady to the Virgin Mary one day.

"Only if the Blessed Virgin never brushed her hair or used a handkerchief properly, Oliver," she answered with asperity. "I'm not sure what your novice master would think of your theology." But at least his ardor distracted him from his sulky self-pity, which could only be a good thing for everyone. Katerinen was oblivious to his devotion, taking his attention, like that of all others, as no more than her due.

The bells that called the monks to prayer reverberated off stone walls and slate tiles, giving form to their days and interrupting their nights. Gebirga attended the divine office when she could, and followed the advice of the mysterious man she met after her first Mass to arrange for her father to be included in the commemoration of the dead on All Souls' Day. The feast began after vespers when the bells tolled once again and the monks chanted the Office of the Dead. At dawn the next morning, her father's name was one of the many read out loud by the boys in their clear treble and he was also the beneficiary of one of the dozens of private masses said that day, the murmur of which could be heard like a steady hum over the office from the side chapels of the church. The pomp and beauty of the liturgy helped temper the grief, guilt, and anger she had about both her parents. When she put her offering on the altar, she felt she was letting go of more than a handful of coins.

She half hoped she might meet her mysterious friend again at that liturgy, but if he was there he did not approach her. When she and Liisa left the church at the conclusion of the feast, it was late afternoon. She was hailed by the voice of a beggar sitting in the shelter of the small door to the left of the main entrance way calling, "Alms! Alms for a poor pilgrim!" Moved by her recent experiences, she hastened to give him a coin and said, "Old father, surely there is a meal for you and a bed for the night in the hospice?"

"They gave me a meal, but I must be traveling on tonight. But thank you for your gift. It is good to see you again, and your dog. I told you I would." Suddenly Gebirga realized she was hearing a familiar voice. It was the beggar she had encountered in Bruges, the one who gave her the shell she still carried, right before she met Katerinen for the first time.

"Yes sir, you did."

"And I told you that you were a pilgrim like me, and here you are, well on your way to Compostela, though you have chosen a roundabout route. I said you were heading for Spain, didn't I?"

She was confused by the beggar's words. It was true; she was going to Spain, and disguised as a pilgrim to Compostela no less. But how could he have known? And how could he know her destination now? The whole journey was a secret still. Had someone revealed their plans? Surely this was impossible; it must be just the lucky guess of a mad old man. She remembered something else that he had said.

"Grandfather, when we met last you said something to me about following the Milky Way. What did you mean by that?"

He laughed, a surprisingly young sound from such an old man. "Yes, that must have sounded strange. Legend has it that Charlemagne, back when he was emperor, followed the Milky Way all the way from France into Spain to St. James's tomb, and that the stars still mark the route there. Look up, look way up."

"But sir, I am blind. I won't see any stars."

"Look up!" he commanded.

She did as she was bid, and as she raised her head she could see a chalky band of stars like a path in the sky, rising above her head and descending to the southwest horizon. Dazed by a wave of vertigo, she looked down and then back up again. It was gone and she was trapped within her black, blind world again. She must have imagined it, inspired by his suggestion.

Before she could question him about what she had seen, the old man asked, "Do you still have the shell I gave you?"

She groped in her purse and drew it out, "Yes, here it is."

"Very good, keep it safe. You have much further to go. Now aid an old man to get to his feet."

She helped him stand. He was sturdy for someone who seemed so old and frail. "Be well," he said, "We will meet again and I hope you will believe me this time." Before he left he turned back to her, "And I promise I will pray for your parents." How could he have known about them, Gebirga wondered as she went back to her quarters.

Clemence returned when the fasting and privations of Advent gave way to the feasts of Christmas. She brought better news of Baldwin. The wounds in his abdomen were healing slowly but cleanly, and only the arrow to his foot was still giving him trouble. It was just a scratch, but it had festered, and he continued to lie in a fever. She also brought news of Gistel. Aude had given birth to a boy, Theodore. With the birth of an heir, Gebirga's last tie to Gistel and her home was severed.

Pope Gelasius was expected to arrive any day at Cluny with Guy, Clemence's brother. Cluny began to fill up with clerics and laymen who hoped the pope's visit would be a chance for them to gain favors only he could grant—a dispensation for an illegitimate child to enter holy orders, the settlement of a dispute between a bishop and a monastery, or an annulment of a now-inconvenient marriage. Clemence was delighted to learn of the arrival of Bernard, the prior of the monastery of San Zoilo, a daughter house of Cluny in the pilgrimage road town of Carrion in Spain. He was an envoy representing Bishop Diego Gelmirez in his efforts to make Compostela an archbishopric. She sought out an audience with him that lasted most of one afternoon to discuss the prospective betrothal and after it was over, she found her daughter sitting with Gebirga, rubbing Liisa's tummy and trying to get the dog to roll over on command. The meeting went poorly. Prior Bernard was stiff, which made Katerinen nervous and over-excited. His awkwardness made Gebirga wonder how smoothly Clemence's meeting with him had gone.

Finally the long-awaited pope arrived with the cardinals who had followed him into his French exile, as well as Clemence's brother, Archbishop Guy of Vienne. The monastery, which had been full before their arrival, threatened to burst, as the new guests squashed into the complex of rooms recently built around the portal of the old church of Cluny. Laymen and clerics all demanded a full complement of militia and attendants both to protect them and to lend them consequence among their peers. Guy of Vienne was the worst offender, and his men-at-arms were at the center of every fight or drunken brawl that occurred over the weeks the multitude remained at Cluny.

Gebirga and Katerinen stood in the courtyard in the cold with Clemence the day the pope and the archbishop arrived, a north wind whipping their clothes. Guy greeted his sister formally and then stood back to take a look at Katerinen. "So this is the girl? She's a bit small and thin. And so pale. Are you sure she's well? In any case, we'll see what we can do with her." Katerinen seemed to shrink under his gaze, and huddled close to Gebirga as if for protection. Gebirga, he ignored completely.

When the pope was assisted off his white mule, a frail, tiny man looking years older than his real age, Clemence was shocked.

"But Guy, the pope is ill!" she whispered.

"Sister, the pope is dying."

"Dying? But then there will be a new pope!"

"There most certainly will."

CHAPTER EIGHT

A Betrothal and an Election

Calixtus, bishop and servant of the servants of God, sends greetings and apostolic benediction in Christ to the most holy monastery and basilica of Cluny, seat of his apostolic election, and to all orthodox persons.

The pope was indeed dying. Gelasius was taken to the bedchamber prepared for him and never left it. He was anointed with the oil for the sick, and the monks of Cluny took turns waiting vigil at his bedside, chanting penitential psalms to keep his mind on the next world. No one else came to visit him; a dying pope was no use to anyone.

Semi-conscious at best and mute, he nonetheless remained the pivot around whom all activity at the monastery revolved. Every day Gebirga heard a new rumour: he was recovering, no he was already dead. Talk of the succession began, and it seemed each night at dinner a new person claimed a miraculous vision that conveniently supported his candidate:

"I saw Pope Gelasius and Pope Paschal together putting the mitre on Guy of Vienne before all the saints in heaven, who were weeping for joy."

"Gelasius was wearing a Benedictine habit and he kneeled at the feet of Abbot Pons while Saint Benedict and Pope Gregory the Great sang hymns of praise."

Other names were mentioned as well but they soon faded, and at the end everyone was talking about Guy and Pons, Pons and Guy until Gebirga was weary. It was none of her affair, and Liisa was fractious and yappy with all the new people around, cluttering the corridors and whispering in antechambers. Could Clemence not finish arranging this betrothal so they could leave?

Some who had come to Cluny to petition the pope, did leave. The rest stayed, waiting to see which way the wind would blow. One of these was an Augustinian canon from Picardy named Aimery who told Gebirga to her great interest that he had recently walked the pilgrimage road to Compostela and back for the fifth time. Squashed on a bench beside him at dinner because of the numerous guests cramming the table, she discovered he was a plump man, despite all his walking. His journey had inspired him with the notion of walking all of the routes from France into Spain and then writing a book about them. He was there, not to talk to the pope, but in the hopes of convincing Cluny to support his venture.

"It would be marvelous! Cluny has so many different houses along the road, each with wonderful relics; pilgrims would travel to see them all, and would think of Cluny and its reach on every inch of the pilgrimage road. Those who could not make the pilgrimage could read the book instead." He spoke enthusiastically between mouthfuls. It sounded like a strange scheme to Gebirga, but listening to him was interesting. She and Katerinen thrilled at his tales of arduous travels, and close encounters with bandits. When no one else was paying attention, he lowered his voice and told them strange stories about the demons still worshipped by the peasants along the route, especially in the wild and dangerous Basque country.

"Have you ever heard of the Basajaim?" he asked. "They're a race of hairy wild men, giants who retreated deep into the Pyrenees mountains when the Christians came. People say they were the builders of the huge and mysterious monoliths that still dot the countryside. And Anbotoko Mari? She's the wife of the demon Majue, who lives in a cave and walks the land, spinning with her distaff, followed by storms that trap careless travelers. But the most frightening of all is Gaueko. He's a black wolfhound who walks upright. In good moods he warns travelers not to be out alone at night, but when he is angry, watch out."

Just as thrilling was his description of the beauties of the new church being built at Santiago de Compostela, the shrine of the saint, with all its magnificent and horrible sculptures. "There are hideous devils, angels with trumpets, and an adulterous woman holding the skull of her dead lover on her lap."

Katerinen said, "Oh that sounds so wonderful. I would love to see it. Gebirga, can we go? And miracles are performed there. Maybe you could even get your eyesight back."

Gebirga changed the subject away from this sore spot. If prayers to her own mother had not cured her, why would the apostle James, object of so many petitions, be willing to listen? So she pulled out of her purse the shell that the old pilgrim had given her and asked, "This is from the pilgrimage to Santiago, isn't it?"

Aimery looked at it. "Yes. These shells come from the sea not far from Compostela and pilgrims take them home as a sign that they have made the journey. Where did you get it?"

She told him about the old man. "He was here a few months before you arrived. I am sorry you couldn't meet him."

Aimery pitched his book to everyone who would listen, but Abbot Pons had no time for the man. Unable to interest the abbot or any of the important Cluniac monks, Aimery pestered Bernard of Carrion whose monastery of San Zoilo was right on the pilgrimage road. "Perhaps he will recognize how a book on the pilgrimage road would attract people to his house," Aimery reasoned to Gebirga.

But Prior Bernard showed no interest in furthering Aimery's visions; he was too full of his own mission, to have the pope promote his master, Diego Gelmirez, from bishop to archbishop of Compostela.

Guy of Vienne used the promise of his own influence with the sick pope to press Bernard on the question of Katerinen's betrothal. Guy strategized with Clemence in one of the parlors, while Katerinen and Gebirga were embroidering. Rather, Gebirga was embroidering and Katerinen was fidgeting and avoiding her own handwork by tossing Gebirga's balls of wool to Liisa.

"Stop that, Katerinen. She drools all over them and the colors get mixed up when you don't put them back in the right place," Gebirga admonished, picking up a soggy ball of wool, when she heard Guy say something interesting.

"Sister, I have good news. I believe I have convinced Bernard of Carrion. We are drawing up documents and settlements, but barring some new problem, the betrothal should take place in a couple of days and Bernard will serve as Alfonso's proxy in the betrothal ceremony." Gebirga pricked a finger with her needle, trying to order her woolbox, and sucked the blood away. She wished Katerinen were not so noisy and restless so she could hear better.

"How did you convince him to do it without word from Diego Gelmirez? He's the sort who waits for his master's permission to sneeze. And all Diego is concerned with right now is the question of his archbishopric and who will be the next pope."

"That played in our favor. I promised to persuade Gelasius, and Bernard thinks there is just enough chance I will be the next pope that he fears to offend me."

"But what of the dispensation, brother? Since Alfonso is our brother's son, he is a first cousin to Katerinen, well within the degrees of prohibited marriage. We hoped for a dispensation from Gelasius but that is out of the question now. Can this marriage take place?"

"That also played in our favor. Bernard knows without a dispensation, the betrothal isn't worth the parchment the contract is written on. He knows if a rival of mine is made pope, the betrothal will be null. From his perspective either I become pope, and become Diego Gelmirez's ally, or Pons becomes pope and the betrothal is worthless. His man wins either way. He thinks."

"But Katerinen needs a protector. We need a marriage. Will we get the dispensation? What if Pons becomes pope? He'll never give it to you."

"Pons will not become pope," said Guy.

"The betrothal contract must stipulate that they will return the dowry if the marriage does not take place. The two are young and many things could prevent the marriage, even with a dispensation—accidents, death, disease. I insist on it."

Clemence told Katerinen about the betrothal later that evening, while Gebirga was trying to fix the brooch Katerinen used to pin her cloak, whose clasp had slipped off its moorings. "I have wonderful news for you, Trintje. Your dear uncle and I have arranged a marriage between you and his ward, the child of our brother, Raymond, and Urraca, queen of Leon. His name is Alfonso. He already is the king of Galicia and one day he will rule his mother's lands as well. Just think, you are going to be a queen!"

Katerinen jumped up, knocking Gebirga's hand and smashing the innocent brooch to the stone flags below. Gebirga fumbled for it on the ground. The dratted girl had cracked the delicate enamel work, tossing it like that. Katerinen shouted, "I don't want to be a queen! I don't want to go to Spain, and I don't like my uncle. He doesn't like me either."

Gebirga knew the truth of that last remark. Guy thought very little of his niece and her emotional ups and downs, and Clemence was made to feel the burden of bringing this imperfect child into the family. He treated the girl with hostility and that only made her behavior worse. "This is a great chance for you. All my worries for your future are gone," said her mother. But now Katerinen was in a tantrum. Exasperated, Clemence said, "You deal with her, Gebirga. The betrothal ceremony is tomorrow, and she needs to be ready for it," and then left the room.

Katerinen was still distraught when her mother and uncle left. "I don't want to go; I don't want to leave home and everyone I know. They'll all hate me there, I know it," Katerinen repeated. Nothing Gebirga promised, not a court of her own nor pretty dresses, worked. Finally, she tried honesty.

"You're right, Katerinen. It is horrible to leave everything you've known and everyone you've loved to go among strangers. I wish I could protect you from it, but it seems to be the fate of women like us to leave. I had to do it, and I was scared, and I'm frightened of going to Spain, which is far away and sounds so strange. Neither of us has any choice." She sat beside the younger girl and stroked her hair, soft and fine as a kitten's fur. "But we'll be together, you know. That will make it better. You and Liisa will be my eyes, and I will do what I can and everything will work out, you'll see. It will be an adventure. And think of all the new churches you'll see on the way."

"Can we go to Compostela?"

"We'll go to Compostela, I promise. You'll see all the statues and the great altar of St. James, and I will stand beside you and you can tell me about everything." Gebirga thought of the old pilgrim. Maybe he would get his way after all.

The betrothal charter was copied onto two large sheets of parchment by Guy's trusted scribes working as quickly as their cold fingers would allow. One would go to Spain, while the other would travel back to Flanders. The scribes would decorate each copy with colored inks, and affix the seals of the countess, her brother, and the Spanish churchmen later, but the formal betrothal could take place immediately.

Clemence summoned Katerinen and Gebirga. She found Katerinen shrieking and struggling while two serving women tried and failed to comb her long hair. Gebirga entered the room behind Clemence, holding the dress Katerinen was to wear at the ceremony. "Katerinen. Stop this nonsense immediately. Don't you want to look your best? And here is your lady mother come to get us and you not even dressed."

Katerinen subsided into small, choked sobs and Gebirga took the comb from one of the women and efficiently started combing its tangles. She twisted it into two tight braids and then pulled the dress over Katerinen's shift and smoothed it down. It was of silk and it felt like ice under Gebirga's hands. It came from far away and they said it was made by worms, but Gebirga knew better than to believe that. Clemence had brought a casket of jewels from her strongbox, and she decked Katerinen with them. Gebirga was wearing a new dress, too, though it was wool, not silk. All her old clothing from Gistel was long gone, replaced piece by piece by Katerinen's mother.

"Are we ready then?" said Clemence, "Katerinen! Where are your shoes?!"

Katerinen began to wail again and Gebirga silently cursed. Why could Clemence not see that her agitation made Katerinen worse? Katerinen was a mirror of her mother's moods; if only Clemence had sent a servant to summon them, instead of coming herself.

Finally, the bride shod, they descended to the chamber where the men waited for the betrothal ceremony, cheerful after a few glasses of good wine and the successful transaction of their business. All eyes were on Katerinen and she shrank into Gebirga. Gebirga was afraid Katerinen was going to cry—she knew the signs. Bernard of Carrion, stiff but kind, said, "The bride is very beautiful and very shy, like a bride is supposed to be." Gebirga felt Katerinen relax and she was grateful to the monk from Spain. But the tension that had built within Katerinen made her giggle and then laugh.

Archbishop Guy intervened swiftly. There was no need for the Spanish to discover now that Katerinen had some odd ways. He summoned her to his side and she subsided.

"Katerinen, give me your hand. I will take you to Bernard, who is standing in for Alfonso of Galicia, your groom."

The archbishop and the young girl held hands and faced Bernard. The rest of the company formed a semicircle around the four, a little cramped in the small chamber.

"We have witnessed the marriage settlement," said Guy, "and since there are no impediments to this union, the betrothal can take place. Both parties will swear a promise, Bernard of Carrion on behalf of the absent prince, that they will marry."

Gebirga held her breath until Katerinen said her line, so many times practiced, "I . . . I, Katerinen do solemnly promise that I will wed Alfonso." There, a little shaky, but it was done and it was binding.

Bernard answered, "And I, speaking on behalf of Alfonso of Galicia, do solemnly swear that I will wed Katerinen of Flanders." Guy put Katerinen's hand in the prior's and then Bernard took a ring from his purse and placed in on the second and then third fingers of her right hand, before sliding it all the way down her fourth finger. The betrothal was complete.

They retired to the guest house refectory, but they had all agreed to keep quiet about the betrothal. Instead, Clemence put forward the story that Katerinen and Gebirga were planning a pilgrimage to Santiago de Compostela, where Katerinen would pray for the health and security of her brother. Later that evening once everyone had left and they were on their own in bed, the strain overcame the girl, and when Gebirga said something to her about how well she had done that day, even though she was afraid, Katerinen snapped and started babbling. "I wasn't frightened at all; it is mean of you to say so. I wasn't frightened, I was just bored, bored from standing waiting while the women poured buckets of water over me, bored while they dressed me, and bored out of my mind as they did my hair. Why did they tug so hard? They'll pull it all out of my head and then there will be nothing to wash! Then what will they do for fun? As if my standing still would make any difference. They tug so hard, I have to move or I'll fall over. It wouldn't take so long to do my hair if only they weren't so incompetent. My shoes hurt. They pinched my feet, so I took them off. But why do I need to wear shoes anyway? I hate shoes."

She bunched the coverlet in her fists and rolled on her side, away from Gebirga. "Mother doesn't understand. And Uncle Guy always looks so fierce. He points that long finger at me and makes me think the earth is going to open up and swallow me whole. But I wasn't crying; I was laughing. Prior Bernard was kind; he smiled at me, and I was going to smile back, but then I was laughing. I can't do anything right so why do they even bother with me?"

A new scandal shattered the peace of the family from Flanders. Oliver missed the first lesson after the betrothal, and then the second. Finally, they learned from the novice master that there would be no more lessons from that quarter. Oliver had been caught writing love poetry and letters proposing plans to run away addressed to a mysterious unnamed lady. The novice master was tactful but it was clear he knew they were meant for Katerinen. Oliver's future as a monk was now in doubt. He was confined to his cell on a diet of bread and water until the abbot decided his fate. Gebirga knew that Katerinen had played no part in encouraging either his calf love or his letters, but she also knew the scandal and suspicion that would fall on her if her name came forward. Even begging the kindly novice master to keep silent would be admitting too much; she had to trust his good sense. Besides, with nothing better to talk about, this would be a popular scandal, but right now everyone's attention was directed to the pope's deathbed.

As the month of January wore on, all over the monastery grounds, knots of anxious people gathered to speculate wildly about the future, stamping their feet and breathing on their hands against the cold. Gebirga escaped the monastery when she could to take Liisa for a run, just to have a moment to herself. The town of Cluny was not large and her walks with Katerinen had familiarized her with its layout. Even when she took a wrong turn, Liisa could now be trusted to return her to the monastery at the command, "Home!"

One day, however, they found themselves completely turned around. A broad street she thought was taking her back to the monastery turned into a wide yard with heaps of rubble and stones. It must be one of the many partly-built houses going up all over town. The builders could not work during the freezing time of the year, so there was no one on the site to stop her from accidentally wandering in. For once Liisa failed to prevent her from tripping as she stumbled on loose pile of rubble and fell to the ground, stinging her hands on the hard ground when she tried to break her fall, and twisting her foot. She maneuvered herself into a sitting position, with her back against a high pile of neatly cut stone blocks awaiting the spring thaw to be turned into a wall or a foundation. She gingerly brushed the sand and dirt off her smarting palms and then removed her shoe to feel her ankle. It seemed fine, painful but not swollen. She decided to catch her breath before attempting to exit the work site, which felt to her like a labyrinth. Liisa curled up beside her, and she appreciated the dog's warmth.

They had not been there long when she heard the voices of two men approach the place where she sat. They came from the far side of the pile of stone, so they would not see her. Were they builders, here to check on the site? She was about to call out when something in one of the men's voices made her pause. It was Archbishop Guy. Yes, she was sure of it, and she recognized his smell, like incense and coins. She did not like Guy and she doubted he would be sympathetic to her plight so she decided to keep silent. Maybe they would keep walking and would not spot her.

They did not walk on, but rather parked themselves on the far side of Gebirga's stone pile. Now she was forced either to be an eavesdropper or to hop up like a jack-in-the-box and greet them. She chose the former. She listened idly to talk of people she did not know and discussion of sums of money but she jumped when she heard Guy ask, "What thinks your lord of this match?" Match? Were they talking about Katerinen? Which lord?

"He says neither aye nor nay to it," said the second man, "As you know, his concerns are elsewhere." Suddenly she realized that she knew his voice too. He was her mysterious interlocutor of the previous October, the one who told her about All Souls' Day and then vanished. What was he doing here? She tried to follow the rest of their conversation.

"I know of his concerns. But does he not know that my friendship is worth having?" answered Guy.

"The friendship of the archbishop of Vienne is a good thing, but Vienne is distant from the struggles we face."

"What about the friendship of the pope?"

"Gelasius?"

"Gelasius is mortally ill, as you know."

"So they say. The friendship of the pope is a good thing indeed, but popes have many friends, sometimes too many, and they need to spread their favors."

"You are bold, for a servant. Whoever facilitates this match will be my very special friend, I promise you."

At last the two walked away and Gebirga could make her way back to the monastery, thinking about the puzzling conversation she had heard. Guy was fostering his niece's marriage. But with whom? She knew she would not ask the archbishop about it. She had a feeling he would not be happy to have been overheard.

The following day, the pope lost consciousness and the infirmarian, trained to recognize the signs of imminent death, set in motion the final rituals that would usher Gelasius safely out of this world and into the next. He spread a hair shirt on the floor beside the papal bed and sprinkled it with ashes. The pope was raised from his bed and laid gently on the rough cloth. Then one monk was sent to beat on the door of the cloister with a billet of wood. This was the signal to the monks that a death was about to take place. They rushed to the bedside chanting the Credo under their breaths, and began a litany of the saints. When that finished and the pope was still alive, though barely, most of the monks left, leaving a smaller group to continue chanting the psalter. Abbot Pons remained with them.

The billet of wood beating on the cloister door was also a signal for Guy to make his move. His first act was to come to the guesthouse, where Clemence sat with Gebirga and Katerinen.

"None of you leave this room until I or one of my servants come for you," he said.

"Why not, brother?" asked Clemence.

"Did you hear that sound of someone beating on a door? That

is the signal that Pope Gelasius is dying. The next few hours could get complicated."

"What do you expect will happen?" asked Clemence, frightened. But Guy was already leaving.

The day was one of grey skies and drizzle, and the women tried to keep busy while rain pattered on the slate roof. Katerinen chafed at the confinement and Gebirga embroidered.

"You've given that woman a blue face," said Katerinen.

"She wouldn't have a blue face if you didn't keep rearranging my wools," said Gebirga, starting to unpick her work, "Come, help me put them in order. Madder root first, then onion skin, chamomile and the rest, and nettle at the very end. I don't know what I'll do when I've used up all of these."

"They must have dyes in Spain."

"I suppose so."

They had just finished when Liisa scratched at the door to go out. "It's a pity she can't use our privy," said Katerinen.

"Well, she can't. I'm going to have to take her out."

Clemence scanned the courtyard for signs of trouble before she let Gebirga go. "It is still raining but it seems quiet. Go, but hurry back."

Liisa pulled the girl down the twisting staircase, tugging hard at her lead. When they tried to enter the courtyard, they were stopped.

"My lady, I'm sorry but my orders are to guard this entrance and not let anyone in or out."

Gebirga recognized the voice of a man in Guy's militia. "But what about my dog?" she said.

"Sorry, those are my orders. Find a discreet spot behind a pillar; that's what I'd do."

She was near the portico outside the papal bedchamber. That was usually empty and it had a number of useful niches. Besides, Liisa was desperate. She could send a servant to come clean later. While Liisa was doing her business, she heard voices coming from the pope's room.

"What is the reason for this interruption? How dare you bring armed men into the pope's bed chamber?" Gebirga heard the distinctive voice of Abbot Pons.

"I have come at the request of the cardinals, to collect the papal insignia, to keep it safe until such time as a new pope is chosen." It was Guy.

"At the request of the cardinals? Everyone knows you have those men twisted round your fingers. This is your idea, we all know that."

There was a pause and the door slammed open. Gebirga pressed herself back against the hard stone of Liisa's niche as Guy charged out of the room. When he was gone, she made her way back to Clemence and Katerinen. She told the older woman what she had heard.

"My brother must have come for the papal regalia—the tiara, the mitre, pallium, and rings—and the papal staff. If I know Guy, he probably wants to pressure the cardinals into electing a new pope the moment Gelasius breathes his last. Or even the moment before he breathes his last."

The women waited distractedly for news, all pretense of passing the time in sewing or talk finished. A hubbub rising from the courtyard made them rush to the small windows that overlooked the square. "What's happening? What do you see?" Gebirga asked the other two.

"Lots of men are gathering below, talking in groups. It is still raining but they don't seem to care," said Katerinen.

"And they're armed," said Clemence grimly, "Pons's men and my brother's militia are eyeing each other. The monks are gathering too. They'd do better to stay indoors, like us."

Then Gebirga heard a huge roar from below. Clemence narrated. "The leader of the Roman cardinals has walked out onto the porch hand in hand with my brother and, dear God, Guy is wearing the papal mitre and all the rest of the insignia."

Even Gebirga knew what happened next when she heard the words the cardinal shouted. "Behold! We have a new pope! God has seen fit to raise Guy of Burgundy, archbishop of Vienne, to the chair of Saint Peter!" Then she heard the distant cheers of those in the crowd, for whom this was good news.

"Well, that's a relief," said Clemence. But she had spoken too soon. "Wait—it looks like some of Guy's own men are rushing him, pushing their way through the crowds. They're stripping him of the regalia and those who can't reach my brother are attacking whoever is standing close to them. It's a riot. Pons's militia is getting the worst of it."

The three women heard one of the men below cry, "For shame! You are taking away our lord and pastor and depriving not just the church of Vienne but all of Burgundy of its protector. Choose someone else; Guy is ours!"

"That does it," said Katerinen, "I'm not waiting in here any longer. I'm going downstairs to take a look." And before she could be stopped, she was out the door. Clemence hurried down the stairs after her, with Gebirga and Liisa following as fast as possible.

By the time they reached the courtyard, Guy had called his militia to order. The courtyard was soaked with spilled blood, now being washed away by the rain that had started coming down even harder. Though no one had been killed, some were seriously wounded and had to be rushed to the monastic infirmary. The cardinals and monks had fled to the church of Saint Peter for protection, and Clemence and Gebirga hustled Katerinen in there too. The cardinals were met in the church by the leader of Guy's militia, who repented of his actions and those of the other men-at-arms, and promised to make restitution for what damages they had done. Then he restored the papal insignia, unharmed, to Guy. But the point had been made. Whoever crossed Guy would have his militia to contend with. Abbot Pons, and anyone else who might have challenged the new pope's election, saw and took note.

Katerinen was excited to see her uncle raised up, but Gebirga was bothered. "My lady, if I may, there is something I don't understand. Why were Guy's men so distressed to see their lord raised to the papacy? Why did they riot and cause such bloodshed? If any group were to be upset, I would have expected it to be Pons's men."

"Yes," said Clemence, "And Guy's riot has neatly preempted any possible armed reaction from Pons's men, hasn't it? They are all nursing wounds of one kind or another, and the superior strength of Guy's men-at-arms has been vividly brought home to them."

"You mean . . ."

"Yes. The whole thing was staged. Did you not realize that was why my brother ordered us to stay in safety? He planned the whole thing from the beginning."

Gelasius died that night. Three days later, Guy was formally elected to the papacy and they had to remember to call him Calixtus now, the papal name by which he would be known forever after.

When it became clear that he was not going to grant any concessions in a hurry, those who had stayed at Cluny hoping to make their case the new pope started to leave. Bernard of Carrion was one of the first to depart. The betrothal of Katerinen to Alfonso was much more likely to lead to a marriage now it had papal weight behind it. Bernard had to rush back to Spain and let Diego Gelmirez know what he had agreed to on the bishop's behalf.

Then it was time for Clemence to say farewell one last time to Gebirga and Katerinen. "I must return to Flanders. There's bad news about the wound in Baldwin's foot. The infection is not going away, and it looks like they might have to amputate. But you two will be fine. You'll travel south as pilgrims with my brother down the Rhone river to the sea, and then west to Toulouse. Then he will turn north and you will continue south across the frontier into Spain."

Katerinen and Clemence knew this might be the last time they would see each other, but neither spoke of it. Spain was far from Flanders, the road was perilous, and life was short and liable to be cut off without warning, especially for a young woman poised to enter the dangerous years of child-bearing. Clemence was formal as usual and, for once, Katerinen lived up to her mother's example. But the girl clung to Gebirga that night in the bed they shared, holding her tighter than usual and whispering through tears, "I'm all alone now. I'm far away and I am all alone and I'm going further. Don't ever leave me, Gebirga. Promise you won't leave me."

Gebirga promised, stroking the girl's hair and soothing her the best she could. Eventually Katerinen said, half asleep, "Your mother left you too, didn't she? We're both the same now." Gebirga stiffened and said nothing. It had been a while since Katerinen had tried to question Gebirga about her family, and it still was not something Gebirga wanted to discuss.

Gebirga and Katerinen were not the only hangers-on joining the newly made Pope Calixtus and his followers on their sluggish meander through the south of France. Abbot Pons himself decided to shadow the new pope, and he had added Aimery Picaud, who was still trying to attract support for his guidebook to Compostela, to his entourage. Aimery planned to travel with the pope as far as Toulouse, and then turn south with Gebirga and Katerinen into

Spain. Gebirga and Katerinen were pleased to have their new friend along for so much of their travels. "Though if he tells us those stories of that demon who ate three shepherds and their herds in one mouthful again right before we travel into the mountains, I won't be able to sleep at night when we're there," said Katerinen.

Less welcome to Gebirga as a traveling companion was Oliver, who had been attached to Aimery as a kind of assistant. Aimery had petitioned Pons for help. "I can compose the stories and describe what I see," he said, "But I am slow at writing. I need a scribe to write for me, someone young who can handle the gear and won't mind an arduous trip."

Pons's choice rested on the disgraced Oliver, thinner now after his diet of bread and water. "This young man will be perfect. He knows some of the road himself already and he is more than able to do the tasks you set him. A penitential pilgrimage to Compostela is an excellent way for him to atone for some of his recent—irregularities. He can return forgiven, and make his solemn vows here at Cluny."

Brilliant, Gebirga thought. Make the boy travel in the same party as the young girl who turned him lovesick in the first place. She spoke to him sternly before they left. "No letters. No outpourings of devotion. No plans to rescue her from her evil family."

"Oh no, you can trust me," he swore, "I see I was wrong now. She deserves far better than me. I am far too lowly for her and I will be content to serve her humbly, teach her Spanish, maybe rescue her from a burning building, or save her from an assassin's arrow only to take it myself, dying for her sake . . ." This was sickening enough that she almost preferred the old, surly Oliver.

"Just behave yourself," said Gebirga. At least they could recommence their Spanish lessons. Closely supervised, Oliver could not get into too much trouble.

Gebirga wanted to make haste, but traveling with a pope was slow work. Guy—no, Calixtus, she corrected herself—seemed to stop at every town and castle, shoring up support for his papacy. It would be June before they reached Arles and the Mediterranean coast, and more weeks of long travel before they arrived at Toulouse and beyond that, Spain.

CHAPTER NINE

The Camargue

Then one should visit, near the city of Arles, the cemetery of the dead at a place called Alyscamps and one should intercede there for the dead with prayers, psalms, and alms, as is the custom. Its length and breadth are a mile. In no other cemetery but this one can be found so many and so large marble tombs placed on the ground.

Aimery made Oliver pace out the length of the old Roman cemetery of Alyscamps, in Arles in the heat of the noonday June sun. The cemetery was full of early Christian sarcophagi and shrines to half-forgotten martyrs as well as the completely forgotten pagan dead. Oliver protested, "But what does it matter, Aimery, if it is one thousand paces long or only eight hundred and fifty? If people visit they will see and if they don't, they'll never know we just guessed?" But he did as he was told and noted this information as well as everything else Aimery told him, scratching it all out with a stylus on the wax tablet he carried.

At Arles, the Rhone divided into a marshy, swampy delta studded with lagoons and salt plains. Most of the pope's entourage had traveled the short distance to St. Gilles du Gard where Calixtus planned to stay for a few days before beginning the long journey to reach Toulouse in time for a church council. Aimery, however, paused at Arles with Oliver. It was a noble and ancient site of pilgrimage, and he wanted to collect material for his book. The city huddled within its crumbling Roman walls, patched with stones taken from the great circus and the other Roman ruins whose sun-bleached stones dotted the area like the remnants of forgotten skeletons. The pair took up residence in the guest house of the convent of St. Caesarius and spent a long day traipsing around the city, trying to see as many of its holy sites as possible.

When there was nothing more to see, Aimery sent Oliver back to their lodgings to transcribe the notes from his tablet onto parchment. Then Oliver could warm the tablet until the wax was soft enough for his scratches to be smoothed out so the tablet could be reused. Aimery continued prowling through the streets of Arles, reluctant to stop exploring this first city on the southern pilgrimage road. He was not planning to visit the market on his walk, but the smell of hot pies drew him. He followed the wafting odors of good beef and onion gravy, setting a direct course through the mass of women shouting the virtues of their chickens, the vegetable sellers displaying what surplus they had been able to coax from the earth, the carts, the wagons, and the press of people wandering aimlessly or purposefully, those lucky ones who had done their marketing clutching their bags of goods to their chests, and those with no money to buy holding only desire and hunger in their eyes. They were strict about beggars in this town, it was clear, but Aimery remembered to keep his hand on his purse against thieves all the same.

The pieman was doing a brisk business. Idly waiting his turn, Aimery noticed a thin, dark-eyed man on the edge of the group who seemed out of place among the plump and jolly burghers. Tall and lean, with prominent cheekbones and a trimmed, dark beard, the man looked foreign, but at the same time strangely familiar.

After a fat woman trundled off with her purchases, it was Aimery's turn. "What's your pleasure, then?" said the pieman.

"What's your price?" said Aimery. The pieman named a price that was almost twice as high as what the fat woman had paid for her pies and Aimery protested.

"Well, see, she's local so she gets a special price. The townspeople keep me in business long after visitors like you are gone, so they get one price. You get another. Besides, she bought six pies. More pies make less cost per pie. That's only natural." The man was aggressive but not belligerent so Aimery recognized this for the game it was. They haggled for a bit until they came up with a figure that was higher than the fat lady's cost but much lower than what Aimery was originally told. Aimery handed a coin to the pieman, one eye on the man's wares, trying to guess which was the largest and most succulent of the pastries. If it had not been for his own greedy inspection, Aimery would not even have seen the thin, brown hand reach forward and snatch a pie.

The pieman was by necessity skilled at keeping track of his merchandise, and spotted the theft right away. His "Hey! Stop! Thief!" drew the attention of everyone in the market and mobilized the bishop's men, there to keep the peace. The thief was unmistakable because he was the only one in the market square who was running. His direction was evident from the people he knocked down and carts he turned over in his effort to flee, cramming mouthfuls of hot pie down his gullet. Aimery half hoped the man would get away. He had passed some hungry days in his own life. Aimery charted his course and estimated that the bishop's thugs would catch the thief in front of the cathedral, so he made his way there without delay, following the pieman who hurried to see justice done. Aimery caught up with the pieman just as the former reached the strongmen. One of them held the thief's arms twisted behind his back, a position that looked extremely painful, while another pointed a knife at the miscreant, prepared to slit the man's nostril or even remove an ear, depending on the mood of a third, who seemed to be the chief.

The pieman addressed himself to this figure right away, "That's him, all right. He stole one of my pies, bold as brass, right off the table! Damned foreigner by the looks of him. He certainly isn't from around here! It is about time you men actually caught a thief and punished him, instead of spending the whole time eating your heads off at the bishop's table and pestering honest merchants about the kind of weights and measures they are using."

Before the man could respond to this claim wrapped in an insult, and with the thief still struggling in his captor's grip, Aimery took his chance, "My good man, what are you doing with my servant? Please unhand him at once or I will have to go to the bishop about this."

"Your servant?" the leader asked with interest, looking at the dark stranger.

"Indeed. I was buying the man a pie when all of a sudden I find him chased across the market place, running for his life and now in danger of losing an appendage."

"You never! He never!" sputtered the pieman, "He grabs it off the table and runs! I'd swear this one was getting a pie for himself. I saw the greed in his eyes, and it wasn't on that one's behalf. Else why not get two pies?"

"Had this man paid you for his pie?" asked the leader.

"Well, yes, but . . ."

"And has he taken a pie for himself?"

"No, but he didn't have time, see . . ."

The leader did not care to listen to the rest. "And does your servant still have his pie?"

The man holding the thief loosened his arms a little, enough that he could bring his forearms before his body. Miraculously, what was left of the pie was still gripped in one hand, a little bit squashed but still edible.

The bishop's man did not wait to hear more. "Fine then. Pieman. You were paid for one pie, and one pie seems to have been taken from you. I do not see what you have to complain about. And," he raised his voice as the pieman tried to break in with further objections, "If you wish to discuss this matter further, perhaps we could do so while we check your flour. We've had complaints that you are adulterating it to make it go further." The pieman stopped arguing, and sulked back to his table.

"As for you," he addressed the thief, "I release you to the care of your 'master.'" He said to Aimery, "You will be responsible for this man as long as you both remain in this town. If he so much as cracks an egg, I'll deal with both of you, bishop or no bishop. And now!" to the crowd, "Show's over! Back to your buying and selling, or I'll have the lot of you for loitering."

The mob went back to its business. Aimery knew that the guard had not believed for a minute that the thief was his servant. He turned to his new responsibility. "You might as well finish that pie. I certainly do not want it. And you look like you could use a good feed." The thief wolfed it down. Aimery was not certain why he had intervened to rescue this complete stranger, a stranger who, moreover, had done him out of his lunch. He very much doubted the pieman would sell him another pie. "Come on. There's a wine shop over there. Let's hear your story."

The red wine poured into the cheap pottery flagons was rough and fresh and they both drank thirstily. Aimery inspected his guest over the top of his glass. Now he could take a closer look, he could see that, though the man was thin, it was the look of recent want rather than long, slow starvation. He looked older on second glance too, probably somewhere in his early thirties. His clothing was better than that of the usual vagrant. His boots were good ones, and the trimmed beard told of someone who cared about his appearance. "You know, instead of stealing my pie you could have sold that short sword and bought a pie for yourself. Watered Toledo steel, if I'm not mistaken."

"You are not. But this sword is my livelihood. With it I can earn a pie for the morrow, without it I am doomed to a permanent criminal career. And next time there might not be a stranger as kindly as yourself."

"What is this livelihood then? And what is your name? I can tell you are not from these parts, but neither am I."

"My name is Yusuf iben Cid."

"A Muslim? It's a good thing the bishop's man didn't know that. You really are far from home."

"I am far from home, but I'm not a Muslim. I'm a Christian, from Toledo. I serve as a messenger for whoever will pay me to carry information, and also as guide or guard, or both, for parties of travelers. As you can see, sometimes they don't pay enough. I heard the papal household was going to be in Arles so I came here looking for work, but I see I was mistaken."

A Christian from Toledo. That explained why the man had a familiar look about him. He resembled people Aimery had met on earlier trips to Spain; Christians who had lived under Muslim rule for generations, trying first assimilation, then intermarriage, before finally fleeing to join their religious brethren in the north. Aimery had heard that in recent years even more refugees were arriving from the south with little more than the clothes on their backs, fleeing the waves of fundamentalist Islam that were sweeping the country. Toledo was the first major Christian city the refugees would reach.

"Greetings, Yusuf iben Cid from Toledo. I am Aimery Picaud and as you can see by my dress, I am an Augustinian canon. The papal household is not here but it isn't far; they reached St. Gilles on the Petit Rhone last night. I am heading there tomorrow, and you may join me. In fact, you have no choice, since the bishop's man expects me to escort you personally past the town limits of Arles. But you may find work with our new pope. Lord knows, he sends enough messages. We are making for Toulouse with plans to reach it by early July. Then I and my companion will turn south into Spain. You and I might come to some arrangement, though since I'm a poor canon and not a rich pope, you may find more lucrative possibilities elsewhere."

So three people, not two, left Arles the next morning to join the papal household at St Gilles down the river. They found the pope and his entourage already settled in their latest temporary home. The abbey was bursting with its visitors, and some had to be put up in the inns that filled the small town, built to cater to the considerable pilgrimage trade. St. Gilles was not only an important stop on the road to Compostela; it was also a destination in its own right. When the men arrived from Arles, they were lucky to get a pile of straw in the abbey stable loft to sleep on.

St. Gilles was a Cluniac abbey so Pons felt right at home. It had not taken him long to start pulling rank. The poor abbot, with a pope and the abbot of his motherhouse both visiting at the same time scarcely knew whose ring to kiss first. But by the time Aimery and his crew arrived and settled in, all the questions of protocol had been sorted out and Calixtus was holding an audience. He received petitioners from the gilded wooden throne that was usually the seat of the abbot. Aimery, Oliver, and Yusuf sneaked in towards the back and found a place to stand close to Gebirga and Katerinen.

The next petitioner was a Benedictine monk. He kneeled before the pope and kissed his ring. Calixtus asked him to rise and state his business.

"My lord pope, I am Berengar de Macon, a monk from the monastery of San Servando in Toledo. I am an emissary of the archbishop of Toledo, Bernard de Sauvetat, and I bear a letter for you from Alfonso, king of Galicia and Toledo."

That got everyone's attention. Most of the petitions had been the usual ones from local priests wanting their sons legitimized so they could inherit the parish or childless men looking for permission to put away their barren wives. A letter from a king would be worth a listen. Oliver nudged Yusuf and remarked on this visitor from his home town but got no response.

The monk handed a parchment dangling a large, oval, wax seal to the pope. He read it quickly through, lips moving as his finger followed the words, and then again more slowly. When Calixtus was finished, he folded the letter up and with a voice like stone asked the monk, "Are the contents of this letter true?"

"My lord, my master the archbishop fears they are. That is why he asked me to bring it to you swiftly." The monk bowed, possibly to avoid looking Calixtus in the eyes.

"Then I summon Gerald of Compostela before me to answer to these charges."

There was a scuffle in the crowd as an elegantly dressed canon made his way forward and came before the papal throne. Gerald had joined the traveling papal party back at Avignon in order to, like Prior Bernard of Carrion, beg the new pope to make the bishop of Compostela an archbishop. But Calixtus had postponed making a decision on this question until the council planned for Toulouse, still several weeks and many miles hence. Gerald had to be satisfied with this, though it meant weeks of kicking around with the papal party, and money spent on living expenses that might be better spent on gifts for those with the power to make decisions.

Gebirga, whose attention had flagged during the long audience, became alert at the mention of Alfonso of Galicia. This was Katerinen's betrothed, and any letter from him to the pope would surely affect her future. And Gerald was a canon of Compostela, a Frenchman in the service of its bishop, Diego Gelmirez, who had sponsored the betrothal.

Gebirga thought that Gerald must know about Katerinen's betrothal from his master, but he never spoke of it and she too kept her silence. He had gravitated to Gebirga, Katerinen, Aimery, and Oliver on the journey south with the pope. He was a little stuffy, and he laughed too loudly at things that were not really funny, but otherwise Gebirga had no objections to him. Aimery and Gerald had formed an instant rapport after Aimery spoke of his project to write a book about the roads to Compostela and the shrine to St. James there.

"A book about Compostela, what a superb idea," Gerald had said, almost dropping his customary pomposity in genuine enthusiasm. "But why stop at describing the shrine? There are the prayers and hymns to Saint James, the beautiful Compostelan liturgy. If you put that in the book, people far away could read it and have a sense of being present at the major feasts of our community. And the miracles! Saint James performs so many miracles, not just here but all over Christendom. You could collect stories on your travels and add them to the ones we already know." They schemed, and Gerald promised to put the project before his master, Diego Gelmirez, whom he was sure would support it wholeheartedly.

But now Gebirga fancied she could hear Gerald shaking in his boots as he groveled and kissed the papal ring. "My lord pope," he said, "I will serve you in whichever way I can."

"Serve me by explaining the contents of this letter from my dear nephew and ward Alfonso. He complains to me of the behavior of your master, Diego Gelmirez. Alfonso writes here that he fears Bishop Diego is plotting to remove him from the throne of Galicia, and he asks me for assistance. He has fled Bishop Diego and sought support from the archbishop of Toledo."

Gerald spluttered, "There's not a word of truth in that. Bishop Diego loves your nephew as a son and lives only to support his reign in Galicia. This letter, brought here by a servant of the archbishop of Toledo I might note, is most certainly a forgery written by the archbishop. We all know the archbishop is jealous of the deep friendship between yourself and my master and seeks to drive the two of you apart. He fears competition, my lord pope, if you raise the see of Compostela to an archbishopric, and he is lying in an effort to persuade you not to make that step."

"And is Alfonso now residing with the archbishop of Toledo, as he says in this letter, or is he still with Diego Gelmirez?"

"Well, no, as a matter of fact, it happens that Alfonso is in Toledo now. But that doesn't mean—."

Calixtus stood, cutting Gerald off in mid-speech. "This audience is over," he said, rising from the throne and, without pausing for the usual protocol, sweeping from the room. His attendants struggled to keep up with him as they pushed through the mob of surprised onlookers.

Once he was gone, the room broke into an uproar originating with those whose petitions had not been heard before Calixtus suddenly ended the audience.

Katerinen whispered to Gebirga. "That monk Berengar, who brought the letter, is yet another French cleric in Spain. Where do they get them all from? Why don't they stay here?"

But Gebirga was not listening. Any news from Alfonso of Galicia was of interest to her, especially news that caused Calixtus dismay. But she was distracted from even these pressing thoughts by a familiar scent.

Aimery said to Gebirga and Katerinen, "Well, that was a dramatic turn around. Good thing we didn't miss it by coming late."

"What do you think, Aimery?" asked Gebirga, trying to remember where she had encountered that scent before, "Is the letter genuine? Is Diego Gelmirez plotting against Alfonso? Or is the archbishop of Toledo trying to cause trouble between him and Calixtus?"

"The problem," the shrewd man answered, "Is that the answer to all these questions is likely to be yes."

The scent was still there. It was coming from someone standing with Aimery. People expected her to have good hearing because she was blind. Less often did they expected her to be able to identity people and places by smell, but even over the normal sweat and dirt of everyday life, Gebirga had found that different places could be identified by their odor, and not just kitchens and gardens. An armory smelled like metal and a sleeping chamber like stale straw and old wool. People smelled differently too. It had always disturbed Clemence to see how Gebirga addressed her when she entered a room before the older woman said a word, but Clemence did not realize how distinctive her scent of rose and lavender was, from the sachets her ladies lay between her folded clothing. Katerinen smelled like the honey on bread and warm milk she insisted on eating every night before bed. Oliver smelled like thin sweat and fear most of the time.

"I know you," she said. "Who are you?"

A man next to Aimery answered. "Yes my lady, you do know me. We met once in the abbey church at Cluny. Perhaps you remember that? My name is Yusuf iben Cid and your friend, Aimery, has been kind enough to bring me into his companionship. I am delighted that our paths have crossed again."

Spices and olive. Yes, she knew that smell, and the voice, low and pleasant. It was the man who had consoled her after her first Mass at Cluny. He was also the man she had overheard talking to Calixtus on the building site. However had he joined ranks with Aimery?

"Yes, I do remember that meeting. How strange to meet you here again. Are you and Aimery old friends?" she said, trying to keep her tone innocent.

There was an embarrassed pause which Aimery relieved by saying, "No, no, a new friend. We met over a meat pie in Arles and I invited him to join us since he is a courier and a guide looking for employment. I thought I could introduce him to the pope."

No need to introduce him to the pope, Gebirga thought, they've already met. Well, if this Yusuf was to travel with them, she would have many chances to determine what his game was, if he had one.

The next day Calixtus remained sequestered in his chambers with his most trusted advisors while Gerald slunk about like a rejected suitor. The tension in the abbey was palpable and it was starting to affect Katerinen, so Gebirga thought she ought to remove the girl for a while for everyone's sake. Aimery, Oliver, and Yusuf were planning to ride down to the coast for the day to visit the priory of Our Lady of the Sea and Gebirga asked if they might join the men. Katerinen was less than enthusiastic but Gerald, passing, heard the plans being mooted and said, "Katerinen, you must go. There are large pink birds that nest there in flocks of thousands, called flamingos. I'll come along too."

"And the Spanish word for them is flamenco, which is the same word we use to describe someone from Flanders, like you, so you really must see them. Maybe you are cousins," Yusuf teased.

Katerinen was intrigued now, so the party set off after begging a picnic from the abbey kitchens to eat on their way. Gebirga left Liisa behind for once so the dog could rest before the long journey to Toulouse. They all rode the local grey Camargue horses of which the abbey had a huge collection, except Katerinen who was on a smaller roan pony. Despite the heat of early June, being out in the air again and away from the crush of anxious visitors at the abbey did them good. Even Gerald began to relax and they all tactfully forbore from talking about his troubles with the pope.

They traveled on one of the long, level roads that criss-crossed the marsh, this one providing access to the salt pans on the shore for the monks of St. Gilles. Their right to the salt in the Camargue was one of their major sources of income, along with the horses that they broke and sold. The road took them through low-lying plains that were submerged underwater for most of the winter. These began to dry to marshland in the spring and now, covered in glasswort and other small plants, they provided ideal grazing land for the horses and also for the small local wild bulls and cows who dotted the horizon. To Gebirga, used to the flat marshes and rivers of Flanders, it felt like home, despite the heat that made the narcissus and asphodel growing in the fields so pungent. There was the same salty, rank scent of vegetation rotting in the sun and the same cacophony of birdsong. She heard the familiar calls of bitterns, coots, and wagtails while her companions remarked on more unusual egrets and ibises picking their way along the shores of the lagoons. But still no flamingos, and Katerinen was getting impatient.

They rounded a corner and Katerinen shouted, "Look!" There before them were some thousand flamingos, resting and eating after the spring mating season and gaining strength for their migration at the end of summer. Whether startled by Katerinen's shout or obeying some unspoken command of their own, the whole flock suddenly took off in a body and wheeled around in flight, passing over the heads of the riders and then out of sight, seeking some new lagoon.

"Gebirga, Gebirga, that was wonderful. I've never seen anything like it. Oh, I'm so glad we came." Gebirga was happy to hear the uncomplicated joy in Katerinen's voice. She too had been awestruck simply from the noise of their big wings beating overhead.

But Katerinen was not finished. "I want to see them again. I want to see more of them. I don't want to go to the boring old priory. Can we look for more flamingos, please?"

"I don't know where they are, Trintje. We could ride around all day and never find any."

Gerald was helpful again. "The biggest flocks will be in the large lagoon to the east of here. It shouldn't be difficult to find them. If you would rather go there than come with us, it will mean much less riding for you since we are still some way off from Notre Dame."

"There's a crossroads up ahead. The left hand road must lead down to the lagoon," Yusuf added.

Gebirga and Katerinen left the men at the crossroads, dividing the food they had brought with them. "We'll meet you back here when the sun is a handspan above that tree," said Aimery, pointing, "Katerinen, you have to pay attention because Gebirga won't know."

The women rode on slowly after the men had gone, enjoying the hot sun. There was lots of time before they would have to turn back. They ate their bread and cheese under one of the few oak trees that grew in the marsh, swatting away gnats attracted by their scent. The noise of sea birds ahead of them promised that their lagoon was not far.

After they rejoined the road, they passed men gathering the reeds that were used locally to thatch their small, round houses. One man pointed in the direction they were riding. "Lou biou," he said, "Lou biou!"

The people in the south spoke a language that bore little relationship to the French they spoke in the north. This had caused few problems when they were traveling cushioned by the papal household but now it created an impenetrable barrier.

"I'm sorry," Gebirga said in French, "We don't understand you. Do any of you speak French?"

The men shrugged and turned back to their work, and the women rode on. They came over a rise in the land and Katerinen cried, "There they are! Even more than the first time." She cantered towards the flocks of unusual birds before her. Gebirga halted her own horse, seeing no need to catch up.

Then Katerinen screamed again but this time it sounded like fear, not excitement.

"Katerinen, what's wrong!?"

The only answer was a frightened squeal from Katerinen's horse and the noise of hooves galloping back in Gebirga's direction. When the nervous horse reached her she discovered it was riderless and panicked.

"Katerinen, where are you? Come back! Are you hurt?" Palms sweating, she urged her horse forward.

The girl screamed again and Gebirga heard more hooves, now galloping from the direction of the crossroads. It was Yusuf. "Don't move," he said, "Here, hold the horse as best you can." He put the reins of Katerinen's horse in her hand. It was still shying and starting, but she did the best she could. Fortunately her own mount remained calm.

Yusuf rode down to wherever Katerinen was. Katerinen shrieked and shrieked, but Gebirga was useless, pinned to the spot by her disability. She heard Yusuf shouting and after what seemed like an age, he and Katerinen rode back, she on the back of his horse. They all three returned to the top of the rise and then dismounted. Katerinen fell weeping into Gebirga's arms, her small body shaking like a frightened bird.

"What happened?" Gebirga asked Yusuf, when Katerinen's sobs slowed and became more rhythmic, a sure sign the younger girl was recovering.

"After we left you, we spoke to some men who told us about wild bulls in the fields and warned us to beware. All the bulls are wild here, but some of them have been attacking people more often lately. The men think it is because there are too many of them and they are jealous for space. I told the others I would follow you and make sure you were safe. I passed some men working in the reeds up ahead and they told me they had warned you but you wouldn't listen. They gave me this stick they use to ward off the bulls."

"Lou biou," Gebirga said, feeling the wickedly pointed metal crescent at the end of the pole that Yusuf held out towards her, "Yes. They did try to warn us. I didn't understand." She cursed her foolishness. Why had she not guessed they might be saying something important?

"If Katerinen had been riding a Camargue horse she might have been fine. They are used to standing their ground. But this one threw her as soon as it saw the bull. I warded it off with the pole and, well, we're here. It all had a good ending. Don't cry."

Gebirga wiped the tears that were beginning to fall and hugged the girl fiercely, as if by doing so she could protect her from harm. She felt sick. If not for her stupid eyes, she might have seen the bulls in the field ahead of them and warned Katerinen. If Yusuf had not come she would not have been able to find Katerinen, far less save her from being gored. Clemence had been wise to worry about putting her daughter in the care of a blind woman. For all the good she could do, she should have stayed in the convent in Gistel.

She and Katerinen were quiet all the way back to the abbey, the girl out of shock and she from shame and the agony of barely averted loss.

In the guest refectory the next morning Katerinen, fully recovered from the scare of the previous days said, "Gebirga, I need new boots."

"Boots?" She felt the foot proffered to her. Yes, there were holes.

Aimery joined in, "Oliver and I should get new soles put on our boots too, before we begin our journey. There is sure to be a good bootmaker in a pilgrimage town."

"Peyrot is the best cobbler around here," someone said, "He is in the town; you can't miss him."

Sure enough, when they went into the small town it was easy to find the one-story shack with the big boot hanging in front of its door as a signpost. Gebirga sniffed the dank leathery interior from the door. "Aimery, if you will help Katerinen find some boots, I want to take Liisa for a run. Gerald told me there is a walled cemetery up ahead, and I do not think the bones will mind if Liisa frolics a bit."

Aimery and Oliver were together more than sufficient to make sure Katerinen found what she needed. Gebirga took Liisa and walked to where she had been told the tiny church of St. Martin lay. She opened the gate to the churchyard and made her way with the dog's help to sit in the shade on the far side of the porch, resting her head on the cool stone. She had not been there long when she heard someone shuffle his feet. There was someone waiting in the porch. Well, it was no business of hers. She let Liisa off her lead and the dog ran off to investigate interesting smells. Then she heard someone else arrive, walking quickly up the path and joining the first under the porch where they were both out of sight of casual passers-by.

"You're late," said the first.

"I was held up. Is there anyone else here?"

Gebirga sat up straight. It was Yusuf's voice. Whom was he meeting this time?

"A woman with a dog came by a while ago. She's probably tending one of the graves. Quick, this won't take long."

"Very well then Brother Berengar, hand it over."

Berengar? That was the name of the archbishop of Toledo's envoy. Yes, it did sound like his voice. Gebirga heard the dull chunk of a purse full of coins exchanging hands and then the sound of Yusuf counting under his breath.

"It could have been more generous," said Yusuf, "I was reduced to stealing pies."

"I will express your views to the archbishop."

"Right then, I'm off. Not much time." Yusuf hurried down the walk to be followed a moment later by the monk Berengar at a more leisurely pace. Gebirga came out of her own hiding place and called Liisa back, her thoughts racing. So Yusuf was being paid by a servant of the archbishop of Toledo. Was that the "master" he had spoken of when he and Calixtus had discussed Katerinen's betrothal back at Cluny? It explained why Calixtus sought his support. Gebirga recalled that Yusuf had not promised Calixtus to support the betrothal. Lost in her thoughts walking back to the cobbler, she was shocked out of her reverie by the sound of a huge crash like the world falling apart and then screams and shouts, male and female. Liisa started barking and she heard Aimery's voice. "Gebirga, thank God you are here."

"What happened," said Gebirga, feeling dust in her nose and settling on her face and hair, shaken for the second day in a row by her own uselessness.

Katerinen was crying again and she clung to Gebirga's arm, "It was horrible. We heard a creak and a groan and then next thing we knew, the whole shop was caving in. Oliver saved me."

"What?!"

"It is true," said Aimery, "Oliver grabbed her just as the building started to shake. It's not much more than a pile of kindling behind you now." Her ears tuned to the sound of the shoemaker wailing and mourning the loss of his business behind her. "It's a miracle we all survived," Aimery said, "I think it was thanks to St. Gilles. I'm going to put it in my book."

That night Katerinen snored peacefully, recovered from this second adventure, but Gebirga did not sleep for a long time. Twice now Katerinen's life had been in danger. The two episodes could have been random accidents, but were they? And was it coincidence that they occurred right after Calixtus received word that Diego Gelmirez might not have the influence over Alfonso of Galicia that they had been promised? But if the incidents were planned, who was to blame? It had been Gerald who had told them about the flamingos, but it was Yusuf who urged them to ride back down that particular road, and who was to blame for Katerinen's unsuitable horse? True, Yusuf had come back to rescue them. But if Gerald was Compostela's man, Gebirga knew now that Yusuf worked for Toledo. Yusuf would have had time after leaving the churchyard to topple the building and from what Aimery and Oliver said, it would not have taken much. Still, they had announced to the whole refectory that they would be buying boots that morning; anyone could have heard, or told someone who was not present. What of Aimery and Oliver? Could she speak to them of her concerns, see what they thought? No: that book they were writing bound them up in loyalties to Compostela and Cluny. And finally what of Calixtus himself? Had the news from Spain made him see his niece as expendable? The bonds of family did not prevent murder. She knew that as well as anyone. Gebirga had not felt so alone since her mother's death and she wished she could speak to Clemence. But Clemence was far to the north tending to her son, and there was no one else Gebirga could trust.

CHAPTER TEN

Toulouse

*Then, on the same road, one should also visit the most
worthy body of Saint Saturninus, bishop and martyr, who
was seized by pagans in the city of Toulouse.*

There was little time for Gebirga to dwell on these speculations however, because they left St. Gilles the next day, hurrying to reach Toulouse in time for Calixtus to preside at the church council. They traveled by boat to Beziers, and Katerinen thrived in the fresh, salty Mediterranean air, so warm compared to the North Sea winds she and Gebirga were used to. Every day was cloudless and sunny, the kind of weather that was spoken of in Flanders for years if they had so much as a week of it strung together. After Beziers, they abandoned the galleys and began a slower trek by horse, cart, and mule on the old Roman road south to Narbonne and then inland to Toulouse.

"Of course, if you're traveling to Compostela, you'll have to be wary of Queen Urraca's husband," said Aimery idly one day as he and Gebirga rode side by side. After the threats to Katerinen and the mysterious appearance of Yusuf in Aimery's entourage, Gebirga was suspicious of Aimery, but she still wanted to learn from him as much as he could teach her about the tangle of Spanish politics; about Urraca and her son, and the competing prelates of Compostela and Toledo.

"Urraca's husband? Are you speaking about Raymond, Clemence's brother? But he's dead I thought," she asked.

"No, I am not talking about Raymond, rest his soul. I am talking about her second husband, King Alfonso of Aragon, the kingdom right beside her own." Aimery settled into his favorite role as storyteller. "Urraca hasn't managed to kill him yet, though I am sure she would love to. And he'd be happy to see the end of her too. Urraca's first act on becoming queen was to fulfill her father's dying command to wed the king of Aragon. They were to rule jointly in each other's realm, and this was supposed to avoid war between the Christian kingdoms. Unfortunately it did no such thing. They separated three years later and there has been constant warfare between them since, so grave that it has been impossible for Urraca's people to cross the Pyrenees into France openly without being captured and robbed and held for ransom by Alfonso, whose realm covers all the passes."

This was disturbing news to Gebirga. Why had Clemence not warned her about this enemy? Wishful thinking that everything would turn out well? "Aimery, are pilgrims in danger?"

"No, Alfonso lets honest pilgrims travel freely through his realm. But woe betide you if he thinks you have business with his wife. Then you'll find yourself in a dungeon before you can turn around. They say he is terribly jealous of his wife because she has an heir in her son by her first husband, and he has never been able to beget a child of his own."

"I can vouch for the danger of traveling through Aragon," said Gerald, who had been silently listening to their conversation, "Alfonso of Aragon will not let any friends of Queen Urraca pass through his domains. Why, to get here, I had to dress as a poor peasant and take the backroads on foot through the mountains until I reached Logroño. Then, I traveled only by night all the way to the mountain pass into France. Even Cluniac monks, like Bernard of Carrion, who should be able to travel freely all over Christendom, fear the wrath of Alfonso of Aragon. If I were you and Katerinen, I'd turn right around now and go home."

This was terrible news. If the king got wind that Katerinen was his step-son's intended bride rather than a simple pilgrim, she would surely be in great danger. Alfonso of Aragon would not be pleased to see his step-son begetting heirs when he had proven incapable of the same. Another thing to add to Gebirga's growing worries.

Yusuf's presence continued to trouble Gebirga too. One day Katerinen artlessly commented that Yusuf was riding a hundred paces behind them, and he seemed to do that every day, and why did he not just join them if he wanted to be close instead of hanging back like that. Gebirga worried again that a blind woman who could not detect pursuit was no fit companion for Katerinen.

They rolled through the countryside, moving from town to abbey, joined by local counts and abbots who planned to attend the council, as well as merchants and other hangers-on who were journeying in the same direction and appreciated the safety of traveling in a group. At each hill-top abbey where they lodged, Calixtus confirmed the privileges of their hosts, and consecrated new altars in the churches being built everywhere. Indeed, the whole of the south of France seemed to be one big building site. Everywhere they went they inhaled the stone dust left by masons constructing yet another monument to God's glory. Katerinen developed an enthusiasm for these building works and dragged Gebirga all over them, Liisa following gamely, as she chattered with the workmen and speculated on the heights that the new buildings would reach. For Gebirga, who could not see to appreciate the towering heights of stone, these excursions were mostly about heat, dust, and the clangor of masons hammering rock.

Without the breezes of the sea to offset the sun, the heat went from pleasant to oppressive. Gebirga was glad she and Katerinen could ride, and did not have to be cooped up in a covered cart. Deeper and deeper inland they rode, exchanging flatlands for rolling hills, each with a little castle or settlement at its top. Dense forests of pine, oak, and chestnut gave way to scrubby uplands on the higher peaks and the air was fragrant with lavender and rosemary as they made their way slowly through the mountains. Katerinen exclaimed the first time she saw the peaks in the distance, "Mountains, Gebirga, higher than anything you could imagine! And snow on them, even in the middle of summer."

At last, someone spotted the spires of Toulouse in the distance—the cathedral churches of St. Stephen and St. James, and the new abbey church of St. Sernin, still under construction. Toulouse was the biggest town the pope had traveled through in the south, an appropriate place for a church council expected to attract bishops from across the Pyrenees as well as from the surrounding towns. An important trading crossroads where the old Roman road crossed a major river, Toulouse could absorb large numbers of travelers. The papal party was able to disperse throughout the town to its many hospices. Gebirga and Katerinen stayed as very insignificant hangers-on with Calixtus in the hospice of the priory of Notre Dame, another Cluniac monastery, across the river from the city proper of Toulouse.

Gebirga wanted to talk to the pope about her fears for his niece's safety, but if she had thought staying with the pope would allow her access to him, she was mistaken. The formal parts of the church council—the solemn masses that opened and closed the proceedings, with all the bishops and abbots in their finest vestments, and the official promulgation of new church law through the canons passed by the council—were the least of Calixtus's preoccupations. He spent long hours listening to petitions from churchmen wishing to shape the content of those laws, whose concerns ranged from worries about local heretics denying the validity of the church's holy sacraments, to those urging the pope to take a harder line against the emperor. They closeted themselves with Calixtus in his apartment, trying to convince him of their views. Gebirga passed her time waiting in the antechamber, hoping to get a few words with Calixtus. Also waiting in vain with her was Gerald of Compostela. His master's petition to be promoted to archbishop from bishop of Compostela was one of the pieces of business to be discussed during the formal council sessions. But Gerald was given no chance to influence Calixtus before that discussion, nor to remove the bad impression left by Alfonso of Galicia's letter. Gerald was not his usual fulsome self, and he made an uncomfortable waiting-chamber companion.

And Katerinen was going wild with boredom, trapped in the hospice with so many fussy old men. So after fruitlessly wasting one full day trying to get the pope's attention, Gebirga gave in to her pleas to cross the river and enter the town to see what there was to be seen.

It was like carnival time in Toulouse. Attracted by the council and the prospect of men with loose silver in their purses, everyone with anything to sell for miles around had flocked to the city. Buskers juggled and tumbled and wrestled for coins, and the two women were buffeted and jostled by the crowds that flowed around them. Katerinen stopped in a group watching a young woman doing a dance with snakes, but they had to leave when Liisa started barking at the serpents. Food stalls filled every corner of the narrow, twisty streets, serving fresh fruit from the countryside, skewered bits of grilled lamb—mostly intestines and other innards—and twists of fried dough, covered with honey and the dust of the streets. The scent of cooked food mixed with the stronger odors of dirt and unwashed bodies pressed close, while beggars and cutpurses did brisk business. More durable goods were also for sale, everything from cheap trinkets and clay ampules of holy water "blessed by the pope," to silks, daggers, and finely carved ivories brought up from Spain. The page boy attending them was soon overburdened by all the things Katerinen felt she could not live without, so they sent him back to the hospice. Gebirga, assaulted by noise and stench, was anxious as always in a large crowd in a strange place, and Katerinen was hot and over-excited. After Liisa sicked up a snack of meat tidbits she had begged for, Gebirga for once agreed happily to visit a building site when Katerinen suggested they leave the crowds behind to see how work was progressing at St. Sernin.

"Shouldn't we go to the church of St. James instead, since we are going to Spain? We can ask him for assistance for our trip," Gebirga teased.

"No, I don't care about any stupid saint," said Katerinen, "There are saints everywhere. I just want to see the walls going up. This church is going to be huge, bigger than any I've seen since we left Cluny."

"I warn you, with all the excitement of the council, there may not be much work going on at the church right now. But that's all to the good as far as I'm concerned since it won't be as dusty or as noisy as all those others churches you dragged me through."

Outside the south door of the church they met a young canon who greeted them amiably and asked if they were visitors, in town for the council. After Gebirga introduced Katerinen as the sister of the count of Flanders and described themselves as pilgrims on the way to Spain, he offered to show them around the building.

"This is the perfect place to start. You see on the left, above the door? That is Saint James. You see his name is written on his halo? Of course you'll be seeing him everywhere the closer you get to Compostela."

Katerinen whispered, "See, we didn't have to go to the boring old cathedral to see St. James."

The canon continued, "And on that capital, up there, you can see the story of the Massacre of the Innocents. It shows how King Herod killed all the little babies after the birth of Christ. You'll see this story carved all over in Spain because they use it to show how the Christians are being killed by the Muslims in our own day. Herod's mother was an Arab, you know."

The tour continued inside the building. The canon was eager to take them to the new ambulatory and to show them the windows into the crypt through which they could peer at the tomb of St. Sernin himself, but Katerinen was more interested in the work done by men on scaffolding high above their heads to raise the brick walls of the nave. Gebirga had been wrong; there was a smattering of workmen taking advantage of the July warmth and sun to raise the walls higher. Liisa trotted obediently beside them as they viewed the sights.

Meanwhile, in the scriptorium of the abbey of St. Sernin, Oliver was fed up. He was tired of traveling all the time, of the disorder and confusion of the road and now the heat. He missed Cluny and his regular life there, and even his fellow monks whom he had disdained in the past for being, to his mind, insufficiently serious about their monastic calling. In Toulouse, he had hoped to join in the services at the Cluniac priory where they were staying, but instead Aimery sent him out to work. Aimery was feeling guilty for having omitted most of the pilgrimage road between St. Gilles and Toulouse, since they had traveled by sea, so he directed Oliver to the abbey of St. Sernin to see if he could copy out the life of their saint for his book, while he himself sat in a tavern collecting stories about the churches and saints they had missed.

At least the scriptorium was cool inside its brick walls. The account of St. Sernin's death was a gruesome contrast to the peace and quiet of the monastery. Each of his limbs had been tied to a savage bull and these had dragged him about before he was finally thrown off the roof of the citadel. The story of the bulls reminded Oliver of Katerinen's encounter in the Camargue, and he gazed into space for a few minutes seeing blue eyes and blonde hair instead of martyred saints. But the tale then told how the saint's head was crushed, his brains scattered, and his whole body torn into bits and Oliver, feeling somewhat ill, copied it all down, recognizing the interest it would hold for readers of the guide.

After he had transcribed the last gory detail, he thanked the librarian and left the scriptorium, passing through the cloister and into the church. As he came into the nave, he spied two women with a big dog talking to one of the canons half way down the church. Oliver was delighted to recognize Katerinen. Maybe the day was not a complete loss after all. Gebirga was engrossed in whatever the canon was saying, but Katerinen looked distracted, and was gazing around. He began walking towards the group when a shout over their heads made him look up. Two men working on the high scaffolding were fighting, pushing each other and shouting. Now Katerinen and the canon were looking up at the workmen too. Oliver walked faster as the men scuffled. He was close enough to hear Katerinen wonder aloud whether they were going to push each other off the scaffolding. Oliver saw the man closest to the newly built wall of the church pick up a hammer, no doubt intending to use it as a weapon. The other man must have come to the same conclusion, because he moved to the edge of the scaffolding.

What happened next must have taken an instant but to Oliver it seemed like forever. He saw the man raise the hammer as if to throw it at his companion, since he was no longer close enough to strike. Oliver realized that if the hammer did not strike its intended target, it would fly right over the edge, down to the threesome on the floor. His startled shout scattered the three and made Liisa bark as he began to run towards them. He barreled straight into Katerinen and knocked her to the ground, just as the hammer crashed to the floor beside them.

"Ouch!" said Katerinen, "Oliver, what do you think you're doing, knocking me over like that? I'll be bruised all over, and you've torn my dress."

The hue and cry brought the other workmen over. The canon shouted at the foremen and the workers shouted at each other, while Oliver and the page helped Katerinen to her feet. The two men sheepishly came down from the scaffolding. It turned out they were apprentices, younger than they looked, and they were taken off to be soundly beaten.

Oliver accompanied the two women back to their hospice. Katerinen was still nattering at him about knocking her over when Gebirga finally said, "Hush, Trintje! Don't you realize that he may have saved your life? If that hammer had struck you . . ." She shuddered.

"Aieee, do you really think so?" said Katerinen, "In that case, I forgive you, Oliver."

"It was a horrible accident," said Oliver stoutly, "But it all ended well at least."

Accident? Gebirga wondered. Could someone have paid those apprentices to scuffle just when she and Katerinen were touring the church, paid them enough that it was worth a beating? It would not be hard to guess that she and Katerinen would make their way there eventually; it was one of the most important sites in town, and the two of them were always recognizable because of Liisa. There were very few Belgian sheepdogs in the south of France. She shook herself for being so suspicious. How could it have been anything but an accident? Building sites were dangerous places; everyone knew that.

The council began formally the next day with a papal mass. It happened to be, Gebirga realized with a start, the anniversary of her mother's death, and she wondered how her mother was being remembered in Gistel. Were they still using the altar cloth Gebirga had embroidered? Maybe Alice had picked out the image of Gebirga and Liisa, as she had threatened. It was hard to believe it had only been a year since her life had changed so dramatically. The nuns said Godeleva's problems started because she went so far away from home to marry, but look how much further Gebirga had gone. She tried to return her attention to the Mass, but she kept thinking of the small chapel at Gistel, incense and candles burning, the priest droning, and the nuns in uneasy truce with the castle for one day in the year.

Her mind went back even further, to the day by the river when her mother died, to her father, and his guilt or innocence in the death. Funny, how it was easier to allow herself to ponder the ambiguities and mysteries of that day now she was far from home. Lord knew, enough of her current situation was just as confusing. Again, she worried about who might want to harm Katerinen.

The cardinals stood with the pope at the altar of the cathedral church of St. Stephen, while everyone else crammed into the nave of the church as best they could, yammering at each other, until they were silenced by the opening words of the hymn, "Veni creator spiritus," swelling throughout the building. Gebirga and Katerinen had wedged themselves beside a pillar where they hoped to avoid being trampled. They could barely hear what was going on and Katerinen complained her view was obstructed by someone's big hat. The pope spoke on the need for unity in the church and everyone trooped out.

The council meetings took place in the hall of the bishop's palace, and fewer people attended these sessions, though the cardinals and most of the abbots and bishops were always present. The matter of Compostela was raised at the end of one of the last days of the council. It was mid-July, and even the brick palace walls were no proof against the midsummer weather. When Gebirga, sweating in her thin wool, complained about the heat, Katerinen answered, "At least we don't have to wear layers upon layers of vestments, like the churchmen. Poor Gerard of Compostela looks bathed in sweat." She added, "Calixtus seems cool, at least, in all his purple and gold." Calixtus had asked Katerinen to be in attendance, because he wished to speak to her afterwards.

All the Spanish prelates were present for this discussion of the elevation of Compostela to an archbishopric. Pons of Cluny was arguing Compostela's case, so Gerald needed to say little. No one mentioned the unfortunately timed letter from Alfonso of Galicia, complaining of his treatment at the hands of the bishop. Finally, Calixtus responded in a formal speech that had obviously been prepared beforehand.

"Dearest sons in Christ, the Roman church is exhausted by many distractions and beaten down by unnameable adversities. God has placed me, although unworthy, over it, and I leap to remedy its oppressions. Please remind your lord, the bishop of Santiago de Compostela, Diego Gelmirez, that he ought to help the Roman church with all those powers in which he so greatly abounds, thanks to God and blessed James. We ask him also to help our nephew, King Alfonso, and the kingdom of Galicia, which his grandfather gave him while both the bishop and myself were present. If Diego Gelmirez helps him freely, then we will grant the bishop's petition freely. Unfortunately, so we hear, Diego Gelmirez has been opposing our nephew. If this turns out to be true, then our friendship for him will turn to hatred. Once, we embraced the church of Santiago—St. James—and its bishop with paternal love."

Calixtus paused for a moment and then raised his voice even louder, "In order that our love for Diego Gelmirez may recover its former strength, we ask that he use his strength to help our nephew, as a father and guardian. We are not able to grant Diego Gelmirez's petition at the present time, namely that the church of St. James be raised to an archbishopric. Since he is not present at this council, it is impossible for me to agree to what he wants. If he had come to Toulouse, of course, we would have granted his petition. Therefore, if he wishes to elevate the church of St. James, tell your master that he should hasten to visit me. This is a letter inviting him to the council of Rheims, which we will celebrate on the feast of Luke the Evangelist in October. If he is present on that occasion, we will satisfy his wish."

Gerald hurried to the foot of the papal throne, where he kneeled and accepted the letter, which he exchanged for a large, heavy sack that clinked. Calixtus accepted it without a word, and passed it to one of the servants standing behind him. "This session of the council is over," the pope announced, "We meet again here tomorrow. Thanks be to God." Those present all muttered, "Thanks be to God," in response, and then filed out, chattering about what they had just witnessed. Gerald said to Gebirga, who was standing close by, waiting to talk to the pope with Katerinen, "Oh well, it could have been worse. At least he promised to hear our petition again at Rheims. But I don't know how we are going to get Diego Gelmirez here, given the difficulties I had traveling through Aragon. And I don't know where I will get enough funds to continue giving gifts to all those whom I need to reward for their assistance. I'm almost cleaned out already." He sighed and left.

Calixtus summoned Katerinen to an antechamber off the palace hall. When Gebirga followed Katerinen, she heard the pope ask the girl sharply, "Who is that following you?"

Gebirga instinctively turned her head behind her to detect the intruder, until she realized the pope was speaking about her. Well, she had only been living in his company and taking charge of his precious niece for the past six months; she could not expect him to recognize her. "Holy father," she said sinking into a deep curtsey that allowed her to hide her irritation, "My lady Clemence, your dear sister, placed the lady Katerinen in my care. I serve her and will escort her to Spain."

"Oh yes, it's you." He finished with Gebirga and turned to his niece, "Katerinen, did you understand how what just happened affects you? No? I didn't think so. I've put the bishop of Compostela off for another few months. I suspect I'll have to grant his request some day, but once I do, he'll no longer have any reason to accede to my wishes. I did not mention your marriage out there, because your betrothal must be kept secret until you arrive in Queen Urraca's domain. You need to pass through the kingdom of Aragon before you reach her lands and you'll never make it if you go as the affianced bride of one of Aragon's rivals. You will travel most of the way in the company of the Spanish bishops returning from the council, and I will send you with a respectable number of armed men. As a pious noblewoman making the pilgrimage to Compostela, you will easily gain safe passage through Aragon. Alfonso of Aragon does not dare scare away the pilgrim trade because it brings him a good income as it moves through his land. For the same reason, I am not going to give you the dispensation for your marriage to your cousin just now. I wouldn't want it to be found on your person."

No dispensation? Gebirga's thoughts flew. She knew that without the dispensation, the betrothal was not worth the parchment that recorded the marriage settlement. Katerinen would be vulnerable in a strange land without it, and she knew that it was something Clemence had insisted on.

"Gracious father," she interrupted, "I will have to write to Lady Clemence to let her know there is still no dispensation."

"You can write her whatever you like," Calixtus said, irritated, "That is all I have to tell you. You may go now. And please be ready to depart promptly at the end of the council."

Gebirga thought about the letter she carried in her purse, the one Clemence had asked her to take to Diego Gelmirez. Long hours pondering its contents had made her endow it with great significance. Now she wondered whether the letter made some discussion or promise of a dispensation. Perhaps it would serve to prove good intent, allowing them to bide their time until the formal papal dispensation reached them.

Gebirga took an exhausted Katerinen back to their rooms. "I don't want to go to Spain, Gebirga. I want my mother," Katerinen said plaintively.

I want mine too, Gebirga thought, as she hugged the girl. We are both so far from home. The food is odd, the air smells different and no one seems entirely trustworthy. Calixtus's reasons for not handing over the dispensation made some sense. If they were captured, its contents would immediately make it clear that they were not simple pilgrims. But Gebirga had to wonder if Calixtus, by refusing to grant the dispensation, was protecting his beloved nephew while sacrificing his beloved niece. And how safe would they really be, traveling through the domains of the king of Aragon as pilgrims?

CHAPTER ELEVEN

The Pyrenees

Along the way of Saint James by the Toulousan road, having first crossed
the Garonne river, one comes to the land of Gascony and then, after
crossing the pass at Somport, to the land of Aragon, and then to the land
of the Navarrese as far as the bridge over the Arga river and beyond.

Gerard left Toulouse the next day at dawn, hurrying to give his
master Diego Gelmirez the bad news about the pope's decision,
and so he could prepare for the arduous journey to reach Rheims by
October. Gebirga and Katerinen woke up to find that Aimery and
Oliver had gone with Gerald and his attendants, hoping to garner
Diego Gelmirez's favor for their book project. "But they didn't even
say goodbye!" Katerinen wailed to Gebirga.

The rest waited to leave until the formal end of the council on the
feast of St. Marina, a virgin who hid her sex and dressed as a man
so she could live in a monastery. On that day, boys chanting "Kyrie
Eleison," led silk-clad nobles and clergy in their best vestments
through streets hung with banners and decorated with flowers to
the cathedral for a final papal mass. Everyone was exhausted with
ceremony and eager to be done.

Katerinen made her final, formal farewell to her uncle the next
day. True to his word, he had arranged a small military escort for
them, one of plausible size to accompany a party of noble pilgrims.
He had also arranged for them to make as much of their journey
as possible in the company of bishops returning home from the
council. Only one was from Aragon, the bishop of Barbastro, but
his presence should be enough of a smokescreen to get them past

the king of Aragon. He had been told nothing of the real purpose of their journey of course, and knew only that they were pilgrims. The Flemish women who had served them had returned home once they reached St. Gilles, and since then they had relied on papal servants, and whomever they could hire briefly during a visit to a town. Calixtus's steward also arranged for two women who spoke French and were willing to travel as far as Jaca, on the other side of the Pyrenees. Completing their party were a couple of pack mules to carry their baggage.

On their journey westward, they skirted the foothills of the Pyrenees, whose distant peaks still amazed Katerinen. "Are we really going to have to cross those mountains?" she kept asking. Each evening they ascended to the nearest of the small walled towns that overlooked the valley and at that altitude, their nights were cool. It was harder traveling as one small group among a crowd of independent traveling parties than it had been traveling with the papal court. Large and cumbersome though that had been, at least there had been some central command and organization. Now there was no one planning when they would start, when and where they would stop, and, worse, there was no one but themselves to arrange for food and lodging. It was up to Gebirga, helped by the leader of their little militia, to decide their plans and make sure they were keeping up with the others. She got better at this although there were a few nights when they reached their destination late to find all the best places to sleep already taken by groups arriving earlier.

Yusuf iben Cid was among those traveling with their group, though it was unclear to whose entourage, if any, he belonged. He seemed to vanish every night, but he reappeared each morning to ride most of the way alongside Katerinen and Gebirga. At least he had abandoned his previous practice of shadowing them from a distance. When Gebirga asked his business, trying not to sound suspicious, he was laconic, merely saying he had been hired to deliver messages. About what and to whom, Gebirga wondered, but it was clear she would get no answers. In other respects, however, he was loquacious and she had to admit, whatever her suspicions of him, he was a welcome traveling companion, skilled at distracting

Katerinen from the tedium of the long trip. Distracting her too, she admitted when she was being honest.

Gebirga thought she might as well make use of him if he was going to stick so close, so she asked him questions about Spain. While they rode, he told them stories about open dusty plains where you could ride for days without meeting anyone, and mountain ranges that touched the sky and were home only to wild shepherds and holy men who could tell you more than you wanted to know about yourself, if you chanced to encounter one of them. He spoke of cities of a size that would dwarf any they had ever seen, each larger and more beautiful than the last, where you could buy goods from every corner of the world: silks, spices, weapons, ivory, and even men, brawny Slavs from the east or black-skinned Africans, and in whose markets you could find metalworkers, potters, dyers and weavers. In his telling, each city was surrounded by lush gardens full of every kind of fruit and vegetable, many unknown to his listeners—melons and lemons, oranges and citrons, pomegranates and figs, as well as the more usual pears, apples, and quinces. "You'll have a chance to try them all," he promised.

"Which is the most beautiful city?" asked Gebirga.

"Seville," Yusuf answered without hesitation.

"Really? What makes it the best?"

"I was born there." They all laughed. "Actually, I left when I was very small so I don't remember it myself. But I have heard the stories. It really is the best. Was the best."

Gebirga's questioning grew more personal.

"Aimery told us that you were a Mozarab but I don't know what that means. It is an odd word."

"It is an odd word. It means, 'like the arabs' and it started out as an insulting term about Christians in Muslim Spain who were living like Muslims. Hard-line Christians, who condemned what they saw as our treachery in assimilating to our Muslim masters called us that. Now it simply means we are Christians who live in Muslim Spain. We speak and write in Arabic and we have Arab names, we dress and eat much like Muslims do, and though we still pray in Latin, our prayers differ from those of the rest of the Christian church."

"Is your name Arabic?" asked Katerinen.

"Yes, Yusuf is just Joseph. Iben Cid, means son of Cid, and Cid means leader. It was not my father's name; he was called Miguel. But he was a war leader, and he served al-Mutamid, the Muslim king of Seville, so his followers started calling him Cid as a mark of honor."

"He fought for Muslims!" said Gebirga, aghast, "Did he fight against Christians?"

"Sometimes. And sometimes he fought alongside Christians against Muslims who were fighting with the help of other Christians. Things are more complicated in Spain than papal crusades would make it seem. At least they used to be. When my father was alive, a long time ago, there was a multitude of Christian kingdoms in the north, and a multitude of Muslim kingdoms in the south, and they were constantly fighting each other, and making alliances without much regard for religion. Mercenaries and soldiers of fortune fought for both sides."

"What happened to your father? Did he die fighting for the king? If you don't mind me asking."

Yusuf was silent for so long before responding that Gebirga feared she had disturbed him. She knew what it was like to be dogged by questions about your family that you would prefer not to answer.

"I said it was a long time ago. Now allegiances are more clear cut. One of the Christian kings became stronger than all the other Christian and Muslim kings—that was Queen Urraca's father. When he conquered Toledo, the Muslim rulers grew frightened. They invited the emir of Morocco to help them defend themselves against the Christians. Instead of helping them, he conquered them. He is the leader of a strict Islamic sect called the Almoravids. They live like warrior monks in castle fortresses. He encouraged our local holy men to preach against our own kings, accusing them of immorality and wandering from the path of Islam, and then when their people wouldn't fight for them, the Muslim kings were defeated. Al-Mutamid of Seville died in a Moroccan prison. And the astronomers, who understood the night sky, fled; the musicians had their instruments smashed as 'un-Islamic' and all dancing stopped; the philosophers were afraid to ask questions; and the poets had their tongues cut out. But the king, al-Mutamid, wrote one more poem in his Moroccan exile." Yusuf recited,

> Will I ever spend another night
> In those gardens, by that pool,
> Amid olive groves, remnants of splendor,
> In the palace of my home, in the spring rain?
> May God will it that I might die in Seville
> And there He might find my tomb at the end of time.

Yusuf stopped. "But what about your father," pressed Katerinen, "What happened to him?"

"The Almoravids despised the Spanish Muslim kings because they showed tolerance to Christians and Jews. Of course, we paid the head tax required of all non-Muslims, but some of us were able to rise to high positions of responsibility, like my father. The Almoravids hated that. When they defeated al-Mutamid, they urged his former subjects to rise against those Jews and Christians he had favored. My father was killed by the men in his own army. His very own men." He paused again. His voice was soft. "We were forced to flee. We left with the household of his younger brother and traveled north. I still remember that ride north, pressed against my mother's chest, her silent tears wetting my hair. In my memory, it is always night, though we must have traveled by day too, once we were far enough from Seville. We stopped at Toledo, which was Christian. There, we were welcomed as extra bodies to help fight the Muslims."

"But how could you survive? Were you able to get enough land for yourselves when you moved up to Toledo?"

"Land?" he laughed bitterly, "We were given as much land as we wanted, as much as we could handle. More. Land where the Muslims come raiding every year to burn our crops, steal our sheep, and even our women if we couldn't get them behind walls quickly enough. There's no shortage of land in Spain. It's not like Flanders, where you have to invent wars in Jerusalem just to get enough people to leave so the rest of you can walk without bumping your elbows. No, the wars come right to us in Toledo, every spring, during the raiding season. It's people we needed, not land, and few wished to move to such a vulnerable spot. Gebirga, if you had grown up in Toledo, instead of Flanders where everyone must be mad, you never would have reached your present age without a husband. Someone would long since have snatched you from your family and set to repopulating the countryside."

Gebirga blushed hotly. She said, "Toledo must be in desperate straits if it needs even blind women. I would be in trouble, because I wouldn't be able to tell a Christian and a Muslim apart."

"Even if you could see, you might have difficulty with that, domna. There's little to tell us apart by sight."

"Are you married?" asked Katerinen, nosily returning to matters of greater interest to her.

"I was. A long time ago, now, it feels. She died, in one of the raids. It was then that I turned my back on making a living farming in the middle of a battlefield. My mother lives with my father's brother, my sisters are married, and I earn my keep far from where I grew up with whomever gives me something interesting to do. And you, Gebirga?" he said, changing the subject. "Katerinen tells me that your mother is a saint."

"Yusuf, I told you not to mention that to her," Katerinen wailed. "Gebirga does not like talking about her family."

"No Katerinen, it's all right," said Gebirga. She felt she owed Yusuf something for being so open with them about his life. And somehow it was easier to speak to someone who, like her, had suffered the loss of his home and loved ones. Slowly Gebirga found herself speaking of her mother's death, the convent, her father, Winnoc, the crusade. "I was right there with my parents on the riverbank, watching them, when my mother died. It was the last thing I remember seeing. I recall the sky, the river, the flowers I was plaiting together, but I do not remember what I saw between them. I probably never will. But I think my father killed my mother, whether it was in a rage or as part of a plan," she admitted for the first time. "It is the only thing that explains why he felt the need for such penance."

"So this pilgrimage is partly your own way of making amends for the past?" he guessed. "And what will you do after your journey?"

Gebirga reddened again. Of course he was not to know that she expected to stay and wait on Katerinen as she began her new life in Spain. "I will go wherever Katerinen goes, and continue to serve her," she answered.

"Always? And is that enough for you, to live by serving someone else?"

She responded to this impertinent question defensively, "I like serving her. It is good to feel needed. And besides, doesn't everyone serve someone? Your father served al-Mutamid. Don't you serve someone too?" She hoped that would draw some kind of answer from him about his own agenda, but instead he merely withdrew.

"Yes, that's true. But I hope I won't be doing that forever. One day soon, when it is safe, if it is ever safe, I'll return to our lands south of Toledo and begin cultivating them again. I hope."

One night, as Gebirga and Katerinen dismounted to stay at the priory of St Martin in Maubourget, he asked her about the small bundle tied behind her saddle.

"That?" she said, "I'll show you. Look." She untied it and unwound the cloth cover to reveal the reliquary chest her father had sent from the Holy Land. Gebirga had intended to load all of her limited belongings onto one of the mules, but at the last moment, she took the chest out and wrapped it in her second best cloak to make a parcel that she could tie to her own mount. "Do you remember the chest I told you my father sent back from the crusade? It was to provide my dowry for the convent. He gave it to me when I left with Katerinen."

"May I?" he gently took the reliquary from her hands, "There is Arabic writing on it. Did you know that?"

"Yes, but no one has been able to tell me what it means. Do you know?"

"It reads, 'Baraka kamila wa ni'ma shamila wa afiya wa izz li-sahibihi—Perfect blessing, complete bounty, well-being, and glory to its owner.' I like that! Let's hope it comes true. What are you going to do with it?"

Do? Did she have to do something with it? "I don't know. Keep it, I think. I suppose I may leave it to a church or monastery some day. It is the only thing I have that is really mine." But she liked knowing the meaning of the strange letters, and got Yusuf to teach her to pronounce its Arabic syllables as they rode.

At Pau, Gebirga had an unwelcome surprise. The raggle-taggle crowd that left Toulouse had dwindled as bishops one by one peeled off to return to their sees. The only bishop left was the Spanish one from Barbastro, along with his entourage and a larger group of merchants, traders, and pilgrims. It was this bishop who, without his knowledge, was to provide Katerinen with cover to get past the king of Aragon. When they arrived at the little village of Pau, huddled behind its wall overlooking the river, Gebirga asked the bishop's steward how soon it would be before they reached the pass of Somport, the gateway into Aragon. That was where she had been told to start being wary of the king's spies on the lookout for friends of Queen Urraca.

"It will take a day and half of hard riding from here. Given the pace of this crowd, I would expect two days, frankly. But the bishop is not going by way of Somport, you know. Our party will branch off from the rest of the group tomorrow and take the river valley of Ossau to the pass of Portalet. Taking that pass will cut our journey on the other side considerably. Do you still plan to ride with us? If so, you will have to look sharp. The bishop wants us to pick up the pace once we leave the rest of this slow-moving crowd. The king is waiting for him."

Gebirga had to make a fast decision. She expected to make their journey with the bishop. But she had also been counting on the protective covering offered by a large traveling group. It seemed most of the remaining party would go by way of Somport. Which way should she choose?

"Is the pass of Portalet safe?" she asked the steward.

"Safe enough. Of course it is a much narrower way than Somport; that is why most favor going that way. And the hills are full of brigands who find thievery more lucrative than sheep herding, but that is true of all of these mountains. A group as large as we are will have no difficulty."

"Then we'll join you," she said, making her decision. Calixtus had impressed upon them the necessity of traveling with the bishop as far as they could. Let's hope that proved to be good advice.

Gebirga, Katerinen, and their women awoke early the next morning, hoping to make a good start with the bishop's group. While they waited out in the courtyard of the hospice for their small militia to get their mounts ready for them, they were hailed by Yusuf, apparently walking his horse.

"I can't stop. My horse has colic. She wants to lie down and roll, but that would be death to her so I have to keep her walking. I've been up since before dawn, when the grooms called me."

"Colic? How did she get that?" asked Katerinen.

"I think the hay they gave her in this miserable place was moldy, but the grooms swear that wasn't so. In any case, I can't leave her here; they won't exchange a well horse for a sick one. I hope it is just a mild bout, but I won't be leaving with you this morning." He sounded worried as well as frustrated. Not surprising—colic could be a killer.

"But you'll catch up with us?" asked Katerinen.

"I'll try to, once she's better. I'll travel faster because I'll be alone, but with any luck, I'll be back with all of you before you reach Somport." He continued his trek round and round the courtyard.

Somport. Gebirga pondered. Yusuf did not know that the bishop and his party were not going by Somport, but by Portalet. Or if he did, he did not know that Gebirga and Katerinen were planning to go with them. Should she tell him? She thought not. She still did not trust him completely.

The roads to Somport and Portalet did not branch off from each other until a few miles south of Pau, so the whole group left together for what would be the last time. When they finally turned aside from the larger group to take the less-traveled road through the mountains, Gebirga felt strangely free. Of all the people she had traveled with over the past year, Clemence and Calixtus, Aimery and Oliver, and then Yusuf, now it was just Katerinen and her. And Liisa too, of course.

The moment the bishop's party left the larger group, it picked up the pace. As they climbed up into the hills, following the river Ossau up to its source, Gebirga's group found it harder and harder to keep up with the bishop's men, who were presumably more used to the steep mountain ascent than they were. They were not far behind, but their isolation made them all nervous and jumpy, even the soldiers. The way was damp and misty, and even Gebirga could sense and feel oppressed by the thick forests that pressed them on both sides. Several times they passed flocks of sheep being taken by their lonely shepherds up to the high mountains for summer pasturing, and Liisa was fascinated by the sheep dogs they passed, as shaggy and white as the sheep they guarded so seriously. The forests of oak and chestnut gave way to lighter woods of pine and beech interspersed with open meadows.

They finally caught up with the bishop's men at the cleft in the rocks called Gabas that was their destination for the night, the imposing Pic du Midi looming over their heads. They were to stay at a small pilgrim's hospice, newly dedicated to St. James. When they arrived, they found they had come on no ordinary day; it was the feast of St. James himself. Their lodgings were even more cramped than usual, but they were promised a very special dinner in honor of the saint. When at table Katerinen found this included, among other dishes, the local specialities of frogs' legs and prune pie, she was less than enthusiastic. The two women lingered in the newly-built church after vespers, having no desire to return to their cramped living-quarters in one of the outbuildings until it was absolutely necessary.

"Do you think we'll ever get there?" asked Katerinen.

"Get there? Of course we will, Trintje. Why do you ask?"

"It is just that we have been traveling so long and I feel like we'll never stop. I never knew the world was so big. It doesn't seem big in Flanders, where the journey from Bruges to St. Omer is a great occasion and takes only a few days."

They walked around the small church a while longer, Gebirga following Katerinen as she examined everything. "Look! That must be a statue of St. James. Oh, I'm sorry, of course you can't. Here, give me your hand. It is not much taller than I am."

Katerinen took Gebirga's hand and raised it to the figure carved out of wood. "Do you feel? Here is his staff and purse, and then here is his hat and it has a scallop shell on it, just like the one you carry. That's how you can tell it is James."

Gebirga's hand lingered for a while on the face of the saint, carved in the guise of an old man on a journey, feeling the contours and ropey muscles the artisan had drawn from the wood. Her action reminded her of the old man who gave her the shell back in Bruges and how he had put her hand to his face, in order, he said, that she might know it again. It was perhaps foolish, but touching the statue comforted her.

They left early the next day and passed the little lakes that dotted the mountains. Skirting the Pic du Midi on their right, they climbed above the tree line and into the narrow marshy valley buzzing with dragonflies that formed the pass of Portalet. The little rivulets flowing through the mountains, which had been running towards them since they began their ascent, were now flowing in the same direction they were riding. Finally, they were descending, after climbing for so long. They must be in Aragon.

The bishop's party was again moving faster than they were, but consultation with the leader of their guard convinced Gebirga that they were making good time and not falling too far behind. As long as they kept up their current pace they would reach Biescas, the small town that was their destination for the night, by late afternoon without difficulty.

Katerinen was not helping, however. She kept stopping to look at the spectacular mountain scenery.

"Trintje, let's go!" Gebirga said, "We have to hurry!"

"No we don't; you even said we'd have plenty of time. I just want to look for a while." Katerinen would start moving again and all was fine until they rounded a bend or came to a crest and she wanted to stop all over again.

They continued in this fashion until, "Oh look! Look! I must get it."

Gebirga said, "What is it now?" very impatient, as she heard Katerinen get off her horse.

"Flowers!" Katerinen shouted from a distance, "I've never seen anything like them before." She returned to where the riders were standing. "They have three big pink petals and then a long yellow and brown tube, like a mouth."

"It's an orchid, my lady," said the head of the militia, "You can find them all over these mountains, in all sorts of colors."

"There are more there; I must pick them," she said and ran off again before Gebirga could stop her. "And mushrooms too!" she said from where she was picking.

"You'll get wet!" said Gebirga to no avail. Katerinen returned with a bunch of orchids tucked in her dress and a bundle of mushrooms concealed in her skirt.

"Let's eat them right now. I'm hungry and we have a long way to go before dinner." It was warmer and drier on this side of the mountains and the militia was in a better mood. The men were enthusiastic and offered a small pan and some smoked bacon to cook with them.

"How do you know they're safe?" asked Gebirga, but she knew she had already lost the battle.

"They're boletus mushrooms," said one of their soldiers as the others set to lighting a small fire and their maidservants sliced the fungi and the salt fat, "Perfectly edible. Delicious even."

They were meltingly tender and juicy against the crisp bacon and Gebirga enjoyed them as much as anyone else, but by the time they were finished, their group was far behind that of the bishop. They continued their journey, winding their way down the narrow path, the river rushing alongside them, louder and louder as it was joined by more mountain streams. At first they chattered about their surroundings and the view, but as the ride wore on they grew tired of competing with the river to be heard and lapsed into silence, eager now for the day's journey to be at an end.

The noise of the river must have concealed the approach of the men from behind the overhang. An arrow found its mark, and the scream of their militia leader was the first sign Gebirga had that something was badly wrong. In an instant, all was a confusion of pounding hooves and the noise of an assault, steel on steel now rising above the noise of the rushing water, and Liisa barking, again and again and again. She heard a feminine scream. "Gebirga!" Praise God, not Katerinen. A rough arm reached up to pull her off her mount but her horse, frightened but sturdy, turned and took off back up the direction from which they had come, and then, dangerously, off the path and over wilder ground. Gebirga had no idea how she managed to stay on the horse, its panic matching hers. Hurtling into a void, whipped by branches as she raced through the forest undergrowth, Gebirga's riding skills were no match for this gallop and when the horse leapt an unseen obstacle, she flew off. Her head met hard ground, and she knew no more.

CHAPTER TWELVE

Ermita de Santa Elena

*This is a barbarous nation unlike all other nations in customs
and in nature, full of every evil, swarthy in color, wicked of face,
depraved, perverse, perfidious, empty of faith and corrupt, lustful,
drunken, skilled in all violence, ferocious and wild, dishonest and
reprobate, impious and harsh, ill-omened and contentious, unversed
in anything good, and well-trained in all vices and iniquities.*

In the beginning there was pain, nothing but pain. She became aware that she had a body and that the pain was in her body, filling its every inch. It was torture to move. Over the pain, she felt air, cool on her skin. From the chill, she realized night had fallen, but she had no idea how much time had passed, nor how long it would be before dawn. She pulled her cloak around her against the chill, and rested against a block of stone she found at her back. Dizzy, she closed her eyes again and tried to think. The effort brought the pain down on her harder than ever. She inhabited a dark world in which the only sense available to her was that of excruciating agony. Slowly, over the pain, she grew aware of the sounds of the night. She distinguished a river rushing some distance away, and birds, insects, and wild animals joining in a strident cacophony.

Smell was the next sense she regained. Lavender, strong lavender. And then, much more surprisingly on this lonely mountain, incense, almost like in a church.

Gebirga opened her eyes. And she could see, really see. And before her was an apparition of horror. A black wolfhound, a giant, but not on four feet like a normal dog. This wolfhound was standing upright like a man. It did not menace or threaten her, but under its gaze she felt herself to be entirely alien, an unwelcome intruder in a land not her own. The hound raised its black muzzle and howled, loud into the night.

Unbidden, she recalled the things that lurk in the dark Pyrenean nights that Aimery had told them about, San Martin Tziki and Anbotoko Mari and the Basajaum who build monoliths. She felt the stone at her back, cold like ice. And Gaueko, the wolfhound who walks like a man. She screamed soundlessly at the apparition, and everything went dark again. She was alone in the night.

She never knew how many hours it took for consciousness to return. This time, her first thought was of the attack. They were riding, coming through the mountains and then they were assaulted. She must have fallen. She recalled the assailants coming upon the company without warning, the sudden confusion as they struck, the shrieks of the men, and the sick sound of cudgel breaking bone. How could such a strong party as their escort be attacked so easily? Her head was too muzzy to figure it out. Other memories surfaced—Katerinen shouting her name, Liisa barking.

"Katerinen? Liisa!" she called. The effort made her head throb more, and was in vain. No one answered and she was alone on the dark mountainside at night. She did not call again. Who knew who might hear? Their assailants might still be close. She strained her ears to distinguish the sounds of the night.

And heard a gentle voice, close by, hailing her softly in greeting, "Gebirga? Well met."

"Who's there? Who are you?" she instinctively drew back. Her retreat was blocked by the hard, high stone at her back.

"A friend. A fellow pilgrim. We've met before. Here, I'm right in front of you now." Her hand was clasped in the gnarled paw of an old man and brought up to his face. He had her trace its contours. "Remember? At Bruges? And Cluny? And I've seen you here and there since then on your journey, but I haven't liked to bother you with all your friends about."

She knew him. It was the old man, the pilgrim.

"But how did you find me? Did you see me from the road?"

"No, you are a ways from the road. Not too far, but concealed from any chance wanderer by this stone you're leaning against. What happened? Were you attacked?"

"Yes, we were," she said and then sat up tall, "Katerinen? Did you see Katerinen on the road? A young girl, the girl I have been traveling with."

He paused before answering, "The girl is not on the road. I don't know where she is."

Gebirga slumped back against the rock. Neither spoke, then the pilgrim offered her his bottle gourd. She took it and drank. The water was clean and cool.

"I saw something in the night," she said, "A black wolfhound, standing on its hind legs."

"Did you?" he said, making no comment about how it were possible for a blind woman to say she has seen anything, far less a standing wolfhound. "It isn't surprising. You are sitting in a holy spot. That stone behind you? It didn't grow there naturally. If you could stand—no, don't try; you're still weak—if you could stand you'd see it is taller than you are. It has a twin a few paces away and another lies on top of both of them, forming a door. They say the Jentilak, who used to live in these hills, built them and that they were doors into the realm of death. But you're safe, on the right side of the door. No one will come to harm you now that I've found you."

"How did you find me?" asked Gebirga.

"Your dog. Liisa, you call her? She's very intelligent. I came as quickly as I could."

"Liisa? You found her? She's all right? But where is she?"

"She's fine. But she's gone to get more help. I can't stay with you, I'm afraid. But what you need most of all is sleep and in the morning, help will come. So, lie down. And sleep." he said, stroking her hair once as she followed his command. And then he was gone without a sound.

Somewhere in the back of her dazed mind she thought she should call to him again, insist that he stay with her, or at least find Liisa. But she found herself obedient to his command to rest, slowly drifting off into a natural sleep, not the concussion of the first part of the night. Her last conscious thought was to wonder how he knew her name. Had she ever told it to him?

When Gebirga woke again, the feel of sun pouring through

dappled leaves told her it was day. Her head pounded and she tried to sink back into the peace of unconsciousness, but pain dragged her back to the world and all its dangers. "Ouch," she heard herself say, as if from a distance. She grew aware of other sources of pain distinct from that in her head, bruises and scratches on every part of her body. Slowly she pushed herself upright, ignoring the crescendo in the throbbing of her head caused by her movement, and leaned against the stone pillar at her back. When she tried to stand however, she grimaced at a new injury found now in her right ankle. She gave up the struggle to stand and lowered herself carefully down again.

Once she was more or less sitting, she took stock of her situation. No food, no water, no friends. No way to know where she was, or where she should go, or how she might get there. Panic tightened in her chest and she fought it down. She found her purse at her waist. With fingers made clumsy by worry she struggled to open it and make sure its contents were intact. She found her coins still there, and the precious letter Clemence had entrusted to her care, destined for Diego Gelmirez's eyes alone. That was a relief, at least. She put her hand up to the worst site of the pain on her forehead and brought it to her nose to smell the metallic tang of her own blood. Her hair was escaping its coif too. But the wound had felt matted and sticky and it did not seem as if fresh blood was pouring from it. She now remembered a wild ride, and being tossed from her horse. Her head must have hit the ground; if she had struck the stone she was leaning against, she would surely be dead. A thornbush growing beside the stone pillar accounted for many of her scratches, no doubt, but must have partly broken her fall. She should make her way back to the road, but she had no idea which direction it was. And what would she find when she did make her way to it? What had happened to her fellow travelers? Had they been taken prisoner or were they all lying up there, dead? The thought of trying to make her way down a path she could not see, tripping over the mangled bodies of her comrades made the panic rise again. What were her chances, alone and blind on a strange hillside peopled with robbers and assassins? She fought again to calm herself.

She remembered her strange visitors of the previous night. The first one, the monstrous dog she actually saw, must have been a nightmare, though her dreams did not often include images. But as she waited in the cool dawn, trying to think of what her next move should be, and feeling pangs of thirst and then hunger when the pain from the abrasions on her body grew less insistent, her second vision, the one of the old man who promised that help would come, seemed more and more like a dream too. Panic gave way to despair.

Then she heard barking. And it was not the barking of some phantom demon come to plague her out of the mists; it was the barking of her own Liisa, loud and insistent. "Liisa?" she called. Her voice was weaker than she expected but it must have been loud enough because she heard the dog come bounding over to her. She embraced the animal and allowed a few friendly licks on her face. "Where have you been? Ouch, watch my head. How did you find me here? Well, you are a sheepdog, and I've always thought you saw me as an oddly shaped sheep that you had to keep from going astray."

Interrupting their reunion, Gebirga heard more noises approaching her in the underbrush. A large animal—a horse? Gebirga froze. Could this be one of their attackers, following the dog to her hidden spot?

"Gebirga! You are here. That dog of yours is a genius; she led me right to you."

Panic subsided. She knew that voice.

"Yusuf?" Her relief was palpable. She forgot all her suspicions of him.

"Yes, it's me." He tied up his horse, then crouched down beside her. "What happened? You look terrible, like someone dragged you through a hedge backwards. And you're bleeding. Wait, let me—." She heard him fumble with something, and then he dabbed a damp cloth on her forehead.

"Ouch! Stop—what are you doing?" She tried to brush his hands aside, embarrasssed by his touch.

"Let me. I want to see how bad this cut on your forehead is, and I have to clean it. It will only hurt for a minute. Don't be a baby." When he was finished with his ministrations, he used another corner of the cloth to wipe from her face some of its accumulated blood, dust and mud. "There, you look better already. Here, have some water. Are you hungry? I've got bread and a little cheese."

After drinking from his bottle, she fell on the food ravenously. The mushrooms seemed very long ago, in another lifetime. She supposed it was a good idea they had stopped to eat them. Or no, perhaps if they had not stopped, they would not have been attacked. She must have looked stricken, because Yusuf's voice was gentle, "Can you tell me what happened? I know you are not hiding behind a stone pillar all alone and covered in twigs by your own will. If you can tell me how you got here, we can figure out what to do."

"We were riding, we were not far from our destination, I think. Biescas."

"Yes, Biescas is close."

"I heard a scream from the man in front of me. The leader of our militia." She gulped, recalling the sound, and continued, "We were attacked. I don't know by how many."

"Were they peasants? Some of the people who live in these hills prey on travelers. There is little land to cultivate here, and families are large. Or, no, you wouldn't be able to tell, or to say whether they wore anyone's insignia."

"I think they had horses, at least some of them. And swords."

"That doesn't sound like peasant thieves. That's helpful. Go on."

"We were attacked. I felt a tug at my bridle—someone must have grabbed it. My horse didn't like it and pulled away. We took off, I don't know how far, back up the path. And then she threw me, and here we are. And I've lost everything and I don't know where the rest are, or if any of them survived or were captured, or are lying hurt somewhere, and I can't reach them. Katerinen . . ." She started shaking, the shock of her situation sinking in deeper. Yusuf pulled her cloak close around her, swaddling her like a child, and then added his own cloak to hers.

"The first thing I should do is go to the place you were assaulted and look around. You say your horse rode back up the path? Then I probably hadn't reached where you were attacked when Liisa urged me off the road to find you. But I did see somewhere ahead that looked like a place I'd plan an ambush. Will you be fine here with Liisa while I go? I won't be long."

Liisa had pressed close into Gebirga's body and the woman had her arms around the dog's neck, holding her tight and drawing warmth and peace from her. She nodded to Yusuf, and as he went, she wondered exactly how many ambushes he had planned in his career.

It seemed like a long time before he returned. Gebirga was relieved to hear his voice, calling ahead of his arrival so she would know it was a friend approaching.

"You haven't lost everything. Look what I found, just where your horse must have left the path."

He put a bundle into her arms. It was her second-best cloak, and concealed inside it was her reliquary chest. She held the chest in her lap with one hand and with the other stroked its Arabic lettering, promising blessings to its owner. "Tell me what you saw."

"I didn't see Katerinen." She slumped with released tension, not sure if this was a good or a bad thing.

He continued, "They killed your whole militia. Alive they were no good for ransom or anything other than identifying their attackers. Your two women were there too, dead. All the bodies were stripped, and the horses and pack mules were gone. That has to be the work of the people in the hills, but it doesn't mean that they were the ones who did the killing. The people who live here will scavenge anything they find, and won't turn their noses up at taking good swords and boots and clothes off the bodies of dead people. But Katerinen wasn't there. That's suspicious."

"What do you think it means? Do you think she is alive somewhere?"

"My hope is that this wasn't a random attack by poor strangers, eager to grab what they could. Everyone knows that the king of Aragon is not friendly to allies of Queen Urraca who pass through his domain. He may have learned that the sister of the deceased count of Flanders was passing through on a pilgrimage, and may have wondered just how authentic that pilgrimage was, and decided to find out for himself. That is what I hope, because then he will have kept her alive."

Wondering who might have informed the king of their travels, her old suspicions of Yusuf crept back. How much did he know about Katerinen's marriage plans? Suddenly, she thought of something.

"Yusuf, how did you know we'd be coming this way, and not by the pass at Somport?"

"I didn't. That's why it took me so long to find you. I waited at Pau for a day with my horse until she recovered and then I rode as fast as I dared to catch up with you. Fortunately, merchants ride slowly. I caught up with the main group just at Somport, and they told me you'd gone the other way, with the bishop of Barbastro, so I had to retrace my steps to reach you. You'd maybe have saved yourself a night alone on the mountainside if you had bothered to tell me your plans, you know. By the way, was the bishop riding with you when you were attacked?"

"Not then. We had fallen behind his party, and were trying to catch up."

"I thought that might have been the case," Yusuf said grimly, "I think the bishop is the most likely candidate to be the king's informant."

The bishop of Barbastro? It made sense. But—"Calixtus himself told us to travel with him. He told us we'd be safer that way." She stopped herself, realizing she had been about to blurt out to Yusuf the fact that their identity as pilgrims was no more than a cover. Then she remembered the conversation she had overheard between Yusuf and Calixtus at Cluny, the conversation in which the pope seemed to be soliciting Yusuf's help to promote the marriage between Katerinen and Alfonso of Galicia. Perhaps he was more aware of the real purpose of their journey that he admitted.

Yusuf did not seem to have noticed her hesitation. "Calixtus may have been misinformed. But if what I am imagining is correct, Alfonso's men could just as easily have nabbed you at the pass of Somport."

"Would King Alfonso really risk the ire of the pope by attacking his niece's party and killing all her servants?"

"Alfonso of Aragon has little need for the pope these days. Calixtus is too closely connected to the king's enemies in the peninsula: Queen Urraca, the bishop of Compostela, and the archbishop of Toledo. And Alfonso has little need for the pope's support for his own crusade against Islam right now. He recently followed up his conquest of the Muslim capital of Zaragoza by taking Tarazona. With these two cities his southern flank is more than well protected and with Zaragoza, he'll have wealth and power to spare. I suspect that the king of Aragon informed some soldiers of fortune that he had an interest in a certain noble traveler, and they would have done the job as they saw fit and collected their reward on delivery. On safe delivery. Killing your servants may have been no part of Alfonso's plan. And he'll treat Katerinen well enough, I expect. He'd throw Gerald of Compostela into one of his dungeons, but he won't do that to her. She'll be lodged as a guest. Even though, so I hear, he has very little personal interest in noblewomen."

"What do we do next?"

"We get out of here as soon as we can. If Katerinen is alive, her captors will have questioned her about her party and they will be able to count. Katerinen is a sweet girl but we both know she'll be as discreet as, well, as any captured young woman alone and scared with violent strangers. She'll tell them you're missing and they will come to look for you. How are you? Can you travel?"

"I'm better, fine, I think," Gebirga moved to stand but when she tried to put her weight on her right foot, she gasped with pain and sank down again.

"Your ankle? Let me take a look." He expertly removed her boot ignoring her winces. "It is badly swollen. But it is sprained, I think, not broken. That's bad luck though. You won't be able to walk. This boot won't go back on. I'll have to bind it." He took a length of cloth and wound it tightly around her foot and ankle and this relieved some of the pain.

He spoke again. "I want to get to Jaca as soon as possible. That's the closest big town and if we're lucky, I'll hear gossip about the king's whereabouts, and maybe even word of a Flemish noblewoman passing through. It will be a strange enough event to cause comment, and her captors will have to stop some time to rest and eat. But with one horse, and you unable to ride, we won't make it together. I'll have to go alone."

"You're not going to leave me here, are you?"

"No, of course not. It may be good fortune that you took this path instead of the one through Somport, because I have friends here. We'll have to avoid Biescas. If anyone is looking for you, they'll expect you pass through there. But there is a village just beyond, where they will take you for my sake, until you heal. They're Mozarabs, like me, who fled Muslim Spain. I got to know them on my travels; some are distant cousins from Seville. We'll have to disguise you. You're so fair and I'm so dark; we'll make a strange couple traveling openly, but if we use your coif to veil you like a Mozarab, you will look like one of us traveling with her husband. May I?"

She did not stop him, and he removed the veil covering her head and said, "So that's what your hair looks like under that coif." Self-conscious with her hair exposed, she waited while he rewrapped her head the way Mozarabic women dressed. It was looser but concealed more of her face. While he worked, he continued, "Considering what happened to you, you are not in bad shape. The fact that this is a holy place must have saved you."

"A holy place?" Someone had said that to her recently. Gebirga tried to remember, a little distracted by his fingers skimming her temple as he secured the veil in place.

"Yes. There is a cave near here dedicated to St. Elena. Usually there is a hermit who serves as its custodian, but the last one died a few years ago."

St. Elena? No, that was not what she had been told. She struggled for the memory, but it remained elusive.

"Ready, then? Good. The hard part will be getting you onto my horse with your bad foot." Eventually this operation was achieved, and they set off, Yusuf leading the horse and Gebirga riding. Liisa trotted alongside of them, glad to be moving again. Yusuf tactfully kept off the main road until after they passed the place of the attack, but Gebirga remembered.

"The bodies! Who will bury the bodies? We can't just leave them there."

"We can't bury them ourselves either. I am sorry; there's no help for it. We have to leave them. I'll have a word with the priest when we get to our destination. I don't dare stop at Biescas to tell the priest there." With this she had to be content.

They plodded along as the sun rose in the sky, making the day unpleasantly hot. Gebirga sweated under her new veil, and the way Yusuf had put it on, so it would conceal her face and her unusual coloring, muffled her voice and made conversation between them difficult. But he alerted her as they approached Biescas.

"I am half tempted to leave the road here in case someone is looking for you. But if we're found wandering in the woods, that will look even more suspicious. I think we're better off just bluffing our way through if we see anyone."

Yusuf was right to be concerned. When they passed the gatehouse that protected the opening of the palisade around the small village, two men stopped them.

"Hey, you! Where are you going?" said one.

"We're peaceful people on our way home after trading in the mountains. What do you want with us?"

Gebirga heard a second voice answer. "We're looking for someone, a thief. A woman. With a big dog." She feared they were looking pointedly at Liisa and she tried to look as Mozarabic and married as she possibly could. But she was pleased she could understand what the men were saying. Oliver's lessons had borne fruit.

"If you want a woman, I bet your sister is willing, but if it is animal acts you are interested in, you'd better stick to your sheep. Wouldn't want them to be lonely."

Gebirga gasped to herself at this deliberate insult. She hoped Yusuf knew what he was doing, goading the men this way.

The first man seemed ready to take up the challenge, "Why you—," she heard him say but the second stopped him and said, "Right now we are interested in this woman. And this dog. Madam, who are you?"

Gebirga kept silent. "This is my wife and if you touch her, you'll pay. And she doesn't know what you're saying. She keeps inside the home, like a good woman should, unless she is with me, and she only knows Arabic."

"Arabic? Well then, let her tell us who she is in Arabic. Speak, woman!"

If she had spoken only Arabic, she would not have understood the man's command, made in Spanish, for her to speak in Arabic. Yusuf must have realized this, because he muttered some words to her in Arabic, presumably translating the man's command. Gebirga was bewildered. What should she do? She repeated the only Arabic she knew, the legend on her box. "Baraka kamila wa ni'ma shamila . . ." She forgot the rest, but that seemed to be enough.

"It's not her," one said to the other, "We're looking for a Frank who wouldn't know any Arabic at all."

"What did she say?" said the other.

"Damned if I know. I don't speak that dog's language." He turned to Yusuf, "Very well, be on your way. Quickly!"

Yusuf did not need to be told twice. Neither he nor Gebirga spoke until Biescas was left far behind them. When the village was long out of earshot he said simply, "Well done."

"Thank you," replied Gebirga. And they trudged on.

It was late in the day, but still sweltering hot when Yusuf announced they had reached their destination, the quiet village of Busa off the main road. Half-wild dogs, sleeping off the afternoon's heat in the shade of a tree, left their refuge and announced the arrival of the travelers with fierce barking that summoned the village's inhabitants from the cool of their dwellings, where they too were resting from the heat.

"Hold Liisa," Gebirga said, worried about the other dogs.

From the voices that clustered around them, it seemed to be a community of women and children. The men must be up in the mountains with the sheep. The women sounded excited and friendly, which was good, but Gebirga could not understand a word because they and Yusuf were speaking Arabic. Eventually, Yusuf returned to French and spoke to her. "All is well. They're willing to look after you for a few days, as long as it takes me to get to Jaca and back. You'll stay in Nazarena's house. She even speaks a little Spanish. You'll be well looked after. We'll all have a meal together, and then I'll set off right away." He paused, "I've told them you are my wife. It seemed best."

Gebirga was gently assisted off the horse with the help of many hands and brought to a bench inside one of the low-ceilinged buildings that circled the tiny village square. One woman took charge of her, and she assumed this was the welcoming Nazarena. She heard what she hoped were the sounds of food preparation in the center of the hot, close room, around a hearth that sheltered a fire of only enough embers to cook over on this July day. Warm, meaty smells reached her nose over the woodsmoke and suddenly she was ravenous. Yusuf had disappeared, but Liisa was at her feet, earning the dog the eternal envy of the animals outside, who were never permitted in the dwelling, and Gebirga was surrounded by curious hands, both young and old. She unwound the veil from her head, trying to cool down a little. The women exclaimed in what Gebirga hoped was curiosity, and not horror. She felt little hands stroke her hair. One child touched her face with a single finger, poking her gently over and over and saying something Gebirga could not understand. It was not frightening, but she was grateful when Yusuf returned.

"Yusuf, what is this little one saying? Why is she so curious about my face?"

"She is saying 'Dots! Dots!' It is your freckles, little brown flecks on your nose and cheeks. Almost no one here has them."

"Do I look so very different from them?"

"Different enough. And while Frankish women do pass through here sometimes, you may be the first one they have seen up close. Your hair is fair, not blond like Katerinen's, but the color of honey, and full of tiny waves and kinks, while most of us have hair that is darker and straighter. And your skin is different too, more reddish, from the sun."

Red skin covered in spots and kinky hair, how lovely. The hair she knew about because of her trials keeping it neat. But Gebirga could not dwell on her looks because Yusuf was offering something to her.

"Look what I found." He put a long staff in her hands. "Now you'll be a proper pilgrim, with a staff. While I am gone, don't rest your ankle for too long. Try to walk on it a little every day, using the staff."

They were handed bowls full of a kind of stew, which they wolfed down with the bone spoons provided. It was only mutton but it tasted to Gebirga like nothing she had ever experienced before, full of strange spices and fragrances. "What's in this?" she whispered to Yusuf. He shrugged and professed ignorance of the womanly art of cooking, and after he finished the second helping that one of the women pressed on him, he rose from the bench.

"Right then. I'm off."

"You're leaving?" asked Gebirga, "So soon? Can't you rest longer? You've been up all night already."

"I want to get on my way as soon as possible before any trail of Katerinen grows cold. I need to ask people if they've seen a blond young woman go by with a party of ruffians go by before their memory of her has been replaced by a passing trained bear or a troup of acrobats or something even more memorable. The sooner I leave, the sooner I can return."

Gebirga felt guilty. She wanted him to start looking for Katerinen as soon as possible, only she was nervous at being left here alone with strangers. Of course, Yusuf himself was a stranger too. It was remarkable how traveling with people made them turn almost into family.

And she could not have been left with kinder strangers. The woman whose house it was shooed everyone out of doors after Yusuf bade his goodbyes. She told Gebirga to call her Rena, an easier mouthful than Nazarena, and when Gebirga started to yawn, she made up a bed for her on one of the benches that lined the walls of the house, and insisted she lie down. The language barrier was too great to allow Gebirga to protest effectively. Oh well, just for a while, she thought, and was almost instantly asleep.

She woke to the sounds of morning in the small house. Rena brought her a basin of water and a cloth, then some bread and sheep's milk cheese in between doing other chores and chivying her children about. There seemed to be dozens of them; Gebirga could get no clear idea of numbers because they never stayed in one place long enough for her to count them. Chastened by the purposeful activity going on around her, Gebirga mustered up her Spanish and insisted she help Rena with her daily work. It had been a long time since she had to perform household chores, but she reckoned she had not forgotten everything. Rena protested at first, but Gebirga stood her ground, so Rena set her to help make the distinctive seasoning that flavoured the stew of her first night. This involved boiling up barley flour and salted water along with ingredients Gebirga had never heard of, like carob, nigella, citron, and sesame, together with others like raisins and anise that were used with what Gebirga from the frugal north thought was reckless abandon. This mixture was allowed to thicken and then it was set outside to dry so it could be crumbled up as needed for flavouring.

Gebirga was doing her best, but she could tell Rena found having to explain everything was more trouble than just doing the work herself. Suddenly, Gebirga was hit with an inspiration. This was sheep country. "Rena, have you any wool that needs to be worked?"

Delighted, Rena set her to card and then spin such a mountain of raw wool that Gebirga feared she had entered the old tale in which a young woman entered the land of faery by mistake, only to be given an impossible task to complete before she could earn her freedom. This thought led her to morbid speculation about what she would do if Yusuf never came back. Why should he help her, after all? Perhaps he thought that having led her to safety, his obligations were finished.

But Gebirga was not allowed to dwell in these gloomy worries for long. Yusuf must have told Rena to make sure she used her bad foot. That was the only thing that could explain Rena's insistence that she get up and go for a walk. Gebirga used her new staff to slowly push herself up to a standing position and she gingerly rested some of her weight on the wounded ankle. It had been bound tight, and while it throbbed a little, the pain was not too much to bear. Rena took the arm not holding the staff and Gebirga hobbled after her, Liisa close at their heels, protective of her mistress.

A crowd of chattering children surrounded them, but Rena warded them off with a sharp word or two. They crossed the village square and Gebirga wondered where they were going. Rena seemed set on a destination, not out for a casual stroll. They stopped, and Gebirga assumed they had reached where they were going.

Rena said a word to her in Spanish and Gebirga searched her memory. Church! That was what she had said. Gebirga sought confirmation, "Rena, is this the church?"

"Yes! Church, church, this is the church," the woman answered, pleased. But Rena was not finished. She took the hand she was holding and brought it up to the arch of the low door. Gebirga understood that she was supposed to feel what was up there, so she leaned against the door jamb to support her weight and felt above her. She was used to feeling bits of stone around the churches Katerinen had dragged her through, but this was really odd. It was a round arch at the top, but instead of falling straight to the ground, it curved in for a bit, right at the level of Gebirga's head, kind of like a horseshoe. But this was not what Rena had wanted her to notice. Rena placed her hand higher, on the arch. It seemed to be carved with some kind of relief pattern, but even Gebirga's sensitive fingers could not tell her what she was supposed to discern.

"It says, 'La ilaha illa Allah,'" Rena said. Words. Were those letters carved up there? "There is no God but God. I pray for you. Find your sister."

Tears pricked Gebirga's eyes at the gentle woman's short speech. Yusuf must have told them Katerinen was her sister. And when Rena suddenly took Gebirga in her strong arms, she did not flinch as she might have once from unexpected physical contact with a virtual stranger, but allowed herself to be held by the other woman as she wept in fear and worry about the future.

CHAPTER THIRTEEN

The Kingdom of Aragon

The Lord has established three very necessary supports for the protection of His poor in this world, namely the hospice of Jerusalem and the hospice of Mont-Joux and the hospice of Santa Cristina, which is at Somport.

"Seven, I win again! That's two hundred pounds you owe me now," said Aimery, scooping the dice off the wet, sticky tavern table into his fist and shaking them madly, ready for the next round.

"Well, I'm never going to see two hundred pounds in my lifetime, so it's not likely you will either," answered Oliver. Clerics were not supposed to play dice because its element of chance was thought to force God's hand, but Aimery had convinced Oliver, by appeals to canon law and quotations from St. Augustine of dubious authenticity, that if no actual money changed hands, he was not doing anything wrong. Then they played for impossibly high imaginary stakes, to keep it interesting. Oliver figured anything that helped them pass the time was worth doing. He would seek forgiveness later, when they got where they were going. If they got where they were going.

The journey from Toulouse started well enough. In the entourage of Gerald of Compostela, they were well mounted and they rode far enough ahead of the others leaving the council that they had little competition for beds and meals. Their problems began after they crossed the pass at Somport and stopped at the great pilgrim hospice of Santa Christina. Aimery decided that this institution was important enough to feature prominently in his guide, so he combed the whole complex, asking the monks for old stories and tales, Oliver diligently taking notes. Aimery's quest for information meant they missed the evening meal in the pilgrim's refectory, and had to scrounge around the kitchens for some bread and pottage. This took more time, so they were late into the dormitory, which was already filled with the sound of tired men's snores. When they arrived at the place where they had left their belongings on arrival, they discovered to their horror that they were alone; Gerald and the rest of their party had vanished.

The man on the pallet next to theirs rolled over and said, "Your friends told me to tell you they had to leave in a hurry. Something about a message arriving for them and needing to get somewhere else quickly." He rolled over again and pulled the thin blanket over his head, discouraging further conversation. Aimery and Oliver were nonplused.

"It's a shame, but we'd best get a good sleep and think about it in the morning," said Aimery, "It's not ideal, but we'll make out, just the two of us. Maybe there will be someone else passing by whom we can travel with."

"Pipe down! Some of us are trying to sleep," a man hissed from a nearby pallet, so they halted their conversation.

Aimery was putting a brave face on it, but it was a huge blow to lose their patron. Had Gerald changed his mind about their book? What would be their reception at Compostela, arriving without his support? And how hard would it be to make it there on their own?

They discovered their situation was even worse than they feared when they went down to the stables the following morning. Their horses were gone. Aimery questioned the stablehand and, sure enough, Gerald had taken them. "We'd scarcely got the horses watered when he came back and insisted we saddle them up again right away. They fled as if the hounds of hell were chasing them, leading your two mounts behind them."

"But why would they take our horses along with their own?" Oliver asked Aimery.

"If they were in a hurry they probably hoped to use the riderless horses when theirs became tired. Never mind. It can't be helped."

They wasted precious days at Somport, hoping to encounter a traveler who might take pity on them and absorb them into their entourage, a lady desirous of pious conversation, or a lord needing someone to write his letters. But no one like that seemed to be passing through, only irritable merchants and poor pilgrims, and the monks who had been welcoming at first, hinted that it was time for the two to be moving on so their beds could be given to new arrivals. They had no choice; they had to leave on foot and hope for better luck in Jaca, the next large town on their route. "This isn't so bad," said Aimery, as they walked downhill out of the mountains into the ever-widening valley before them, sown with wheat and rye already golden from the summer sun, "A walk will do us good. This is the way real pilgrims travel." Just then, it started to rain.

By the end of the day, tired, footsore and damp, they made it to Jaca where they cooled their heels in the hospice of the Holy Spirit, hoping their luck would change. They spent most of their time in the small tavern next door that catered to the traffic of pilgrims and merchants who flowed through the town, hoping to find a new patron, and growing steadily more bored with each other.

It was with great joy then that they greeted Yusuf when he unexpectedly put his face through the door and scanned the inside of the tavern. "Yusuf! Well met!" called Aimery, "Come and join us for a cup of this vinegar they call wine. I believe you still owe me a cup anyway, after the one I bought you in Arles."

Yusuf looked just as pleased to see them, and came over to sit at their table. "Aimery, Oliver, good to see you. What brings you to this dank tavern? I thought you'd be half way to Compostela with Gerald by now."

Aimery and Oliver competed to tell him about their woes since the pass of Somport, while Yusuf signaled the tavern keeper to bring them another flask and an extra cup. They were half way through their first draught before Oliver thought to ask Yusuf what his plans were in Jaca.

Yusuf told them about finding Gebirga on the mountainside, and about the attack and the loss of Katerinen. When he got to the part about Katerinen's likely abduction by the attackers, Oliver slammed his fist on the table and railed at Aimery, "I knew it! I knew it was her and that there was something wrong and we should follow her, but you said no, it wasn't her, and why would she be traveling without Gebirga!"

"Oliver, you kept seeing Katerinen everywhere we went; first she was a tavern girl in Auch, then a nun at Pau, and then you saw her in the crowd at the pilgrim's mass here in Jaca at the Church of Santiago. You can see why I was skeptical. And how can you be sure it was her?"

"It was her, I tell you, I'd know her anywhere."

The argument would have continued for who knows how long if Yusuf had not intervened, "Wait, stop—when did you see her? What did you see?"

"It was the day before yesterday," Oliver began, eager to speak to someone who took him seriously, "We had just come out of our hospice, right opposite the royal citadel, the fort at the cliff edge. I saw her riding out of the fort, surrounded by men."

"How many?" Yusuf asked.

"I don't know—six, maybe seven. Anyway, they were riding fast, heading for a city gate. I ran after them and even called her name. She turned her head, at least I think she did. But they were riding too fast and were beyond the city walls before I could reach them."

"She didn't turn her head; you're imagining things," grumbled Aimery. "Besides, the sun was in our eyes when we came out of the hospice. There was no way you could recognize her."

Before the two could start arguing again, Yusuf interjected, "Oliver, what can you say about the men riding with Katerinen? What did they look like? Did they wear any special badges or colors? That could help us find them."

Oliver answered with a voice full of woe, "I didn't see. I'm sorry. I was concentrating on Katerinen."

"I can tell you what mark they wore," said Aimery surprisingly, "Some of us have eyes for things other than girls. It was a badge of alternate red and yellow stripes—the king of Aragon's mark. Like the ones those fellows at the back of the tavern are wearing." He gestured subtly at a table of youths who were drinking together, occasionally breaking out into bursts of song, oblivious to everyone else in the room. They had just been served bowls of the tavern's specialty, a thin broth with blobs of blood sausage floating in it, and were greedily tucking in. They were dressed in identical livery, and each wore a square badge of red and yellow stripes.

"Of course," said Yusuf, "The tower belongs to the king of Aragon, and those are his men."

He sounded pleased, but Oliver was horrified, "The king of Aragon? What's he doing with Katerinen? Do you think it was his men who abducted her, or have they rescued her? We've got to find her!"

"Oliver, keep it down! That's what I'm here for, and this is my first good lead. I'm afraid it does look like the ambush was done under the king's orders. Gebirga and I were stopped by two men of Aragon while I was getting her to safety."

"What good is it to know that she was taken by Alfonso's men? We have no idea where they went. And it won't be easy to get her away from the king, wherever she is," Aimery said.

"I have a notion how we might find out a little more," said Yusuf, "Aimery, loan me those dice of yours." Yusuf swallowed the last of his wine and then threw the dice on the table, "Damn!" he shouted, "I've lost again. Time to play someone else." He stood up, as if unsteady from too much wine, and looked around the tavern, which was almost empty. He approached the table of youths and said, "Good men! Care for a game of dice? I'll stand you a flagon if one of you will take me on."

"I'll play you," said one, and they made room as Yusuf gestured for a pitcher of wine from the tavern keeper.

Aimery and Oliver waited for what seemed like hours, as Yusuf sat with the men, laughing, drinking, and playing dice. Finally, they all rose from the table, visibly the worse for wear, the men departing the tavern and Yusuf heading back to his friends. It must be about time for the change of the watch and Aimery hoped great things would not be expected from those about to go on duty—they would scarcely be up to it after drinking all afternoon. "What took you so long?" he said to Yusuf.

"Gathering information without incurring suspicion takes time. But it wasn't in vain; I found what we needed to know. They didn't tell me her name—probably didn't know it themselves—but there was a young woman of high birth kept in custody in the tower last night. They also told me that she was taken to the care of the sisters at Santa Cruz, not more than half a day's ride from here, so that's where I'm headed, once I retrieve Gebirga."

"Are you sure the woman is Katerinen?" asked Aimery.

"Almost certain. The physical description fits, though I didn't want to question them too closely about that, lest they grow suspicious. They told me she bit one of the guards, and that she screamed all night once she had been put into her chamber, keeping them awake, even through stone. You'll be pleased to know, Oliver, that your language lessons bore fruit. They said she wasn't from Spain, but they were very impressed with her collection of Spanish curse words."

"That's Katerinen," said Aimery, and Oliver nodded.

Yusuf continued, "But I need to ask you—will you come with us to Santa Cruz, and maybe beyond? A larger party may make a better impression on the sisters and we are more convincing pilgrims with some clerics with us."

"Of course we will!" said Oliver.

Aimery was amenable. Gebirga could pay for their journey, and that would get them out of Jaca at last. But he had one question. He knew why Oliver wanted to help. The boy was still infatuated with the young noblewoman. But—"Yusuf, why are you so interested in finding Katerinen? If you're a messenger, shouldn't you be busy delivering messages, instead of rescuing damsels in distress."

"Let us just say that I am a citizen of Toledo, and like all good Toledans, I have an interest in keeping a daughter of the houses of Burgundy and Flanders out of the hands of Aragon."

With this somewhat cryptic reply, they had to be content. Aimery knew there was more to Yusuf than met they eye, but he liked and trusted the man. "Very well then, pay the account, Yusuf, and we'll be off. The sooner you get Gebirga, the sooner we can find the girl."

"Pay the account? But Aimery, I lost all my small coins to the soldiers. I'm afraid you'll have to pay this time."

"Playing all that time and you couldn't win enough for a pitcher or two? What kind of a dice man are you?"

"Aimery," Yusuf said, "As you well know, those were weighted dice you gave me. If I'd won from them and those boys had noticed, I would have lost an ear or been thrown in the fort's dungeon, and

I wouldn't have found out what we needed to know. Now, pay up, and let's go. I want to get back to Gebirga by nightfall.

"Weighted dice!" said Oliver to Aimery, "No wonder you always beat me."

He had only been gone for a couple of days, but Gebirga was relieved to hear Yusuf return to the village as she sat spinning on a bench outside Rena's house to catch the evening breezes. "I have some news," he said. He sat beside her and took her hand, so she feared what he would say. Apprehension turned to hope as he related his tale. She stood up. "What are we waiting for? Let's go right away!"

"Gebirga, night may be the same as day for you, but on a night without a moon, it is difficult for the rest of us to see to ride. The gates of Jaca will be closing soon, and Aimery and Oliver won't be able to come out to meet us, nor will we be able to get in. Besides, if we arrive at the monastery in the middle of the night office, the sisters will think we're invaders, not friends. If we leave first thing tomorrow, we'll have plenty of time to meet Oliver and Aimery, and still reach Santa Cruz in daylight."

Gebirga reluctantly agreed to be patient, and they set out the next morning, leaving Busa well-hugged by Rena and her fellow villagers, and carrying enough food to feed a small army. The journey was an easy one, along the river valley to Jaca. They took a back road, so villagers would not be surprised to see Yusuf passing through for the third time in three days. They made Jaca in good time, and there found Aimery and Oliver, who had already chosen mounts and were just waiting for Gebirga to pay for them. She did so gladly, though the money in the purse Clemence had given her was vanishing more quickly than she had expected. Worry about Katerinen tempered the joy she felt at the reunion with her old friends.

The four of them left Jaca by a different gate than the one Gebirga and Yusuf had entered. They rode only for a short time before they stopped to picnic in a field of sheep at a bend in the river whose valley they were following. Cuckoos calling to each other from the oaks behind them and the rushing of the river were the only sounds to disturb their meal. They feasted on the provisions that Rena had packed—garlic sausage, cold chicken, dark bread and a skin of sheep's milk—and discussed strategy.

"As Katerinen's companion and the only one among us who is gently born, you will have to speak for us at the abbey," decreed Yusuf. "Aimery and Oliver are your priest and his assistant, and I, of course, am your humble servant," he finished, perhaps unaware of the irony that the humble servant was giving all the orders. His plan was good, but Gebirga was nervous; the only abbess she had ever spoken to was Alice, back at Gistel, and she had had no luck charming her.

The men were inclined to linger, but Gebirga pressed them to resume their journey. Soon they left the river valley and turned south towards the monastery. She was surprised to feel her horse gently ascending again.

"We're going up? I thought we had left the mountains."

"You've never completely left the mountains behind, no matter where you are in Spain. To the south of this river valley, a high mountain range rises, not as high as the Pyrenees, but still impressive," said Yusuf, "We won't climb too far into it today, though, to get to Santa Cruz."

Sure enough, before long the men signaled to Gebirga that they had arrived at their destination and that they should all dismount. Yusuf went to see about admittance and Aimery described the monastery to Gebirga. "The nuns have built themselves quite a nice church, small but new and in the latest style. It is surrounded by a perimeter wall, nothing I would like to depend on in a siege, but the church is defensible enough, if it came to that. Small windows, and the walls are four feet thick if they're an inch. And the mountains rise sharply behind the abbey, so no one can approach from that direction. The buildings inside the walls must be where the nuns sleep and meet for meals. Their farm looks like it has seen better days however, judging by the outbuildings." Gebirga could smell the manure and straw that suggested the presence of a large number of animals somewhere.

Yusuf returned and signaled for them to enter the monastery gate. There they waited for the portress, who introduced herself as Sister Gracia. Gebirga was glad to discover she understood this woman's Spanish easily, and she introduced them and their mission in the same language. "Sister, we are pilgrims to Santiago de Compostela." The lie caught in her throat, but she pressed on. "We became separated from one of our party, the lady Katerinen of Flanders, and we have learned that she may have received your kind hospitality in this place, so we have come seeking her."

"There was a young lady, just yesterday . . . Come, you would better speak with the lady abbess. Iñigo," she said to one of the men manning the gate, "Take these three men and their horses to the stables, and then show the men the guest quarters. That dog can stay in the stables with the horses."

"Sister," Gebirga interjected, "I need the dog with me. I'm blind and she helps me find my way."

"The dog helps you find your way? Very well, but she can't come into the church. Will she wait quietly outside and not chase our cats?" Gebirga assented and they began to walk towards the church, Gebirga leaning on the staff Yusuf had found for her. Her foot was much better already but she still appreciated the security of having the staff with her. Several times Liisa manouevred Gebirga around obstacles in her path, a flock of chickens and then a stray duck, and the nun was frankly astonished. "A dog to do that—I never would have believed it. The Lord's ways are indeed strange. We're at the church in any case, so you'll have to leave her now."

Gebirga admonished Liisa to stay, and Sister Gracia watched as a fat tabby walked right in front of the sitting dog without eliciting so much as a whimper from the larger animal. She watched the cat saunter off and then took Gebirga's arm and drew her into the church. "Careful of that step. The abbess is in the palace. It's a large room over the nave of the church, and we call it the palace from when the countess used to live here. That's her tomb over there on the right, may she rest in peace. Oh, of course, you can't see it. Never mind. We'll have to take the staircase up to the palace over here in the left side of the church. Can you manage it with your staff? I'll follow you up." She put Gebirga's left hand on the thick rope hooked into the wall that served as a banister. They climbed the wooden steps up the inside of the church, and Gebirga felt dizzy, knowing that if she tripped and fell to the right, nothing would prevent her from falling down to the stone floor below.

"Only a few more, three, two, one, that's the last step, dear. Come and let me introduce you." Gebirga found herself at the doorway of a stone room. Gracia went in and whispered to someone, and then returned to bring Gebirga into the room. "I am the abbess, Mother Andregota. Sister Gracia says you are looking for someone," a woman said in a youthful but firm voice. From the direction of her speech, Gebirga could tell that the abbess was seated before her. She curtsied. "My lady abbess, I am Gebirga of Gistel, in Flanders. My party was attacked, most of our guards were killed, and we became separated from one of our number, the lady Katerinen. We heard a tale that she might have found refuge here. We are pilgrims," Gebirga finished.

"Pilgrims?" answered the abbess shrewdly, "Hmmpf. I can set your mind at rest. Lady Katerinen is here, and she is unharmed. She arrived two days ago."

The heat of the day, the climb up the stairs, residual pain in her foot, and this sudden good news all became too much for Gebirga and, to her deep embarrassment, she started to swoon. She was caught by the able hands of Gracia and the abbess herself, and was lowered onto the abbess's heavy wooden folding stool. Gracia pulled up another stool for the abbess, and brought Gebirga a drink, which she held to the young woman's lips. The abbess began to question her.

"What is your relationship to the lady Katerinen?"

"Her mother, Clemence of Burgundy, appointed me as her companion, to bring her to Spain. And back again," she added hastily.

"So she is your office, your duty? And when your journey is completed, you will return home, perhaps back to your parents? The girl has only been here for a few days, but I can already see that she is a handful."

"She's not! Well, she can be, but most of the time she is a dear, lovely and enthusiastic. Maybe sometimes too enthusiastic . . . but it is no duty. It is my privilege to be her companion. My parents are dead, and my home is with Katerinen. I—I love her, and it is a joy to serve her," Gebirga finished, and realized that she had been more open than she planned. The abbess's "Thank you. That is helpful," caused her to wonder what she had given away.

"The first thing we must do is find Katerinen," said the abbess, "I believe she is sewing with some of the nuns. She will be relieved to see you and know that you are safe. She has been speaking about you, you know. And then you and I must talk. Do you think you are well enough to make it down those awful stairs again? Yes? Good, let's go."

They made their way to the church door, where Gebirga retrieved Liisa. Sister Gracia chattered enthusiastically to the abbess about Liisa's awesome powers, and wondered if they could find a dog like that for the nuns who had gone blind in old age.

When the abbess opened the door of a low, stone building that served both as a day parlor and a bedroom for some of the nuns, Gebirga was relieved to hear Katerinen's voice, laughing and chattering with the other women in the room. The abbess said, "My lady Katerinen, here is a visitor for you," and the girl's mood changed instantly. She dashed over to Gebirga, embraced her, and started sobbing hysterically, "You're here, you're here; they said you were dead, but you're not." Gebirga rocked the younger girl in her arms and said, "Here I am, and everything is going to be fine. And I have Aimery, Oliver, and Yusuf with me, and here's Liisa. She's the one who really saved the day." And to calm Katerinen down, Gebirga told the story of how Liisa had gone to find help when she had been tossed from her galloping horse. Katerinen bent over and gave the dog a hug and a kiss between the ears, but when she stood up, she clung once more to Gebirga.

The abbess intervened, "Now Katerinen, as you can see, your friend Gebirga is well and safe. But she and I have many things to discuss, so we are going to leave you now. No—," the abbess stopped Katerinen when the girl protested, "You will have plenty of time to be together later. Gebirga will be staying in here with you. But now you must go back to your sewing." Katerinen subsided, to Gebirga's surprise. Very few people had that kind of authority over Katerinen. The abbess must be a formidable woman indeed.

The abbess sent Sister Gracia on an errand, and she and Gebirga returned to the church. But instead of ascending to the palace, the abbess brought her to a raised sarcophagus in the right aisle of the church, perhaps the one Gracia had spoken about earlier. This was confirmed by the abbess's words. "Here is the tomb of Countess

Sancha Ramirez, the greatest patron of our monastery. She was sister to one king of Aragon and aunt of another. She lived here as a widow until her death about thirty years ago, but we were only just recently able to afford to have a suitable resting place made for her. We moved her remains here last year." She took Gebirga's hands in her own, "Feel the stone here—that is the countess, seated between two of her sisters, who were nuns. Over here," she moved Gebirga's hands to a new place on the sarcophagus, "Is her blessed soul, ascending to heaven. And on the back, around here," they walked around the tomb, "Is a woman prising open the mouth of a lion, showing her strength. The lion is a symbol of the house of Aragon. There are lions carved on the cathedral at Jaca, and on the tympanum above this church's main door. But we feel more like Daniel in the lion's den now. In Countess Sancha's day, this was an important royal monastery and a crucial fortification against attack by the Muslims who possessed the plains on the other side of these mountains. We protected the northern approach to the men's monastery of San Juan de la Peña, just up the mountain behind us. We held land in every river valley north of here. But after the Christian kings conquered the Muslim strongholds south of us, Barbastro and Huesca, and most recently Zaragoza, the frontier moved south, we lost our royal patronage and with it our importance. Once, we influenced kings. Now we do what we are told or have more of our lands granted to others."

The abbess clarified the reason for her mysterious digression into Aragonese history with her next words. "Katerinen was brought here by servants of the king of Aragon, and we were told that she was the only survivor of an attack by brigands. We were asked to keep her with us as an honored guest of the king, and we have done so. Now I know that you say you are pilgrims destined for Santiago in Galicia, but I also know the reasons why a young noblewoman makes a pilgrimage to the kingdom of an eligible unmarried young king, and if I can figure this out, you can have no doubt that the king can too. Stop!" she said as Gebirga began to speak, "The less you tell me the better for all of us. Frankly, I don't want to know. I want to say something else to you, something about Katerinen herself. From the moment I met her, I saw that she is not like other girls; she's moody and strange, ecstatic one minute and in despair the next. My youngest sister was like her and they used to say she was possessed by a demon. I want to ask you, whatever your plans for her were, to let me keep Katerinen here with us. A regular life, safe and protected among loving sisters, with simple food and an easy routine is what she needs, I believe. She is not a girl cut out for the drama and intrigue of this world, and least of all for marriage and children. You would be most welcome to remain here too."

Gebirga was distressed. What the abbess said rang true, and was nothing she had not wondered herself. Indeed, who better than she to know the dangers of a bad marriage? Gebirga had never thought much of the other option open to women, monastic life, but this community seemed very different from that at Gistel. Perhaps she and Katerinen could both stay? But memories of her oath on Clemence's cross smote her. "Katerinen's lady mother expects her to make this—pilgrimage. And I have sworn to assist her," she finally answered.

The abbess replied grimly, "I expected as much. And that was why I asked whether you served Clemence of Burgundy or Katerinen of Flanders. Well, think on it. I am sworn to the king not to let her leave in any case so you may have no choice. Come, I'll return you to Katerinen. You can sleep in the room with her. We've turned over that parlor for her use. We don't have enough nuns to fill all of our buildings anyway at the moment."

The abbess left Gebirga at the door of her new lodgings saying, "Good day. Dinner will be in the refectory in a few hours. Sister Gracia will fetch you."

Before she left, Gebirga asked, "Mother Andregota, what became of your sister?"

"My parents married her to a local lord, a nice young man. She killed herself by jumping from the tower of his castle when she was pregnant with his first child. She was a dear girl, gentle and sweet unless she was in one of her moods. It never should have happened."

CHAPTER FOURTEEN

A Feast and a Fair

*These are sacred apostolic feasts to be honored, celebrated by everyone,
and cultivated by all nations. On these feasts, heavenly rewards are
given to the just and eternal salvation is promised the sinners.*

Gebirga settled into the routine of the monastery with Katerinen.
It was easy to forget she was here for a rescue, and to simply
enjoy the ease of regular meals, the same straw pallet every night,
and no need to pack up and move on in the morning. With the
words of the abbess in her mind, if it had not been for the presence
of Aimery, Oliver, and Yusuf, all plotting a moment to escape,
Gebirga might have been content to let events take their course.
Not that it was easy for anyone to plot. The freedom of their life in
the monastery was deceptive. Gebirga and Katerinen shared their
dwelling with three other nuns, one of whom always seemed to be
present. They unrolled pallets for sleeping at night and put them
away during the day, so the space could be used as a sitting room.
On one of the rare occasions when Gebirga could snatch a moment
with Katerinen alone she asked the girl whether she might like to
give up their plans for the journey, and stay at Santa Cruz.

"Stay here, in the monastery? Not go to Galicia? Not marry
Alfonso?" she responded, confused.

"Shhhh! Not so loud," answered Gebirga, "Yes. Maybe we should
just stay. You seem happy here, and it would be safer than trying to
escape and make that long journey."

"Gebirga, everyone always tells me I am mad, but you are the mad
one now. Mother expects me to marry; she has planned everything.
She would be furious if we didn't carry out her arrangements. We

need to leave as soon as we can." Katerinen shifted around restlessly as if she intended to march out of the monastery right then and there. Gebirga did not raise the subject of staying at Santa Cruz again.

It was even harder to make plans with the men, since she was never able to speak to all of them at the same time. Yusuf was nowhere to be found; evidently he was out reconnoitering the area. She had the most contact with Aimery who, in the guise of being their priest, had a good excuse for occasional private communication with the women. It was Aimery who first warned them it might be difficult to free Katerinen.

"Couldn't Katerinen and I just walk out of here, and meet the rest of you in the woods with the horses?" asked Gebirga.

"I doubt you would be allowed to leave, the two of you. This monastery seems very free and easy, but there are two men wearing the livery of the king of Aragon at the gate. But try it. Just say you want to go for a walk, and we'll see if they let you leave."

So Gebirga and Katerinen begged some bread, cheese, and sausage from the kitchen for a picnic and made to exit the monastery compound. Sure enough, at the gate, they were stopped by a man who pleasantly but firmly forbade them from leaving.

As planned, Gebirga said, "But we just want to go a short way, to see the hermitage of St. Caprasius and have a meal outside, since it is such a lovely day. We won't be gone long." She pleaded without success. He insisted they remain where they were, "for their own safety."

"There are all kinds of dangers outside the monastery walls, domna. We couldn't guarantee your well-being out there."

"Just as I expected," said Aimery, when Gebirga told him what happened, "But we have another plan. The monastery is dedicated to the Holy Cross and also to the Virgin Mary. It is the feast of the Assumption in a few days, and they hold a procession, a mass with the bishop of Jaca, and a sheep fair here. You may have heard the shepherds bringing their flocks down out of the mountains for it."

Gebirga had. More than once, their sleep had been broken at dawn, not by the monastic bells, but by the bleating of dozens of sheep moving to lower pastures. "Do you think it will be easier to escape during the fair?"

"It may be. There will be more armed men about because the bishop and any local lords who come will all bring their men. But there will also be more confusion and a better chance for us to slip away. We just need to figure out how to get you two outside the monastery wall."

It was Katerinen who inadvertently came up with their plan. She ran to Gebirga one day. "The sisters are having tableaux on their feast day and they want us to help! Do say we can, Gebirga, it would be such fun. The guilds in Bruges used to have them and I always wished I could be in one instead of riding in the boring procession."

"Tableaux? What are you talking about?"

"They're for the procession. The procession leaves from the church, and at every stop on the way, outside all the other churches in the neighborhood and a few other places, there is a scene from the life of Mary. They finish back at the monastery church and do the part where Mary flies up to heaven. Sister Blanca told me the person playing Mary gets drawn up on a wire and disappears through a window of the church. Do say I can be that Mary, Gebirga; I would love to be drawn up on a wire."

"Certainly not! Besides, I am sure the nuns get to be Mary in all the tableaux." That was a pity, Gebirga reflected. For if she and Katerinen were Joseph and Mary on the flight to Egypt, they would already have one donkey to escape on. They would have had to deal with the baby somehow, though. She had a better idea. "I know, Katerinen. Tell them that you and I can be shepherds at the Nativity. That will be fun because we can take care of the animals. Maybe Oliver can help us too, and Liisa can play our sheep dog. She is a sheep dog, so she won't need a disguise at least." But we will, Gebirga thought. And then dressed like shepherds, like every single other shepherd at the fair, we may be able to slip away unnoticed.

The abbess was agreeable to their choice of roles, possibly because the Nativity scene took place inside the monastery walls. It was preceded by the angel Gabriel's annunciation to Mary at the church doors and it was only with the flight into Egypt, that Mary was cast out into the cruel world beyond the monastery. As Gebirga had expected, different nuns were chosen to play the roles of Mary, and there was some bad feeling among those not selected. The whole community was turned upside down with preparations for their big day. Gebirga quietly made her own plans. They would sneak out of the monastery gate with the rest of those following the procession. Aimery would meet them and take them to where Yusuf would be hiding with their horses. With luck, they would be miles away before anyone noticed.

Oliver assented to being a shepherd. Katerinen was jealous of his costume when they were assigned their garb by a harried sister holding a long list on the morning of the fair. "I wish I could wear leggings and a tunic. You and I look more like shepherd-wives, Gebirga, in these dresses. And mine itches."

"That's nothing to the itch you'd feel in a pair of woollen leggings," said Oliver, "Whoa, Gebirga, watch where you're swinging that crook. You almost hit me!"

"Sorry," she said, shifting the staff.

They received their lambs, one for each of them, from one of the abbey shepherds, rather nervous to see his darlings in the hands of rank amateurs. For all her skill with wool, even Gebirga had little experience with it on the hoof. But Liisa helped keep the bleating animals in order and they made their way through the crowds already starting to fill the abbey precincts to the place where they were supposed to meet the angels who would direct them to the makeshift hut where Mary and Joseph were admiring their new babe. The day was already burning hot and the scent of unwashed bodies in close proximity mingled with the rank lanolin smell of the sheep and the sweeter odor of roast mutton, turning on spits to feed the assembled hordes at the conclusion of the Mass. Gebirga was disoriented by the presence of so many unfamiliar bodies around her, and she was grateful when they got into their positions.

"Look! Back over at the doors of the church. That must be the bishop, all clad in gold," said Oliver.

"Where? Oh, I see. He's just put on his mitre. The procession must be starting. Good, because I am bored standing here," said Katerinen.

They had to wait a good while longer though, as the procession formed in ranks before the bishop. First was a young acolyte from a local church, swinging the silver abbey thurifer, full of burning incense. He was followed by two more, one of whom carried the abbey's tall gilt cross, and another with the crossed Greek letters X and P, the first two letters of Christ's name, on a long pole. The nuns not participating in the tableaux processed two by two, with the abbess and prioress bringing up the rear. They were followed by local clergy, and then the clergy brought by the bishop, who came last in the procession, garbed with all the insignia of his office and carrying a staff much like that of the three waiting shepherds, although theirs had no gold or gems. The procession made a lengthy stop at the first tableau, which showed Mary receiving word of her impending child from the angel Gabriel. Everyone from local lords down to simple peasants cheered as Mary humbly received the angel's news. Then the crowd lumbered over to the Nativity scene. The abbey had only one set of angel wings, the other having been found crushed under a pile of Christmas decorations that morning, so they had to wait for the single angel Gabriel to hustle over to them to begin. The angel finally arrived, brought them great tidings of glad joy, and Oliver, Gebirga, and Katerinen made their way over to Mary and Joseph, Liisa diligently nudging their lambs. They kneeled before the manger and tried to look awe-struck, and the crowd cheered again, enjoying the familiar story. Gebirga was glad they were so easily amused; a satisfied audience would make a better cover for an escape.

Mary was helped onto the donkey that was to take her and Joseph out of the abbey gates and into Egypt, and Oliver whispered to the two women, "Now's our chance. Let's try to blend in with the rest of the crowd following the procession. The king of Aragon's men are all over, but none of them are looking our way at the moment."

Gebirga panicked a little as they entered the swell of the crowd, but Oliver held her left elbow and with her other hand she grasped Liisa's lead. It worked better than they could have expected. They were swept with the crowd out of the gate and down the road to the church of St. Caprasius, where Mary and a much older Christ were to perform the scene of the Marriage at Cana. They waited until the crowd was absorbed in watching Jesus turn water into wine, no doubt hoping for a sample, then slipped away, unnoticed among the young couples sneaking off for a kiss, and the mothers taking small children, overcome by heat, excitement, and eating too many sweets, away to be sick. To provide some cover, they stopped at a stall and purchased rounds of dough fried in sheep fat and soaked in honey syrup.

As planned, Aimery was there to meet them. He led them behind the stall and up the path to the clearing where Yusuf was supposed to be waiting with their horses. When they made their plans, however, they had not realized the path would lead right behind the area where the king's knights had sent up their own tents. "Most of them are watching the procession," said Aimery, "But I see a few people wandering about wearing the insignia of Aragon. We must be very quiet." They walked a little further until Aimery announced they had reached their destination. "But where's Yusuf? Maybe we are here too early." They munched their fried dough and waited, wiping sticky hands on the grass. They could not talk for fear the men below would hear them and the silent waiting made them all edgy, although they had not been there for very long.

Suddenly they heard, "Meep? Meep?" on the path behind them.

"What's that?" whispered Aimery.

"Meeeeeep!"

"Oh Lord, it's those blessed lambs," said Oliver, "They've followed us. What will we do now?"

The three lambs came into the clearing and made a huge racket. Then Liisa started barking, trying to get them in order.

"Hi! What's all the noise up there?'" cried someone from below. "Sheep and shepherds are all supposed to be on the green. Come down, right now!"

"We're sorry! Some of our lambs escaped, and we're just rounding them up." Aimery called down below, "We'll come down as soon as we can."

"Not good enough. Here, we'll help." To their horror, they heard people crashing through the undergrowth, climbing up to meet them.

"Quick, Katerinen, hide!" said Oliver, "They'll recognize you out of any of us."

But Katerinen was so frightened, she could not move, and soon she had no opportunity. Four men reached the clearing, all wearing the badge of Aragon. Liisa had just managed to pin the three lost lambs against a hedge. The leader, the one who had spoken first said, "Four people and a dog to catch three little lambs? What kind of shepherds are you?"

"There are more of them up there," said Oliver hopefully, pointing up the path, "Maybe you could help us catch them!"

"Hmpf. You may be holding a shepherd's crook, but I'll wager you're no shepherd. Grab these two, we'll have to take them all to the count," he called to his henchmen, gesturing to Aimery and Oliver. The struggles of the clerics were no match for the brawny men. Oliver was cuffed hard when he resisted. Gebirga and Katerinen held hands, terrified. The leader walked over to Katerinen and pulled off her head covering. "Hello blondie," he said, "We don't see that color much around here. Just as I thought. We'd been told you might use the fair as a chance to go where you're not meant. I don't think you are supposed to be wandering all over this mountainside. We'd better get you back where you belong. Men, tie them up."

Gebirga was grabbed by a man smelling strongly of garlic, who bound her hands in front of her before she had time to do so much as gasp. From the sounds of it, Aimery and Oliver were handled by their captors with equal efficiency. Katerinen was putting up more of a struggle. Perhaps her captor was afraid of hurting his noble prisoner. "Ouch! She bit me!" Gebirga heard someone say. Finally, they were all subdued and told to march, back down the path.

"Wait!" said Gebirga, "I need my dog. Liisa! Liisa!" She called, but heard no answering bark.

"Your dog's run off. We wouldn't take her with us in any case." the leader told her, pushing her ahead of him and getting her to walk as quickly as she could down the path.

"I can't just leave her here. Liisa, Liisa!" she called fruitlessly, stumbling and tripping down the path, hoping in vain that the dog might catch up with them.

They were led to the encampment below and presented to another man. "My lord, we found these four skulking around in the clearing above our camp, " said the leader of their captors.

"Very good. Katerinen of Flanders, I believe, wandering outside the abbey grounds. How unfortunate. We'll have to restore you to the convent. Take Katerinen back to the abbess and tell her to take better care of her this time. The rest of you, take these three and lock them in the shed behind our campsite. The king will want to know their business here."

"No!" screamed Katerinen, "Don't take Gebirga away! I need her." The younger girl pressed herself against Gebirga, almost knocking her over. But the leader pulled her away as easily as he might pick up a kitten. "Gebirga!" Katerinen shouted one last time as she was taken away.

"Trintje, don't give up hope," called Gebirga after her, "Be brave and strong and make your mother proud of you. We'll be together again soon, I promise."

She and Aimery and Oliver were manhandled into a nearby building, and the door was locked securely behind them. Gebirga sank onto the hard packed dirt floor, and started to weep, overcome by shame and fear, the loss of both Liisa and Katerinen too much to bear. Aimery sat down beside her and tried to comfort her as best he could. "We'll get her back, Gebirga, you'll see. The abbess likes you and won't let them keep you apart," he said, with more optimism than he felt. "But I'm puzzled," he continued, almost to himself, "That was Count Bertran de Risnel. He is the king of Aragon's cousin, but the land he holds is far to the west, in Carrion, part of Queen Urraca's domain, where he protects the king's interests in the kingdom of his wife. I recognize him from when I passed through Carrion last time. It is right on the pilgrimage road. What is he doing back here?"

"Will he recognize you?" asked Gebirga, trying to pull herself together.

"He might. I hope not."

Meanwhile, Oliver was exploring their prison. He used his shoulder to try to force open the door, until someone outside called for him to stop. "It's too bad this building doesn't have a window." Oliver said, "Even if it were too small for us to get through, at least we'd have some light. I begin to understand how you feel all the time, Gebirga." He felt his way around the small single room. "They keep carts here usually, but now there's not so much as a log to stand on. The carts are probably all being used for the fair. He sat down beside Aimery and Gebirga.

Gebirga could not respond. How could the day, which had begun with such promise, have gone so very wrong? Why had Liisa not responded to her call? It was so unlike her. As for Katerinen, she must be so lonely and scared on her own. At least the abbess could be trusted to be kind. Whomever the abbess blamed for this escape attempt, it would not be Katerinen who would bear the brunt of her anger. But would the abbess be allowed to keep custody of Katerinen, now her care had proved so porous? And whatever had happened to Yusuf? Why had he not met them as planned? Gebirga recalled his previous mysterious behavior, and wondered whether he had betrayed them.

Time passed slowly. Gebirga measured it by the bells she heard, calling out the different services, almost drowned out by the sound of revelers still enjoying the fair. Dusk came late in these Spanish summer nights, and they had been waiting for hours before someone finally opened the door, but it was only to thrust in a hard loaf of bread and a bucket for them to use as a privy. The door was slammed shut and locked again, and they were no better informed of their ultimate fate.

"I'm afraid they mean to keep us here all night," said Aimery, dividing up the bread as best as he could do with his hands tied. His glum prediction turned out to be true. Gebirga was glad of her double layer of clothing, as she tried to rest on the hard earth floor and the night grew steadily colder. She knew she should try to sleep, since the trials of the next morning would be easier if she were well rested. But her mind churned with chilling prospects of the future while her body sought in vain a comfortable position on the hard ground. She fell asleep just before dawn, only to be awoken much too soon by an argument right outside the door of the shed.

"I have my orders, domna. No one goes inside until the count gets back."

"You're on my land and this is my shed. If I tell you to unlock the door you will do so."

It was the abbess. Gebirga struggled to her feet. If only they could speak to her, she might have some news about Katerinen. Whatever the abbess was saying must have been persuasive, because Gebirga heard the key turning in the lock.

"You may lock us in, if you wish," said the abbess to the guard, "I won't be long."

The door shut behind her, and the abbess addressed Gebirga, "First of all, Katerinen is fine. She's upset, of course, but she is back with us and she is safe. We'll take as good care of her as we can."

"Bless you, my lady . . ." Gebirga began, but the abbess interrupted her.

"Whatever possessed you to think you could to escape? You never had a chance; you were watched every minute, you know. No, not by me. But now you've put yourself in a position where I can't protect you. You'll have to take your chances with the king."

"The king?"

"Yes, Alfonso of Aragon. He is at his castle at Loarre, not too far from here, and Count Bertran de Risnel, the man who had you locked in here, will take you to him today. The king is hostile to those traveling through his lands in order to reach Queen Urraca, so your safety might depend on how well you can convince him that you are ordinary pilgrims. He might pop you straight in the dungeon, but I have written him a letter to try to persuade him that you would be more useful to him free. Even if he does think your final destination is Urraca, not Compostela, they have a fragile truce at the moment, and that might stand in your favor. Their truce allowed Alfonso to turn his attention from his Christian to his Muslim enemies, and that is what let him conquer Zaragoza. A new war with Urraca would ruin all that, and might allow the Muslims to retake what they have so recently lost. Your papal connections should impress him too. I have given my letter to Count Bertran and he has sworn to pass it along to Alfonso."

"Thank you, my lady," said Gebirga.

"I've brought you some food and drink, before your journey. Guards!" she called banging on the door. They responded by unlocking it and peering in. "You can untie these people's hands so they can eat. Yes, I insist. You can stand guard and watch them if you must, and if you think two clerics and a blind girl can overcome you and escape, then you are not worthy of your hire."

The guards did as they were bid, and the three stretched their arms, trying to get the feeling back into their wrists and hands. The abbess summoned her servant to open the parcel he had brought with him, and he drew out bread and cheese and water skins for each of them. They ate and drank, and saved the rest of their skins for their journey. He also gave a smaller parcel to Gebirga.

"My casket!" she said, unwrapping it.

"Yes, I wondered if I should keep it safe for you here, but then I decided you might find a use for it in your travels. And now I must leave you," said the abbess.

"My lady, before you go—have you seen any sign of Liisa? She ran off when the men took us."

"Liisa? No. But if she comes back here, we'll take good care of her."

At that moment, the count arrived with the rest of their escort. "Lord Bertran, I am glad you arrived before I had to leave," said the abbess, "Now remember, these are not dangerous villains, they are foreign pilgrims and travelers who are chastened enough after a night in a dark shed. Treat them with respect; you'll have no trouble with them on your journey. Farewell, all of you, and God speed."

"My advice to you, my lady, is to take better care of your own protege, the girl from Flanders, and let me worry about my prisoners."

With that, the abbess was forced to leave, and Bertran took charge. "The abbess has convinced me, somewhat against my better judgement, that it is safe to let you ride. There are six of us coming with you, and each one can draw a bow faster than you can fall off a horse, so there'll be no funny tricks. Look sharp, we have a long day today, and hard riding through the hills."

Soon they were all mounted and on their way. They took the narrow road that led south of the monastery, twisting back and forth on itself as it climbed up into the mountains. Aimery rode close to Gebirga and described what they were passing, and the condition of the path in an effort to keep her calm as possible as they rode into the unknown. "The woods are very close to the road around here. I don't think we have too much further to climb. We're just passing the monastery of San Juan de la Peña. How I wish you could see it; you would be amazed, Gebirga. The whole thing, cloister, church and all, is built into the side of the cliff, in a fold of the rock. The cliff above looks like it is going to fall and crush the monastery at any moment."

"Hey priest," Bertran addressed him, "You are very chatty. Who are you, and what brings you to this part of the world?"

"My name is Aimery Picaud, and I am an Augustinian canon. I am engaged in a pilgrimage, with my friends here, as I am sure you've been told."

"I thought I recognized you," Bertran responded, "You were at Carrion last year, weren't you? Making a pilgrimage and telling everyone you wanted to write a book. The bishop of Compostela will love that idea, which is unfortunate for you now, because the king of Aragon loathes Diego Gelmirez. But if you're a canon, you'll feel at home at Loarre. The castle is royal, but it is held for the king by a community of Augustinian friars. You may find a permanent home there."

With this dismal thought they rode on. Oliver whispered to Aimery, "What do you think happened? Why was Yusuf not there with the horses? Do you suppose he's been captured too?"

"I don't know. Have you noticed that no one has spoken about him? It seems strange; everyone knew he was traveling with us."

Gebirga debated sharing her own fears about Yusuf, and then decided their straits were dire enough that she owed frankness to the others. "Aimery, Oliver, has it occurred to you that Yusuf might have betrayed us to Aragon's men? He might have told them when and where we were meeting, so they could trap us."

"I suppose it is possible, "Aimery said cautiously, "But what would he gain from it?"

"And why would he do that?' asked Oliver, "He was the one who figured out where Katerinen was in the first place. Why lead us to her, just to have us taken away again?"

Gebirga did not have an answer for them. In the face of their skepticism, she did not want to tell them about the money purse he had received from the archbishop of Toledo's man back in St. Gilles, and she could not yet see what the archbishop's interest in Katerinen might be. But Yusuf's absence at the crucial moment of their capture did not look good.

It was a long journey and the sun was hot. They stopped several times to water their horses, and once for longer to eat. Their route led them up and down, twisting up mountain paths and snaking through narrow gorges. Bertran must have decided they were not about to make a break for it, because he unbent a little and became almost friendly. He commented on the river they were traveling beside, "That's the Gallego, and if you followed it downstream, you'd find yourself in Zaragoza. I was there when we took it last year. That city is a sight, full of palaces and fountains and gardens. And there were riches for everyone; they're still dividing up the spoils. That victory made Alfonso of Aragon the mightiest ruler in all the peninsula, more powerful that any other, Christian or Muslim, immeasurably stronger than his shrew of a wife."

It was almost dusk when they began their final ascent to the castle of Loarre, passing through olive groves and almond trees laden with fruit, the scent of sweet pine heavy in the air. Oliver whistled as they approached its impressive gateway, and Aimery muttered under his breath, "By God, these Spaniards know how to build a castle. That heap is impregnable. No one could get in if the defenders didn't want them to."

"And I bet no one could get out either," said Oliver grimly.

Once inside the castle wall, they dismounted. Their guards greeted familiar faces, and laughed and joked. Their duties towards the three were over. Oliver was right; no one could escape from this fortress once inside. The count escorted them through an ornate arched gateway and into the castle. As they ascended a wide staircase up to the main level of the castle grounds, Gebirga thought she heard singing coming from over her head. "What's that sound?" she asked.

Bertran answered, "This staircase passes under the nave of the church. The crypt, with the bones of St. Demetrius, is beside us. The canons must be singing vespers, and that is what you are hearing."

They passed through a series of corridors and into the castle yard before ascending yet another staircase, this time a twisting circular one. Gebirga felt like she was wandering around in a labyrinth. Aimery kindly took her elbow and directed her, but he was not nearly as good as Liisa. She could never escape from this place; she had barely been able to find the privy. Bertran took them to a small room at the top of the staircase and told them, "You'll have to share this room, I'm afraid. I'd put you in the women's quarters, Gebirga, but they don't exist here. There are screens to divide the room, and pallets rolled up in the corner. I'll have food sent up, but I'll have to lock you in again tonight. We'll see what the king says when you speak with him tomorrow. Right now he's out hunting, I've been told. You'll hear when he returns." He bade them good night and left, turning the key behind him. He was as good as his word though, and sent up a meal, some plain roast meat and pease pottage. Exhausted from their long day, and trying previous night, they went to bed as soon as they could, only to be awoken almost at once by the sound of horns and rowdy huntsmen. That must be the king, Gebirga thought sleepily, but even if the whole court had traipsed through their room, it could not have kept her awake for long.

The next day they were wakened by brilliant sun streaming through their windows. "Look at that view!" said Oliver.

"Yes," said Aimery, "Our window faces south. To the north, the castle has its back to the foothills of the Pyrenees, but before us the land opens into a wide plain that stretches to Zaragoza and beyond. I almost feel like I could see Zaragoza from here, though it is a good two days' ride." Gebirga wondered if the bright sun in this strange, southern world she could not see was causing the dull headache she was feeling.

Their appreciation of the view was interrupted by the sounds of breakfast at their door. A servant also brought a very welcome basin of water. Gebirga had worn her shepherd's costume over her gown and shift all day yesterday, and the night before, and she was glad to lose a layer and to be able to clean up from the rigors of traveling and a night spent on a dirt floor. She hoped this meant they would be brought before the king soon. She was dreading that encounter, but the waiting was even worse.

Gebirga got her wish. They had barely finished eating and washing up when Count Bertran appeared at their door. "The king is waiting for you. Hurry up."

They did their best to follow him, but Gebirga found going down the narrow circular staircase even harder than going up it. Bertran waited for them impatiently at the bottom, and then set out across the castle yard to the large keep where the king was. They need not have hurried. When they entered the dim interior, they found the king on a throne in a great hall, attended by his knights, servants, and the canons, listening to petitions from local people, eager to press their demands on him during one of his rare visits north, away from the frontier. One canon was beside him, assiduously taking notes. Gebirga and her friends would have to wait their turn.

Gebirga listened closely to the stentorian voice at the front of the hall meting out justice and settling disputes between neighbors, trying to get a feel for what kind of man King Alfonso was. His voice was strong and authoritative. The audience seemed simple after the display and rhetoric of the papal court. He was a man who did not want to waste time listening to flowery honorifics and empty praise. Finally, it was their turn. Count Bertran addressed his royal master.

"My lord king, I have returned from the monastery of Santa Cruz where, as you directed, I checked on the welfare of the domna, Katerinen of Flanders, currently your most serene majesty's guest at the monastery. As the lady abbess, Andregoto, informed you, she had been joined by three people claiming to be her traveling companions. They are here before you. A fourth, a servant, has since vanished. I found them in the middle of what can only be construed as an attempt to spurn your majesty's gracious hospitality, and leave the monastery.

"How regrettable," said the king, "You did the right thing to bring them to us, cousin. And the girl? You left her at the monastery?"

"Yes. The lady abbess assured me she would be safe there with her adventurous friends removed from the scene. She has also sent a letter for you to read."

Count Bertran handed the parchment to the king who unfolded it and read it slowly. When he finished, he twisted the tassel that hung from the abbess's wax seal through his fingers, meditating on its contents before passing it to the scribe, who scanned it in turn. The king spoke. "Come forward, you three, name yourselves, and state your business in my kingdom."

Gebirga, Aimery, and Oliver approached the throne, Gebirga in the middle, guided by the other two. The king addressed Aimery. "I see by your habit that you are an Augustinian canon, like my companions here. I understand that you call yourself Aimery, from Picardy, and that you claim to be writing a book about the pilgrimage road to Compostela. That will surely please Diego Gelmirez."

"Your majesty, the fame and glory it will shine upon the blessed route should please all those through whose lands the road runs, not least yourself. I have spent much time in your own towns of Burgos and Belorado, Castrojeriz and Carrion, all of which shine in the reflected glory of the road."

"We shall see. And who is this?" he asked, pointing to Oliver.

"Sire, I am Oliver d'Asquins, a monk of Cluny. I serve Aimery Picaud and help him with his book."

"You speak good Spanish for a monk from Asquins, young Oliver."

"That's because I grew up in Spain, your majesty. My parents live in Logroño."

Gebirga groaned inwardly. She was certain he should not have admitted that to the king, and the king's next words confirmed her fears.

"Then you are either a loyal subject with a perfectly good right to be traveling through my kingdom, or a traitor, exposing its secrets to foreign spies. We shall have to see which. And you," the king turned to Gebirga, "Who might you be? It is rare to find a blind woman caring for a noble lady. Why are you roaming the countryside and not safely in a monastery back in your homeland?"

Gebirga was used to counts and lords, but this was a king, one of God's anointed. True, she had spent time in the presence of the pope, but Calixtus had barely acknowledged her existence. Papal indifference was less intimidating than having the full force of royal attention directed towards her. Her voice shook as she responded. "Your majesty, I am Gebirga of Gistel, daughter of Bertulf the Cross bearer who bravely fought at Jerusalem." She paused for a moment before adding, "And I am daughter of Saint Godeleva whose bones are raised to the altar at Gistel." It was the first time Gebirga had ever claimed connection to her mother in public. Both of them made her who she was; both deserved mention. "I am in service to Katerinen of Flanders and her mother, the lady Clemence. I was escorting Katerinen on pilgrimage to Compostela when our party was sadly attacked by thugs." Gebirga's accusation was clear in her tone. "All were killed except for myself and Katerinen, but we were separated. I found Oliver and Aimery in Jaca, and they agreed to help me find Katerinen. They have nothing to do with our expedition, and you should have no grudge against them."

"In the days of my deceased father-in-law, it was said that a young virgin could walk from one end of Spain to the other, carrying a bag of gold without molestation. It pains me that this is no longer so. Only if Spain were again united under one Christian emperor, could this be possible." The king then addressed the objective of the two women. "On pilgrimage, you say? And what do you hope to accomplish by your pilgrimage? What sorts of sins do two such nice ladies have to atone for? Are you hoping for a cure for your blindness? Could you not have saved yourself the journey and asked your sainted mother for help?" he mocked.

If her mother had not cured her, why would some distant apostle do it? That was the implication of his words and she winced for it was something she had often asked herself. But she knew she had to give the king a convincing reason for their journey. "Your majesty, we go to Compostela to ask St. James to protect the health of Count Baldwin, my lady's brother, wounded in battle against the English, and to protect the county of Flanders."

"You pray for Count Baldwin's health? I am afraid you are too late for that. Haven't you heard? Count Baldwin died over a month ago."

CHAPTER FIFTEEN

A Hunt and an Escape

Therefore, he who has not violated those pilgrims, but has behaved himself properly with them will without doubt obtain a reward both now and in the future from the Lord. But he who has violated them, or has taken anything from them by theft, plunder, or deceit, his share will doubtless be with the devil.

Gebirga was speechless. Baldwin, dead? And not recently; well over a month ago, the king had said. Why did they not hear? And what would it mean for Katerinen to no longer be the sister of a count?

"This is news to you? Word of his death did not catch up to you on your travels?"

"No. Your majesty, may I ask if you have heard who is to succeed the count?" she asked. She hated to seek information from this hostile source but realized she needed the answer to this question to know how best to protect Katerinen.

"The succession is still somewhat in doubt, but I believe Charles of Denmark has claimed Flanders and it looks like he will prevail."

This was terrible news. Charles was no friend of Clemence and cared nothing for her daughter. Gebirga wondered what Clemence was doing, if she was already negotiating a new marriage for herself in order to shore up her own position. Knowing Clemence, she must be. But wait—if the death had occurred over a month ago, surely Calixtus would have known about it by the time of the council in Toulouse, if not before. Would Clemence not have written to her brother as soon as possible to tell him the news, so he could rally behind her? The more she thought about it, the more likely this seemed. Clemence would have passed along a letter or at least a message for Katerinen about the news, since it affected the girl's prospects so deeply. If Gebirga's fears were correct, Calixtus must have deliberately suppressed news of the death. This cast a chilling light on his failure to produce a dispensation for Katerinen's marriage. Had he sent them to Spain merely to abandon them?

Gebirga realized she had been silent for far too long, and everyone was waiting for her. "I'm sorry, your majesty, your sudden news has shocked me."

But the king had moved to other subjects. "Abbess Andregoto speaks well on your behalf. You are fortunate. She seems to feel that whatever your original intentions, you may prove a friend to Aragon. We shall see, but I am disposed to be lenient." The king addressed Count Bertran, "I see no reason not to give them the run of the castle while we are here. They will feast with us this evening. And tomorrow, they may come with us when we go hunting. I have a fancy to go after the wild boar that plague the locals in the mountains north of here. They must be prepared to ride at dawn, so see to it that they are kitted out properly."

This was a new shock for Gebirga. Hunting? Alarmed, she spoke out, "But, your majesty, I am blind. I won't be able to hunt from horseback."

"We can always put your horse on a leading rein," Alfonso answered, "And we'll certainly make sure not to give you a spear, lest you accidentally stick our royal self with it. But with a good dagger and some guidance, even you might be able to land a telling blow. Enough now. Next petitioner."

With this dismissal, the three left the hall and walked through the castle yard, enjoying their new semi-freedom. They made their way to the queen's belvedere, a large opening in the inner castle wall with a view over the vast, golden plain below, named for some long deceased queen who used it as a lookout to spy her lord returning home from fighting the Moors. Gebirga could not appreciate the view, but she stared with them, feeling the sun burn her sightless eyes and thinking over the news she had learned.

"This is an odd court," ruminated Aimery.

"Really? How so?" she asked.

"Well, there are almost no women here. In fact I don't think I've seen one. It is more like a monastery than a royal court. A monastic fortress."

"I noticed that too," said Oliver, "But I thought that was just because of the canons who control the castle when the king is not here. It seems strange to me to have canons guarding a castle."

"I understand King Alfonso got that idea from the very Muslim enemies he is fighting now. The Almoravids are known for using fortresses full of warriors dedicated to religious life and jihad," said Aimery.

"What's jihad?" said Gebirga.

"Holy war. You know, 'Allah be praised, fie on the infidels.'"

"But we're not the infidels, they are," said Gebirga.

"They have a different perspective. But it is more than just the canons who make this such a masculine castle. None of the lords have their wives with them. That is odd."

"King Alfonso is well known for forbidding his lords to have their wives and daughters with them when are they are in attendance on the king. He says it makes them womanish and distracts them from fighting. He says the only proper companion for fighting men is other fighting men," said Oliver.

"He may not like beautiful women about," said Aimery, "But he does not seem to have the same feelings about beautiful men. Did you notice the slaves who act as his pages? My tastes do not run in that direction, but even I can recognize that he must have picked the cream of the crop out of his captives at Zaragoza for his own service."

"There are rumors about that too," said Oliver, "People remark that although he is in his forties, he has never fathered a child, and has never even taken a mistress. They say Queen Urraca believed it was safe to marry him because she knew the marriage would never produce an heir to challenge the rights of Alfonso of Galicia, her son by Katerinen's uncle."

Gebirga finally realized what they were saying about Alfonso of Aragon's tastes. "Oh my goodness," she said, thinking about the rumours that had swirled around the friendship of Count Baldwin with Charles of Denmark and William Clito, back in Flanders. A practical thought struck her. "But if he has no heir, who will inherit his kingdom when he dies?"

"No one knows," said Aimery.

When they returned at last to their quarters, Gebirga was delighted to discover that clothes had been left for her for the feast that evening, and for the hunt the following day. Somewhere in this masculine castle they had been found for her, probably locked up in a forgotten chest, judging by their scent of tansy and mugwort, protective herbs against moths. She thrilled to find insets of icy silk in the soft sleeves. Dressed like this, she would feel like royalty. Maybe they had belonged to the queen for whom the belvedere was built. Since she had been wearing the same clothes since before the attack in the Pyrenees, she was grateful for a change, and tried the gown and shift on right away, then used the length of cloth they had left her as a veil to fashion one of her coifs, securing it tightly so not a strand of hair would show through its folds.

"I think you're supposed to lie the veil loosely over your hair, secured to your head with this embroidered filet," said Oliver timidly.

"Nonsense," said Gebirga. "I might as well go down naked as with my hair showing like that."

The feast itself was an assault on her senses. The close hall and crowds of people were disorienting, and knowing she was the only woman in the room made her feel even more vulnerable. Having Oliver and Aimery on either side of her comforted her, but she missed Liisa at her feet. The wine was superb, though she asked for hers to be well-watered; she was told it came from the royal holdings in the Rioja valley. The food was unusual but delicious, and available in copious variety. She was served a dish of marinated lamb with a pungent, grassy herb Oliver told her was cilantro, a plate of lentils cooked in strange spices and gilded with a layer of baked egg, and a chicken stew thick with olive oil, garlic and breadcrumbs. At least she was used to olive oil by now. There was one dish, a kind of paste that they ate using small pieces of flatbread as spoons that puzzled her completely, and even Oliver was no help. She questioned the page who was serving their part of the table, wafting perfume over them every time he refilled a glass, or set down a new dish, but he turned out to speak only Arabic. He kept saying something that sounded like, "badinjan muhassa," until one of Gebirga's neighbors took pity on them both. "It is eggplant, roasted and pounded to a paste with raw onion."

"Thank you," said Gebirga, but she was none the wiser. Eggplant? What was that? The candle smoke, the noise of the hall, and the boy's perfume were making her head hurt.

When the savory dishes had all been taken away and the pages had brought out trays of confections—layers of pastry filled with sweet cheese or nuts and drizzled with honey, as well as hardened sesame seed candy and sweetmeats made of pounded dates and walnuts—King Alfonso called for entertainment. The tumblers who responded to his summons were cheered by the rest of the hall, and they made plenty of noise crashing about, though Gebirga could scarcely appreciate their skill. But they were followed by a musician who played a strange, stringed instrument, unlike any Gebirga had ever heard at a northern court, and he sang a sad lament that brought tears to her eyes. Though he sang in Arabic, the melody and tone made her think of her loved ones, all gone or left behind—her parents, Mathilde, Winnoc, Katerinen, of course, and even poor Liisa, vanished on an Aragonese hillside. She wondered again what had become of Yusuf. Lost in the beauty of the music and the unfamiliar language, she was surprised to understand the conclusion of the song, which was in Spanish.

> What can I do? What will become of me?
> My love, do not go away from me.

The young man sang these lines in a higher pitch, as if he were impersonating a woman. A few final chords on the oud, and his song was done. The hall erupted in cheers, and the king summoned the singer to take a gold cup, full of wine, as his reward.

The rest of the evening was anticlimax, and Gebirga was glad when the king rose so she could finally return to her room. The rhythms of the song, and its sad closing lyric, stayed in her mind when she tried to sleep.

They were wakened before dawn by a servant at their door bearing a simple breakfast and urging them to get ready. They dressed rapidly, wanting to give no occasion for their host to be angry with them. While they were dressing, Gebirga said, "Aimery, is there any chance we might be able to escape while we are out of the castle today? I know the king seems friendly, but I am afraid of him, and this might be our only chance to be outside the walls."

"I doubt it. We'll be surrounded by armed men on horseback who know the countryside like the backs of their hands. But we can stay alert to any good opportunities to make a break for it. Take with you anything you don't want to lose, just in case."

For Gebirga, this only meant her casket. Wrapped in a cloak, it could be tied to her saddle. At the last minute, she added the dress she had worn the previous night to her bundle. It was not as if anyone else would wear it in this masculine preserve. "I can't eat this breakfast," she said, "I'm still full from last night."

"Me too," said Oliver, "But let's take it with us. We have no idea when our next meal will be." So she added her share of the breakfast to her bundle. It was a small loaf and a triangle of fried egg and onion so she slit the loaf and wedged the egg inside.

The castle yard was a cacophony of dogs, horses, and hunstmen in rawhide boots and leather leggings testing out their hunting horns. Many of the grooms had been out all night with the tracking hounds, searching for traces of boar and to locate their lairs so they could be flushed out by the dogs when the royal party arrived. Boar was not usually hunted until the autumn, but nearby villagers had complained of attacks, and one young girl had been gored to death. Hunting boar was a way for the king to pass time, and please the local population too.

Gebirga and her friends were given the same horses they had ridden on to Loarre. She tied her bundle to her saddle and covered it with the green cloak she had been given to wear. Aimery and Oliver were given bows while Gebirga received a sharp dagger, and after what seemed like a lot of waiting around, the whole party set off in the direction the grooms had gone, the king at the center on a lively horse, both resplendent in figured Islamic silks. They descended the mountain, retracing the path they had taken to come to Loarre. But instead of returning north along the river valley, they crossed it and ascended into the foothills on the other side. The way was dense with scrub and holm oak, and the party of riders spread out. The forty or so dogs who would be used at the kill, massive alaunts who were used to taking on boar and other large game, were kept in check by blasts of the huntsmen's horns. They came to a wood between two high mountain spurs, and there the party organized itself into a long line, each hunter choosing a favored spot from which to begin moving forward.

At the call of a horn from the king's chief huntsman, echoed up and down the line by the other horns, the alaunts were released and the hunt began. The hunters went forward slowly, trying to keep the line steady and even, while the grooms were supposed to push the game towards them so it could be killed. The king and his favorite lords were at the center, where they would encounter most of the prey.

Aimery had maneuvered himself, Gebirga, and Oliver to the far end of the line where, with any luck, an escape might be possible. He would have preferred to be at the east end of the line, closer to the road that led back to Santa Cruz and Katerinen, but they found themselves at the other end, far to the west, deep in the wilds and distant from signs of human habitation, with only a few hunters further west of them still. To Gebirga, the baying of the dogs and the noise of the hunters and their horns was terrifying, and it was all she could do to keep her seat, riding through the dense undergrowth. Aimery kept a tight hold on her leading rein. They could hear excited cries down the line, when the hunters came in contact with their quarry. The dogs barked as they attacked their prey, howling when they came in contact with the vicious tusks, subduing the animals so they could be safely finished off by the spears of the men on horseback. Gebirga and her friends were just as glad to be far away from the center of the hunt; they had no wish to encounter an angry boar. But crashes through the undergrowth ahead of them indicated that they were not going to escape unscathed. A boar, shrieking with rage, two alaunts sharp at his heels, rose up before them.

A wily and experienced animal who wanted to evade the men with spears would try to run around the hunters rather than towards them, and might attack those on the end of the line who encountered it without sufficient support from other hunters. The boar ran straight for Aimery and Gebirga and then mercifully swerved west, towards the last hunters. Normally, the dogs were to keep the boar at bay until it could be finished off by a spear thrust from a hunter on horseback, but there were not enough dogs on this particular boar, so the hunters dismounted and prepared to stab it from on the ground, a much more dangerous method, though it would earn them praise and admiration from their fellows if they were successful.

When Aimery saw the hunters dismount, he said to Oliver, "Quick! This is our chance! Let's see if we can circle back to the road while everyone else is occupied."

But when they tried to ride east behind the line of hunters, in the direction of the road, their way was blocked by straggling hunters and grooms. Riding further south, in the hope of avoiding detection, they found themselves in a shallow valley that veered over to the west, taking them further from their destination. What was worse, Oliver, looking behind, spied a rider observing their route from the ridge above them.

"We could try to go around the hunters to the north, and get to the road that way," said Oliver.

So they picked up the pace and continued riding west. But when they tried to turn north, they found another mounted man blocked the way. "I didn't think there would be any hunters this far west," said Aimery, "Let's ride a bit further and see if we can turn south."

But the way south continued to be barred by a man on horseback. "Do you think that is the same man as before, Oliver?" said Gebirga.

"It is hard to tell against the sun. It might be."

They rode further and further west, picking up their pace as much as they could. Finally, they felt they had left behind anyone who might have been tracking them. But they were miles to the west of their destination, and the rest of the hunting party. The reached a small stream, rising cool and fresh from the mountains to the north, and Aimery suggested they dismount to water their horses and make plans. They filled their own water bottles and sat underneath a tree to eat a belated breakfast, tearing with their teeth at the bread and egg they had brought with them.

"What do we do next," said Gebirga when their most immediate hunger pangs had been sated, "Admit defeat and return to the king's party? We can always pretend that my horse got scared by a boar and you had to come rescue me. Or should we press on? Is there any way through the mountains north of us?"

Aimery said, "The mountains in this ridge are at their highest just here. We'd have to go further west, to the pass at Sos, at least two days ride away, and it would be almost impossible to get back to Santa Cruz. And knowing we were gone, surely the king would guard the monastery carefully, expecting us to be heading there. Our only hope was to make it to Santa Cruz before anyone knew we were on our way. It is almost as if we were being guided away from the road to Santa Cruz."

"I agree—we were being guided in this direction, away from Santa Cruz," said Oliver, "Every time we tried to ride in any direction other than west, we were blocked."

"If you're right," said Gebirga, "Then the king wanted us to escape, and he wanted us to go this way. If his men were able to block us, they could have stopped us. But why?"

They sat, glum and silent, trying to figure out how they had been manipulated and to what end. Why would the king make such efforts to have them brought to him, only to let them go right away? Gebirga spoke first. "I think King Alfonso wants us to go to Queen Urraca, but without Katerinen. That way, he still has her as a pawn, while we open negotiations between the two monarchs for her safe passage. And much though I would like to hasten to Katerinen this very moment, I am afraid that it is probably in her best interests for us to do what the king wants. Queen Urraca may be our only hope for securing Katerinen's freedom. We have nothing to offer the king, but she does."

"What you say makes sense, and he may be expecting Oliver and me to forge a connection between himself and Bishop Diego Gelmirez," said Aimery, "We're on the old frontier of the Aragonese kingdom, before King Alfonso captured Zaragoza and moved the frontier south. All along the road here are royal fortresses held by lords loyal to Alfonso—Biel, Uncastillo, and then Sos beyond the pass back to the pilgrimage road, which is the way we must take to get to Urraca. The towns on the pilgrimage road are all loyal to Alfonso too. The king doesn't need to have us guarded or escorted;

this is the only direction we can travel, and his allies and friends can keep him informed of our movements at every step. I agree that we should go to Queen Urraca, but we must remember that at all times we are under the eyes of the king. Come, we can reach Biel in good time if we leave now. It is west of us on this ridge, if I am not mistaken."

"I hate this," said Oliver, "I keep thinking of Katerinen back at Santa Cruz, wondering what has befallen us and worried about what is going to happen to her."

Gebirga was impressed. The old Oliver would have been full of dubious schemes for impossible rescues that would make him look like a devoted hero, whatever the consequences. Finally he was learning to imagine how Katerinen might feel and to take her best interests into consideration. "I know, Oliver," she said gently, "I hate it too. But the sooner we reach Queen Urraca, the sooner we'll be in a position to help Katerinen."

As they urged their horses to ford the cold, narrow stream so they could resume their journey, Gebirga kept silent about her worst fear. What if Queen Urraca had no interest in securing Katerinen's freedom? What would they do then?

Their fear that their presence at Biel would be noted was well founded. Unlike the towns on the pilgrimage road, Biel was not set up for visitors, and there was no hospice where they could stay. But a question to one of the guards at the gatehouse pointed them to a wine shop that sometimes had a square of floor in an attic to let for a night, as well as room for their horses. While they were getting directions from one guard, Aimery spotted another leaving the gatehouse, heading to the castle perched on the top of the hill, no doubt informing the garrison of the strangers in their midst. Much the same phenomenon was repeated the next night at Uncastillo, and then at Sos, which they reached after a hard day of riding through the steep mountain pass. Each fortress town was located a day's ride from the next, and it was clear what an effective chain of fortifications they once had been.

Their journey the next day was a short one. When they were half-way between Sos and the next town, Sangüesa, where they would rejoin the pilgrimage road, Oliver brought down a partridge with the bow he had been given by the king. Gebirga's knife gutted the bird and they plucked it by the simple measure of removing its skin, feathers intact. Roasted over a fire, it made a good change from bread and cheese for lunch. "They taste better if you hang them for a few days, of course," said Oliver, "but this isn't bad."

As they gnawed on the bones, Aimery made a suggestion. "There is a small monastery on this road, about a mile before we reach Sangüesa. It is called San Adrian de Vadoluengo and I understand that it has ties to Cluny. Why don't we try to stay there tonight? We won't escape the king's notice for long by avoiding the town but I am tired of being tracked like an animal and I'd like one night out of the king's eye."

The others were agreeable, so after they put out their fire and replaced the sod they had removed in order to clear a spot to light it, they set out for San Adrian. This turned out to be a humble community, only a modest church and a few outbuildings surrounded by a low wall. The monks were rather unwelcoming too, despite Oliver's efforts to play up his Cluniac background. "One night, and that's it," they were told. They were shown to a guest house that was not much better than the shack they had been locked in overnight at Santa Cruz, and rather ungraciously offered a basin of water for washing up. And their feeble hopes to avoid detection by the king also seemed in vain, since the moment they were shown to their dwelling place for the night, Oliver spotted the monk porter speaking to a servant, who was next seen riding out of the monastery gate, no doubt headed straight to Sangüesa to announce their presence. Oh well, Alfonso might be tracking them, but he was not impeding their journey, so there was nothing else to do but keep moving forward and hope for a sympathetic hearing from the queen.

After a meagre supper of barley gruel and soured milk in their quarters, Aimery and Oliver decided to attend vespers in the small abbey church.

"Ugh, you're not going to abandon me in this horrid room," Gebirga said.

"You could go sit outside," said Aimery, "It is a lovely night, and it is starting to cool down."

"I would, but I'm afraid of tripping over something or walking into a wall. How I miss Liisa!"

"There's a bench not far from our door. We could take you there. And there's a staff leaning in the corner of this room. You could use that to feel your way in front of you if you want to go back inside before we get back."

"It was probably abandoned here by a would-be pilgrim who gave up after a night in this place. Very well, that's a good plan."

The toll of a bell revealed that vespers was about to begin. They left Gebirga on her bench and headed to join the monks. Gebirga felt the last sun of the evening warm her face. The air was sweet and pleasant. She wished she had her embroidery wools with her, and a piece of linen. She supposed they were adorning a hovel somewhere back in the Pyrenees. She stretched, unknotting her muscles after her day of riding. After so much travel the last year, she was beginning to get used to packing up every morning and sleeping in a new bed every night. Who would see in her now the shy woman who had been afraid of a visit to Bruges? Worried thoughts of Katerinen never quite left her mind, but for a short moment she tried to set them aside. Though she missed Liisa. How lovely it would be to have the big dog curled up at her feet right now, or begging for a belly scratch.

And with that wistful thought, she heard a bark. It almost sounded like—no, she must be imagining things. All these thoughts of Liisa were making her fancy she heard phantom dogs. But then there was another bark, and another. That was Liisa, there was no question of it. She would know that bark anywhere.

"Liisa, Liisa, are you there?"

More barking. But how could it be? Had Liisa somehow followed them from Santa Cruz? Was that even possible, when they were on horseback? But it was Liisa, that was unmistakable.

"Liisa! I'm coming!"

But how? She rose from her bench, glad of the staff Aimery had found for her. The monastery gate was to the right of the building where they were staying. If she walked forward, surely she would walk straight to it. She began feeling her way, probing the ground in front of her with the staff. From time to time, she heard another bark, which encouraged her to keep moving forward.

"Domna, are you certain you want to leave the monastery grounds," a voice spoke to her, unexpectedly close.

"Is this the gate?" she asked, "You don't sound like the porter who let us in this afternoon."

"The porter is at vespers, domna. I keep the gate for him while he is gone."

"Have you heard a dog barking?" Gebirga asked.

"There are always dogs barking around here."

"But just now! There was only one. I heard it. Can you tell me which direction it came from?"

"I might have heard something coming from that direction, on the way into Sangüesa. If you walked that way, you might find it," he positioned her in the right direction. "But why are you looking for a dog?"

She did not answer, but started feeling her way down the road in the direction he had indicated. She was not sure she was on the right track—surely if Liisa had somehow followed them, she would be coming up the road in the other direction, from Sos. She almost decided to turn back and wait until Oliver and Aimery were finished with the service, so they could help her. But then she heard more barking, coming from the direction she was heading. She walked as quickly as she could and called for her dog again.

The staff was helpful, but not infallible in the rutted road. She stumbled and almost fell over a stone in the middle of the path, feeling a twinge in the ankle she hurt in the Pyrenees. She managed to stay on her feet but just as she righted herself, she sensed the presence of people close to her. "Who's that? Who's there?"

The staff was wrenched from her hand and she shouted, "Aimery! Oliver!" Then a gag was tied around her mouth. It was not painful, but it effectively stopped her from calling out. A large sack that smelled like turnips was thrown over her head. One man picked her up, while the other tied the bottom of the sack, impervious to her struggles. She was unceremoniously placed on a cart among a crowd of unidentifiable warm bodies, and the cart began moving in the direction of Sangüesa. "Uuungh, uuungh" she tried to call, attempting to make herself heard through the gag and the sack. She tried to pound her feet against the floor of the cart. At this, the other occupants of the cart, who turned out to be a small herd of goats, added their own bleats to her cries. She would never be heard over their din.

There were no more barks from Liisa, or whichever dog that had been, as the cart rolled towards its destination. Gebirga struggled in her sack, but it was just small enough to impede free movement. The cart rumbled along for about a mile or so before it made one sharp turn and then another, suggesting they were driving through the narrow streets of a town. The cart paused and she heard one of its drivers leap down, and then the creak of a door, before it started up again. It did not go far before it stopped for good.

She felt someone fiddle with the bottom of the sack, and she tried to kick out. "Stop, please, I am just trying to untie you," an unfamiliar voice said. Two men pulled the sack over her head and then one gently restrained her while the other somewhat gingerly untied her gag. They were large men, and her nose caught their scent, a confusing mixture of expensive things like musk and fragrant wood, not what she expected from the goat cart and the turnip sack. "This way, domna," one said, leading her forward.

"Why should I follow you?" she asked, hoping her defiance masked her fear.

"All will be explained but, please, come inside."

Feeling she had no choice, she let them lead her. One offered her a cup of watered wine. She took it but did not drink.

"I insist that you return me to my friends at once! Who are you and why have you brought me here? Where am I?"

"You are in Sangüesa la Nueva, the new town of Sangüesa," said a new voice behind her, his words punctuated by a friendly woof. Yusuf had just walked through the door, and with him was Liisa.

CHAPTER SIXTEEN

Sangüesa

Pilgrims, be they rich or poor, whether going to or returning from the way of Saint James, are to be charitably received and cared for by all. For whoever receives them and attends diligently to their lodging will have not only Saint James, but also the True Lord Himself as guest.

Yusuf. So he had finally turned up.

"What are you doing here? Why have you abducted me? Why did you let the king's men capture us? Why weren't you at Santa Cruz with the horses? And unhand my dog!"

This last was a bit late because Liisa had already hurtled forward, placing her paws on Gebirga's knees and licking her face. Gebirga found it hard to sound fierce while she was hugging her dog. "Stop, Liisa. That tickles." But under her relief to see Liisa, she was furious and frightened. Whose side was Yusuf on? It was time to find out.

"It is good to see you, Gebirga," said Yusuf.

"You have a lot of explaining to do. And you can do it while you are taking me back to Aimery and Oliver. They will be frantic."

"I'm afraid that isn't possible. You'll be safer here with me and my friends."

"According to whom? And who are these friends of yours, who treated me like a sack of onions? Using my own dog as a decoy!" She was so vehement, the wine sloshed in her cup, splashing her hand.

"I understand that you are angry. I am sorry we had to abduct you like that, but it was the only way to get you away without implicating Aimery and Oliver. You can see that it is important that no one can blame them because you have disappeared."

"Yes, I am angry! And scared. And confused."

"I will explain, but it will take some time, and it is complicated. Please, come and sit at the table. Food is coming, if you are hungry, and you can drink your wine."

All four moved to a nearby table, but instead of chairs or benches, Gebirga was surprised to be directed to sit on cushions on the floor. Liisa liked the arrangement; she laid her head in her mistress's lap and stretched out full length. The whole room smelled faintly of citrus and fragrant wood. Gebirga suspected her new prison was no hovel and her captors were no farmers, despite their goats. A woman entered the room silently from the back and Gebirga smelled the musk and flowers of her perfume as she laid a platter of food on the table before retreating again. The men poured wine out for themselves while Gebirga took a sip from her cup. It was good, very good. She had better not drink too much of it before she learned what she needed from Yusuf. She took a deep breath. "Very well, Yusuf, begin at the beginning. Why didn't you come to the meeting place with the horses as we had planned? Why did you let us get captured?"

"That isn't really the beginning, but it will do. When I went to the stable that morning to collect our horses, I found the building guarded by two of the king's men, who refused even to let me enter. That made me suspicious. I argued with them for a while, which made them decide they wanted to keep me in custody until someone with more authority could take a look at me. That plan didn't suit me at all, so I made a break for it. Fortunately, the guard who chased me was slow, so I got away. I feared that our plans were doomed to fail, and I wanted to warn you that we'd have to cancel them. I couldn't find Aimery and I couldn't reach you and Oliver and Katerinen, because the procession had begun and you were in the middle of it. The only thing for me to do was to go to the meeting place and warn you off there. But I had to take the long way around, through the woods, in order to avoid any men who might be looking for me. I was walking down to our meeting place from the path above when I heard you being taken by the guards. That's when I had to make a quick decision. Did I let myself be captured with the rest of you, or should I try to escape and help you from the outside? I had reasons for thinking the king would be harsh with me, but I believed he would treat you well enough, better if I weren't found among you. Still, it was a difficult decision and I only had a moment in which to make it. If I'd been wrong . . . but here you are, so it turned out to be right, thank God. Liisa bounded up to where I was hiding, and she's been with me ever since. I was sorry about that because I knew you'd be worried and somewhat helpless without her, but if she hadn't come with me she'd still be at Santa Cruz, or with the king, so it is just as well. Since then, Liisa and I have been waiting, hoping you'd turn up."

It could be true. Or it could be a fairy story from beginning to end. "How did you know we'd come through Sangüesa?"

"I didn't know for certain, but I hoped you might. It wasn't hard to learn that you'd been taken to Loarre. Sangüesa is a major crossroads and if the king let you free, as I thought he might, there was almost no way you could reach Queen Urraca, except by traveling through here. So I came to my friends and waited. I have people who tell me things and the king's guards have a hard time keeping a secret. They were tracking you rather ostentatiously."

"Yes, even we noticed that."

"I heard you'd reached Sos, and then we made our plans. I'm sorry we had to grab you that way. I hope my friends didn't hurt you; I told them to be gentle."

She had to admit that, though the gag and the sack were unpleasant, she had not been harmed. It would have been far easier for them just to hit her on the head to keep her quiet, and they had not done that.

"But what if the king hadn't let us go free? What if he had kept us prisoner at Loarre?"

"Then I would have taken the castle apart stone by stone to get you out. But I'm just as glad it didn't come to that."

He quickly took her hand in a strong grip but he released it before she could register shock. She would have to mull that over some other time. Right now she had more pressing questions. "So tell me then, Yusuf, who are you working for, and what is his interest in Katerinen?"

Yusuf was silent for so long that Gebirga thought he was not going to answer. Finally he spoke. "There is no harm in you knowing the truth, and maybe some good at this point. I am a loyal servant of Archbishop Bernard of Toledo. I run errands from him and act both as his messenger and his eyes in distant places."

Gebirga remembered hearing Berengar, the archbishop's monastic envoy, paying Yusuf's wages back in St. Gilles. She pressed Yusuf further. "And what is Archbishop Bernard's interest in Katerinen?"

"Before I answer that question, Gebirga, it is time for you to be honest with me. What kind of pilgrimage are you and Katerinen making through Spain? What is your real goal here?"

Now it was Gebirga's turn to ponder before speaking. Was there any harm admitting the truth to him? She was sure he knew already, from his conversation with Calixtus that she had overheard back at Cluny. "Send your friends away first."

"My friends stay. They are helping you at considerable risk to themselves, and they deserve to know what the stakes are."

Did she have any choice? He could tell his friends anyway, whether she spoke or kept silent. With a silent apology to Clemence, the latest of many in the week since the attack in the Pyrenees, she decided to speak. "As I believe you are well aware," she began, "Katerinen and I are not in Spain for the good of our health, or our immortal souls. Katerinen is betrothed to Alfonso of Galicia, the queen's son, and we are here to plan a wedding."

"Yes, I thought so. Thank you for telling us."

"Now it is your turn again. Will the archbishop let the marriage take place? Are you here to ensure its failure?"

"This is where it gets complicated," said Yusuf, "My master has no objection to a marriage between Katerinen and Alfonso of Galicia. She is of good lineage, even if Clemence is less powerful than she once was, and her papal connections are not to be rejected lightly. But her presence here threatens to disorder an already complex political situation."

"I think I understand a little of that, but explain it from your perspective."

"My master, the archbishop, is one of Queen Urraca's most loyal supporters. Without him, she would have lost her kingdom years ago. Right now, she's in a relatively good position. She's at peace with Aragon and her son is established in Toledo, with my master as his guide. But two factors threaten to upset this fragile peace. The first is that the king of Aragon, in the absence of heirs of his own, will not want his stepson to marry and beget heirs. But even more important is the role of Bishop Diego Gelmirez. He wants two things: he wants to be made archbishop, and he wants to regain control of Alfonso of Galicia. In both he is the enemy of my master. Queen Urraca can't afford to side against Diego Gelmirez because she needs him to hold the western part of the kingdom against her half sister Teresa who is claiming to be queen of a new realm called Portugal. But she doesn't trust him. And some of her nobles are afraid of her truce with Alfonso of Aragon, and have allied with Diego Gelmirez against Urraca, or at least against the man who is her lover, Count Pedro de Lara. They have imprisoned him in the castle of Mansilla, near Leon and right now she is attempting to free him. You can see how precarious the whole situation is."

Lovers, sisters, bishops, and archbishops. Yusuf was right when he said this was complex. "So tell me how Katerinen's marriage fits in?"

"A marriage between Katerinen and Alfonso of Galicia sponsored and fostered by the archbishop of Toledo preserves the balance in the kingdom. The archbishop and the pope strengthen an allegiance that helps Queen Urraca. Diego Gelmirez remains in check. A marriage between Katerinen and Alfonso of Galicia sponsored by Diego Gelmirez disrupts the kingdom. Diego is made archbishop of Compostela by a grateful pope, the balance of power between him and Queen Urraca shifts decisively in his favor, the nobles are angry, the queen must make concessions, the kingdom is weakened, and Alfonso of Aragon, Teresa of Portugal, and our Muslim enemies rejoice."

"I begin to see why you wanted to detach me from Aimery and Oliver."

"Yes. I like Aimery and Oliver, and they mean no harm, but their aim to write a pilgrim's guide to Compostela puts them squarely in Diego Gelmirez's camp. If you arrive at Urraca's court with them in tow, the whole marriage project takes on a Compostelan cast. I'm hoping they'll pause for a few days to look for you and we'll reach her court ahead of and independent from them. But that's not the only reason. I also want you out from under the eye of the king of Aragon.

He controls the pilgrimage road, almost all the way until we reach Urraca. As long as you travel with those two, you are easily tracked."

Her head was spinning, and she changed the subject. "You mentioned Clemence. Did you know about Count Baldwin's death?"

"Yes. I debated telling you but thought it would have sounded strange coming from me. Besides, I thought the pope would tell Katerinen." He sounded rueful.

"When did you learn of it?"

"At Toulouse. It wasn't common knowledge, but word got around."

Her fears were confirmed. Calixtus had suppressed the knowledge of Baldwin's death. But why?

Yusuf seemed to read her mind. "Gebirga, have you ever thought that maybe Calixtus doesn't have Katerinen's best interests at heart?"

"I have wondered." She decided to share her worries about the "accidents" that had threatened Katerinen while they were traveling with the pope. If he had been the perpetrator, he would know about them already, and if not, he might have some ideas about who had been responsible. "Strange things happened to Katerinen while we were with Calixtus. The encounter with the bull you know about already. The next day a building almost fell on her. And then when we were in Toulouse, we got in the way of a fight between two artisans that almost ended with her being bludgeoned by a hammer. I know King Alfonso was responsible for the attack in the Pyrenees, but I wonder about the other events. They seemed too coincidental."

"And you think Calixtus might have been involved?"

"I don't know." She felt tears spring to her eyes and put her hand to her face to conceal them.

"This is a lot for you to take in all at once, I know." A reassuring hand on her shoulder this time. "Here, try some of the food that Blanca brought us. You'll like this, but watch out for the pit in the middle. Don't eat it."

With the hand he removed from her shoulder, he reached to the platter and put something oval and firm and slightly damp into her fingers. She put it in her mouth and took a tentative bite. It was salty, sour, sweet, and bitter, all at the same time. She was not sure she liked it. "What's that?"

"It's an olive, the same fruit they get the oil from. These are cured and then marinated in oil and vinegar and herbs."

She took another bite. It could be an acquired taste. She reached out to the platter herself and took something else, a firm, leathery round. "And what is this?"

"It's a dried fig, a fruit. It's sweet; you'll like it."

She did not put it in her mouth, but returned to questioning Yusuf's own actions and motives. "What you say is all very well, Yusuf, but how do I know any of it is true? How do I know you are not a servant of the king of Aragon, and this is not part of his plot?"

"You don't; you can only trust me. And what choice do you have? I'm sorry. But the king is a man of war. I've seen enough war in my lifetime; I am a man of peace. A balance between all the powers in the peninsula, Muslim and Christian, is the best way to achieve that."

Yusuf was right. What choice did she have indeed? As long as she was heading towards Queen Urraca, maybe it did not matter in whose company she traveled.

"Very well, then, what's your plan? How do you expect to hide me from the eyes of Aragon's men? They seem to be everywhere."

"People see what they expect to see. They are looking for a woman traveling with a fat old canon and a thin young monk. They are not looking for a Jewish woman with a dog traveling among Jewish merchants engaged in trade along the pilgrimage route."

"A Jewish woman? You mean me? In disguise? With you?"

"Yes, and with my friends here, and a few others."

"Your friends … are they… you mean…your friends are Jews?"

"Gebirga, I would like you to meet Mosse Toledano, on your left, and Sason ben Raguel, here on my right across from you. This is Mosse's house, and it was his wife Blanca who brought us the food, including the fig you have in your fingers. They are merchants and traders."

Gebirga considered the piece of dried fruit she still held. It was a Jewish fig. This was a Jewish house. She remembered how Katerinen had teased her in Troyes about her reaction to the Jewish bankers Clemence had dealt with, and how she had been too afraid to go down the street where the Jews lived. And now she was inside a Jewish house, sharing their food and drink.

"I knew this wouldn't work," the one called Sason said to Yusuf, shifting uneasily on his cushions, "See how scared she looks. These Christian women from the north, they're terrified of us. We see it with the pilgrims all the time. And beginning with a kidnapping was hardly the best way to gain her trust."

"Don't worry, Sason. It will work," responded Yusuf.

"Why would they help me?" asked Gebirga, speaking of the two Jews as if they were not there.

"Let's just say that they owe me a small favor."

"It is more than just that," said Mosse, "She should know. Domna Gebirga, Yusuf has been a true friend to my family. I live in Sangüesa now, but ten years ago I lived with my family in Toledo. Every summer, the Muslims would ride north to Toledo to burn our fields and sack our communities; maybe they still do, I don't know."

"They still do," said Yusuf, "And sometimes we do it back to them."

"We were used to it, but one year, we faced a much stronger attack than usual." Mosse continued, "The Muslim governor of Granada attacked and utterly defeated the Christian army at the fortress of Ucles, just south of Toledo. This was in the time of the king, Urraca's father, and her brother was leading the Christian army. He perished with all but one of his counts, and that was when the king decided Urraca would inherit his kingdom. The Muslims claim they took three thousand Christian heads on that day. It was a disaster, but it was worse for us Jews when the remnants of the Christian army reached Toledo. They said the Jewish merchants cheated them on supplies. Mostly they wanted to hit someone weaker than themselves. They broke into the Jewish quarter and started beating everyone they could get their hands on. When we defended ourselves with sticks, they used their swords. They set fire to our homes, our synagogues, our shops, and our warehouses. We had the right to arm ourselves for protection, but we were no match for the knights. Yusuf persuaded the archbishop to send the militia out to protect us. If he had not, the whole community would have been destroyed. My family almost was. The fire in the silk warehouse spread to other buildings. It was dry in Toledo, as it always is in the summer during the season for war, and there was no way to put out the flames. I was out in the streets with a sword gash in my right arm and abdomen, and my father was old and sick. My mother and sister wouldn't leave him. Yusuf helped get them out of the burning building, and took my father to safety. And that is why I am going to help him get you past the eyes of the king of Aragon. We've helped each other often since then."

Gebirga considered his story. "Why are you in Sangüesa now?"

"The rest of my family are still in Toledo, but I decided to leave. I heard tales that the king of Aragon was encouraging Jews to settle along the pilgrimage road, so I married Blanca and we moved north. The old town of Sangüesa is huddled under the castle across the river; we're in the new part of the town here. I have a vineyard outside the town and a good business trading with my family back in Toledo and elsewhere."

"And if we get caught by the king as we travel to Queen Urraca?"

"Yusuf is a known servant of the archbishop; his punishment will be harsh. Even if we can convince the king we know nothing of his and your mission, we'll probably lose our right to live in this town and have to pay a crippling fine. You will most likely be expelled from the realm and have to return north."

"So you see Gebirga," broke in Yusuf, "We're doing this because we think it is important, because we think the chance it will preserve peace is worth the risk. We didn't kidnap you just for the pleasure of your company on the journey. Well, maybe I was motivated a little by the pleasure of your company."

Gebirga felt color rise to her cheeks at this last comment, and hoped he would not notice. She took a bite out of the fig in her hand. It was chewy and sweet. She was not sure she believed Yusuf yet, at least not completely, and it would be strange to travel among Jews. But it was not the strangest thing that had happened to her since she left home. She took another bite from the fig, chewed thoughtfully, and after she swallowed, she spoke. "Thank you Mosse ... and Sason. I am truly grateful that you are willing to help me. Yusuf, what is our plan? How are you going to disguise a woman from Flanders as a Jew?"

At her words of acquiescence, everyone in the room relaxed. Yusuf explained, "We won't have to do much. Mansilla, where the queen is now, trying to rescue Pedro de Lara, is a two and a half week journey from here. We'll travel with Sason and Mosse while they trade goods on the pilgrimage road. They are well-known in the towns we will go through. As I said, people see what they expect to see. Traveling with Jews, most people will assume we are Jews too. We'll wear the same clothing that the Jews in these parts wear. Most people won't look beyond that. We will also stay in the Jewish quarter of whatever town we find ourselves in, with friends of Mosse and Sason."

"But they'll surely know you and I are not Jewish. And won't we be putting them at risk?" She twisted her fingers in her lap. How was she going to cope with this masquerade?

"Yes, they will know, but they'll protect us for Mosse and Sason's sake. We'll have to follow their laws though, while we are with them, eating what they eat and so forth. And that reminds me. We need to leave first thing tomorrow. I want to get as far as we can away from Sangüesa before the Sabbath starts and we are unable to travel. We should be able to make it all the way to Estella. It has the biggest Jewish community on the road, and it is a good place for us to lose ourselves over the Sabbath." This was all a mystery to Gebirga. Laws? Eating? No travel on the sabbath?—but she was tired of asking questions.

She did not sleep much that night though. Every time Liisa turned over in her sleep, Gebirga woke, and worried about her friends. The next day, Blanca helped Gebirga dress. Her woolen dress was bundled away and Blanca helped her don a light long, flowing gown with tight sleeves, and a cloak of the same material. Too fine for wool and too soft for linen, Gebirga had to ask what it was.

"It is cotton, domna. We wear it in summer," Blanca answered, pinning a veil of the same stuff under Gebirga's chin and securing it with a filet on her crown. Her hair felt strange, unbound under the light cloth after so many years tied up in her coif.

The next day was hot, as they wound their way through the low hills west of Sangüesa. The guard at the gate did not pay much attention when they left the city, but all four were tense until the town was far behind them. They had four mules who took turns pulling the cart, two at a time. The cart was loaded high with goods, mostly woolen cloth and skins of olive oil, but also treasures like saffron, pepper, musk, and even some silks hidden at the very bottom. Traveling this way was slower than going by horse, and Gebirga chafed at the extra time it might take to reach the queen, and help for Katerinen. There were no Jewish communities between Sangüesa and Puente la Reina, so they spent the night camping in a field by a river, the men taking turns to guard against local bandits. Despite herself, Gebirga enjoyed sitting around the campfire, listening to Mosse and Sason sing nonsense songs in Hebrew. They tried to teach her to sing them too, but her tongue twisted around the unfamiliar sounds until they all laughed at the strange noises she was making.

The following day they reached Puente la Reina. Gebirga had a nervous moment as they wheeled their cart through the gate, but apart from making them pay a toll, the guard did not question them or their identity. The town had grown up around a bridge spanning the Arga river, built by a forgotten queen, and the Jews lived clustered behind a wall close to the main street. The hosts were cousins of Sason who had been warned he was bringing along some unusual guests. They were welcoming, eager to hear what news the travelers brought of the world beyond, and they passed along gossip of their own.

"Calixtus was in Toulouse you say? He's a sharp one; you've got to beware of him" said their host, and his wife nodded sagely. "But the big news here is that Alfonso of Aragon is on his way north. A man selling sheepskins came through with that story yesterday. He's supposed to be heading towards Soria, fortifying his western border. But my guess is Queen Urraca will think that is much too close to her for comfort. I expect she'll have to move east to face him. I hope you won't get caught in the middle."

This was bad news, and there were more immediate dangers to think about. "You'll be staying with some second cousins of mine in Estella," said the wife, "But do be careful. The Franks who have moved there recently from across the Pyrenees have been making trouble lately for our people, knocking over market stalls and so on. They think the Jews were given too many concessions by the king. They're worried there may be riots."

It was a short journey to Estella, and they arrived there long before the beginning of the Sabbath, which began late on the short summer night. Unlike their hosts in Puente la Reina, their new hosts, Natan and Jamila, seemed anxious about having Christian houseguests, though they were welcoming enough. Relations between the Jews and the Franks in Estella were tense, as they had been warned. "It's a brushfire waiting to happen," worried Natan, "We have always gotten along well with out neighbors, but there are some new arrivals from France who don't like sharing the town with us. 'Why should we go south to fight the Muslims when there are Jews in our midst?' they say, that sort of thing. The usual, but more serious this time. We'll have a good Shabbat here, the Lord willing, and then you can be on your way. But it might go ill for us if anyone outside our community learned we had Christian guests at our house."

Jamila was worried about the same thing. She took Gebirga back to the women's quarters to settle herself in and gave her a basin of water to wash off the dust of the day's journey, but she seemed uncomfortable having a Christian woman in her house. "I must tell you, Domna Gebirga, that tomorrow when the men go to the synagogue, the women all come here and we pray together. We meet in this room. We have the only house big enough to accommodate everyone. And it would look suspicious if I canceled it; we meet every week. I hope that won't disturb you."

It did disturb Gebirga. Jewish prayers? What might they be? But she said, "Oh, not at all."

"Well then, that's settled. Now, do you have everything you need? I mean, I'm not sure what a Christian woman would want."

"No thank you, everything is simply wonderful. You've been so kind, really." Gebirga found herself compensating with excessive politeness for the discomfort she herself felt.

"You'll have to excuse me. I must go back to the kitchen. I have many things to do before sundown to prepare for Shabbat. I have to do all the cooking since I gave our Christian servant the day off to get her out of the house while you are here. It seemed safest."

"May I help?" asked Gebirga suddenly, "I'm not that much use, since I can't see, but I can chop things if you give them to me. And I can wash dishes." It would be better than staying alone in this room feeling useless.

"Really? You wouldn't mind? It would be a great help." Jamila unbent a little.

"Not at all. And you can tell me about Shabbat," Gebirga said bravely.

That was the right thing to say. Jamila set Gebirga to chopping onions for a stew of lamb and white beans, Liisa quiet at her feet, and told her everything she could about Shabbat and how they celebrated it. Gebirga listened with curiosity. It seemed a little like Lent with its rules and Easter with its celebrations. And they did it every week.

"But if you are not supposed to cook after sundown, how will you cook this stew?"

"We share a bakehouse outside in the courtyard. I took my bread there this morning to be baked, and also a chicken for our dinner and a pastry filled with vegetables for tomorrow evening. In a little while I'll pick them up and you can come too. Then the fire will be extinguished, and I'll leave my stewpot to sit in the cooling oven. By tomorrow at lunchtime it will be done. All the women do that. The pots are marked with our initials, so we don't take the wrong one."

When all the ingredients for the stew were in the pot, Jamila broke an egg for each person who was going to share their meal, slipping each one gently onto the top of the stew. "Would you like to come with me, Gebirga? You can meet the other women; we all come at around the same time, and share news. I am going to tell them that you are a cousin from France. They'll know that is not true, but it is easier if they all have the same story, in case something goes wrong."

They set off, Jamila with the stewpot and Gebirga holding onto Liisa. They did not have far to go. There was already a cluster of women around the baker, exchanging their savory kettles for the newly baked bread. Jamila introduced Gebirga to them, but they were distracted.

"Did you hear?" said one, "Someone broke into the slaughterhouse last night. They spilled the large vat of blood all over the floor and defaced the walls with excrement." Horror greeted this news.

Jamila explained to Gebirga, "We keep the only slaughterhouse in town, and sell meat to Christians and Jews. Some of the newcomers in town don't like buying what they call Jew meat and have been agitating for it to be closed."

It was Jamila's turn at the front of the line. "Gebirga, can you count the breads? There should be twelve." Gebirga counted out a dozen large, round flatbreads as Jamila handed over her pot to the baker and retrieved her pastry and her chicken, whose fragrant scent filled the air. With calls of "See you tomorrow!" they left the knot of women and returned home.

Once home, Jamila lit the candles and said the prayers that officially began the Shabbat. They all had a cup of wine, before the men traipsed off to the small synagogue for prayers. Gebirga was surprised that Yusuf went with them, and that he was prepared to go with them again the following morning.

"There's only one God," he answered her question, "Does it matter where He is worshipped? And it is a way of showing gratitude to our hosts."

Gebirga thought about this as the women arrived for their own small service. If Yusuf could pray to God with the men at the synagogue, could she send a small petition for Katerinen's safety to her mother in the service with the women? It had been a long time since she had asked her mother for anything, but it made her feel better about being present for their prayers, even though she could not understand what they were saying. Jamila tried to explain what was going on under her breath, "Next we have a prayer for the safety of the community."

The women had barely begun when they heard a commotion coming from outside. "Pay no attention," said Jamila, "The door is bolted and we're safer in here."

But it grew louder and louder, and they could no longer concentrate on their devotions. They rushed to the windows at the front of the house and someone spotted a plume of smoke in the distance. "Fire!" said one.

"Not the synagogue!"

"No, it is further down, closer to the river. It must be the slaughterhouse."

The Jewish quarter in Estella was a narrow street that straggled up the hillside, widening at the top into the courtyard where Jamila and Natan's house and the bakeoven were located. The synagogue was nearby. A gate at the bottom protected by their own guards sealed off the quarter from the rest of the town. The slaughterhouse was outside the gate, close to the river for hygienic purposes.

"Let's go see!"

The women ran out of the house. The men were already out of the synagogue and down the street in front of them. As they opened the gate so they could go outside to try to put out the fire, they saw an angry mob surrounding the slaughterhouse. There was no way to put out the fire until they dealt with the mob.

Natan and the other leaders of the community took charge as the Jewish men flooded through the gate to face the angry citizens outside.

"What is the meaning of this? How dare you disturb our peace?"

"Get Richard!" people in the crowd shouted, "Let him show the Jews what he found."

Someone was pushed to the forefront of the mob. He stood in the no man's land between the Christians and the Jews with a crucifix raised aloft in his right hand.

"See this, Jews? With my very own eyes I saw one of you this morning down by the riverside throw this crucifix in the water. But instead of sinking and drifting away, as was no doubt his dastardly plan, the cross stood affixed in the river, right beside the slaughterhouse. The Jew tried to pull it and move it, but it wouldn't budge, and at the very moment he laid hands on it, the slaughterhouse burst into flames."

"It's a judgement," cried someone from the back of the crowd, "We are going to build a church on this very spot."

"Nonsense," said Natan, "Who was this mysterious Jew?"

The man called Richard scanned the crowd and then stopped and pointed a finger. "Him! It was him, I'd swear to it."

"Oh no," Jamila said to Gebirga who was standing beside her with the women, just inside the open gate, "He is pointing to Yusuf."

"See his ugly Jewish face?" said Richard, "He's the one who performed the sacrilege. Let's get him!"

Yusuf did not have to wait to be accused twice. He took to his heels immediately, leaping over stray carts and market stalls and disappearing into the town. About half the mob chased after them and their progress could be tracked by the noise they made running through the town. The rest turned on the Jews with cudgels, fists, and short daggers. The Jews responded in kind. Missing half their number, the attackers were no match for the Jews and the battle was over quickly. The Jews retreated behind their gate, and the Christians took their own wounded away to be patched up and bandaged. The slaughterhouse burned to the ground, and it was only luck that the fire did not spread to other buildings.

It was a glum party that finally sat down to Jamila's stew. Sason had lost a tooth and Natan had a gash over his right eyebrow from being hit with a staff. They were all worried about what might have happened to Yusuf.

"If only I hadn't asked that liar whom he had seen with the crucifix," lamented Natan, "That was inviting him to make a false accusation."

"But if half of them hadn't chased Yusuf, you might not have had enough men to put down the rest of the mob. And I'm sure we would have heard if they had caught him by now," said Jamila, speaking while trying to clean Natan's wound. "Sit still and it won't hurt, Natan!"

"Yusuf may not know Estella as well as he knows Toledo," said Mosse, "But he's a fast runner and as tricky as can be. I'm sure he's given them the slip, and we'll find him when we leave Estella in the morning."

Brave words, and maybe they were correct. But Gebirga was not reassured.

CHAPTER SEVENTEEN

The Pilgrimage Road

All the rivers that lie between Estella and Logroño are deadly for both men and beasts to drink, however their fish are good for eating.

"I can't say I thought much of those vespers," grumbled Oliver as he left the small church of San Adrian de Vadoluengo, "I think half of the monks were asleep."

"I've heard better," admitted Aimery, "Wait, where's Gebirga? The bench is empty. Has she gone inside?"

But when they stuck their heads inside the door of the guest-house, they found Gebirga was not there either.

"That's funny," said Oliver, "I wonder where she went. We can wait for her outside. I don't fancy spending more time than we have to in here."

So they sat on Gebirga's bench and discussed plans for their journey on the following day. Time passed and the shadows lengthened, but still Gebirga was nowhere to be found.

"I don't like this," said Aimery, "Where could she have gone? Do you think something has happened to her?"

They started calling for their friend, to no avail.

"Could she have left the monastery?" asked Oliver.

"Why would she do that?" But they found the monastic porter, who professed to know nothing, "Of course, I was at vespers with you at the time you say she vanished. The servant who guarded the gate for me then might have some news."

It took time to track this man down, but at least when found he had some information, "Why yes, she did leave the monastery. She heard barking and wanted to find out where it was coming from. She took the road to Sangüesa."

"And she never came back? And you didn't think that was suspicious?"

The man's attitude indicated that he was not paid to be suspicious. Aimery and Oliver begged a lantern, which was given rather grudgingly, and set out to search for their friend.

"She may have fallen and be lying somewhere, hurt."

They called and called until their voices were hoarse, but there was no reply except the cry of a night bird. It had not rained in weeks and it was impossible to tell anything from the road. There were tracks that might have been a cart, but there was no way to say when it had passed by. They walked until they reached the gate of Sangüesa, which was locked tight until morning.

"There is nothing more we can do tonight. We'll come back tomorrow and see if anyone has seen her. Things will look better in the morning."

But they did not. They spent the next three days fruitlessly looking for signs of Gebirga, their frustration mounting with every false lead.

"There's nothing else for it," said Aimery at the end of the third day as they relaxed in a wine shop, "We'll have to give up. In the morning, we'll sell Gebirga's horse and continue our journey. Maybe Queen Urraca can help us when we reach her. But if King Alfonso is still tracing our progress, I don't know what he is going to think when he discovers there are now two rather than three of us."

Oliver could tell that Aimery was in a bad mood as they left town. It made sense; they were both worried about Gebirga and feeling guilty that they had abandoned their search for her. "I'm sure the people we spoke to were hiding something," Aimery muttered, "How could she just disappear like that? Those monks at San Adrian surely knew more than they were telling." His mood translated into a growing suspicion of all the Spanish people they met, and it only became worse after they were cheated by an innkeeper their first night in Monreal. "A bed and a meal," Aimery grumbled as they left the next morning, "If you can call a wooden board shared with four others a bed, and a bowl of thin soup a meal." He only allowed Oliver to water their horses in certain streams for fear of poison, and told him dark tales of local men who tempt travelers to allow their horses drink, and then skin the animals when they drop dead. Oliver thought it best to humor him though he wondered how the people who lived here could survive if all their rivers were tainted.

Aimery seemed happier during their stay in Estella, which they reached late on Monday. The Jewish quarter was quiet, and the two travelers learned nothing about the disturbance two days before. They stayed in the French quarter and speaking his native tongue again to compatriots seemed to revive Aimery. He even found some people from his native Picardy. The French were excited about his project to write a guide for the road, and they plied him and Oliver with good food and wine. "Just think of all the people who will come through Estella after you write your guide. You must say good things about us so they will stop here."

After being assured by their hosts that the river running through town was clean, Aimery decided they could safely water their horses. Their hosts led them down to the river, where they saw a building destroyed by fire, with a crucifix proudly standing in the ruins. Their hosts told them of the wicked Jew with the crucifix and the building bursting into flames. "We're going to build a church here to commemorate the miracle," they said.

"But what will you do without a slaughterhouse?" asked Oliver practically.

"Not to worry, Richard wants to build one in the French quarter. The Jews will need to have their own from now on."

Two days later, in Logroño, Aimery and Oliver stayed again in the French quarter, but this time Oliver's parents were their surprised hosts. They fussed and fretted over their son, and the next morning, Aimery and Oliver left loaded down with food, as well as socks and new woolen underclothes for Oliver, which his mother pressed on him no matter how many times he told her he would not need them in heat of high summer.

Their next stop was Najera, and this stay proved bittersweet for Oliver. The monastery of Santa Maria where they found lodging had been given to Cluny in the last century so that the renowned Cluniac liturgy for the dead could be used to pray for the deceased kings and queens of Navarre who were buried here. The tiny kingdom of Navarre had been swallowed up by Castile and Aragon and few now cared for the long-dead monarchs except for the monks still dutifully commemorating the anniversary of each death with special prayers and masses. It was strange for Oliver to find himself among all the old familiar customs, rituals, and prayers from Cluny, and yet still be an outsider. He had always thought he would return to Cluny after his mission with Aimery was complete, and he had longed for that day. But in Najera, he found himself looking back at his life as if from a distance, and for the first time he was not sure he wanted to return. But what else could he do?

Oliver was still distracted by this question the following evening. They were staying at a hospice and church founded by one of Aimery's heroes, a man named Domingo who had dedicated his life to keeping open the road to Compostela and helping pilgrims. Aimery had met Domingo once before he died a decade or so ago now, and he was hoping they could collect some tales of the man and his deeds to prove his sainthood. Oliver was transcribing anecdotes about Domingo and stories of miracles but he kept losing focus as he considered his own future.

". . . And when the German family returned from Compostela, they found that their son was still alive on the gibbet he'd been hanged from. He'd been supported by St. James the whole time. Or some say it was our own Domingo holding him. Boy, you're not listening to me!" The old peasant woman who was recounting the story stamped her cane on the ground to get his attention.

"Yes I am, yes I am," he said hurriedly, "German family, gibbet, still alive, I've got it all."

"Very well, so then the family went to the city official who had ordered their son be hanged to tell him of the miracle. He was eating dinner and he scoffed at them and said their son could no more still be alive than the two chickens he was eating could stand up and start crowing. And I'll be blessed if those chickens, roasted and all, did not leap up from the platter, with all their feathers and innards and everything, and start crowing, thus proving the miracle," she finished, triumphant.

Oliver, who had been transcribing everything diligently to make up for his earlier inattention stopped and looked up from his wax tablet, "The chickens came back to life? That's impossible, old woman."

"It most certainly is possible, and I can prove it." She led him to the door of the church Domingo had built. "See? Those are the very chickens themselves. We keep them in the church in memory of the miracle. They're fed with alms from pilgrims."

Oliver looked where she pointed and, sure enough, there were two chickens, contentedly rooting around in a coop inside the church.

"Yes, those are chickens all right," he had to admit.

"See? I told you," the woman gloated.

Oliver was no nearer to solving the problem of his future when they reached Burgos four days later. Their final two days took them through a wilderness barely marked with a road. Relieved to have finally arrived, they made straight for the hospice of Saint John after a longer than usual interrogation by the guards at the gate who wanted to check every bag they brought in. But Aimery and Oliver had not even reached the door to the hospice when they were stopped again by armed guards.

"Aimery Picaud and Oliver d'Asquins?" they were asked.

"Why yes," said Aimery, surprised.

"You'll have to come with us." The guards surrounded the two and escorted them through the streets of the town and out through another gate. They led Aimery and Oliver across a bridge and away from the city, and Aimery asked, alarmed, "Who are you? Where are you taking us?"

"You'll know soon enough," was the only answer he received.

As they rode west on the south side of the riverbank, a large fortress rose ahead of them. Realization dawned on Aimery, and he said under his breath to Oliver, "That's the royal palace up ahead. That must be where they are taking us."

Their journey had been so uneventful since Sangüesa, they had almost forgotten that King Alfonso was tracking them. Now it was clear his men had been marking them their whole journey, lazily knowing they could be reeled in at any time. And this was the time.

Aimery's suspicions proved correct, and they rode into the courtyard of the palace. Burgos had changed hands several times in the contest between Urraca and King Alfonso over the region, but the burghers preferred Alfonso. The city had been firmly in his hands for the last few years, and he kept his residence at the palace. Aimery and Oliver were told to dismount and follow one of the guards. They had the presence of mind to grab their belongings before their horses were taken away. Then they were taken up a flight of twisting stairs to a small room behind a locked door. The room was not empty, however. Sitting on a chair was Count Bertran de Risnel, the man who had captured them back at Santa Cruz.

"We meet again," he said, "Our plan had been to allow you to travel to Queen Urraca, but when you so carelessly lost your traveling companion, the blind woman, it seemed safest to have you travel with us. We expect to catch up with Queen Urraca in a couple of days in any case."

"We?" asked Aimery.

"The king of Aragon and his army. The king is here in the palace and his army is camped south of the town. You won't meet him tonight, alas, but there is somebody else here who is eager to see you again. You can come in now, Domna," Bertran called to someone in the next room to enter.

"Aimery! Oliver! It is so good to see you. I am tired, tired, tired of traveling and it has been so boring. But now you're here, everything is going to be better. Where's Gebirga? I'm longing to see her."

It was Katerinen.

Gebirga spent a bad night in Estella after Yusuf disappeared, chased by the mob. Her hosts tried to reassure her, but she was still worried. The experience of being targeted by the mob drew Gebirga closer to her hosts, and to Mosse and Sason. The latter two told her that she could travel with them, even if Yusuf could not be found. "We'll be going at least as far as Leon, and I'm sure we'll meet the queen before then." In bed that night, Gebirga debated with herself whether to go with the Jews, or whether she should wait in Estella in the hopes of meeting up with Aimery and Oliver, assuming they were behind and not ahead of her on the road. She finally decided to continue with Mosse and Sason, to get help for Katerinen as soon as possible.

They left early on Sunday, wanting to avoid the Christians who would go to church later in the morning. They were silent as they passed the horror of the burnt slaughterhouse which stank of charred wood and flesh. When they reached the town gate, it had only just opened, and after they were safely through, Sason said to Gebirga, "You'll see. The moment we are out of sight of the town, Yusuf will pop up out of nowhere."

But it took a long time and several miles journey before they were hailed by a voice, "Can a poor traveler get a ride to Los Arcos with this mule cart?"

"Yusuf, you made it!" called Mosse, the relief in his voice suggesting that he had not been as confident of his friend's safety as he had pretended to Gebirga.

The mood of the travelers, increasingly subdued the further they went from Estella, rebounded. They questioned Yusuf about how he had made his escape from the mob.

"It was a close thing for a moment, but they weren't expecting me to swim the river twice. Luckily, it was a hot day. Once I gave them the slip, I decided I should get as far from town as I could, so I walked long into the night. I'm exhausted now, of course."

"Never mind," said Sason, "We don't have far to go today."

The next stages of their journey were pleasant, since the mountains of the Rioja funneled light breezes through the wide valley, and most of their way led gently downhill. Gebirga could smell the fertile fields of ripening vines and wheat on both sides of the road. The next towns on the road—Los Arcos, Logroño, Najera, Grañon, and Belorado—all had Jewish communities, and they stayed in these with a confusing array of cousins, in-laws, and business associates of Mosse and Sason. Fortunately, these communities had more peaceful relations with the Christians they lived among than Estella, at least for the moment, but everyone listened with horrified curiosity to news of the mob and the burning of the slaughterhouse. Between travel, meals, and conversations, Mosse and Sason traded with both Christian and Jewish merchants, and the mound of goods in the cart slowly diminished as they replaced bulky wool and oil with smaller, more precious objects. They banked some of their money with a moneychanger they trusted in Logroño so they would not have to carry it all with them.

Between Belorado and Burgos, the way grew more difficult as villages and cultivated fields gave way to a landscape of difficult hills and scrubby wasteland thick with oak and pine. Their hopes to spend a night at Villafranca before tacking the worst of it were dashed when they were refused admittance to the town.

"No Jews here. You'll have to press on. Try Burgos."

"But Burgos is two days ride from here. Can't we spend the night? Our Sabbath begins this evening, and we are not allowed to travel."

"Jews not welcome here. And don't try camping outside the walls either." The guard at the gate slammed the door on them and refused to speak to them any more.

"I don't like this," said Sason, "We've had troubles here before, but never as bad as this. The hills ahead of us are not safe. They're full of thieves and the road is unclear in many places. And I hate the idea of spending Shabbat out in this wilderness."

"Never mind," said Yusuf, "Although the sun is low in the sky we still have plenty of daylight ahead of us. We should find some place to camp before long. Come on, I'm eager to shake the dust of this unfriendly town from my feet."

The road ascended steeply once they left Villafranca. As they wended their way through scrubby bluffs and twisting woodlands, they found that the sun was hidden by the steep hills and thistle-filled gullies they traveled through. The light dimmed further as the sun set, and they were chilled to hear the distant calls of wolves answered by packs that seemed frighteningly close. The mules grew skittish hearing these howls and, "No camping here tonight," said Mosse, sounding anxious.

Worse, after a time the Jews, who knew the way best, realized that they had lost the path. After anxious consultations with each other, they announced their worries to Yusuf and Gebirga. "This wilderness is almost trackless and we must have veered onto a sheep run or goat path without knowing it," they said, "But we should keep pressing forward. Maybe we'll find a shepherd's hut or even a house. I don't like to travel on Shabbat but we are permitted to when it is a matter of safety." A house full of thieves, Gebirga worried, but kept her thoughts to herself.

The first stars were just peaking out in the sky when Mosse announced that he saw a small light in the distance. They proceeded cautiously towards it, waiting to see if it belonged to a friend or foe.

"It is only one old man with a small fire," Yusuf said, relieved.

"Be careful. Sometimes they use one person as a decoy so they can ambush travelers."

But no one burst out of the dusk to surprise them when they approached the old man. Though the days were hot, it cooled off quickly at night, and once they got nearer, Gebirga had the sensation that she was feeling warmer, as if from the man's fire, though it could hardly have cast its heat to where she was sitting on her mule.

"Greetings, pilgrims," the old man called out.

"I am afraid we are not pilgrims, old man, just simple travelers who have lost our way. Can you help us?" asked Sason.

"At least one of you is a pilgrim." the old man said, "My dear girl, I am overjoyed to see you have made it this far, despite your many reverses and distractions."

Gebirga was startled. That voice—it sounded like the strange old man from Bruges and Cluny. And from the attack in the Pyrenees too, though surely she had dreamed that part of her horrible adventure. "Wait, I think I know this man," she told her companions.

"But in answer to your question, good sir," the old man continued, not acknowledging Gebirga's response, "Yes, I can help you. There is a refuge up ahead that was built by my friend Juan. He welcomes visitors who brave these inhospitable mountains, and he will be delighted to give you a bed for a night. Or two. It will be simple lodgings, but safe. I ask one favor from you in return. My old bones are weary of walking. May I ride in the back of your cart until we get there?"

This seemed like a fair exchange. At the old man's suggestion, they lit torches from his small fire before they extinguished it carefully. He leapt onto the cart with surprising agility for one so old, and started giving them directions. After a few hundred yards, they rejoined the old road, which was well marked. "I can't understand how we lost the path," said Mosse, "And to think we were traveling so close to it all the time."

"Just continue in this direction," said the old man, "It isn't far ahead. And I'm going to have a small nap on this cart until we get there."

Happy to be close to the end of their journey, they went as quickly as their tired mules would allow. Before long, the path met a clearing where two small stone buildings with wooden roofs stood around a well. One had smoke coming from its chimney.

"Do you think this is it?" asked Mosse.

"Probably," said Yusuf, "Let's see who is here."

They dismounted and a big yellow dog ran out and barked at them. He seemed friendly though, not like the wild dogs many villages used to keep away intruders. He and Liisa found each other, and soon the two were involved in an intricate and happy game of chase-me-chase-you-roll-over. A man came out from the building with the chimney.

"Alfonso! Alfonso! You are supposed to welcome our guests, not fight with their dogs." The dog ran obediently back to his master, as Gebirga took hold of Liisa. "He's still just a puppy, though he looks so big," said the man, "I named him after the king and sometimes, like the king, he thinks he is in charge of the whole world. But welcome, welcome, all of you. I was feeling sad that I was going to have to eat my dinner alone tonight. I am Father Juan, and I take care of this hospice. All pilgrims are welcome here."

There was an awkward silence that Mosse broke. "Father, we aren't pilgrims. We're Jews, at least the two of us are," he gestured to Sason. "We tried to stay at Villafranca but they wouldn't let us. Because we are Jews."

"Jews eh? No room at the inn in Villafranca? Well, you are welcome here. Bring your mules and cart through this door. After that you can come inside for some soup, and we'll see about finding you places to bed down for the night."

There was more, but Mosse hated to ask the generous priest. Yusuf knew what he was thinking though, and made the request himself. "Father, it is the sabbath for my friends here and they are not supposed to travel tomorrow. Would it be possible for us to stay two nights?"

"The sabbath? Yes, yes of course, not a problem," said the priest, already opening the door to the shed where the cart and the mules were to stay. "Stay as long as you like."

As the cart was wheeled in, it was Sason who noticed something strange. "Where's the old man? We left him sleeping here on the back of the cart, and now he's gone."

"Could he have fallen off?" asked Gebirga, worried.

"Not possible. The back was up, and I checked the latch myself. He's vanished without a trace."

"Old man?" asked Father Juan.

"We were lost, Father," Gebirga explained, "We came across an old man, a pilgrim and he told us how to get to you. He knew you; he said you were named Juan and he called you his friend. He asked to ride on our cart." She decided to tell no one that she thought she had met him before. Now that he had vanished before she could question him, she had no way to be certain it was the same man.

"Perhaps it was Saint James himself, guiding lost pilgrims to my door. That is just the kind of thing he does. You must give the apostle a hug from me when you get to Compostela." If the two Jews were doubtful that a Christian saint would come to their aid, and if Gebirga thought it unlikely that her journey would take her to the shrine, none of them wanted to contradict this man who had been so kind.

When their gear was safely stowed and the mules had been given water and fodder, the priest turned his attention to his human guests. Once again, he proved sensitive. "You'll be able to eat this, you know," he said to the two Jews as he brewed the soup. "Nothing in here is prohibited. It is just garlic and bread and water and salt with a nice egg cooked on top. I eat no meat myself. It is part of a vow I took." Humble though the ingredients sounded, the priest had performed some alchemy putting them all together. Gebirga thought she had eaten nothing more delicious even at the king of Aragon's table. When they had finished eating, Yusuf tried to get some information from the priest about the situation in Burgos, their next stop, thinking the priest would learn much from pilgrims passing through. But Juan proved to be utterly unworldly in that respect. "I don't pay attention to kings and queens and lords and ladies, unless they want to build me a bridge or help clear a road," he apologized.

The following day of enforced rest was a welcome break from their hectic travels. Gebirga was moved by the priest's gentle piety and hospitality to be the sole congregant at the mass he celebrated in the tiny church, while Mosse and Sason performed their own devotions in the main dwelling. After the mass was over, Gebirga remained for a long time alone in the chapel, allowing herself to pray for Katerinen's safety and a happy ending to their journey, willing herself to sense a response to her prayers. When she came out at last, the priest approached her.

"Domna Gebirga, might you bring this flagon to your young man, Yusuf? It is full of the beer I make myself. He kindly offered to help me with tasks that are beyond my old age and I set him to chopping wood, but the day is hot and I am sure he would welcome refreshment."

She agreed, resolutely refusing to ponder the implications of "your young man," and accepted a wooden beaker filled with yeasty-smelling liquid. The sounds of chopping wood had interrupted her prayers while she was in the chapel. A command to Liisa to "Find Yusuf!" led her to where he, wood now all split and waiting the winter's fires, was working on a small bridge over a creek that bounded Father Juan's compound.

"Gebirga, you're a welcome sight," he greeted her. "Is that a drink you have for me?"

"Father asked me to bring it to you," she said, handing him the wooden cup, suddenly shy. He smelled like hard work in the hot sun.

"He's a good man, for a priest." He drained fully half of it in one long draught and said, "Come sit on the bridge and keep me company while I finish this. I have been replacing the stones washed out by winter rains that support the wooden top of this bridge. I am due for a break."

They sat side by side at the end of the bridge and Gebirga let Liisa off her lead so she could investigate interesting smells at the river's edge. Yusuf took a drink from time to time, but neither spoke. The only sounds were the trickle of the river, shrunken after the long summer, and occasional chatter from birds when Liisa disturbed their rest. After a while Yusuf said, "It is rare to find someone with whom silence feels so comfortable."

Gebirga had been thinking the same thing. In her world, men and women had little to do with one another, unless they were married. And look how that could turn out. She had no precedent for the quiet companionship she and Yusuf enjoyed. She made no reply, but she did smile. Yusuf spoke again. "I have a house, a villa south of Toledo with olive trees and vineyards and land extending as far as the horizon. It is closed up now, but I have always wanted to open it up and live there again. Gebirga, once you and I have rescued Katerinen and seen her safely married, I want you to come back there with me and live with me there and help me rebuild what has been lost. I can see you there, beside me."

And Gebirga could see it too. She imagined herself feeding the chickens and supervising the servants, and sitting before the hearth with Yusuf, drinking wine from their very own grapes, peaceful and safe, running away from all of her cares, and free from worry about the doings of kings and counts. The thought filled her with guilt. She put her hand on the purse that hung by her side. Through its thin leather she could feel the parchment of the letter that Clemence had entrusted to her care, the sign of the vow she had sworn to protect Katerinen and stay with her always. She struggled with her conscience. Maybe Clemence only meant for her to swear she would always remain in Spain. Maybe it would not matter if she were with Katerinen all the time as long as she were close. No. Her face flooded with shame. How could she have for one moment dreamed of finding Katerinen only to abandon her again?

She stood. "It's not possible, Yusuf. I'm sorry." And she summoned Liisa and walked quickly away before he could tempt her further.

The rest of their stay with Father Juan, Gebirga avoided Yusuf, but he made no move to speak to her again as he had done on the bridge. They set off the next morning for Burgos, fond farewells from the priest in their ears, not knowing what they might find ahead. Sason knew the town well; he had grown up there and his sisters lived within its Jewish quarter. His father had been a wealthy banker before being cheated in a bad debt contracted by a lord too powerful for the Jew to challenge. He had died a broken man, and it had been up to his many children to try to restore the family fortunes. They were still working on it.

The Jews lived in their own walled quarter with their own guards protecting its single gate, and it was there that the travelers hastened the moment they reached the city. It was the largest town Gebirga had been in this side of the Pyrenees and the noise of its crowded streets disoriented her. She was relieved to enter the courtyard of the house of Sason's sister and her husband, and this made her laugh to herself to think how recently it had been that she was afraid to be in a Jewish house.

Their hosts had bad news for them.

"If you are trying to avoid King Alfonso, you've leapt right into the frying pan by coming here. His army is south of the city, and he is at his palace on the other side of the river. Whatever his other plans, I am sure he plans to enter the city to collect our taxes."

"We'll try to be gone before that happens," said Yusuf, "Do you have any knowledge of the whereabouts of Queen Urraca? The last thing we heard, she was besieging Mansilla, trying to rescue Pedro de Lara."

"Yes," said Sason's brother-in-law, "I heard that she abandoned the siege about a week ago, the moment she heard King Alfonso had left Soria and was on his way north west, and is heading this way with her army. Most of the towns on the road between here and there are held by nobles loyal to King Alfonso, like Count Bertran de Risnel, but the territory on either side of it is held by the Lara family. Count Pedro was captured because some of her nobles feared the pair of them were getting too cozy with King Alfonso. I think she hopes a show of force against Alfonso will be as good as a siege for ensuring the release of her lover."

Gebirga finally asked a question that had been bothering her. "How is it possible for a queen to take a lover like that, without being married to him?" She thought back to Clemence. There was no chance she would have been permitted to be anything other than a chaste widow and mother of Count Baldwin.

But things seemed to be different in Spain. Her listeners all reacted with confusion that she should even ask such a question. Yusuf tried to explain. "It is more of a political union, Gebirga, than a love match. The Laras are among the most powerful lords in Castile, the region where we are now, and allied to them, she keeps some control over it. They even have two children together, a boy and a girl. Pedro de Lara has been seeking formal recognition of his status, and some believe he is seeking support from Alfonso of Aragon. Partisans of her son and people who fear Alfonso of Aragon, see this relationship as a threat, and have captured the count."

It still sounded very strange. Pedro de Lara seeking help from Urraca's husband? But the only important thing was how it would affect Katerinen, and this was the next question she asked.

Yusuf said, "I expect this show of force between the two monarchs is nothing more than spear rattling, a show of enmity to convince the nobles that their truce is just that: a truce, and not an alliance. For that to be convincing, however, each side will have to make some public, mostly nominal, concessions. I hope one of the concessions Urraca can get is the release of Katerinen."

CHAPTER EIGHTEEN

Queen Urraca's Court

Once past the woods of Oca, towards Burgos, the land of the Spanish continues with Castile and Campos. This is a land full of pastures and gold and silver; rejoicing in fodder and very strong horses; well-provided with bread, wine, meat, fish, milk, and honey. Nevertheless, it is devoid of wood and full of wicked and vicious people.

A t Burgos, Yusuf and Gebirga changed their mules for horses so they could travel faster. The news they had learned the previous night of the movements of the royal armies pressed them to reach Queen Urraca as soon as they could.

"Sorry, Liisa," said Gebirga, "You'll have to walk faster. And no more riding in a cart when you get tired."

Gebirga wore her own coif and dress under the Jewish cloak and veil, which she stripped off once Mosse and Sason, who had accompanied them out of town to give them protective cover, turned back. If she was going to meet the queen today, she wanted to look like herself, so she sweated in her wool dress under the hot sun. She was shy traveling alone with Yusuf, and wondered if he would speak again of marriage. But Yusuf was strictly businesslike as they made their way across the sun-warmed plain, and if she was disappointed, she did not admit it. He made sure she was safe in the women's guest quarters at the monastery of San Baudillo, where they spent their first night, and then he was off.

When they set off the next day, they could tell they were getting closer to the queen's army. They passed carts laden with provisions brought by eager farmers and traders, hoping to garner a profit from the hungry knights in their midst. They asked one man with a donkey bearing a load almost the size of the animal, how far away the queen was.

"Not far. They tell me she is mustering south of Fromista, near the village of Tamara. You see the break in the low hills up ahead? Follow the southern mesa, and you can't miss the army camp."

They followed the trail of supplies when it left the main road and headed southwest through farm country. The day was hot and the screech of insects drowned out conversation, but Gebirga was too tense to want to chat in any case. By mid-afternoon, Yusuf finally announced they had arrived. Gebirga could hear the noises of an army setting up camp, a scene of controlled chaos. The clang of hammers pounding on tent pegs rang out on all sides.

"Good. Where's the queen?" asked Gebirga, eager to complete her mission.

"Queen Urraca has situated herself brilliantly here," he said, admiration in his voice. "The town of Tamara is on a low hill just to the north of the mesa we've been following all day. She can post sentries who will warn her long in advance of King Alfonso's arrival. Her troops can easily climb the top of the mesa and take up a strategic position before his army reaches the plain. Meanwhile, she will stay safely within the walls of the village with a perfect view of everything from the top of the hill."

"Yes, but where will she be now?"

"Unless I miss my guess, she will have commandeered the small church perched on the top of the hill for her headquarters. But slow down. I must talk to the archbishop of Toledo first. He will be in one of these tents somewhere here on the flat."

The archbishop? Gebirga was dismayed. She had thought of trying to find Diego Gelmirez, if he was here, so she could give him Clemence's letter, and she wanted to speak to the queen as soon as possible. Surely it would be better if she came to Urraca as an independent agent, not under the aegis of the archbishop of Toledo. But she could hardly strike off on her own. She doubted that an anonymous Flemish woman could march into a walled town and demand an audience with the queen, so she followed Yusuf.

Challenged by a sentry, Yusuf identified himself and was directed to the archbishop's camp. "Go past where you see the men digging latrines and keep riding. Archbishop Bernard and the king are at the far west end of the camp, closest to the town gates."

The king? Gebirga was confused. "It's Urraca's son, Alfonso of Galicia," Yusuf explained, "He is king in Toledo and Galicia. I didn't expect him to be here. I imagine he's not happy about it. Since he entered his teens, he has tried to separate himself from his mother and exert his independent rule. But he depends on my master, who remains loyal to Urraca."

So Alfonso was estranged from his mother, Gebirga thought. Another complication for the betrothal. She was excited by the prospect of meeting Katerinen's betrothed. When Yusuf told her they had arrived, she dismounted. Grooms took their horses, and they were directed to enter the tent. Gebirga entered through the door flap behind Yusuf, Liisa at her side. The tent was hot and close, and it seemed full of men. Someone was speaking in a petulant voice.

"I don't see why we're here. I don't want to make any kind of truce with Alfonso of Aragon; I want to fight him. He's no friend to me, whatever his relationship with my slut of a mother, and I know I can beat him." Something was thrown to the ground with a loud crash.

Goodness, was this Alfonso of Galicia? She could make excuses for youth and royalty, and she would not say that Katerinen was all sweet unselfishness, but Gebirga wondered what a marriage between two such headstrong and self-centered people might be like.

"You'll have the rest of your life to fight, your majesty. Right now it is worth helping your mother preserve her kingdom so you will continue to have something to fight for," said an older and wiser voice, with a trace of a French accent. Gebirga thought that must be the archbishop and her suspicions were confirmed when he hailed Yusuf, who introduced her to the aging prelate. She kneeled down and kissed the ringed hand he offered, then he said to the young king, "I have some tedious business to discuss now, your majesty. Why don't you return to your own tent and make sure that everything is being set up to your liking? And take these men of yours with you."

The king and his followers filed out of the tent, and with them gone, there was finally room to breathe. "Now we can talk frankly," said the archbishop, "Yusuf, tell me your news."

It did not take Yusuf long to fill the archbishop in on Alfonso of Aragon's involvement in the events of the past few weeks—the capture of Katerinen, the use of Gebirga as a decoy, and their secret journey across Spain. Also significant was that he obviously did not need to tell the archbishop about the betrothal between Katerinen and the young Alfonso. Gebirga was glad to hear Yusuf make a powerful case to Bernard for helping free Katerinen in terms that would most appeal to the archbishop. Yusuf suggested that if the archbishop married Katerinen to Alfonso, then Calixtus would favor him over Diego Gelmirez, and he would not make Diego Gelmirez archbishop. The archbishop sounded almost persuaded. But he had a surprise of his own.

"You say that Katerinen of Flanders is in the custody of the sisters of Santa Cruz? I am afraid that is no longer true, even if it once was. I have it on good authority that she has been removed from the care of the sisters, and that she is now with the king of Aragon outside of Burgos. The king knows that if you are going to play a piece in a game, you need to have it close at hand."

Gebirga was stunned. Katerinen at Burgos? Why, they must have ridden right by her. How awful to think they had been so close without knowing. And the archbishop's next question was unpleasant in a different way. He turned to Gebirga and asked, "Can you show me the dispensation Pope Calixtus gave for the marriage, my dear?"

Gebirga had feared this moment ever since Toulouse. "My lord, Calixtus did not send the dispensation with us. He feared it would give our purpose away if we were captured and it were found with us. As it happens, that was a wise decision." She hoped she sounded convincing, but the archbishop's reply was perceptibly cool.

"That is a very great pity. And if Diego Gelmirez ever received a betrothal charter, he has not shared it with us. It is going to be difficult to get the queen to take this case seriously without these documents."

Gebirga thought of the letter concealed in her purse. Surely it spoke of the betrothal and maybe even the dispensation. True, it was destined for the bishop of Compostela, not the archbishop of Toledo, but did that matter now? It was the archbishop on whom Katerinen's safety seemed to rest now, and that was the only important thing. "My lord, I have a letter from the girl's mother that I believe will explain everything." She took it from her purse and unfolded it before handing it over.

The archbishop scanned it quickly. "There is no mention of a betrothal in here. She doesn't even speak of her daughter."

"That's not possible," said Gebirga.

"But I am afraid it is so. Let me translate what the Latin says, and you will see: "Clemence, countess of Flanders, sends greetings with love to the bishop of Compostela. I rejoice with you if you enjoy prosperity, and I send condolences if you suffer adversity, for the apostle says, 'Rejoice with the rejoicing but weep with the weeping.' Beloved lord, I give so many thanks to you for so kindly and mercifully raising the children of my brother, Raymond. I beseech your goodness that you write and tell me whatever is happening to them now." That's all. You see, domna Gebirga, there is nothing in here except pious good wishes from Clemence to her nephew Alfonso and his sister, Sancha. Commendable, but useless for our purposes. No matter. We will do our best."

Gebirga was speechless. That letter contained nothing; a loose-lipped messenger could have broadcasted it at every tavern between here and Flanders with no harm done. Why had Clemence asked her to carry it in such secrecy? Was it a decoy, something to throw people off the trail if she had been captured and the letter found? Or had it been intended to make herself feel important and to bind her closer to Katerinen and her mission, as if Clemence had not trusted either Gebirga's oath or feelings for Katerinen. She had a sick feeling both explanations were true.

The archbishop was busy concocting a plan. Eventually he spoke. "We must consult with the queen. She should be in her headquarters in the village."

They abandoned the dust and mud of the army camp and entered the gate to ascend the hill that housed the town. The queen, as Yusuf had predicted, had taken the town's church for her headquarters, but a lingering scent of incense was the only thing that suggested its usual purpose to Gebirga. If the archbishop's tent had been a masculine environment, the queen had made over her borrowed space in a manner wholly feminine, but equally crowded and just as overpowering in its own way. The floor was softly carpeted, and over the sound of chattering voices, Gebirga could hear the soft thrum of an oud. Where the archbishop's tent had smelled of male sweat, leather, and metal, the queen's domain was a bewildering mixture of rose and musk over the incense. When the archbishop entered, with Yusuf and Gebirga and his followers, all attention turned to them.

"My lord archbishop, how good of you to come see us. I recognize your servant Yusuf, who has helped us on so many occasions. But who is this blind woman with the very large dog making dirty footprints on my carpets?"

Gebirga did not wait for the archbishop to speak for her. "My lady, I am Gebirga of Gistel and I am in the service of Clemence of Flanders and her daughter Katerinen, who is a captive of the king of Aragon as we speak."

"Clemence of Flanders, ah yes, my late husband's dear sister. Who communicates so often with everyone in my kingdom except me. One might have thought that if she wished to contract a marriage between our children, she would have had the grace to consult me about it, instead of relying on her brother the pope, and Bishop Diego. A mother likes to see to the marriage of her own children. But I hear Clemence is sadly bereft, now that her beloved son has died, leaving her without influence or friends in Flanders. So sad to see a formerly strong woman brought to such a pass."

This was terrible, worse than Gebirga could have imagined. Urraca sounded completely unfriendly to Clemence and her plans for their children. How could Clemence have been so foolish as to ignore this woman in her machinations for Katerinen? But Gebirga fought back. "I know the countess will be grateful for your kind sympathy, your majesty. She is also fortunate in having the support of her brother, Pope Calixtus. He keeps her well-being, and that of her last remaining child, close to his own heart."

The queen got the message. "Yes, it is always a good thing to have the favor of a pope."

Gebirga pressed her advantage, "Katerinen of Flanders was on her way to see you and to bring you her mother and uncle's warmest regards when she was waylaid by the king of Aragon. Now that the king is so close, I hope Katerinen will be able to make the rest of the journey to your side. The lady Clemence, and her brother, would be relieved to hear of Katerinen in the company of such a friend as yourself."

"We shall do what we can to bring her to our side, and we will love her as our own daughter. And we will keep you by our side until she reaches us. Mumadona," the queen said to one of her female attendants, "Take Domna Gebirga and find her a place in your quarters. Find her something more suitable to wear than that travel-stained rag, before you return, and get rid of that queer headdress she is wearing. She must be terribly hot."

The two women left the church, followed by Yusuf and the archbishop. Before the women left the men, Yusuf hissed in Gebirga's ear, "You were wonderful in there. She likes people who can stand up to her; few try. And reminding her that Calixtus's friendship is worth having was the perfect strategy."

Gebirga was pleased with herself too. Though she had not received any indication that Urraca would support Katerinen's marriage to her son, that possibility had not been ruled out. And she had achieved her main goal, a promise from the queen that might soon reunite her and Katerinen.

The king of Aragon's army rumbled into the vale of Tamara the next day and set up a camp at the far end of the valley, two good bow shots from the queen's encampment. Oliver was glad to be traveling with Aimery and Katerinen, because he felt out of place among the many Aragonese lords, knights, churchmen, servants, followers, and hangers on who accompanied the king to this meeting with his estranged wife. Of course, he realized, if it were not for these two, he probably would not even be traveling with the Aragonese army, a prisoner, albeit chained with a silken cord. It did not help Oliver's feelings of unease that the reason for the meeting of the two monarchs was not entirely clear. Was it a battle they had been invited to, or a fond reunion, or something in between?

Oliver was also experiencing for the first time the full force of Katerinen's extravagant personality, untempered by the wisdom and good sense of Gebirga. That first night back at the palace outside Burgos had been horrible once Katerinen realized that Gebirga was not with them and even worse when she discovered they had no idea where Gebirga was. She wept and beat her fists against Aimery's substantial chest when he tried to calm her. Count Bertran had wished them the joy of their reunion with a thin-lipped smile. "We have found her quite a handful and we are glad to pass her back to the good offices of her priest," he mocked them, as he left the room, and Katerinen descended into hysterics.

"Please stop, please stop, Katerinen. We'll see Gebirga soon, I promise." Oliver kept repeating in vain. What on earth had Gebirga said to get her to stop when she was like this? They found the women's quarters in the palace and gratefully left her with a servant who promised to get her to sleep, while they went to see if they could find food from the palace kitchens.

The next day they were roused early and set off with the king to join his army, to meet Queen Urraca. Katerinen was full of a strange kind of excitement and elation, rather than the weeping of the night before. Oliver's relief at this mood shift turned to consternation, however, when they were riding through the open plain at the center of the army. Katerinen challenged him to a race and then set off at top speed before he could stop her. There was nothing he could do but race off after her to try to catch her, and he could hardly blame what felt like half the king's army for chasing after him. He only wished they had not been so strenuous in knocking him to the ground. He had to ride bound, and on a leading rein for the rest of the day, but at least Katerinen had been taken off her horse and put in a cart with some of the women. He felt sorry for the women, but he was angry with the king and his men. Surely they had seen enough of Katerinen to know she was capable of a stunt like that? Why had they not kept a better watch on her from the beginning? As for himself, he still cared very much about Katerinen's welfare, but the experience of being her co-guardian with Aimery was doing wonders to cure the last remnants of his calf-love.

Although they reached their destination by the following morning, it took the rest of the day for the king's camp to be set up with a magnificence suitable for receiving envoys from the queen, so it was not until the next day that negotiations could begin. The two chief envoys were Count Bertran de Risnel, their old friend, acting for the king, and Count Diego Lopez de Haro, for the queen. This boded well for a peaceful solution: since Bertran held lands in the queen's domain and Count Diego likewise held territory in the region claimed by the king, they each had an interest in avoiding conflict between their masters. It also pleased those in the queen's camp who feared her relationship with Count Pedro de Lara, since Count Diego was no friend of his.

It took a day of travel to and fro between the camps, a day of courteous public flattery, ceremonial welcomes and hand washings, meals of delicacies accompanied by light entertainment, not to mention hours of back-room hard-boiled horsetrading, but finally news of a settlement filtered through both camps. There was to be no battle. The king and queen would each withdraw from the field and return to the heart of their respective realms. The king promised to respect the rights of her vassals in his kingdom, and the queen promised to give up more territory on the salient the king and his followers held on the pilgrimage road. This last provision was going to benefit Bertran de Risnel at the expense of the Lara family, and thus might convince Pedro de Lara's enemies to free him, as he had suffered enough. The armies were to line up against each other the next day in ceremonial fashion; there would be a few symbolic bowshots, the horns of truce would blow, and the peace agreement would go into force. Everyone was satisfied, but still anxious. Until the last moment, anything could still go wrong.

Count Bertran took it upon himself to fill Aimery and Oliver in on the terms that were of greatest interest to them, "Your friend, Katerinen of Flanders will be allowed to pass over to the queen tomorrow. I am sure the queen will be as delighted by her little ways as I have been. And, at a discreet interval, the two of you may continue your travels also." This sounded better than they could have hoped.

To Gebirga waiting anxiously the next morning for the treaty to be signed and Katerinen to arrive, it took an age for the two armies to array themselves on either side of the field. Each noble wanted to face his equal in the opposing ranks, and to be as close to his own monarch as possible, so they jockeyed for position and precedence before they all found their places. They were dressed for display rather than battle, from the king and queen, and their lords, down to the Muslim mercenaries who served both sides as archers. Gebirga was rescued from her position among the queen's ladies by Yusuf. "Let's see if we can find Katerinen," he said, and they found a place to stand not far from the queen's archers, Liisa obedient at their feet.

The armies preened and postured as they waited for something to happen, tense until the treaty was signed. The noise they made surrounded and disoriented Gebirga—horses snorting, eager to be moving, mock fighting among the squires, the trumpeters who were to announce the truce warming up their instruments, and the boom of the war drums that accompanied the Muslim archers. "Yusuf," she turned to her companion, "Do you see Katerinen anywhere? Can you tell where she might be?"

"She is probably somewhere over towards the center of the field, not far from the king. I see a group of women on horseback, and some priests. She might be with them."

"Can you tell which one is she?" Gebirga asked, anxious worry in her voice.

"It's too far. Except—maybe that one in the blue dress? I think that is her. She is on horseback and she is talking to two clerics on foot. And, wait, I think they are Aimery and Oliver. Yes, it is, I'm sure of it."

"Where?"

"Over there, on the far side of the king of Aragon's archers, between them and the royal party." He took Gebirga's hand in his own and pointed it across the field in the direction of the girl.

Gebirga tried to wait patiently. The noise around her shifted its rhythm, an order growing out of the cacophony.

Yusuf said, "It won't be long now. The king has arrived. He's all in gold. There will be a mock battle first, probably two knights from either side engaging in some sword play on horseback. No, wait, it looks like it is going to be an archery display. There are targets in the middle of the field. After that is over, horns on both sides will call for a truce, the agreement will be signed and we can all celebrate."

But Gebirga still looked apprehensive. "Don't worry Gebirga," he said, clasping her hands in both of his to reassure her, "Katerinen is with Aimery and Oliver. They will take good care of her."

But over on the Aragonese side of the field, Aimery and Oliver found taking care of Katerinen easier said than done. Perhaps it had been a mistake to tell her ahead of time that the truce meant she would pass to the custody of Queen Urraca. Half-forgotten worries of husbands and marriages were resurfacing in her mind and she was skittish and nervous.

"When will they start, when will they start?"

The reply, "Not long now," began to ring hollow after the fifth time.

"Why do I have to wait? Why can't I go over to the queen right now? It isn't far; I see her over there with her ladies and I could ride right over."

Oliver, remembering her wild dash of two days ago put a protective hand on her bridle while Aimery answered, "You can't, Katerinen. I told you. There is a whole ceremony and protocol that we have to wait for."

Oliver was scanning the queen's ranks when he spotted something odd. "Look, by the archers, that dog. Doesn't it look like Liisa?" Realization dawned quickly. "It is Liisa. Because that's Gebirga behind her. And I see Yusuf too."

"Where? Where is Gebirga? Tell me, Oliver!"

"Over there," he said, taking his hand off Katerinen's bridle to point.

She did not hesitate.

Yusuf saw her first. "Wait! What is she doing? Is she mad?"

"What?" cried Gebirga, knowing.

"It is Katerinen. In the blue dress, I am sure of it. She is riding through the middle of the field."

"Gebirga! Gebirga! It is me, your Trintje! I'm coming." They heard the thin cry across the empty field. At that moment, the Muslim archers on both sides let loose their arrows and even Gebirga knew what had happened as she heard them whine through the sky.

"No!" shouted Gebirga, and moved convulsively forward, to rescue her beloved. Yusuf caught her in his arms and held her with all his strength as she struggled to get free. "No! You can't help her. It is too late."

It was too late. Yusuf saw one arrow and then another find the fast-moving girl in the blue dress as she rode across the line of archers to the other side of the field, an easy target. She fell off her horse and cartwheeled to the ground like a songbird shot by a reckless hunter. The horns blew for the truce, but not soon enough for Katerinen.

CHAPTER NINETEEN

Aftermath

*Once you have seen the burial ceremonies properly completed
for your dead friend, and after you have spent the night in
prayer in the usual way, you may begin your return. You
should meet up with your friends in the city of Leon.*

Somewhere very far away people were happy. War had been averted, peace was preserved and there was music and acrobats and feasting, and contests of strength, and fighting with bulls. And all this had happened without anyone getting hurt, except one young woman whom no one knew anyway. But for Katerinen's friends, this joy was as distant as Jerusalem, as they waited for news of her state. The news came quickly, and it was not good.

"I'm sorry," said the queen's Jewish doctor, summoned as soon as the young girl fell, "There is nothing I can do. She was dead even before I arrived. You see the arrow piercing her neck here? It severed a vessel and she died very quickly."

Gebirga insisted on going with the doctor and his assistants when they took Katerinen back to their tent to prepare her body for burial. Aimery went along to see if he could be of any comfort, but there was no room for Yusuf and Oliver. First they removed the barb of the vicious arrow, then they washed her body thoroughly. They wrapped her in a winding sheet, starting from her feet, interleaving sprigs of hyssop and boxwood between the bands of linen. Aimery described each stage to Gebirga. "Stop!" she said to the doctor's assistants, and before they could cover Katerinen's face with the linen shroud, Gebirga traced her features with her hand, running her fingers over the lids of the blue eyes she had never seen, now shut forever, and stroking her hair one last time.

"Domna, where will your friend be buried? asked the doctor, "There is a cemetery here, in the village."

"No, not here!" she said instinctively.

Aimery said, "Gebirga, not far away, in Fromista, there is a Cluniac monastery dedicated to Saint Martin. It has a beautiful new church, just the kind that Katerinen so loved on her travels. And I am sure her mother would appreciate Katerinen being laid to rest in a Cluniac house."

Dear God, Katerinen's mother. However was Gebirga going to explain to Clemence what had happened? Clemence would never forgive her. But what did that matter when she could scarcely forgive herself?

"Fromista. Very well," she said dully, "But I want to leave right away. Can we take her now?" Gebirga could not bear the thought of enduring the hoopla outside the tent.

The doctor assured them that it would be possible. Aimery could collect the others and find a coffin—these had already been prepared in case the encounter between the two monarchs was a battle rather than a celebration—and could commandeer a cart to carry it to Fromista. "The sooner you bury her the better," said the doctor, "In this summer heat."

Aimery finally arrived back with the others and they departed, not missed by the happy revellers around them. As they rode on the long, dusty road to Fromista beside the slow moving cart with its precious burden, Gebirga asked for the first time the question that would torment her in the next days as she tried to make sense of what had occurred.

"Why did it happen? Why did Katerinen have to die?"

"It was my fault," blurted out Oliver, uttering the thought that plagued him since Katerinen dashed across the field.

"No, Oliver, how can it be? I am sure you didn't do anything wrong," said Gebirga.

"But I did," he said, miserable. "I told her you were across the field. I even pointed you out to her. If I had not done that . . ."

Aimery intervened. "Oliver, I was there and I saw what happened.

Katerinen would have dashed across that field whether you had spoken or kept silent. You remember how agitated she was? You mustn't blame yourself. Gebirga, it was an accident, a horrible accident. She did not have to die, but she did. I suppose we could call it God's will," he finished, trying to comfort her and sounding like he did not think much of God.

"No, I don't believe that. She wasn't there because of an accident and we weren't separated because of an accident. If we hadn't been separated none of this would have happened," said Gebirga.

"In that case," said Aimery, considering, "You could blame Alfonso of Aragon and Count Bertran of Risnel. They separated you and Katerinen in the first place. And we know that Alfonso played us like chess pieces until you managed to get away—you'll have to tell me how you did that, and where you found Yusuf again, by the way. Furthermore, they placed us where we were standing, and made sure Katerinen had a horse while we did not. Everyone could see how reckless she was; it would not have taken much imagination to suspect she would cause some disturbance or another."

"And Alfonso had no desire for Katerinen to marry Urraca's son," Gebirga sighed, and as Oliver and Aimery made noises of surprise, she realized what she had given away. Oh well, it did not matter now. "You might as well know. Katerinen and I weren't on pilgrimage; she was betrothed to Alfonso of Galicia, and I was bringing her here to be married."

Aimery and Oliver were silent, and Gebirga's thoughts wandered in a different direction. "The arrows. Had they started flying before Katerinen began to ride? Or did they only begin after she moved into the field? And which side started shooting first?" They could see what she was asking: Did Katerinen wander into a field of death by chance, or was her movement into the field itself the signal for the arrows to rain down. And if so, a signal for whose side, the king's or the queen's?

Yusuf answered. "That's a very good question. And I don't know the answer. But I didn't notice any other signal for the archers to begin." Aimery and Oliver confirmed that they were uncertain if Katerinen rode off before or after the archers began their display. "I suspect the former," said Aimery, "Because foolish though the dear girl could be, she would hardly have ridden off into a hail of arrows."

Trying to piece together the events that had led up to that horrible day reminded Gebirga of how she had been interrogated over and over in the days following her mother's death. She feared that, like then, she would have no rest until she could come to an understanding of what had happened. Only this time, she would be the one asking questions.

It was late afternoon before they reached the adobe huts and narrow alleys of Fromista, and entered the gate of the monastery, whose monks made no demur at burying the niece of the pope in their precincts. "We will place the body before the altar of the Virgin, and we can begin our prayers at once. We will keep vigil all night, singing psalms, then perform the burial mass in the morning." said the abbot, leading them to the guest quarters. Though she rebelled at his reference to Katerinen as 'the body,' she was grateful for the way he took charge. Shock was settling in. After a generous meal in the guest refectory, of which she could only eat a few bites, she spent the evening in the cool and calm of the monastery church, listening to the monks pray for Katerinen and breathing in their potent incense. The familiar psalms and chant took her back to the cold autumn last year at Cluny, to her days with Katerinen learning Spanish and exploring the town. Gebirga wondered what she would do now her reason for being in Spain was gone. She still did not weep for Katerinen. That would have to come later.

She did not weep the next morning either, when they buried Katerinen in the churchyard, though as the clods of earth were tossed on the coffin, Gebirga felt as if she herself was being buried, and was almost surprised to find herself still walking around in the sunshine after the pit was once again filled.

The queen's party caught up to them at Fromista shortly after the service was concluded, and Gebirga was content to be reabsorbed into the chattering circle of noblewomen who formed the queen's attendants. These murmured condolences to her—"How awful, your good friend," "So sad, such a terrible accident on such a happy day"—but soon settled back into their own concerns.

Only one woman showed real empathy. This was the Infanta Sancha Raimundez, Queen Urraca's unmarried daughter. She was close to Gebirga's own age, almost a decade older than her willful younger brother, whom she loved greatly and bossed every chance she could. "I had a dear friend who died a few years ago. We were inseparable, and when she was gone, I was beside myself. Come with us at least as far as Leon. You shouldn't be alone right now, and then you can think about what you want to do next."

It was Sancha who found Gebirga a scribe to write a letter to Clemence for her. She did not want to use Aimery or Oliver for this task. It was as hard to compose the letter as she had feared. How to begin? "My lady, I regret to inform you . . ." "My lady, your daughter is dead." Gebirga knew Clemence's grief at her daughter's death would be tempered by frustration and anger that her daughter had once again failed her, had once again, by her impetuosity, upset the plans carefully made for her. She wanted to protect Katerinen from this last display of maternal disappointment. One way was to tell Clemence that, through no fault of Katerinen's, the marriage had been impossible from the beginning. But Gebirga could not tell Clemence anything about the diplomatic machinations and intrigue that had led to Katerinen's death on a plain in Castile, machinations she herself still poorly understood, because she knew her letter would be read a dozen times between here and its destination. And although Aimery blamed the king of Aragon for Katerinen's death, Gebirga was not yet comfortable with the role Urraca might have played. She needed to rely on one of Urraca's messengers to carry the missive, and anything she wrote would be scrutinized before it even left the castle. So she decided to be vague about the cause of Katerinen's death, to speak of it as the accident everyone wanted to believe it was.

Gebirga remembered Clemence's descriptions of Katerinen's troubled childhood. Katerinen had been difficult from the moment she was born. Never did she sleep and smile like other children. Sadness became rage. Happiness was expressed in a dizzying euphoria of dancing and laughing at the top of her lungs until she tripped over something or made herself sick, and then the rage would begin again. She had no peace as a child; would the demands of being a wife and mother have brought her peace? Gebirga thought not. Now she was with God. Surely that was better. But had there been another option between marriage and death for Katerinen? Could they have lived out their days at Santa Cruz? Too late now.

After the letter was sealed and the scribe left, Yusuf came to her, full of anger, though not at her.

"Gebirga, I have to leave. I'm sorry; it's the archbishop's orders. He wants me to travel with him south as far as Palencia. But this is the last time, I swear. You're going to Leon with the queen?"

"Yes, I suppose so."

"Good, then I'll meet you there. And Gebirga…?"

"What?"

"Never mind. It is probably too soon. I'll see you in Leon. Wait for me."

She was glad to have him go, and she avoided Aimery and Oliver on the journey west to Leon. Though she had needed them in the first awful moments after Katerinen's death, now their presence felt like a reproach; they were alive when she was dead. Also, after Oliver's revelation that he had told Katerinen where she was on the other side of the field, she found herself blaming Oliver as he blamed himself, though she knew in her heart it was not his fault. Aimery and Oliver still hoped to join up with Diego Gelmirez, notably absent from the bishops attending Queen Urraca. Word was he was still trying to find a way to get to Rheims by October to present his case for being made archbishop to the pope. But with the king of Aragon still refusing him passage, and the queen suspicious of his treachery, Diego Gelmirez's prospects did not look good.

Traveling with the queen and her entourage across country was slow, like their travels with the pope had been. The way was level and straight, which made the journey easier, but it was dusty and hot. Sancha Ramundez kept close to her, and it was good to have the woman's companionship, although they talked little as they rode. Gebirga was surprised to discover that Bertran de Risnel had not left with the king, but was coming with the queen's party. "He holds the town of Carrion, our next stop, and other places on the pilgrimage road," Sancha explained, "He's here more often than he is in Aragon."

Carrion. Gebirga had known Count Bertran held land somewhere on the pilgrimage road; she just had not remembered where. But she had heard of Carrion before, and it had not been in connection with the count. She struggled to recall what the connection was.

Her memory was jogged when she heard the voice of the man who welcomed the royal party to stay in the monastery of San Zoilo at Carrion. She sought out Aimery. "I know that man, I'm sure of it. Do you recognize him, Aimery?"

"You do know him. That is Bernard, the prior. San Zoilo is a Cluniac house, and Prior Bernard was at Cluny while you and I were there, last winter. He stayed until after Pope Gelasius died, then left in a hurry. I was sorry; I thought I had almost convinced him to support my book. He and Count Bertran are welcoming us to stay. They seem to get along well."

Bernard of Carrion. Of course. He was the man who stood in as proxy for the betrothal of Katerinen to Alfonso. And when Calixtus became pope, he left as fast as he could to inform his master, Diego Gelmirez. And also to inform Count Bertran of Risnel? Was that why the count was so conveniently available to capture them at Santa Cruz? It seemed likely. Gebirga wanted to confront Bernard, but found the prior elusive and suspected he was avoiding her. When she missed nabbing him after vespers, she realized she would not know what to say, even if she could speak to him. Whatever he had done or said to affect Katerinen, he was only a pawn of more important people.

They were under the sheltering arm of Cluny again two nights later at Sahagun, another Cluniac monastery. She gained renewed appreciation for the powers of Cluny and its ability to extend its reach and influence far from its mother house in Burgundy, the same form of life replicating itself at each stop on the pilgrimage road. At Sahagun she went with Sancha to the tomb of the queen's father. Sancha knelt and prayed at the tomb for a long time and Gebirga knelt beside her in courtesy, though her mind felt dead and no prayers came.

Mansilla, where Count Pedro de Lara still languished, was the queen's objective. As they approached the castle and the small village at its feet, however, Sancha asked her if she would like to make a detour. "I have to go to San Miguel de Escalada. It's not far; we can spend the night and be back the next day. And mother is going to be preoccupied here for a while." Gebirga agreed, so they crossed the river and rode along its northern bank, with some of Sancha's servants.

"What is San Miguel de Escalada?" Gebirga asked, trying to make conversation.

"It is one of my monasteries," said Sancha, "It isn't the richest, but it is one of the prettiest. But they're terrible managers there. I have to visit with my steward from time to time to make sure they haven't reduced themselves to water and nettle soup."

"What do you mean, one of your monasteries? How many do you have?"

"About a dozen, but that only counts the large ones. Many of them have dependent daughter houses and such. It is part of an inheritance handed down to all the women of my family. They're ours; we govern them."

"And what happens when you marry," Gebirga asked, curious.

"Oh! We don't marry," Sancha laughed as if the very idea was absurd. "Why would we marry? If my mother married me to some-one, I would be that man's hostage and my mother would be in his power. Look what happened to mother when she married the king of Aragon—constant warfare. She only married my father because grandfather had no sons. Her aunts never married and neither did their aunts. We live in the monasteries we control, and travel with the court, and we pray for the good of our family and for the king-dom. Of course, we've been able to amass quite a bit more property than my great-great aunts ever held."

This was a novel approach to the notion of the proper role for a well-born daughter. She wondered what Clemence would have made of it.

They reached Escalada and Sancha quickly transacted her business with the abbot. They spent the night, and before they fell asleep, Gebirga asked another question. "Sancha, my friend Katerinen, and her death . . . I feel we stumbled into politics we barely understood, and Katerinen paid the price."

Sancha answered the question concealed in Gebirga's words.

"If you want someone to blame, I would look no further than the archbishop of Toledo," she said decisively.

The Archbishop? Yusuf's patron? "But why?" she asked.

"I know he has supported my mother all these years and I know she trusts him, but look how he keeps my brother under his control, trapped like a fly in his web. He has his fingers in every pie, Gebirga, and messengers to do his bidding all over Europe. And I would be careful of that Yusuf of yours too. Where is he now? Back with the archbishop, I'll wager, getting his next set of orders."

This did not make much logical sense and it did not fit with what she had learned about the relationship between Count Bertran and Bernard of Carrion, but it triggered Gebirga's worst fears of Yusuf, as if the other woman had read her mind. She had much to think about.

Returning to Mansilla, they arrived to find that the custodians of the castle had agreed to free Count Pedro. What shocked Gebirga was the news that Queen Urraca and Count Pedro had agreed to betroth their young bastard daughter, barely seven years old, to Count Bertran of Risnel. She remembered Yusuf telling her that Count Pedro had been imprisoned because people thought he was too friendly with the king of Aragon. Gebirga had thought it unlikely that Queen Urraca's lover would be seeking support from her estranged husband, but this was confirmed now that Pedro and Urraca's daughter would marry a cousin of the king.

But, "Things aren't always what they seem," said Sancha. "King Alfonso may find it harder to hold onto his cousin's loyalty now he has this close alliance with my mother's house. I think mother has made a brilliant move, and no doubt this was always part of the count's plan."

Maybe, but if this alliance had been Count Bertran's intention all along, what had been the purpose of his intervention in Katerinen's life and their journey? Had he been working for two sides all along? Had his capture of Katerinen been as much to the queen's benefit as to the king's?

Gebirga was surprised the next day, when they rode into the town of Leon, to be joined by Count Bertran himself. "You're moving up in the world," he said, "Once a king's prisoner and now a queen's honored guest."

"You are too," she answered, "Once a king's lackey, and now a queen's prospective son-in-law. I do hope this bride will live to see her wedding day."

"You blame me for the lady Katerinen's death, I know," he said, "But you're wrong. If anyone is to blame, it is Queen Urraca herself."

"What do you mean?"

"Your story that you and the girl were on a simple pilgrimage was easily recognized for the fiction that it was. It was obvious that Katerinen was intended as a bride for the young Alfonso."

"Especially obvious to an ally and friend of Prior Bernard of Carrion," she interjected crisply.

"Indeed, especially to an ally of Bernard," he acknowledged her suspicions freely. "But don't blame Bernard too harshly. I am an old friend so it was natural for him to tell me how he passed his time at Cluny when he returned to Carrion. His news meant only that I could make it to Santa Cruz in time to find you. And who knows? Maybe it went better for you that it was I who captured you. Who do you think persuaded the king to let you escape so easily during the hunt? As for Queen Urraca, the last thing she wants is for her son to marry during her lifetime. A queen of his own and an heir would further weaken her own position. She was negotiating with Alfonso of Aragon for custody of Katerinen not to free her for a marriage, but to have her under her own control. I do not know if Urraca had a hand in the unfortunate timing of the archery display; I wouldn't put it past her. But whether she did or not, there are many ways for a young girl alone and far from her family to die, and I assure you Urraca would have found one of them before long."

It was sickly plausible, just like all the other theories that had been advanced since Katerinen's death. Fortunately, having planted this new seed of doubt in her mind, Count Bertran did not wait for a response, and rode on ahead.

Their lodging at Leon was in another of Sancha's monasteries. "This is the most important of them all," Sancha told her. "It is a royal palace as well as a monastery, and it is also the place where most of my ancestors are buried. My aunts are here, and so are my mothers' aunts, and their aunts. And the kings, their brothers, too, of course," she added almost as an afterthought.

She took Gebirga to the church to admire the two most important reliquaries there, each one holding the bones of one of the monastery's patron saints. "This one holds the bones of Saint Isidore and has figures in silver all over it."

Gebirga traced figures of Adam and Eve eating the apple, done in raised silver gilt. They reminded her of her own casket, now long gone. "I used to have one like this, only smaller," she told Sancha, "But it was lost on my journey. I left it at the monastery of San Adrian in Sangüesa and I suppose I'll never see it again. The monks there were not very friendly, and I doubt they will give it back to me if I ask on my return."

"About your return," said Sancha, "You don't have to leave you know. You could stay here with me, or even become a nun. If you got your casket back, it could be your dowry."

Gebirga was touched by Sancha's offer but she did not know what to make of it. Stay in Spain? That had been her intention when Katerinen was alive, but now she was dead, should she not return home? On the other hand, what home did she have? Clemence would not be glad to see her, and Aude at Gistel would be even less welcoming. Could she find Trude and Winnoc somewhere in the wilds of Germany? Her head hurt. "I can't think about this right now," said Gebirga, "But you are kind to offer."

She left the church to take Liisa for a walk through the narrow streets of the small town, mulling over Sancha's invitation, when she bumped into Aimery hurrying in the opposite direction. She was still avoiding Aimery and Oliver, knowing their company would remind her too much of Katerinen, but she could not escape a conversation now.

"I am glad I ran into you, Gebirga," he said, "Oliver and I set out later today. Diego Gelmirez is not far from here, and we want to catch up with him as soon as possible. I have a bundle I need to give you, though. If I don't see you back at the monastery, I will send a messenger to put it in your room. But what I most want to say is this. I know you have agreed to stay with Urraca's court for a time. I think that is the right thing to do. But I want you to know that

Oliver and I won't be in Compostela forever. We will surely return to France by this very road before long, and if you want to travel back with us, you would be welcome."

Moved by his offer, she embraced the canon and bade him a safe journey. A return to Flanders would be easier to contemplate if she could do it in the company of friends. She did not think to ask what was in the bundle he wanted to give her until he had gone. She would know soon enough.

She had been given a tiny unused cell of her own in the part of the monastery abutting the town walls to sleep in. Normally sleeping alone would be a strange experience. But she was glad to have a place to go where she could get away from the chatter of Urraca's women, and even the sympathetic Sancha for a while. She retired there after returning from her walk, and begged a servant to bring her bread and cheese so she would not have to join everyone in the hall for supper. She wanted time alone to meditate on her future and on all the divergent views she had heard about who was responsible for Katerinen's death. When the servant returned, bearing also a small flask of wine, Liisa followed him out again, hopeful that he would lead her to the kitchen where she might find a bone to gnaw on or some scraps.

Gebirga sat on the hard bed and ate quickly, savouring the crusty bread and the sharp nutty tang of the sheep's milk cheese. She had just poured some wine into an earthenware cup when she heard a knock at her cell door. Who could that be? Aimery, perhaps, with the bundle he promised. She opened the door.

"Gebirga. They told me I'd find you here. I just arrived. May I come in?"

It was Yusuf, travel-worn and smelling of sweat and horses.

"Please," she said, a little shy. He sat beside her on the bed, which was the only place to sit in the small room. She offered him her cup of wine and he drank it down in one draught. The second cup, he sipped more slowly.

"I would offer you food but I'm afraid I've eaten it all."

"Never mind. I'm not hungry. I have something for you. Aimery asked me to bring it. I passed him and Oliver on my way in. They were just leaving."

He handed her a shapeless cloth bundle, which she unwrapped. She recognized her second best cloak, the dress she had worn in Loarre, and protected deep under both, her casket. She traced the raised figures and letters with her finger. "Thank you."

"It was left behind at San Adrian when you were so violently abducted. Aimery brought it with him, hoping to find you again. There is something else too."

He moved the contents of the bundle to the floor, and put a metal object in her hand, a brooch. She clasped it tightly, barely noticing when the pin pierced her palm. It was Katerinen's. "It must have fallen off when the doctor was attending her," he said, "He found it later and gave it to me. I knew you'd want it."

Katerinen had been buried with all her meagre belongings. This was the only remnant of her now above ground. Gebirga held it tighter and tighter, willing the pain in her fist to make the pain in her heart less acute. Finally, the tears that had waited for so long started, first silently running down her cheeks, and then in ever more convulsive sobs. She was too far gone in her grief to be surprised when Yusuf took her in his arms. He became a focus for all her sadness and anger; she pounded her fists against his back, railing against him in lieu of untouchable fate. He kissed her, roughly, and she responded, just as roughly. His mouth tasted like wine. The floodgates were open.

Deliberately, he stripped her, then took off his own clothes. Their love-making was fierce and rough on both sides, as much a battle as a union, but that was what she wanted, and Yusuf gave as good as he got. Gebirga was a virgin and the physical pain when he entered her balanced the misery she felt inside. "What am I doing?" she thought quickly at one point, before falling, careless, back into the whirl of sensation he was summoning from within her.

By the time they finished, she had stopped crying. He took her in his arms as they lay on the small, hard bed, and held her close. With her face buried in his chest, he stroked her hair as gently as she once stroked Katerinen's to calm her after a tantrum, as gentle now as before he had been rough. And then suddenly he fell asleep, deep and steady breathing rending the silence of the room. She lay there in wonder, sticky and damp with sweat. And then she too slept.

She woke once in the night and was startled to find a man's arm encircling her waist. Then she remembered. They had shifted in the night; they were both on their sides, her back pressed against his chest. He was still deep in sleep. She experimentally tried to move away from him; in sleep his grip tightened and he pulled her close again. Astonished at what had happened, she was not ready to think of its consequences. Once again, she drifted back into sleep.

CHAPTER TWENTY

Pilgrimage

*All languages, peoples, and nations go to him in troops and battalions,
discharging their vows to the Lord with thanksgiving, and bearing
tributes of praise. Whoever sees these choirs of pilgrims keeping vigil
at the venerable altar of Saint James, marvels with great joy.*

She was the first to wake in the morning. Their bodies had
separated in the night, and he was lying on his back, snoring
gently. She lay there questioning what had happened the previous
evening, what she had done. All of a sudden she felt shy and
claustrophobic in the small room. Surely there was something she
should be doing, somewhere she could go. Maybe she could slip
away before he wakened. She swung her legs down to the floor and
sat on the bed.

Her movement woke Yusuf, who reached out a hand to touch
her. He drew her back under the covers and made love to her again,
as slow this morning as they had been fast the previous night. This
time when they were finished he did not fall asleep. He turned on
his side towards her, kissed her hand, and said, "Marry me."

"What?!"

"You heard me. I said, marry me."

"That's ridiculous. I can't marry you."

"Why not?"

She felt panicked. "I'm too old to marry. And I have no dowry,
beyond my casket."

"Irrelevant. You know I don't care about any of that."

"I can't marry you because . . . because I'm blind." That was the
truth; no one wanted to marry a blind woman. Whatever Yusuf

said, she knew that. Oh, she had been groped in the corners by young neighbors a few times during the celebrations for Christmas or the harvest back in Gistel. But no one had ever really wanted her, and good thing too. None of the local couples were a good advertisement for the joys of marriage. Liisa had been good at scaring them away when they grew too forceful in their attentions. Despite herself, she smiled at the memory of Liisa taking a bite out of one pimply-faced boy's bottom. Wait, where was Liisa? She should have been protecting Gebirga last night against this—

"You're smiling," he said.

"No I'm not!"

"Gebirga, I don't care if you're blind. Look, I have to leave this morning, right away in fact. I have one more message to deliver for the archbishop but after that I have told him I no longer want to be in his service. When I have delivered this message, I will come back here and find you. I told you, I want to go back to Toledo, back to my family's property and put it into cultivation again. And I want you to come with me. I only came back yesterday to tell you, to ask you to wait for me. I wasn't planning for what happened between us last night, but I can't regret it. We're good together. In every way. You know that."

"But you said it wasn't safe around Toledo," she said weakly.

"It is getting better. Now that Alfonso of Galicia is there, whatever you think of him, the region is coming more under control. I want to be part of that. With you."

Whatever response Gebirga might have made was cut off by a knock at the door. A servant opened it and stood in the jamb. "Domna Gebirga, your dog has been lying outside here all night." He sniggered a little when he saw that domna Gebirga was not alone, but recovered to deliver the real part of his message. "The queen asks that you attend her immediately. She is in the palace hall." He turned and left.

Gebirga groped around on the floor feeling for where her shift and gown had fallen the previous night. She left her hair loose under a simple embroidered circlet; there was no time to arrange it, and many ladies wore their hair uncovered at court.

"Gebirga. . ."

"You heard him. I must go to the queen."

"Promise that you will wait for me."

She was not sure why his words made her so sad. "I can't promise anything, Yusuf. I'm no good to anyone right now," she said as she pulled her boots on over her hose. She left the cell, retrieving Liisa to help her find her way to the queen, and they winded through stone passageways and twisted up a narrow staircase.

The queen was sitting in the low barrel-vaulted hall, surrounded by her ladies and her daughter. "Domna Gebirga, awake at last," she said.

"Your majesty," Gebirga made a deep curtsey, bowing her head to hide her blushes.

"I wanted to learn something of your plans for the future. Our Sancha has told us that she has invited you to stay."

Why was everyone pestering her about her future? What did it matter to anyone but herself what she did? Why could she not be left alone to think, just for a short time, without someone wanting a decision? Gebirga wanted to say all of this, or rather, to shout it, but instead she replied, "I don't know, your majesty. I haven't decided what I am going to do."

The queen made a noise of disgust at this equivocation. No doubt there had never been a time in her life when she did not know exactly what she would do at every moment.

"I know what your problem is," the queen said. "You're still mourning that girl, probably wondering whom to blame. I can tell you whose fault it was the girl died, for what good it will do you now. You need look no further than Diego Gelmirez, my situationally loyal bishop of Compostela. Ah, I see you look surprised. I don't know why. If he hadn't stuck his fingers in this ill-fated attempt to marry off my son without my consent or knowledge, your Katerinen would still be doing her sewing in front of a fire in Flanders. Foolish man, since a bride would draw my son as much away from Bishop Gelmirez as from me." The queen suggested even darker plots. She lowered her voice, more for effect than to prevent anyone from hearing her next words. "It would not surprise us if he had some double agenda. Make the marriage to please Pope Calixtus, and then see to it that it never took place to preserve his own position. I don't know whose signal the archers obeyed to fire, but I can guess."

This was too much. "Your majesty, may I be excused?" asked Gebirga, not caring how rude this might sound. The queen, her point made, gave her assent.

Gebirga could not stand to be in the palace monastery any longer, and she did not want to take the chance of returning to her cell and finding Yusuf still there, so she donned the cotton veil Blanca the Jew had given her, which she had been wearing instead of her coif since the first day she met the queen, then took Liisa and went outside. It was a beautiful day, warm and sunny and not too hot. She and Liisa found a stone bench and sat on it, joining several people who sounded like they were having an outdoor meal there.

Gebirga drifted in her own thoughts for a moment. Despite herself, she kept returning to her night with Yusuf. Her body was acutely aware of every sensation, the sun on her face, the caress of her veil on her cheek, the material of her dress. She felt completely changed, like a different person. Overnight? No, she admitted that the changes had begun long before; last night merely set the seal on them. She could scarcely remember the Gebirga who had set out from Gistel in the castle boat with Winnoc and Trude.

She began to listen idly to the conversation of the people beside her. Suddenly she realized the language they spoke sounded like Flemish. It had been a long time since she had heard it; even she and Katerinen had started speaking together mostly in French.

"Waar komt u van dan?" she asked the woman sitting beside her. "Where are you from?"

"Ah, you are Dutch!" the woman replied, delighted. "I would not have thought you were one of us in that headdress."

"No, I am from Gistel, in Flanders," she answered.

"That's pretty close. We are from Dordrecht, in Holland, and we are making a pilgrimage to Compostela. Our friend Anneke is suffering from a tumor in her breast, which she hopes Sint Jakob will cure, and we all have our own petitions to seek and penances to perform, of course. My name is Aliit."

Gebirga introduced herself and Liisa.

"And what are you and your dog doing here?" Aliit asked and

then without waiting for a reply, she answered her own question. "How silly of me—of course, you are on pilgrimage too, to ask Sint Jakob to cure your eyes. But surely you do not travel alone?"

Gebirga ignored the question about her destination. The woman could think what she wanted. But she did answer her second question. "I had a friend whom I was traveling with. But she died. I buried her in Fromista."

Aliit was instantly sympathetic. "How terrible for you to be alone and to be in such a strange land. The food they eat here is so odd. What I wouldn't give sometimes for a good salt herring and goose fat on rye bread. But you must join us. We can travel together. Truth to tell, we are a little tired of each other's company after walking most of the way from Dordrecht. We could do with a new face who can tell us some different stories."

Gebirga was about to say she could not possibly, when she reconsidered. She remembered the old man who kept calling her a pilgrim despite her denials. Maybe she should be a pilgrim for a while, a real one, on foot with a staff and a purse and a destination. It would get her away from Leon and from having to make a decision about her future. The rigors of the walk could serve as the penance she felt she badly needed for her failure to protect Katerinen from the forces arrayed against her. She put her hand on the purse hanging from her girtle and felt the contours of the scallop shell she still kept there.

"Aliit, I would be delighted to join your party. When do we leave?"

The next morning, carrying her small bundle and with Liisa in tow, Gebirga met Aliit and her friends at the hospice of San Marcelo at the first light of dawn, as directed. "We walk early, to avoid the heat," Aliit explained. "If all goes well, Compostela is a fortnight's journey." Yusuf was long gone on his errand by the time Gebirga had returned to the palace the previous evening, and she left a message with a servant to be delivered to Sancha that she was traveling with a group of friends and would be leaving Leon for a time. Leaving early meant she did not have to explain to anyone else where she was going and why.

Traveling the pilgrimage road on foot was a very different matter from journeying on horseback. They covered only a little less ground each day than by horse, but it took them much longer, and they left their hospice before dawn each morning to avoid as much of the heat of the day as possible. Gebirga was much closer to the ground in every way. She could feel every cobble of the crumbling Roman roadway under her boots, which she hoped would last her to Compostela and back. The periodic throbbing in her head she had endured since Loarre continued under the hot sun, and she experienced occasional disturbing bright flashes in her eyes. But she was connected to the land she was walking on in a way she had not felt riding through it from a high perch on the back of a horse or a mule. The success or failure of their journey depended on the kindness of the people whose small adobe farms they passed, and their willingness to give water to the travelers, both for themselves and for the donkey that carried their possessions. And they needed lots of water because, although it cooled down each night, the heat by day as they crossed the dusty plain beyond Leon was like a wall they constantly pushed against to keep moving forward. But the people they met were friendly, giving them water and sometimes even small local cheeses and bread, asking only for prayers on their behalf when they reached Santiago in return for their generosity. The only ones who were unfriendly were the wild dogs that congregated at the outskirts of every village, barking and snarling. Gebirga was afraid for Liisa, and her new friends acquired for her a walking staff she could use to beat them back.

"Just hit them on the head if they come too close."

Gebirga doubted she could do that, and hoped seeing the staff might be enough to scare them away.

It was a relief to be with strangers who knew nothing of Gebirga's history. There were seven of them. Aliit and Anneke each had husbands, Dirk and Hugo, who were so silent most of the time that Gebirga kept forgetting which one was which and who was married to whom. Aliit's brother, Pelgrem, and his two grown children, Piet and Sara, made up the rest. Their mother had died a year before and Gebirga had the awful feeling she might have been invited to join their walking party as a prospective step-mother. Pelgrem was pleasant enough, though a little shy, but she tried to avoid too much time walking alone with him lest she encourage unrealistic expectations. She avoided Sara too, who was close enough to Katerinen's age to bring back sad memories.

To pass the time, they sang walking songs in Dutch, many of which were familiar to Gebirga from childhood. It seemed strange to sing these so far from home in such a different landscape. Though they were far from home, her friends traveled in a cocoon of Dutchness, remaining almost untouched by their strange new surroundings. They were all in the wool trade back in Dordrecht, and Gebirga found herself endlessly discussing wool quality, weaving techniques, and sheep diseases, subjects she had not thought about for months. It all came back to her quickly. One of them, Dirk or Hugo, was excited about the sheep he had seen in Spain. "They have the whole country for a pasture, and they travel all the way to the Moorish lands and back every year. I've never seen such wool. We need a way of getting it to the north."

They gave her the first night off but, as she had expected, on the second she had to pay for their company by telling stories. They were inside the walls of Astorga, enjoying bowls of stew, heavy on the chickpeas and vegetables, light on the meat, at the pilgrim hospice of San Esteban when Anneke said, "Tell us a tale, Gebirga; entertain us." Gebirga racked her memory, trying to think of what might amuse these people who had welcomed her so kindly. She had so many experiences worth telling—the court in Flanders, the papal council in Toulouse, even her night at Loarre with the Muslim entertainers. But no, under their good spirits, these people were homesick. With winter coming, they might not make it back home until spring unless they could find a ship to take them. So that night and the nights that followed, after they had taken off their boots, soaked their feet, and eaten whatever meal they could find or that the hospice provided, Gebirga entertained them with tales of her home, of Gistel. She told them how Helligond had built the first castle, of the fight between the brothers, and even about her own father and his journey to Jerusalem and back. The only tale she did not tell was the one about her mother's death. She did not want to hear repeated the old questions of why prayers to her mother had not cured her blindness.

The road out of Astorga continued flat for a while, but then began to climb steeply. The houses they passed were built of stone and thatch, rather than adobe and straw, and the air was perfumed with the scent of wild thyme as they climbed past the treeline and through a landscape of scrub and brush. By the time they reached the hospice near the top of Monte Irago, Gebirga was weary, and it was all she could do to stay awake long enough to eat at the great communal table. "This was nothing," she was warned the next morning by the hospitaller who bade them farewell, "The pass at Cebreiro a couple of days hence is much higher, and harder to do in any weather."

His warning was prophetic. When they left the hospice of a small Cluniac monastery at Villafranca two mornings later, the day was warm and sunny and their path wound up and down, mostly up, through the valleys and hills that led to the mountain pass of Cebreiro. All was well, until they began the final ascent. At first, though steep, their way was sometimes sheltered by trees that protected them from the sun. When they left the trees behind, however, the weather changed suddenly. The sky clouded over and a wind picked up from nowhere. A sudden cloudburst drenched them. Though this would have delighted them during their hot walk across the Leonese plain, here it was unwelcome. The wind soon dried them, but left them chilled through. Whichever direction they walked, it seemed to blow straight into their faces. Worse, when they rounded a bend they found themselves in a dense fog, and the way ahead was scarcely visible. Gebirga was not bothered by the fog, though she felt its soft tendrils touch her face, but she was forced to inch her way along with the rest. The climb was hard; every step she took felt like a knife stabbing through her feeble boots straight to her spine. Pelgrem walked beside her when he saw how slowly she was moving. A sudden gust blew someone's belongings right off the donkey and far onto the hillside below, where they were irretrievable. The donkey brayed its displeasure and had to be strongly encouraged to keep moving. They climbed for what seemed like hours with no knowledge of how far they had come or how far their destination for the night still was.

At last the monastery and hospice of Santa Maria loomed above them out of the mist. They left the donkey contentedly munching turnips in a thatched, round barn, and fled inside the hospice where they were welcomed by the monk in charge of guests. Once inside, the sound of the wind as it rushed around the contours of the land and the stone buildings was unearthly, like rampaging horses and wild beasts howling.

"La Compaña is out tonight, the Wild Hunt," said the monk. Seeing their confused faces he explained. "The souls of the dead who wander through the land. Did you see a lantern while you were walking? No? Good. Seeing their light brings bad luck." He fed them hot soup, and eventually they thawed, but the noise of the wind haunted them all night long as they tried to sleep. If it was only the wind.

They woke the next morning to a different world, one of sun and birdsong, and the previous day's difficult journey seemed like a bad dream. By contrast with the ascent to Cebreiro, their next days of walking seemed much easier, though they still had many ascents and difficult descents to master. The landscape transformed itself once they were over the pass, from a dry country of wheat fields and plains almost empty of human and animal life, to a verdant, fertile landscape of sudden showers and mists, dotted with small hamlets and crooked stone fences. Proud of conquering Cebreiro, the normal challenges of a day's walk were as nothing to them now, though they did have a bad moment at Portomarin, where they discovered that the bridge over the Minho had been destroyed by Queen Urraca's forces after a battle with Diego Gelmirez seven years before. They managed to ford it, but at the cost of a good wetting.

The walkers retreated into their own thoughts and there was less of the song and common conversation that had maintained their morale up until now. They walked in ones and twos, and often Gebirga found herself alone. She welcomed this chance to take stock of her own situation.

She mulled over the fate of Katerinen, and wondered where fault should be assigned. Oliver blamed himself; well, that was typical of Oliver, though he had matured from the self-involved boy she had met at Cluny. Sancha had blamed the archbishop of Toledo and Yusuf. It was her worst fear that Yusuf might be involved—and why was this her worst fear? She needed to think about that some time— but she had to admit that Sancha's scenario seemed the most unlikely. It was far more likely that Queen Urraca hesrself was to blame in some way, if not by a sin of commission, at least by one of omission. This was the main reason Sancha's proposal for her to remain with her in the monastery appealed to her so little; she did not want to be close to Urraca for the rest of her life. Gebirga had a harder time remaining angry with Alfonso of Aragon, though he was more evidently culpable than anyone. Perhaps that was because his actions and aims seemed to be so transparent. Besides, she had liked him. The same could not be said for Count Bertran and Bernard of Carrion.

But the person she kept returning to in her cogitations was Pope Calixtus. With all his talk of family loyalty, she knew Alfonso of Galicia was as much his nephew as Katerinen had been his niece, and a king in his own right and heir was a more powerful ally than the daughter and sister of two dead counts. He had been close by when the various "accidents" happened to Katerinen, and he had arranged for the escort of the Aragonese bishop who had betrayed them to Alfonso of Aragon and arranged for the attack in the Pyrenees. And even if Calixtus were not directly culpable, he had been well informed about all the factional struggles going on in Spain. He must have known Katerinen's presence would be like flint set to tinder. Gebirga admitted that there was not one single person, apart from herself and Clemence, who was truly interested in promoting a marriage between Katerinen and Alfonso of Galicia.

And what if Calixtus was ultimately to blame? What could she do to bring him to justice? Nothing: this was not the court at Ghent and she was not Count Baldwin to mete out justice among recalcitrant subjects. And Pope Calixtus was no subject. Telling Clemence would do no good; even if the countess did believe her, she was more dependent on her brother than ever now her son was dead. It would upset her to no purpose. As Gebirga was upset to no purpose. She would have to let Katerinen go. There would be no justice for her, as there had been none for Gebirga's mother. But Godeleva was remembered, loved, prayed to. Gebirga could not found a monastery in Katerinen's honor, but she could remember her. She resolved to begin by making her tale part of the nightly story sessions she shared with the other pilgrims.

Then there was Yusuf's proposal. Recalling this made her feel sad. She could almost imagine a life with him. But had he meant it or did he just feel he needed to offer her something after the night they had shared? He must have realized she had been a virgin. And how could she bind someone to herself when everyone she loved, died. What if they had children? Blind, she seemed no more capable of protecting the people she loved from harm now than she had been as a young child.

But the thought of remaining with Sancha and perhaps occasionally seeing Yusuf, especially if he did marry again, bothered her also for reasons she did not want to identify. Perhaps the sisters back at Santa Cruz would take her. And then she would have to face the fact of her failure to protect Katerinen every day of her life. No, there was no other choice but to leave Spain and return home. But if she went with Aimery and Oliver, she would have to retrace all the steps she had taken to get here and the memories would break her heart. After their adventure at Cebreiro, her companions had decided to take a ship home from one of Diego Gelmirez's new ports, rather than retrace the road they had walked. They invited her to travel with them, and she supposed she might as well. Who knows, she might even marry Pelgrem after all and become a cloth merchant's wife in Dordrecht. Aliit had certainly dropped enough hints about it, and an aging widower with grown children would have fewer expectations than a man her own age.

She told Aliit her plan to return with them by boat.

"That is wonderful! I am so happy you will be joining us. But are you sure? You won't change your mind?"

"It would take a miracle to change my mind," Gebirga said, a little sadly.

Arca was their last stop for the night before Compostela. There were more pilgrims than just their group spending the night in the hospice of Santa Eulalia, though none had traveled as far to get to their destination as the group from Holland. Their mood as they left the following morning was giddy and joyful, and Gebirga found it infectious. They kept up a brisk pace all the way to Lavacolla, the stream where by tradition, pilgrims bathed themselves before entering the town of Compostela and the cathedral dedicated to Santiago.

It was not much of a stream. They might have done better to bathe in the Minho, a few days back. And the road was full of hawkers, trying to persuade travelers to stay at this inn or that tavern when they reached Compostela, and even offering samples of the wine and food they might get there. But some enterprising person had dammed the narrow stream to create a couple of deeper basins for bathing, and after all, it was tradition.

The women's side of the river was downstream from the men's. Gebirga waded past the point where her companions timidly entered the cold water, though she was still well within hearing of their voices. She stripped down to her shift and entered the stream, Liisa paddling beside her. The shock of the cold almost made her cry out as she submerged her body as well as she could in the shallow river, slithering through the reeds like an otter, feeling the current tug at her and taking care not to let it pull her too far away from the rest. When she came up for air, she could hear Aliit, Anneke and Sara giggling and splashing not too far away, as well as the more distant horseplay and jesting of the men. It sounded like the four men were having a mock battle, Piet and Hugo on the shoulders of Dirk and Pelgrem, trying to knock each other off into the river. This swim was a badly needed break, a chance to release the tensions of their long walk, and to soothe their aching muscles in the cold water; a chance to let off steam before the solemnity of the final approach to Compostela, and before the encounter with the cathedral and its precious relic. Though her companions did not talk much about it, Gebirga knew they were longing for that spiritual encounter, to hear the cathedral clergy tell them, "Yes. You did the right thing making this journey. You are almost at its end. All will be forgiven." And Anneke of course hoped the end of her journey would bring healing to the tumor in her breast.

Gebirga was not certain how she felt about the end of this journey, or what she expected from it. She had not set off on this trip as a pilgrim, whatever the old man from Bruges had thought. Her goal had been to get Katerinen to Spain and see her safely married, and at that task she had failed. She had taken her purse into the stream with her, and she pulled out the scallop shell the old man had given her. She felt its rough surface and smooth interior before she put it back. Her eyes hurt, and as she rubbed them she saw the bright flashes that had been bothering her intermittently. She plunged under the water again to soothe the pain with its cold. Could it be that her eyes were getting worse? It seemed a poor reward for her pilgrimage, however long she had delayed undertaking it properly.

She sat on the bank, letting her hair dry in the sun, working her fingers through its tangles, until she was joined by the other women. Their shifts dried quickly, and soon they were dressed and veiled again and ready to join the others for the last stage of the journey. It was Piet who raced first up the low hill that marked their last ascent before they reached Compostela. When he reached the top he called to the others, "I see it! I see the cathedral! There, in the distance."

His companions soon reached him and fell to their knees, weeping at finally seeing what had been their objective for so many months. Only Gebirga remained standing, unable to be moved by what she could not see, though she was glad for her new friends that they had made it.

"Well done, Piet," said Dirk, "Reaching the top before the rest of us makes you the king of our group. Piet Konig. It is a good name that you will be known by from now on, and everyone will know from it that you made the pilgrimage to Compostela."

Anneke spontaneously started singing a familiar hymn, "Te Deum laudamus, te Dominum confitemur—We praise You, God; we acknowledge You as Lord," and the rest joined in as they walked the remaining distance. When they finished all the verses they knew, they began again from the beginning, only stopping at last with faltering voices when they reached the city gate.

The pilgrims headed straight for the cathedral, but when they got to the large square in front of the northern door of the church they disagreed about their next step. In the square were booths selling everything a traveling pilgrim might want—new shoes, purses, staves, belts, water bottles, and herbal poultices against blisters. "Gebirga, they even have scallop shells like the one you keep in your purse," said Sara.

As at Lavacolla, there were also inn-keepers trying to lure the arriving pilgrims to stay in their inns and no other. The men were all in favor of finding a good place to stay for the night, having a bite to eat and then a rest before returning to the cathedral the next morning. "That's the way you're supposed to do it," said Hugo, "In the morning you bring your offering and attend Mass, and then you pray at the shrine."

But, "No!" said Anneke, "I have not walked all the way across Europe to wait until tomorrow to see the altar of Sint Jakob. I'm going in right now."

Gebirga did not mind what they did, as long as they got out of the square. It was hot and the sound of the stone masons' hammers was making her headache worse. Clearly this cathedral was still a work in progress. She had a pang, thinking how Katerinen would have loved to be with her to see the men at work, how she had promised they would come here together.

Anneke prevailed and they entered the church, heading straight for the great altar to Santiago in the middle. "It's beautiful," breathed Aliit, "I wish you could see it, Gebirga. The front of the altar is worked in gold and silver and there are figures and letters all over it, just like your casket, but much bigger. And the whole thing is covered with a canopy like a pavilion, carved and painted with saints and angels."

A pleasant canon there invited them to place their offerings on the altar and then kneel to pray. Gebirga had not thought about making an offering. What should she leave? Leave that which is most precious to you, a voice seemed to say inside of her. She warred with the voice. Not that. Surely some coins would be enough. Or even my scallop shell. That is what brought me here. But the voice was silent. Finally, head pounding, she unhooked the pin she had used to tie her cloak together ever since Leon and laid it on the altar. It was Katerinen's brooch.

Once it was gone, a huge emptiness filled her. Perhaps Aliit sensed her distress because the other woman said gently, "You may not be able to see the beautiful altar, but beside it, against the pillar, is a wooden statue of Sint Jakob, Santiago as they call him. Some pilgrims kiss its foot. You could do that."

She took Gebirga to climb the two steps up to the statue and the younger woman prostrated herself on the floor to kiss its foot. Many had preceded her; the foot was almost worn away by thousands of soft pilgrim kisses. Hers joined theirs and then, inspired by she knew not what, she stood again and reached her hand to its carved face, only a few inches above hers. She felt the ropey contours of the saint's visage, its big nose and short beard. It's him, she thought. It's the man from Bruges and Cluny and the Pyrenees and the Montes de Oca. He's here; he's real.

A sharp pain and a flash worse than any previous stabbed through both her eyes so she shut them convulsively. When she opened them, all was changed. She could see blobs and colors and odd patterns and movement. Disoriented, she tried to take a step. Her staff was no help to her, and Liisa was waiting patiently outside. She fell forward onto the hard stone floor, hitting her head. She lost consciousness.

CHAPTER TWENTY-ONE

Sight

From the time when it was begun up to the present day, this church is renewed by the splendor of the miracles of Saint James. Here, health is given to the sick, sight restored to the blind, the tongue of the mute is loosened, hearing is given to the deaf, easy movement is granted to the lame, liberation is given to the possessed, and what is more, the prayers of the faithful are heard, their vows are accepted, the bonds of sin are broken, heaven is opened to those who knock, consolation is given to the grieving, and all the barbarous peoples, crowding here from all parts of the world, come bearing with them gifts of praise to the Lord.

When she came to, she found herself lying flat on her back on a pallet. Her head throbbed, and when she raised her hand to investigate the source of the pain, she touched a bandage that had been tied over her eyes. She tried to raise herself and was stopped, both by the pain in her head, which increased when she moved, and by the gentle pressure of a hand belonging to someone sitting beside her bed. An unfamiliar voice said, "Lie down and rest. No need to rush."

"Who are you? Where am I?" said Gebirga.

"My name is Robert, and I am the canon infirmarian at the cathedral. You are in the pilgrim's infirmary."

"Why? What happened?"

"You fell down and hit your head. You had some kind of a fit and you were rubbing your eyes, which is why we bandaged them. Your friends told us you were blind."

Her eyes. She remembered now, seeing something strange just before she fell. Seeing something.

"Where are my friends?"

"They left you with us. No doubt they have found lodging somewhere. They can come visit you here."

"Would you . . . would you please remove this bandage?"

The canon did as she bade. Gebirga looked straight up. Grey, flat above her. She turned her head to the right, towards the source of the voice. Grey and brown and pink in the middle, with blobs, lumps. She closed her eyes and put her hand to her own face. A nose, a chin. Yes, it was a nose and a chin, a face, that she had seen. She opened her eyes again and looked straight at the canon's face.

"I can see," she said.

"I thought that might be the case," he said, his face shifting into a contortion that startled her, until she realized it must be a smile, and those white things were teeth. She touched her own teeth experimentally, comparing them with what she saw. "From what the canons present when you fell described, I prayed it might be so. What a wonderful miracle for the honor of Saint James." he said, elated. "Canon Gregory, send for a scribe! We must record this tale."

When a scribe arrived, wax tablet in hand, Robert asked her questions about her journey and what she had done when she entered the cathedral. "And have you been blind since birth, or did it come upon you later in life."

"I could see when I was a small child. I must have become blind when I was around three or four years old. The last thing I remember seeing was my mother and father." Tears ran silently from her eyes.

Canon Robert was gentle with her, "This has been a shock to you, I know." He waved the scribe away, "We can finish hearing your story another time. In all my years at the cathedral, I have never known someone to regain their sight, but my master had a patient who did once, and he told me it takes a long period of adjustment."

The infirmarian had not been exaggerating when he told her it would take a while for her to get used to being able to see again. She found that out right away when she tried to leave her bed to use the privy. With her eyes open, the room whirled and swooped and she did not know where to place her feet. She had to close her eyes in order to be able to walk straight. The bump on her head healed weeks before she learned to walk with her eyes open.

Faces were easier to get used to. Her traveling companions visited her, first Aliit. "You have blonde hair," said Gebirga, "And you are so pretty."

"Piff, I am too old to be pretty," said Aliit, pleased.

Aliit had brought Liisa with her. The dog had not been permitted to stay with Gebirga in the infirmary so the pilgrims had taken her with them, but after Gebirga's miraculous cure was confirmed, their prize patient was moved to a cell of her own with room for Liisa. Each day one or another of the canons came to help her get used to her new sighted life. When she was alone, she spent hours just staring at her hands, curling them into fists and then opening them again. She passed as much time as she could with her eyes closed, comforted by her old, dark world in which her hands and feet were where she thought they should be, and not flailing around out of her control at the end of long appendages.

Her cell was plain, whitewashed with no decoration, and that helped her avoid overloading her new sense. The open window mystified her, and she kept putting her arm through it and wondering how the houses outside could be so small. A canon patiently explained that the things she could see through it were all located at different distances. "Look, you see these two apples?" he said, putting one into her hand. "And you see when I put the second one all the way over here, it looks much smaller? That is like the houses and buildings outside. The further away, the smaller they look."

"But your second apple is smaller than this one in my hand," she said, taking a bite out it.

The canons kept meticulous records of any miracles that could be attributed to their saint. The scribe of the first day returned and took as much of her story down as he could and she made sure he recorded as much as possible about Katerinen too; not about Gebirga's suspicions, but about their friendship, and her tragic death. Then one day the infirmarian asked if she would repeat the story to someone who was putting together a miracle collection. She reluctantly agreed, and that afternoon was greeted by two voices she knew well. "Gebirga! We were sent to hear a tale from a Dutch merchant woman. We had no idea it would be you."

It was Aimery and Oliver. Of course, they must have arrived at Compostela a few days before she did. "I was traveling with

Dutch merchants, and the canons had no way to know I was not one of them. But look at you. It is so good to see you." They laughed a little awkwardly. "Yes," she said, "To see you. And you both look exactly as I thought you would. But tell me everything. How have you been received? Are you going to write your book?"

"Bishop Diego thought it was a wonderful idea. But he wants much more than a simple guidebook. We are to include miracle tales, and liturgy for the feasts of Saint James, and the story of the arrival of the bones of the saint in Spain. Oliver is copying stories of Charlemagne in Spain. It is going to take much longer than I expected, and I will have to stay in Compostela for a good while. The bishop is not here, or he probably would have dropped in to see you. He is interested in anything that redounds to the credit of Saint James, and so onto him. We have been speaking mostly with Gerald—you remember, from our travels with Calixtus? Oh, and one mystery was cleared up that will interest you. Remember how he abandoned us at Somport in the Pyrenees when we were traveling with him? Something about receiving an urgent message? It turns out that the message was from Pope Calixtus and it was about the death of Katerinen's brother, Count Baldwin. He had to let Bishop Diego know as soon as possible. You can draw your own conclusions from that."

Indeed she could. Bishop Diego had to know that Katerinen was no longer the marriage partner for Alfonso of Galicia that they had hoped. Gebirga was glad the bishop was absent and she would not have to face him. But she had a few things she wanted to say to Gerald.

"And you, Oliver, what are your plans? Are you free to travel back to Cluny now?" she asked, trying to change the subject to happier things.

"I could. But I have decided I don't want to. I have decided to stay in Spain, but not on the pilgrimage road, where my parents are. I am going to go to Toledo and enter the Benedictine community there. I think I would find Cluny dull after all I have experienced and there would be sad memories for me there of the way I used to be. And of Katerinen."

This was a surprise. But it reflected the changes she had seen in him over the past weeks. And in his own way, he had genuinely cared for Katerinen too. She could understand why he needed a fresh start.

After their first visit, Aimery and Oliver came as often as they could, and helped the canons teach Gebirga how to use her eyes. Her Dutch pilgrim friends were frequent visitors too. One day, however, almost a fortnight after Gebirga's strange recovery, Aliit came alone.

"You look sad," said Gebirga, proud of her new-found ability to read mood from people's faces.

"We have learned that there is a ship leaving from port soon that will take us all the way home if we can make it there on time. To do that, we have to leave tomorrow."

"Oh," said Gebirga.

"You're not going to come with us, are you, Gebirga." It was more of a statement than a question.

"No, it doesn't look like I am after all. Not right now, not after what has happened to me. I need more time to adjust."

"But what is there for you here?" Aliit burst out, almost sounding angry.

"I don't know. I'll have to see. I have spent too much time trying to live in the past and in the future. I need to live in the present for a while now." This did not satisfy Aliit.

Then Gebirga impulsively reached under her bed and found her casket, the relic chest she had brought all the way from Gistel. "Aliit, could you do something for me? I won't see Anneke again, but could you give this to her, a gift from me? It holds the forefinger of St. Nicholas. I don't need it any more and maybe it will help her."

Aliit seized Gebirga in a fierce embrace, "Thank you my dear girl." Anneke had not said so, but they all knew it had crushed her not to have her tumor healed, when Gebirga had been the recipient of such a spectacular miracle. But with St. Nicholas on the boat with them back to Holland from Spain, who knew what the future might hold for Anneke?

"Tell everyone I said goodbye," Gebirga said, "And have a safe journey."

Compostela was emptier after her Dutch friends left, but Gebirga had much to keep her occupied. She started walking further and further afield. Doors were difficult; she could never quite see how to go through one without hitting herself on the jamb, but she could navigate across a large, open room. Stairs were still beyond her.

News filtered in from the outside world. At the end of October, great cheers went up all over the complex of cathedral building when it was learned that at the council of Rheims, Pope Calixtus had finally agreed to raise the status of the diocese of Compostela to an archbishopric. Diego Gelmirez had been unable to travel to Rheims himself, prohibited from leaving the country by Queen Urraca who still feared he was plotting to put her son on the throne. Instead he sent another bishop, Hugo, to speak on his behalf. But Diego Gelmirez would be bishop no longer; he was now Archbishop Diego. Gebirga wondered how Bernard of Toledo would take that news. That thought led her to wonder about Yusuf, and whether he had ever returned to Leon to look for her. She pushed the thought out of her mind.

Other news from Rheims was of more personal interest. Clemence had been given permission by her brother to marry Godfrey of Brabant. This marriage allowed her to be a constant thorn in the side of the new count of Flanders, Charles of Denmark, her enemy. Gebirga yawned. She was glad that Clemence was settled, but all that politics seemed so far away. Maybe she would just stay here at Compostela forever. She could help take care of the women pilgrims in the infirmary. Maybe she could even learn how to take their stories down. Or she could enter a local convent. Somehow none of these possibilities filled her with much enthusiasm.

She grew tired of her life as a semi-invalid and began to explore the cathedral and its many buildings. With her staff and her dog she could navigate slowly, eyes open, and the infirmarian told her she needed the practice. She ventured further afield, sometimes to the courtyard where she would sit in the crisp autumn air and watch the pilgrims arrive, footsore and elated, new ones every day, chattering in every language she knew and many she did not.

One day, feeling lonely, she went looking for Aimery and Oliver, hoping to find them in the cathedral scriptorium where they spent much of their time digging through old texts about St. James and

Compostela and copying them. She looked into the room and saw two clerics sitting together, one writing on a wax tablet while the other spoke. She entered the room so she could see whether they were her friends.

"I made it all the way to Logroño, disguised as a simple pilgrim, but then someone recognized me at the hospice . . ."

It was not Aimery; from the tale he told, it had to be Hugo, the bishop who had been Compostela's hero at Rheims. He must be recording his story for posterity. The other man, she had never seen before, but when he replied in a plummy voice, she recognized it immediately.

"Do go on, Hugo, this is fascinating. Such a wonderful story for our history."

It was Gerald, the canon who had pleaded with Calixtus on Diego Gelmirez's behalf. She had last encountered him at Toulouse. And she had questions for him.

Gerald saw her. "Excuse me madame, but pilgrims are not allowed in here. You'll have to go back to the cathedral."

"Gerald of Compostela," she said, "You don't remember me? After our travels together, down the Rhone and to Toulouse? You must remember the flamingos at least, the pretty flamingos that Katerinen so loved."

She saw horrified recognition dawn in his eyes and then he turned to his companion. "My lord bishop, I think I have taken down enough for today. Perhaps we could meet again here tomorrow, same time? Yes? Good."

When the bishop was gone he said, "You can see."

"Yes. You hadn't heard? I thought I was the talk of the cathedral."

"I only arrived back yesterday. They said . . . but I did not hear a name."

Gebirga was not here to talk about herself. "It was you, wasn't it, Gerald. With the flamingos and then at the cobblers, and with the workmen in St. Sernin in Toulouse? You tried to kill Katerinen. How did you do it?"

He mopped his forehead with a cloth. Maybe it was because she could see that he did not bluster and deny everything; maybe he could not lie to one so recently touched by a miracle from God.

"It wasn't to kill her, never to kill her. You can't think that. Just maybe to wound her enough so she couldn't travel, or even to scare her. You know how fragile she was. A good fright might tip her over the edge and she would spend her life in a nice, safe convent instead of coming to Spain."

Gebirga was sickened. Until he admitted his fault, a part of her had hoped she was mistaken. "How did you do it?" she repeated.

"Oh, it was easy. Bribes here and there. And then to bribe the apprentices at St. Sernin to stage a fight. You and Katerinen were sure to go there at some point. But Gebirga," he pleaded, "You can't think how awful, really unbearable it was for me after Pope Calixtus received the letter from the archbishop of Toledo while we were at St. Gilles. Once Calixtus learned that Alfonso of Galicia was so close to Archbishop Bernard, there was no way Compostela could benefit from the marriage anymore. It would only have served to link Calixtus closer to Toledo and that could have dashed all our hopes. I knew Diego Gelmirez would be furious, and I was the only one there who could do anything about it. But please believe me. I never meant to kill her. Only, you know, incapacitate her." His pleading changed to defiance. "And you'll never prove a thing," he finished.

"Tell me," Gebirga said, "Was Calixtus involved?"

"Of course." He sounded surprised she would even ask, "He gave me the money for bribes."

She had learned enough and left the scriptorium, wanting to get as far away from Gerald as possible. Weary and sad, she did not return to her cell immediately, but went into the cathedral, bringing Liisa with her in defiance of the rules. She chose the altar dedicated to St. Faith, a virgin martyr with a reputation for curing eyesight. She spent a long time kneeling there, sometimes in prayer, but mostly just thinking about herself and Katerinen, barely aware of the other people in the church or the hard stone beneath her knees. She had lost Katerinen's brooch and the casket she had since childhood, but she knew what she gained here was far more precious.

When she finally got back to her cell, she found someone there, sitting on her bed. He was tall and thin, dark and bearded with an ascetic face. Liisa went over to him and fawned at his feet. Gebirga stared and stared but did not speak.

"Yusuf," she said finally, "It's you. You found me." He was smiling at her, as if he had just found a treasure beyond price. Her smile copied his, and she sat beside him on the bed, shy.

"How did you know it was me?" he asked finally, "You've never seen me before."

"How could I not know it was you." She looked down at the floor.

"I had a devil of a time finding you. No one in Leon knew where you had vanished to. I took a chance that you might have continued on the pilgrimage road. Fortunately, everyone remembered the blind women with the big white dog who had passed through, so I soon knew I was on the right track. I found Aimery and Oliver here, and they told me what had happened to you and where to find you."

"Oh, did they?" she said weakly.

"Yes. You have no excuse now, you know."

"No excuse for what?"

"You said you wouldn't marry me because you were blind. Of course, I didn't care either way, but you're not blind any more. You have to marry me. I've been back to Toledo, and mother is reopening the house. My sister can't wait to meet her new sister-in-law and her children are looking forward to meeting Liisa, who will have nothing to do but grow fat in front of the fire, now she no longer needs to make sure you don't fall in a ditch."

Gebirga closed her eyes and thought a moment. "It wasn't only that I was blind. It was Katerinen, and my own parents...," she trailed off, uncertain how to explain the restraints that had held her, restraints now eased, not only by her pilgrimage with the Dutch family, but by the whole of her journey from Flanders and all that had happened, good and bad. "I will marry you," she finally said.

He put his arm around Gebirga and kissed her forehead, and she knew he understood. She relaxed against him, her curves fitting into the side of his body. She tentatively encircled his back with her own arm. There was something more she had to tell him.

"Yusuf, it was Calixtus after all. It was Calixtus all the time. He never meant the marriage to take place. From the time when we were in St. Gilles he did everything he could to make sure his niece would never be wed, might not even survive. And there's not a damned thing I can do about it or anyone I can tell, except you. All I can do is go on with my life and not forget her." It was a relief to share her burden of knowledge with him, and know he understood this too.

"He tried to stop the marriage from the moment at St. Gilles when he learned via my former master that Alfonso had severed his ties to Diego Gelmirez," Yusuf said, "It is what I had feared."

She sat beside him on the bed and they remained in silence for a while as if to preserve this moment of finding each other.

Too soon Aimery and Oliver popped their heads through the open door. Gebirga moved to separate herself from Yusuf, but he continued to hold her tight. "I thought I told you two to give us some time alone," he said to the men.

"Well, did she say yes? Did she?" said Aimery, ignoring him.

Yusuf looked at Gebirga and she smiled up at him and that was the only answer the two clerics needed.

Epilogue

*The Poitevin Aimery Picaud of Partheney-le-Vieux and Oliver
d'Asquins and their friend Gebirga of Flanders gave this book
to Saint James of Galicia for the redemption of their souls.*

It was twenty years before Yusuf and Gebirga returned to
Compostela and many changes had happened in the meantime.
Calixtus had not enjoyed the papacy for long. He died four years
after Gebirga regained her sight, and Queen Urraca followed him
two years after that. On her death, her son Alfonso of Galicia, now
Alfonso VII, was able to pursue at last the vigorous policy against
Alfonso of Aragon that he had dreamed of for so long. Count
Bertran of Risnel switched his alliance from the old Alfonso to the
young one, and his treachery helped Urraca's son gain back control
over the pilgrimage road. Alfonso of Aragon finally died himself
in 1134. Clemence had died the year earlier, far away in northern
Europe, but it took a long time for news of this passing to reach
Gebirga. Archbishop Bernard of Toledo was also dead, replaced
in Toledo by another Frenchman. Only Diego Gelmirez lived on,
though word was he too was failing.

Alfonso VII's strength meant good things for the frontier in
Toledo and, as Yusuf had predicted, life there grew easier, though
no one could tell how long it would last. Yusuf and Gebirga's house
was more fortress than farm dwelling, but in it they managed to
endure the Muslim raids, and even sponsored a few raids of their
own in response. The country around Toledo was as different from
Flanders as possible; where Flanders had been green, flat, cool,

damp, and cultivated, Toledo was golden brown, hilly, wild, hot, and dry. Gebirga would not have traded it for anything. They had two children; a boy, whom they called Miguel after Yusuf's father, and a girl named Godeleva after Gebirga's mother. Young Godeleva was most often called by the shortened form, Gota, a more common name in those parts.

They saw Oliver often, in fact he traveled with them to Compostela. He had been made prior of his community and he often grumbled to them about the novices. "They are so self-important and earnest; you'd think no one had ever decided to be a monk before."

They enjoyed traveling with him once more after so long. Aimery had summoned them all back to Compostela. He had spent the last two decades traveling between Compostela and Cluny, collecting material for his book and pleasing his patrons. It was a fond reunion when they were finally together again.

"But I didn't ask you to come here just to see me," he said, "I have something to show you." He took them to the cathedral library, where a large book sat on one of the long library tables.

"Oh Aimery, is that it? Have you finally finished it? How beautiful," Gebirga said, with eyes shining.

"Open it, open it," said Aimery, "Take a look."

So they opened the cover and turned the parchment pages, admiring their colors and decoration. Oliver read out a few words in Latin from time to time, and then translated for the benefit of the others. Gebirga was fixated by an image of Charlemagne lying in a field, the Milky Way stretching overhead. "He followed the stars there just as I did," she said, "Even though I couldn't see them at the time, they were there."

Their reaction was everything Aimery could have hoped for. "But you haven't seen the best part yet." He turned a few pages to find the section he wanted, and pointed an aged finger to the right place. "There, Oliver, read that aloud."

Oliver did as he was bid. "'Aimery Picaud of Parthenay-le-Vieux and Oliver d'Asquins and their friend Gebirga of Flanders'— Aimery, you've put us in your book!"

"Of course. I couldn't have done any of it without you."

"My name is in there? Show me," said Gebirga.

Oliver pointed, "See? That big letter there is a G and what follows is your name. And everyone who reads it will see your name and wonder who you were."

"My name is in a book," Gebirga said, satisfied.

About the Author

Lucy Pick became a historian at age eight when she saw her first castle during a visit to England. She later studied history at Queen's University and the University of Toronto, where she fell in love with medieval, and modern, Spain. Lucy now teaches at the University of Chicago Divinity School and has published a book and numerous articles on the history and culture of the Middle Ages. *Pilgrimage* is her first novel.

CPSIA information can be obtained
at www.ICGtesting.com
Printed in the USA
FFOW02n1234251116
29670FF